BORDER CROSSFIRE

TODD BLOMERTH

Editor: Susan Rock Gower

Cover Design: Karen Phillips, Phillipscovers

Project Manager/Interior Design/Formatting:

Tarra Thomas Indie Publishing Services

To Patti

ONE

The Truck Driver

THREE MONTHS BEFORE PRESENT

The leash tightened as the drug dog pulled the U.S. Customs agent toward an idling tractor trailer rig in the line of vehicles whose drivers were waiting to be questioned by the agents. The dog ignored a '64 Chevy truck with Nuevo Leon plates, spewing exhaust fumes from a tailpipe held in place with baling wire, and let out short yips as the tractor trailer's air brakes released and the rig edged over the speed bump, up to the stop sign. The air brakes let out a squawk. The driver, ready to talk to the lead lane agent, didn't get the chance. Instead, after glancing at the dog, the agent motioned the driver to a tall steel-roofed building and held up three fingers, indicating Inspection Bay 3.

As the rig's driver's window rolled down, the smell of rotting vegetation and churned up mud from the narrow river he'd just crossed, cotton candy from vendors just across the international boundary mark, along with various fluids oozing from vehicles, wafted into the cab.

Shrugging, he swung his arm back inside the cab with the entry paperwork still clutched in his fist. He tossed the clipboard up on the dash and released the brakes, easing up to and stopping at a line marked PROCEED TO HERE. Affecting casual alertness, two nearby agents stood next to concrete pylons placed to make runners zig and zag. One made a throat-cutting sign, and the diesel engine died.

The driver stepped down out of the cab, clutching cargo manifests and logbook. He was a small moon-faced Anglo, and he wasn't happy. Another agent appeared, this one wearing sergeant rank. He motioned the driver over to a table where the rig's driver spread his papers out for inspection.

Any driver slowing for the speed bumps and curious enough to care could look off to the right and see the short Anglo gesturing angrily to the taller and darker officer. Most weren't that curious. The few Anglos were simply happy to get out of what they had heard was deadly Nuevo Laredo without the cartel cutting their throats, or having to buy Chiclets from the urchins working the line of traffic. The Hispanics were more interested in breaking out of the increasingly backed up traffic heading up from Mexico. A few of all shades even had a few choice words to say to the agents which they said quietly, with minimal lip movement.

The crossing time had gone from bad to worse with the drug killings in Nuevo Leon and Tamaulipas. Cussing out an agent because of delays and officious attitudes guaranteed a vehicle being torn apart. Besides, outside Encinal, 50 or so miles up Interstate 35 toward San Antonio, the process could be repeated. Even if you got away with telling the Border Patrol agents that you thought they were all a bunch of pricks, the chances were good that a phone call would get you searched and questioned up the road.

Most agents didn't like to work the bridge crossings anyway. They took pleasure in dicking with those whose travels in and out of that God-forsaken country south of the old U.S. of A had put them there to begin with.

Meantime, the dog, a female German shepherd, crossed with any number of wire-haired breeds, continued to pace back and forth. The agents engaged the driver in conversation, asking casual questions as to what he'd just hauled across from Mexico. The agents' eyes belied their ease in discussion. No one, including the rig driver, was missing the dog's behavior.

Undeterred by the noise of other vehicles being inspected or waved through, and the foot traffic of Nuevo Laredo residents walking into the States to menial jobs on the north side of the Rio Grande, the bitch kept pulling her keeper toward the front end of the trailer. The logo on the enclosed trailer's dirt-filmed side gave notice that it belonged to a Laredo plumbing supply firm.

"God dammit. I'm hauling porcelain toilets and PVC in from Monterrey, just like always. This shit ain't going far. Just over to the warehouse district on the north side. I'm on a tight schedule. Why the hell are you pulling me over this time?"

The agents had a reasonably high tolerance for whining bridge crossers. Everyone had someplace they'd rather be than in an inspection bay in downtown Laredo. No one was paying much attention to him, except to note that small rings of sweat were developing in the armpits of the plumbing supply company shirt, which told them his name was "Luther."

The dog handler disappeared around the far end of the rig. As he did, three more agents, one with another dog, appeared from the glass-fronted border entry building. The Shepherd bitch's behavior was soon mirrored by the actions of a brindle great Dane/lab mix, which immediately pissed on a tractor tire, and then pulled its handler toward the front end of the trailer.

The sergeant, now holding the truck's manifest and entry papers, motioned the driver into a small covered office area adjacent to the bay, and then nodded at a nearby man wearing jeans, scuffed Tony Lamas, a white vented shirt, and narrow-brimmed Stetson.

"Luther." He glanced at the passport. "Uh, Luther Wellington, this here is Mr. Eddleman."

Luther didn't offer to shake hands, and neither did Eddleman, who seemed busy fishing snuff out of a Kodiak tin.

"As you can see, them dogs of ours seem to be highly agitated by something going on in that rig of yours. Can you think what that might be?"

Luther glanced over his shoulder at the truck, and then turned back toward the sergeant, who was flipping through paperwork on a clipboard.

"Uh, well, mister—I mean *sarjento* Gutierrez." He made a point of checking the agent's name tag. "I ain't seen you before. Maybe you been up at Columbia." He motioned upriver toward a lesser used crossing accessing the Mexican state of Nuevo Leon. The sergeant, a stocky man in his early forties, didn't try very hard to look interested.

"I've been bringing supplies in for three years at this here Number One Bridge. Everyone knows me. Everyone knows what I bring is sealed in there at the *maquíla*. And everyone knows I don't and wouldn't allow someone to put something in that trailer that don't belong there."

Taking off his baseball cap, Luther pushed his thinning hair back. "You got my manifest. You know it's going to Vasquez Plumbing Contractors. If you ain't from here, maybe you don't know, but it's local, it's legit, and I'm getting pissed off." Luther paused, winded by his oratory.

The man introduced as Eddleman handed him a printed form. "Luther, then you don't have anything to worry about, do you? This is a Consent to Search form. You wouldn't mind signing it, would you?"

"Why in the hell should I do that? I let you break the seal on that trailer, I'm up shit creek. There's enough toilets in that box—it'd take you boys a good day to pull all that off. And all it's going to do is piss off my boss. Besides, who are you? You with the Border Patrol or something? Why ain't you in uniform?"

Eddleman ignored him. "Sit down, Luther. Here's a chair." He slid over a scratched folding chair. "We need to talk."

Luther sat.

Eddleman pushed his hat back on his head, showing a high forehead but no hair. "You can sign the consent form," he nodded in its direction, "and quit worrying about our inconvenience. We'll set stuff off nice and proper, and you can call and get your folks to come on over and help re-load when we're done. Or," he paused, his eyes getting squinty, "we'll just get a warrant and tumble everything out the back of your goddamned rig."

This last exchange set Luther back a tad. Crossings hadn't been any problem for him. All he did was get up, eat breakfast, shit, kiss the old lady goodbye, deadhead to a Mexican plant on the outskirts of Monterrey, load up toilets. Home by six, six pack and supper by eight. Sleep, wake up, and start the whole thing over again—Sundays off. He wasn't getting paid $22.75 an hour to buck up against the federal government. He cogitated for a minute.

"Hell, I'm just a truck driver. I'll sign the damned thing if you want."

TWO

Present Day – A Friday:

PURDY KENDRICKS

K ickapoo County was noted as one of the poorest of Texas' 254 counties. That was saying something. Needless to say, scrambled 900 MHz police radio equipment was not on the top of the Commissioner's Court Christmas list. So, when I got the call, it was shared with the several hundred some-odd scanners located on windows, kitchen counters, courthouse personnel desks, and wrecker drivers' dashes. In fact, to not be within hearing range of a scanner was like not having a cell phone if you lived in the big city. I pulled up on a gravel road coming up from canyons overlooking the Rio Grande, turned on the police radio, stopped, and stepped out.

Hot. Long summer coming.

"Purdy, what's your twenty?" Jake Nichol's readily identifiable voice came through on my six-year-old Dodge county car. I was in an awkward stance, getting rid of the better part of four glasses of sweet tea from the Cenizo Diner that came with the Wednesday lunch special of a meat, three vegetables, and a dessert, all for $6.99 plus tax. A 1:30 p.m. inquiry as to my location was unusual enough that I pissed the transformed tea onto the tops of a cracked and dried up pair of brogans I wore with my Kickapoo County Sheriff's Office uniform. An iPod earplug hung in one ear, while the other dangled to my waist, entangled on its own cord as I tried to multi-task.

"Shit," was the first response, which didn't get on the air. I zipped up. It was 96 degrees and only the middle of May. The cruiser was also

5

in need of Freon or a compressor; I wasn't sure which. I reached through the open window and grabbed the mic.

"Yeah, Jake. I'm out by the gas plant. What do you need?"

Behind me stood the largely automated collectors, fracturing towers and pipelines of a Shell facility that, much to the consternation of Kickapoo County officials, scrubbed and processed natural gas from wells enriching adjoining counties. After running a low-lying country road that followed the river and was in its entirety a dead zone for radio transmission, I had turned north and upland to make a largely ceremonial law enforcement check of the perimeter fence of the facility. This was mainly so the pump station foreman could pass along law enforcement's vigilance and concern in the wake of 9-11 and assure Sheriff Thomas Jefferson, or TJ, Johnson a hefty contribution in the upcoming November election from company officials.

Strangely, TJ had done something most incumbent sheriffs fail to do in Texas—piss off the populace to the point of drawing an opponent. That opponent was the long time Santa Rosa Marshal, Clarence Livermore. As this was his fourth term, and the first with any opposition, he was having to learn the fine points of county politicking, including letting folks think he gave a rat's ass about their law enforcement problems. He didn't, but suddenly my shift work now included showing the County vehicles in places rarely visited.

"Been trying to reach you for over half an hour. You been out of reach?"

Yes, with the radio turned off and taking a nap.

Jake had a good idea of my after-lunch "patrolling" hiatus. It wasn't mentioned.

"Been working down toward Lágrimas. Thought I spotted new tire tracks." True I'd been sniffing around the crossing there, but I'd also taken about half an hour to just be left alone—completely.

"Meet the Sheriff over at the Griffin place." Jake sounded miffed, as if his dispatching required an immediate response, and I had somehow failed him. To his credit, Jake also knew that my job was on the line, and little things like response times to dispatches were the things coffee shop conversation revolved around. TJ's re-election efforts now dictated much of the patrolling. Dead air in response to inquiries, at least in my case, would be talked about. Since TJ was spending more and more time in the four coffee shops in the county, creating new and lasting bonds of friendship with retired ranchers and widows, this delay would eventually end up on the cutting edge of speculation as to what I had actually been doing. My star was not in the ascendant with TJ. He would as soon jettison me as not if he could squeeze ten more votes out of it.

The Griffin place could have been one of six properties now, due to the break-up of the old family place. I didn't know exactly which one Jake was referring to. "He say what for?"

"Not sure. Being as how you were in the bottoms, I guess you didn't hear all the call-outs."

Well, he was right about not hearing anything. Leave it to Jake to try to cover me and make it sound even worse.

Sheriff TJ Johnson had little use for me right now. The idea of him actually asking for my services puzzled me.

"TJ will meet you at the old ranch house. He's out there now. He says to tell you that the north pastures don't look to have any cattle in them right now, so don't worry about closing the gates."

The old ranch house. At least I knew which of the properties to go to now. The Griffin place held memories for me—some good, some bad. It also was home to two people I held dear. I hoped whatever was going on didn't involve them.

THREE

The Watcher

THREE MONTHS BEFORE PRESENT DAY

B ridge Number One in downtown Laredo extends south from a gaggle of one-way streets, filled with *ropa usada* and low-end furniture stores. The small square around La Posada Hotel is a bright spot in what some would say is just an extension of Mexico, which was true.

Try communicating with any store clerk in English. Either feigned or real, no one gave you the time of day. The area's make up made it easy to blend in—if you were brown skinned.

The small Hispanic was inconspicuous. His employers dubbed him, "Watcher." Watcher fit in. He carried a roll of American money that he used to grease the skids when he needed access to the roofs. He had paid for uninterrupted usage earlier and lay prone on the roof of three-story building with a clear view of the border crossing.

Watcher ensconced himself with a set of binoculars and watched traffic ooze through the border checkpoint. The rig with a plumbing supply logo on the trailer inched across the river and eased up to a uniformed officer. A dog was running back and forth in the lane of traffic, and then showed interest in the rig's trailer. Watcher focused in on the dog. Why was the damned thing getting excited? Watcher was there to make sure no one was in bed with the Border Patrol and Customs agents—that drivers weren't passing notes or appearing too chummy with any of the border officials.

Watcher knew just enough to do his job—and not much more, at least that he would admit to. He was not stupid. He knew, or at least heard enough, to wonder why the dog was alerting on a shipment in the trailer. It wasn't all that uncommon to have a vehicle checked over by the *pinche norteamericanos.* They assumed that they could catch at least some of the drugs coming in just by random chance. However, there was no reason to believe any drug dog was going to alert on product well-hidden and not likely to be leaking any odors.

As the semi eased into the inspection bay, Watcher could see additional uniformed men slowly coalescing around it, some not uniformed and looking unkempt. DEA? Something was up. The Anglo driver, gesturing angrily, was escorted over to the small glassed–in booth area. Something was up.

Punching in pre-set numbers on his cell, Watcher saw a young agent produce a pry bar to break the metal seals on the back of the cargo box.

"*Oye. Tenemos una problema.*" He was sweating. Part of his job was to ensure there *wasn't* a problem.

"*Onde?*" Watcher assumed that whoever was on the other end of the conversation was keeping tabs, and probably was seeing exactly the same activity.

I know you are watching me, carbrón. Do you think I am a fool?

"*Puente Uno. Los pararon el mek.*" It was actually a Kenworth. "*Parecen que los gringos van a sacar todo del remolque.*"

The agents were now pulling up with a fork-lift, and new agents, freshly gloved, were climbing in the back of the fully loaded trailer.

"*Piensas que ese pinche chofer hablo?*"

What am I, a fucking mind reader? Can I read lips?

"*Tu me digas. No vi nada. El parece enojado y nervioso—nada mas.*"

Moreover, he hadn't seen anything to suggest the driver was in cahoots, but then from his vantage point there was no real way to be sure. Besides, the *gabacho* was just a mule, and shouldn't know anything, anyway.

"*Quedase a ver si rescatan algo aparte de inodoros.*"

Fine, but the longer I'm up here watching them unload shitters, the sooner some helicopter or barrio snoop wanting to make some dolares off the pinche americanos will spot me. First thing I see coming out the back of that fucking truck that doesn't look like a commode, I'm off this roof.

He was paid to watch—not to be a sacrificial lamb.

Watcher rang off. He punched in another pre-set number. This phone was answered by a man sitting in the top floor of the Mexican customs building across from the American inspection stations.

"*Tu vistes?*"

Of course, he saw. Who wouldn't have seen the stop?

"*Si. Que parece?*"

"*Que la pinche patrulla paró a la troca. Los perros estan dando demasiado atención al remolque.*" In fact, the dogs weren't the only ones paying too much attention to the trailer.

"*No dices mentira. Parecen como pulgas.*" Just mentioning fleas caused Watcher to scratch a sudden itch between his shoulder blades.

"*Ahora que?*"

"*Pues, llamame pa tras si hallan algo.*"

The trailer's position in the inspection bay will make that a bitch. I pray they find something before it gets too dark. And I need to piss.

So, a truck that crosses nearly daily was suddenly being swarmed like *pulgas* on a street cur. The gringo's hand-held scanners weren't good enough to detect anything in the trailer. There was no way that dogs would alert on the product as packed. *Hijo de la chingada. Had some* puto *created another stash that dogs could sniff out?*

If this beehive of activity resulted in some expensive product being seized, someone was going to have to answer for it. Someone would die. It wasn't up to Watcher to decide who it would be. He just reported what he saw, and occasionally coordinated the street vendors, lottery ticket sellers, and kids selling Chiclets, all part of Watcher's cartel controlling Nuevo Laredo's river crossings. That was all. His boss watched the watchers. He no doubt was monitored as well.

Watcher just hoped that logic made sense to those for whom he worked. Sometimes it did. Sometimes, they cleaned house, rounding up everyone remotely associated with a blown crossing, and either strangled or shot them. Then decapitated them. Then cut off their nuts. *Madre de Dios*—he couldn't see Jesus in that condition.

FOUR

The Truck Driver

THREE MONTHS BEFORE PRESENT

L uther Wellington did indeed live in Laredo, and worked for Vasquez Plumbing and Construction, LLC. He was 47, had a wife and a girlfriend, two grown kids who hadn't turned out worth a shit, and arteries to his heart half-clogged from years of smoking and fast food.

He'd been escorted from the booth into an interior, windowless room of the large building housing immigration and customs offices. Someone asked him to take a seat before closing its door. The smell of stale coffee struck him almost as strongly as the awareness that the door closing behind him automatically locked. He continued his quest to convince himself that whatever was happening outside really didn't have anything to do with him—that he'd make it to the house before dark. It wasn't working.

It had taken five Mexicans two hours with forklifts and dollies to load the trailer. A bunch of wet-behind-the-ears government employees weren't going to be motivated to do anything quickly. He'd seen enough vehicles being torn apart by the Border Patrol. None of them would make it in a chop shop, for sure. But he couldn't fault them on thoroughness. It was going to be a long afternoon.

Luther subconsciously reached for his cell to call his dispatcher. Then remembered that Eddleman had relieved him of that device as he'd been escorted away from the public area and into the office area. *Shitass.*

Looking around the room, he found some old *Car and Driver* magazines. Settling down to look at someone's version of road art, he farted into the plastic cushion of the straight back chair. The hard surface enhanced the sound and caught two DEA agents by surprise. The speaker just over their heads and above the one-way mirror did everything but waft the redolence into the darkened room where they stood.

"Do we talk to him now?" asked a raw-boned agent with a beard and dark glasses. His equally scruffy partner snorted.

"Fuck, no. I'm not going in there now unless you can shit a can of Lysol. Let him stew. He needs to sweat awhile anyway."

FIVE

Present Day — A Friday

PURDY KENDRICKS

My return to Kickapoo County wasn't the one I had envisioned, if I had ever thought about it at all. Short of family ranches, there just wasn't much to keep young people here. Still isn't. Life has a way of telling you that you don't control as much of it as you think. At least that was the case with me.

By the time I graduated from high school, Daddy was dead of a heart attack. I was sixteen when that happened. My dad was a full-time water well driller and a part-time evangelical Bible-thumping preacher. I was getting used to my newly won freedom as a teenager from mid-week church attendance. A bunch of us with newly minted Texas driver licenses were parked at the Dairy Queen in Santa Rosa when Clarence Johnson drove up. None of us had been drinking, so whatever prompted him to talk to a bunch of pimply faced boys had to be out of the ordinary. I just didn't know how much out of the ordinary it would be.

"Purdy, I need to talk to you." He motioned me over to the old Chrysler cruiser the city provided for his town marshal duties. I didn't like Clarence; probably because my Dad thought he was a windbag who was rumored to ill-treat Mexicans, but I couldn't think of a reason for him to single me out. I walked over to the car, and in a show of decidedly unusual gentleness, he awkwardly put an arm around me.

"Your mama's been looking for you. Your Daddy's had a heart attack, and they want you at the hospital."

Daddy had died in his pulpit in a Wednesday mid-week service, which I think would have pleased him. His death meant the end to his KW Drilling Service. Mama eventually sold the business and went to work for the school system as assistant librarian. We moved into Santa Rosa and closed up the tiny house in Lágrimas. The well service's shop was adjacent to the house, so Mama rented the house to the new owners, who let some of the hands live there.

I finished up high school and went off to Texas A&M with a scholarship. College gave me a larger world to look at. Between stints in the Army and the Houston Police Department, I'd been away for over 20 years when, lugging a young child, an unhappy wife, and a lot of baggage, I had come back to take a job as the Sheriff's Office chief—and only—Investigator.

Mama was in the Golden Horizon Nursing Center by this time, suffering from early onset Alzheimer's. I was trying to figure out how to raise a son, mollify a wife, care for a mother quickly headed toward a vegetative state, and find an AA meeting that would, hopefully, help me maintain some new-found sobriety.

It wasn't the best of times.

The radio chatter was endless. EMS and off-duty deputies, along with elected constables and, it seemed, anyone with any sort of badge, were enroute to the east side of the county. Whatever had happened or was happening was substantial.

Son of a bitch! This quiet little place with absolutely nothing going on, and I take a quick snooze, and the shit hits the fan.

The guilt interspersed itself with worry about what I felt I was about to find.

At least I can explain it away if I have to. And no booze—this time.

After 15 miles, I got decent cell coverage and pulled over to the side of the highway. I punched in the sheriff's phone number. TJ once smoked unfiltered cigarettes at a two-pack-a-day rate. His wife had finally nagged him into quitting, but his voice still showed their effect.

"We got a call from Pete Vasquez," he rasped. "His grandparents hadn't checked in with him for awhile. He drove up from Laredo to check on 'em and found something at the main house."

"What is it?"

"It's a goddam mess is what it is. I'll meet you there. The north pastures don't look to have any cattle in them right now, so don't worry about closing the gates."

"Are Otabiano and Raquel okay?" My gut tightened.

"Far as we know they are. Pete says they aren't at home, but their truck is there. I'm hoping they got a ride into town or to Del Rio and just left it there."

"Oh, and stop by the office and get all your investigator type stuff."

Huh, I still kept most of the gear in the trunk of the patrol car. I guess I was back to my old job title of Chief Investigator.

I knew the layout of the Griffin ranch like the back of my hand. I had worked there part-time in summers and on Christmas holidays before its break-up, doing whatever needed doing on a large cow-calf operation.

My usual job was as an extra hand on a water well drilling rig. Daddy had a couple of full-time men, and work could be spotty. I viewed working for anyone else who actually paid wages, no matter how hard the work, as a vacation. After the KW sold, I had looked to the Griffin place as a way of saving money for college.

The headquarters buildings, which included the old ranch house, ended up as part of the property partitioned to the youngest child, Laura Griffin Sandler Saenz. It wasn't much to look at. Nothing man-made in this part of Texas was, unless someone with a lot more money than sense poured that money into something that was more art than utility. At least out here, utility counted for most everything.

In appearance, the ranch house had the rock and wood mix typical of structures built in the 1920s, when the better land in Texas had been snatched up, and folks found themselves poking into marginal areas for farming and ranching. This border area with Mexico, with an average rainfall of less than ten inches per year, was definitely marginal. A cow and her calf needed at least forty acres of grazing land a year to survive.

Water came from deep wells, *tinajas,* the Rio Grande, and earthen stock tanks, usually dug without the benefit of tractors by cheap labor eager for anything resembling a paying job. A night's sleep away from marauding revolutionaries in the arid northern Mexican states came as a bonus. Feed came from grama grass and some dry land hay production. When things got particularly bad, the ranch hands used butane pear burners to singe the thorns off prickly pear tunas. The cattle then ate them.

The main house had once been part of the headquarters for a reasonably good size operation, for its place and time, owned and operated by Clayton Griffin. It had totaled a little over 120 sections with five miles of Rio Grande frontage. The river allowed for pumping and irrigating with the precious water when it wasn't too droughty. Most of the time, the Rio's lazy meanders allowed easy ebb and flow of people, cattle, horses, and, on occasion, other less legal commodities.

The ranch had been split up between feuding heirs over the years, and the old house became not much more than a glorified deer camp for family and visitors. Occasionally, they would come from San Antonio, or Houston, or Dallas to test their marksmanship against South Texas whitetails. Except during the fall and winter, no one spent any time there.

Otabiano Vasquez and his wife Raquel looked after Laura's part of the land. Otabiano was born on the Griffin land. He had nursed calves, broken horses, mended fences, and raised a family on the land. After the split-up among the heirs, he had been kept on as a sort of majordomo. It was more out of loyalty than need. There wasn't a lot to do these days. Otabiano had an old tin-roofed, rock house down by the river, some three miles from the headquarters.

The old vaquero or Raquel would sweep out the floor, replace broken window glass, check for skunks, snakes and other critters, and generally keep an eye on the place so it didn't become a hideout for wetbacks crossing a porous border looking for a better life.

The Vasquez family had consisted of Otabiano, Raquel, and a daughter, Concha. Concha had been a huge disappointment, not because of her pregnancy in high school—that was almost a border rite of passage for much of the teenage population—but because of her refusal to care for the resulting child, Pedro, or Pete, as we knew him. She high-tailed it to California, where she eventually died of shock after her second leg amputation, caused by too much booze and untreated diabetes.

It was normal standard procedure for whoever was dispatching to use at least some kind of "10" code of what was to be expected at the scene. Originally, these codes had been to abbreviate the police messaging system. It also helped not being so obvious to the public, when, say, a call went out where someone's kid had been killed on the highway by some drunk. However, loneliness in my county reduced the need to truncate calls, and besides, anyone with a scanner knew virtually any "10" sign. 502: drunk driver; 415: disturbance; 187: homicide; 20 (like Jake's earlier call to me): what is your location. Mostly it was 10-4: understood; 10-20: location; 10-21: use a telephone and call.

Jake was right not to give a description. Besides, TJ's presence, along with anyone else with a badge, was perking everyone's ears now.

TJ didn't make many investigations, generally handing that responsibility to underlings. Maybe the election was also giving him a new appreciation of the personal touch in police work.

I had been up since 3 a.m., helping Department of Public Safety Trooper Clete Morales with a hit and run investigation on U.S. 90 that had gotten nowhere. I had met Morales five miles west of Santa Rosa. Flashers and take-down lights illuminated a fifth-wheel camper with a 10-foot scrape down its left side. Fortunately, no one was hurt. A tourist from Nebraska was left cursing drunk Texas drivers and the delay in getting to a Good Sam get-together at Big Bend National Park.

Recently demoted to line deputy, I was now on shift work, and well over the eight hours allotted. According to the federal regulations we learned about in continuing education, I should expect comp time or overtime at time-and-a-half. Receipt of either was problematic, but at least I could try and claim it. If I pushed it, TJ would merely "undemote" me into a salaried, and thus exempt, position I had held for three years as investigator.

A rutted road of sorts in Mexico crossing into Texas at a low water crossing up by Lágrimas was rarely patrolled by law enforcement. Even there, it was rare to hear of anything of consequence. The county's remoteness spared this stretch of river most concerns about smuggling. There were easier places to access from both sides of the border than at the Griffin place. Miles of nothing in Mexico except some half-starved *ejido* dwellers.

I was digesting all this as I hit the tarmac of US 90, turning east. It was a 42-mile run from the gas plant road to the county road into the

Griffin properties, and another six through pastures back to the old house. I had promised my wife that I would pick up our only child, Forrest, from school today. As bad as work was, it was keeping my mind off what I faced daily on the home front. Everyone in the county knew my marital situation was dicey, and I risked the additional ire of my wife by waiting till I hit cell coverage going through Santa Rosa, to call and give her the good news.

"Betty Kendricks, Kickapoo Valley Electric Cooperative. May I help you?"

I took a deep breath, let it out, and broke the news. "Hon, I've got a call of some kind at the Griffin ranch house. I can't pick up Forrest like I promised." Pause. Promises were a big issue with Betty, and right now I was in the middle of what seemed to be a streak of broken ones.

"Purdy, you promised. This is my one chance this year to ride over to San Antonio with the bunko club." The local club gave one of the few social occasions outside of church and sports that were readily accessible to women. The club had planned an annual trek to eat and drink on the River Walk in San Antonio, with an overnight at Holiday Inn. My interference with those plans was a decidedly risky bit of business. It sounded trite, but there were few outlets for women in what many considered a God-forsaken spot. The chance to blow off some steam in the big city was looked forward to by all involved.

I could feel the sigh on the other end of the line. I almost wished for anger, but that effort had gone away awhile back. Resignation had settled into a relationship where neither of us had the guts to call it quits.

"I know, and I didn't expect this either." Logic said that it's about as often as the Second Coming that a sheriff *and* a Ranger were demanding my presence in a county of less than 2,500 souls at the exact time school let out. But logic didn't have much to do with it. I could feel my anger overpowering a well-ingrained sense of guilt. "Look, I don't expect this will take that long, but whatever it is, I've got to be there. Have Paula pick him up when she goes to get KayCee."

The Co-op has a scanner. You know damned well there was something that has everyone's attention.

Paula Richardson was Betty's sister, and the consolidated school system meant that kindergarten through high school was on one campus on the edge of Santa Rosa. I took a deep breath before saying, "Go on to San Antonio. I'll get the boy fed and homework done and see you when you get back."

I was relieved when cell coverage broke down as I went out the east side of Santa Rosa and through cuts in a string of low hills. I heard what I thought was a disgruntled *okay*. Paula and her family lived in town, and KayCee and Forrest were close enough in age to get along like sister and brother. Paula ran the CutNCurl and knew enough about her sister's marital situation to regard me with little favor. She was a good enough person that I never sensed her feelings being communicated to our son, and she had a knack for keeping KayCee and Forrest occupied, even while perming, polishing, and visiting with customers.

Just before the cutoff, the highway made its long winding drop toward Snake Creek. This generally dry watercourse marked the eastern county line. I eyeballed a tractor trailer rig coming up behind me that didn't seem to notice or care that I was slowing down. The driver jake-braked it, blasting his air horn at me as it went by. Probably a regular on this highway and fairly sure no local yokel was going to cross county lines for getting too close.

It was five miles to the Laura's portion's front gate, and another mile to the house. Because there were several adjoining ranches, and because of a fish camp farther downstream where john boats and v-hulls were kept for catfishing, it was a dedicated county road. You still had to know which tracks were the county's and which was some rancher's going off into trackless pasture. I did, and everyone knew I did, which is why it puzzled me to see TJ's chief deputy, Johnny Reagan, standing outside his truck some 200 yards off the highway.

He waved me over. I leaned out the window. Reagan stepped on his half-smoked cigarette, grinding it out in the dirt. Sunglasses hid his eyes, but they couldn't hide the ashy look on his face.

"The high sheriff and you don't gee and haw." He paused. "But right now, I need you to promise me that when you get out there, if asked, you'll agree to step up and be the Sheriff's Office investigator again. No puffing. No acting like your pride is too damaged. None of that. Can you do it?"

Uh oh.

My mouth went dry. My personal woes disappeared like thin smoke.

This is bad.

Ohshitohshitohshitohshitohshitohshit.

I nodded and started to ask for more information. Reagan was already turned around, heading to his truck.

————————————————

SIX

Present Day – A Friday

PURDY KENDRICKS

B ecause of the County Road designation, every three years or so a maintainer leveled the potholes and graded out the rock outcroppings that bared themselves after the infrequent rains. Unfortunately, I calculated we were in year two-and-a-half. I drove the Sheriff's Office car as fast as I dared, hoping not to get a hole the oil pan.

The far southeast end of Kickapoo County was marginally different in landscape from farther west and north. There was more chance for rain, and more arroyos. The land ran more to a loamy sand than the hardpan gravel and rock outcroppings farther west and away from the river. This gave the ranchers who had been fortunate enough to settle here a better shot at making a go of it. Down by the river, there were even old acequias once used for flooding alfalfa fields and small melon patches. It was, relatively speaking, the greenest part of the county.

I steered off the county road and headed crossed the cattle guard into the ranch. Laura had married and divorced well, perhaps more than once. Laura Saenz, if Saenz was still the last name she was carrying, did not rely on her portion of her family place to support her lifestyle. She had, however, made some efforts at keeping the place looking respectable. Now, fences had come unstapled from old mesquite and cedar posts. The windmill near the road was freewheeling, the sucker rod not connected to the pump. It seemed apparent that no real living was being attempted on her 25 or so sections.

23

I drove the last half mile looking out over pastures that had once held Brangus cows and calves. I saw nothing there. There seemed little pretense of a viable ranching operation. Maybe some neighboring rancher leased some pastures to keep the place's agriculture exempt status with the local taxing authorities. I didn't know, and right now, didn't care.

Laura hadn't shown much of an interest in the place since long before her parents had died. She'd used the place to get away from it all during divorce proceedings. There'd been one or two impressionable males she had trysted with soon afterwards, or so I heard. Nowadays, the feed store and grocery in Santa Rosa got intermittent business from mostly strangers stocking up during hunting seasons. I couldn't see why she held onto the place.

In the years I'd had anything to do with Mr. Griffin's property, it had been a ranch where I was proud to work. Otabiano and Laura's father had made sure of that. Mesquite infested much of this part of the county because of the sandy nature of the soil and proximity to the river. For years Otabiano had worked to control its spread with D8 Caterpillars and chains. The pernicious thorn bush was quickly reclaiming the place. The untended look puzzled me and deepened my feeling of dread.

There was a small dip down to the ranch house, which had been built in the shelter of some small hills. To one side was a stock tank, fed by an old Aerometer windmill. It still worked. Water spilled into the earthen structure that had for years held catfish and black bass. The water always had its share of reeds, but now seemed choked with vegetation. The recent runoff from heavy thundershowers had churned up the tank's silt, raising the level to near full, and turning its normal green color to brown. TJ's personal truck and an assortment of law enforcement vehicles were strewn along the outside of a corral fence. The assemblage included a local EMS ambulance and what I recognized as Texas Ranger Abner Selman's state sedan.

What the hell is a Ranger doing here from Del Rio on something that just got called in?

Men in a variety of uniforms bunched in the available shade of the east sides of outbuildings and an out-of-place live oak that stood next to the house.

Hope no one is robbing the bank in Santa Rosa. From the looks of it, anyone remotely involved in law enforcement is here.

Someone had shown the presence of mind to run crime scene tape around the general area, but if this was a crime scene, I had a feeling it had already been compromised.

God, please, please, make whatever has happened be here, and not down by the river.

I killed the engine. As I stepped out, TJ and Selman came up, offering me their hands. There were no pleasantries.

TJ took a deep breath and nodded to the Ranger. "Go ahead, Abner; tell Purdy what we've got."

One of the anachronisms of rural Texas was the availability, some would say potential for interference, of the Texas Rangers. Whatever their original basis for being, they now often lent a hand, and occasional easing of political pressure, to beleaguered and undermanned rural law enforcement with limited resources.

TJ didn't take kindly to anyone getting in his business. Unless there was something involved with an ongoing Ranger investigation, or TJ had asked for outside help, Selman wouldn't be butting into a strictly local issue. Ranger assistance in a hot election year would not be abided unless it was for something profoundly troubling.

Selman hadn't just happened by. This was getting stranger and stranger. He brushed an imaginary dust speck off his pressed slacks.

"There's a mess in the house. We've got a body in there. You'll see what I mean in a minute. I'd be glad to call Laredo or San Antonio and get some criminalists out here, but TJ says you should handle it. You can cover this about as much as they can."

I glanced at TJ. He made a small nod.

That's as good as it's going to get.

Remembering Reagan's request, I kept my mouth shut.

The bile in my throat suddenly reappeared. "Where are the Vasquezes?"

"No one was at the river house, and their truck is there. Pretty sure they went into town or Del Rio. Pete's the one who called this in. He said he called and got no answer, so he drove up from Laredo to check on them and spotted the door open to the porch. Saw this." He nodded toward the house. "He went toward the river. He used the old folks' landline."

This was a long speech for TJ. He paused.

"I sent Sanchez and Wilson down at their place looking as well, but so far, nothing. House is unlocked, but Pete says that's normal. Nothing disturbed. Hell, they may not even have been here."

Maybe, but if Otabiano's truck was there...Please, God, don't let them be somehow hurt.

Selman looked around as he added, "I'm here to help, and TJ knows I'm not going to step on any local toes to do it. But we've had some problems all along the border, and some may have shifted here."

Well, we always have trouble on the goddamn border. What are you doing here, right now, you sneaky bastard?

TJ blew out a burst of air. He looked frazzled. "This may just be some outlaw wet crossing the river and killing someone, but I doubt it."

Farther west a few years back, a county sheriff had been caught hauling horse trailers full of cocaine. It had been going on under the nose of that area's Ranger.

Selman wasn't here without a reason, and a remote ranch killing wouldn't get him here unless he was asked, or had a vested interest in something going on in the area to begin with. I was betting that "trouble on the border" translated to drug smuggling.

"TJ, whose case is this, ours or the Rangers'?"

TJ glanced at Selman before responding. "Right now, it's ours."

Right now?

It was hot, and whatever was in the ranch house had got me promoted back to investigator.

Johnny Reagan grabbed a clipboard and walked toward the screened in porch. "Come on, Purdy, I'll show you what we've got."

The smell hit me before I went through the porch door. It was a scent of rotting flesh. With it came the sound of blow flies. Two paramedics nodded as we pulled up the tape and stepped up on the porch. Both were pasty faced, and it didn't take a lot to see that there were no life-saving efforts being made in the house.

"You go inside?" I asked them.

"Yeah," one replied. "We didn't touch anything, but wanted to make sure. Whoever it was has been dead awhile. Goddamn, I've seen some shitty stuff, but this takes the cake."

Both headed toward some shade, as I stepped inside.

SEVEN

Present Day – A Friday

PURDY KENDRICKS

Just off the porch was the kitchen, and through the kitchen was the old living room. The smell of death permeated the whole house. A sink full of dirty dishes and a scattering of magazines, mostly of the checkout stand variety, cluttered the two rooms. A sleepy drone of engorged flies came from the bedroom.

Once you smell dried human blood, it never leaves you. It has a cloying, metallic bite to it. Reagan walked toward the bedroom door, and I followed, regretting not bringing some Vicks to put under my nose.

Blackened blood and viscera were splattered all over the back of the room and on the bed. The bed itself held what could only be described as the desiccated remains of something once human. Like an Edward Munch painting I'd seen in a museum, the mouth described a surprised and pained oval of shock. One hand clearly had been shot to pieces, and there was only half a head to go along with the mouth. An eyeball was incongruously draped over the iron bedstead. It had once fit into the left eye socket that was now a maw of blackened flesh.

BB-like holes permeated the wall behind the bed. It was easy to see someone had been killed with a shotgun.

I'd worked a lot of homicides in Houston, and I had taken a lot of crime scene courses in order to keep my Investigator certification alive. I stood in the doorway trying to take it all in. Peering in a screened window were couple of deputy constables looking like vultures on a fence. They watched me eyeball the dead body.

"Instead of gawking, someone bring my kit and camera cases out of the trunk." I unlatched the window screen and pushed my keys through the opening.

They skittered off. The trunk slammed as they retrieved the criminal investigation kit and two camera cases.

Worrying about what might be found at the river wasn't helping my disposition.

"Do we know who this is?" I opened the two camera cases, and loaded batteries into the cameras.

Reagan stood outside the room. "Purdy, no one has a clue, and I've never seen him before—at least so far as I can tell from what face he's got left. I was down at Otabiano's place with Pete and called dispatch on the land line from there to see if anyone can track down Laura to see if he was a guest out here."

Johnny Reagan's family had lived in Kickapoo County for three generations, and if anyone would know whether what I was looking at had been a local, it was him.

Most rural law enforcement comprises one part keeping feuding neighbors calmed down about their next door transgressors, one part trying to pen cattle that break out of their barbed wire pastures, one part dealing with break-ins and assorted thefts, and one part dealing with drunk drivers and the mayhem they create on highways. My exposure to dead bodies, since I had returned to Kickapoo County, was mostly in assisting fire and EMS pull maimed remains out of car wrecks, or ensuring that things termed "natural" deaths were in fact just that. Because of Kickapoo County's proximity to the border, I occasionally worked cases with illegals who couldn't buy any luck at all and got caught in some eddy or hydraulic when the Rio Grande was in one of its rare moments of anger. We didn't have a true border crossing, and while there was no doubt that the river was of little impedance to incursions of the U.S. border, the county hadn't seen the gang-related violence downriver associated with Nuevo Laredo and Matamoros.

At last count, the county only had five beer joints, one frequented by the Anglos, and the others primarily by the Hispanics. None had an atmosphere that lent itself to violence.

The poverty and hopelessness I'd seen in the wards in Houston had created a hotbed for cheap deaths. The casual violence of gang drive-bys, drug snuffs, with an occasional unhinged lover's rage thrown in had pretty much numbed me at the time. It was one of several reasons I came home.

I could see in the Griffin bedroom that someone had been killed in a very deliberate fashion. The blow flies and acrid, rotting smell of old blood emphasized that thought. This mayhem hadn't been seen in Santa Rosa County in a long while.

I felt the gorge rising in my throat, but caught Reagan eyeing me. I swallowed and reached for a set of elastic gloves, paper booties, and a filtered mask.

I thought my protective shell still was still in place.

It wasn't.

EIGHT

Present Day – A Friday

PURDY KENDRICKS

Johnny Bonavita, 22 years old and six months in the department, took my digital camera out of its case and stood in the doorway to the bedroom.

"Want me to take some shots?"

Johnny's family was from Lágrimas. Sensing some sort of bond between us, he occasionally hounded me about stories of being a "real" investigator in Houston. Johnny'd been president of the high school photography club, and was a quiet, nerdy type. I liked him. I'd shown him a few things about photography at the Sheriff's office.

To give him something to do, I agreed.

"Keep back but stay behind the door right now. Don't touch anything, including the doorframe, okay?"

He nodded but couldn't conceal his appreciation at getting to do more than just stand around.

His eagerness to help made me feel somehow beholding.

"Deputy Reagan," I hollered. He wandered over from the shade. "I'd appreciate it if you could get someone to make a list of anyone in the room." I paused. "We just need to rule out prints and stuff. Thanks."

Reagan nodded. "How long is this going to take, Purdy? I'm not rushing you, but we've got everyone in uniform over here it seems. I'd like to turn some of them loose; like to know if you'll need anyone else."

"I'm okay here. What about the river house?"

"Still nothing, but I'll let you know." He looked around. "I want to send some more folks down there." He pulled on his cigarette and tossed the butt into the gravel. "Hope you won't be needed down there."

Mercy, no.

"Need a favor, Johnny. Can you call Paula and tell her I'll be late for the boy? Maybe ask her to bed him down?"

Reagan nodded and walked off.

Plugging in the iPod ear buds, I found my playlist and punched play. *Back in the Saddle Again* played to an audience of one. It wasn't long before I was there with Gene Autry on the open range.

I reached down and pulled some baggies out of the kit and started marking items to be sampled or collected. With the video camera, I was shooting as I described what I saw. I then got the digital from Bonavita and systematically took pictures of all marked items, as well as the body. Bonavita got the array of plastic baggies and paper bags ready for use. Mostly, we collected and bagged steel shotgun pellets and dried chunks of human flesh.

The assortment of onlookers milled around outside the house, anxious to be gone. They were stuck there until something came of the search for the old folks on the river. I moved around the room, and something grabbed my insides. I couldn't figure what it was for a few seconds. Then it hit me—I was doing *real* police work—again. As I pawed through the detritus of death, Eddie Arnold's looping yodels of *Cattle Call* rang in each ear.

Bonavita coughed. I turned, thinking he was going to toss his cookies. He stared at me.

I pulled out an ear bud. "What?'

"Purdy, you okay?"

"Yeah. Why?"

"I think you're yodeling."

Oh, shit. "Sorry." I cut my eyes toward the bedroom's one window. The conversations around the vehicles had stopped, and everyone was looking toward the house.

"Everything okay in there?" shouted TJ.

"All good here. Sorry, Sheriff. I'll tone it down."

I'm in the middle of some nasty shit, and I'm acting like a damned fool. I plugged in the ear bud, and went back to work, quietly.

A fingerless claw of a hand stretched out near the bedstead. Something had blown off the digits. The webbing between the first finger and thumb showed a jagged tear that looked somewhat different that the other wounds, but I didn't give it much thought. The body's injuries were so extensive, I'd let someone else sort out if there was any significance.

The body showed some lividity, and blood pooled in the back and lower legs, which dangled off the bed. Shit from a suddenly relaxed bowel was smeared on the sheets and back of the legs. Fluid ran from the rigor-relaxed mouth. Bloating was aggravated by the heat.

Bonavita coughed loud enough for me to hear.

"How long has he been dead?"

"Can't say, but at least two days, given what I'm seeing here."

Damned lucky this was found when it was. Although I have no idea how this happened in the middle of Bumfuck, Egypt.

A few more days in this heat would have left partially mummified remains.

"Uh, you remember Peter Vasquez?" Bonavita seemed on a fishing expedition.

I more than just remembered Pete. Growing up, we were closer than brothers. Of course, things changed.

"Yep." I left it at that.

"He was the one who found this guy."

I knew that. Bonavita was a lot younger than I was but had to know at least some of my history with Pete and his family.

My lack of response wasn't dampening his desire to talk something out.

"Well, me," he squared his shoulders as if to deliver a homily. "If I lived darned near three hours away, and I called to check on my grandma and grandpa and got no answer, I'd a called someone to go check on 'em. Or at least not waited a whole day to go up here."

He had a point, one that had been kicking at my insides for a while, as well. Pete could have called any of a dozen folks to check on his grandparents in a pinch, and he knew it. It was a good 2-1/2-hour drive from Laredo. Something didn't ring true, but I couldn't put my finger on it. But right now, Pete's motives in not using locals to check on his grandparents weren't my concern. What I wanted to do was drop what I was doing and drive the additional three miles down to the Vasquez house.

As Bonavita and I labored, a long-buried memory suddenly washed over me – my mom had been coming to pick me up at Tommy Hudson's house on the highway after his birthday party. I was swinging in an old tire in the back yard, when we all heard a horrific smash of cars, and a keening of one of the occupants. Somehow, I knew Mom was in one of those cars. I ran screaming at the top of my lungs toward the accident.

It was dusk, and two vehicles lay in various pieces scattered across the highway. The keening continued, and vaguely, one of the cars looked like my mom's old car. I heard the Hudsons and other adults running behind me, screaming at me to stop. I had outrun my endurance and had to stop and catch my breath, as the lactic acid boiled up in me. I bent over, took some breaths, and ran out into the highway toward the noise in the first car I came to. I was six years old, and I was screaming "Mama" at the top of my lungs. I remember trying to breathe, yell for her, and pray to God, all at once.

I got to the car about the time that the Hudsons reached me. In the gloom was a fiftyish woman in the passenger seat of a car from Iowa, screaming for help. Her feet were caught up under the crushed dash, and there was blood all over her forehead where she had hit the metal. I was shocked. I'd never seen anyone in pain. I'd never seen so much blood. No one else was seriously hurt. But this was the big thing—the woman in the car wasn't my mom.

Relief flooded over me like cold water dousing a fire. As the Hudsons pulled me back from the shattered glass and pieces of metal, I saw Mama and our sedan pulling around on the shoulder, and I started crying, partly from pent-up fear, and partly from just knowing I was going to be all right. I was elated—she was all right—it wasn't Mama! The fact that another human was in agony didn't matter right then. For a six-year-old what was important was that the horrible imaginable loss hadn't happened.

Pulling more baggies out of the kit, I felt a wreck being played out in my mind, along with the physical and human detritus involved in its most horrible way. I could see myself running toward the scene—only this time, I knew that whatever had happened to the Vasquez family wasn't something that was going to be someone else's problem. No, this time, whatever had happened directly involved two people I deeply loved.

NINE

Present Day – A Friday

PURDY KENDRICKS

TJ, Reagan, and Selman helped with the inventory and search of the place. The small dresser held several changes of clothes. Beneath the underwear and socks lay a large manila envelope. Selman lifted it by the corner and opened the unsealed flap.

"Sheriff, we've got money in here."

He scooped up the envelope with gloved hands and took the time to count out the bills, placing the money in stacks on the rug in front of the bedroom door. Mostly hundreds with a few twenties mixed in, it came to $40,320. I bagged the money, marked the evidence tag, and handed it to Bonavita.

"That's a shit load of money for this poor sod," Selman gestured toward the body.

The afternoon's work had accumulated several cardboard boxes that would go into the trunk of my cruiser for transport to the Texas Department of Public Safety lab in Austin.

The bedroom closet held years of accumulated junk—old puzzles, a Monopoly game, some faded insulated coveralls, and the scent of mothballs. Next to the nightstand on the floor lay an alarm clock; the AA battery was still in place, and it still kept time.

The dead man wore some Munsingwear briefs and nothing else. A pair of jeans and a denim shirt were draped over a chair adjacent to the dresser. Dirty boondockers lay underneath. A small pile of dirty laundry emitted a sour smell that overtopped the copper smell of the blood. The sheriff picked up each bit of clothing, bagging it separately. In the mix were two sets of mud-encrusted camouflage pants and shirts.

"Huh," TJ uttered. "These smell like the river. What's this ole boy been up to?"

Selman paused, raised a muddy pant leg to his nose. "Yep."

After the tete a tete they went back to bagging evidence. There was no weapon, no wallet, nor any sort of identification. No credit cards in the pockets on the jeans . . . whoever had killed this guy hadn't done it for the cash.

The old ramada had been screened in at some time in the past, and dusty day beds, extra mattresses, sliders, and rockers sat in various positions of disuse on the hand-poured concrete floor. Turning into the kitchen, I checked an old-style fuse box. The only circuits that looked in use were those feeding the bedroom and kitchen. Several new looking 20-amp fuses sat on a windowsill next to the sink.

A compressor kicked in, and I jumped at the unexpected sound. An old Kelvinator refrigerator still operated, but its compressor rattled and chugged like it was giving out. Its interior light bulb was as dead as the guy in the next room, but the machine worked well enough to cool unwrapped lunch meat, bottled water, some bread going stale in its original wrapper, and a half-empty bottle of Smirnoff's vodka.

A bar code sticker on the bologna pack showed it to be from the Busy Bee. The expiration date on the pack had passed two days ago. The Smirnoff's had a sticker from the liquor store in Santa Rosa. Whoever I'd taken pictures of had shopped locally, or someone did it for him. No way this guy's presence hadn't been known to the Vasquez couple.

We gave EMS the okay to remove the body. It wouldn't go to the local mortuary, but to San Antonio for an autopsy. Like most rural counties, we contracted with a large county's Medical Examiner's Office to do postmortems.

Seth Roberts, Justice of the Peace for County Precinct Four, where the ranch was located, waited with the onlookers in the shade. Like most rural JPs, his was a part-time, low-paying avocation. Its duties let him cut loose from his job with a local propane dealer, which suited him fine. Seth had once applied to DPS in Austin, didn't get accepted, and never pursued it or any other kind of law enforcement job after that. Once, over coffee I joked that he didn't have the appropriate level of paranoia to be a cop. He'd laughed, sort of. I liked him and had since we were kids.

State troopers tried to file any traffic tickets in other precincts, as Seth was a soft touch for any excuse. TJ also saw few possible votes to be gained by making his deputies run radar, so most deputies' ticket books got dusty or lost before they got used up. Since writing tickets was something I detested, I didn't have a lot of problems with either of their viewpoints.

"Seth, we need an autopsy on this one." TJ nodded toward the departing ambulance.

"No shit, Sherlock," Seth grinned. "But I can save the county some money. I got a look. I *know* what killed him." He seemed pleased with his attempt at humor.

TJ scowled.

"All right. Just kidding. I'll fax the order up to Bexar County."

As he spoke, paramedics walked by pulling a gurney with the black body bag strapped to it, headed for one of Kickapoo County's two ambulances. The gurney rocked and bounced in the uneven soil, but the corpse in the bag wasn't going to complain about the treatment. The trip to San Antonio would leave the county shorthanded in that area for a good half a day, but it also meant that a couple of underpaid county employees would draw some overtime. The ambulance crew collapsed the gurney's legs and shoved it into the back of the ambulance. The back door slammed, and dual rear tires cut a dusty path back to the ranch entrance.

Chief Deputy Johnny Reagan had had the presence of mind to move some of the vehicles out of the general area, in hopes of finding footprints, tire tracks, or anything else that would show how the killer had gotten to the house. He sure as hell didn't walk in from the highway. From Mexico? Well, that would be another story. Emergency vehicles and personnel had pretty well messed up any chance of this being a fruitful operation.

Late afternoon heat and torpor reclaimed the ranch house, as humans, both living and dead, departed. Abner and TJ headed toward the river and the Vasquez house.

Clete Morales's black and white pulled in. Clete was on the downside of a 30-year highway patrol career. He'd decided a long time ago he wasn't going to make sergeant without moving to Dallas or Houston, and settled for corporal stripes and rural policing. We were close enough in age to have some experiences in common, and my renewed sense of impending misery helped me appreciate his company.

Clete locked his cruiser and climbed into the county car. No sense in risking having to explain to Austin how he scratched up a new black and white, I guess. I started the engine on the county car. We inched down the tracks, and I filled him in.

"Pete's down by the river looking for his people. Apparently he hadn't heard from them, couldn't get them on the phone, got worried and drove up. He found the mess back at the main house."

"Pete doesn't get up here too often now. It's not like him to just show up, as I recall."

He was right, but his assessment rubbed me the wrong way. Clete had transferred to Kickapoo County long after Pete had left. As far as I was concerned, it was still family we were talking about. The two old folks were as honest as the day was long, and I couldn't see either of them trucking to any sort of illegality. I was edgy and on the verge of getting upset. Clete apparently sensed it. He'd seen me worse. He settled back in the seat and decided to change the focus of conversation.

"What shit music you listening to now?" He gestured toward the iPod ear buds and wires dangling from my shirt pocket.

"Hell, Clete, this is some of the greatest *tejano* music around."

"Didn't know you liked it. Who is it?"

"Greatest Mexican import in last couple a years. Guy named Carlos Gardel. Got a new hit out that's cutting across Tex-Mex to mainstream as we speak. Called *Mi Noche Triste*. Good little shuffle beat."

"*My Sad Night.*" Like all of us, Clete spoke passable Spanish. "Sounds like something me and the missus could dance to. I'll try to find him on Pandora," he said.

Good luck with that. I wondered why I was jerking his chain, although it did take my mind off things for a bit. He wasn't going to remember, and probably didn't care what music I had downloaded. I doubted he'd take the time to figure out that Gardel had been dead since 1935, and "he and the missus" would play hell trying to tango.

The sun dipped below a bluff. It would be dark soon. Canebrakes and salt cedars choked the riverside. Finding bodies in the dense growth—assuming the Vasquezes were dead—would get harder, unless they hadn't been taken over the border, or tossed in the river.

"What do you think?" Clete rolled down the passenger window, trying to get some air circulating.

"I don't know, Clete, but something isn't right. Pete's out looking for the folks, and I'm hoping the two of them are just off shopping."

I wasn't buying it. Clete glanced over and tried to offer a little comfort.

"Don't you think if they'd found something down there, we'd heard about it by now?"

Good point, but there were places on the riverbanks where it'd be damned impossible to search.

"I just came from Santa Rosa. I didn't see Otabiano's old truck around town or at the café." He paused. "Of course, he could be any of a dozen places, I guess, but I didn't pass him on the way out here either."

The car dipped down into a sandy track that led into the alluvial plain. Any wind moderating the heat stopped with the drop down to the bottom land.

"Goddamn, Purdy, when are you going to get some A/C in this car?" He was trying to keep things light, but I could tell he had some of the same feelings I had.

"I suspect it'll get done about time of first norther, if history is any indication. Course, we could have used yours."

"Shit no, Purdy. This car," he tapped on the dashboard, "this here is just the ideal automobile for where we're headed."

A Ford pickup, which I took to be Pete's, was parked near a pole barn that normally provided some shelter for the old Vasquez Dodge three-quarter ton diesel Otabiano had bought third-hand years before.

A deputy was filling TJ in. "It," he gestured toward the truck's hood, "was hot as hell on this metal but it's not from the engine. I don't think Otabiano has gone anywhere in this thing anytime recent."

The Vasquez house was wide open, and I assumed no one had been found inside. We sat there for a minute just taking in the area. Cooling metal from our vehicles ticked and pinged. Off in the distance, the usual late afternoon buzzards rode the air currents, looking for a meal. A tethered goat from across the river bleated and rang its collar bell. Grasshoppers snapped and fizzed as they made for some piece of greenery to chew on. Nothing seemed out of place, except that the old folks had always had at least one dog on at the place.

Abner didn't know the Vasquez family, but knew enough of folks around the border to know that dogs were necessary equipment this far from civilization. "Don't these folks have a dog?"

"I don't know," I shrugged. "It's been a year or two since I've been out here, but they always have had, and I can't imagine them not." Dogs scented snakes and both two- and four-legged coyotes.

The last one I had seen was an Alsatian cross of some kind, too old to ride into town in the back of the pickup. So Otabiano kept him chained inside the run when they were gone. Talk stopped again. No barking. I walked around the back of the small house, and sure enough, the dog run I had remembered was still in place. The food bowl was empty, but there was a cut-down plastic bucket under a dripping faucet extending from the back wall of the kitchen. Every time a drop hit the surface, the surface tension broke, and a small amount ran down its side. There had been enough run-over to attract a bead of piss ants.

"They have one, or at least did."

The clothesline held three pairs of old jeans and a row of socks and underwear. The wicker clothes hamper still had washing in it, along with an old plastic bread wrapper half full of clothespins. Several sheets and pillowcases remained unhung. I stuck my hand into the hamper. There was no indication of dampness, even in the deep folds at the bottom of the stack.

Reagan came around the edge of the house. "No one's found anything yet. The boys are trying to do a systematic search, but trying to keep Pete on a short leash hasn't worked. They tell me he hasn't slowed down since he got here. Won't let them do their jobs."

Just then shouts erupted upriver from where we stood. The noise then settled into gasps of "Oh, Gods," and "Oh, Jesus Christs."

We both knew who it was, but I guess we were both frozen as if bidden to honor someone else's private descent into a very personal hell.

Pete had found his grandparents.

We huffed down to the river on a sendero that led toward where Otabiano kept his small boat.

Following the sound through the thickets, I spotted a white-shirted, black-headed man who could only be Pete Vasquez. As I got near, I saw him moving his hands up and down, and pacing in a small circle, as if caged. Sounds continued to emanate from him, but I was too busy trying to catch my breath to hear what was being said.

Clete caught up with me just as we came to a grassy area where Otabiano had his boat chained. Pete turned and saw us. He kept shouting, not at us, but like he was trying to drive something malignant away from him with sound alone. He pointed over to a cane-brake upstream. Then he turned and pushed into the foliage as we ran to keep up.

"Here. Here. Here. They're here," he screamed, his voiced hardly muted in the cane.

Ignoring thorns and the chance of meeting rattlesnakes, we came to a small opening. The old couple had had their hands bound with what looked to be plastic and nylon clothesline. Raquel had been shot once in the back of the head. She'd dropped face down. It didn't look like she had had the chance to even try to avoid what was about to happen. I knew when we turned her over that the front of her face was going to show an exit wound that was much bigger than the small black dot surrounded by a mat of blackened blood.

Otabiano had gotten a harder death. He must have known what was coming, because his body showed he'd put up a fight before he died, probably resisting being trussed. Blood had soaked into the sand and discolored the grass all around his abdomen. I guessed he'd been gut shot first, maybe trying to protect Raquel. Another round had caught him in the forehead, and powder tattooing was apparent around the wound. The second bullet had been fired within three feet, probably as the *coup de grace*. The old man's caked and glazed eyes seemed to be looking at his wife's still form. Ants trailed to and from the wounds, eyes, nose, and mouth.

I pulled my eyes off the two bodies and watched Clete pinning Pete's arms to his side, embracing him in a bear hug. Pete kept trying to move toward the bodies, and Clete wouldn't let him. It was like trying to calm a wild animal. Pete started coming back into some sort of self-control, almost made it, and then broke loose again. Clete kept saying "It'll be okay." Those words never make sense at a scene like this, but we had all used them. TJ grabbed and bear hugged Pete, but he was struggling. Selman, Reagan and Clete wrestled Pete down and sat on him.

"Fuck. Fuck. Fuck. I'll kill the motherfuckers. I'll kill them."

"Pete. Pete," I shouted. "Look at me, Pete."

He turned his head, his forehead bleeding where it had hit the ground.

"Oh, Purdy. Goddam. Goddam."

His screaming now was reduced to grunts.

"What motherfuckers, Pete?"

Pete began to sob.

TEN

Smith And Jones

EIGHT DAYS BEFORE PRESENT–A FRIDAY

The two men waited impatiently by the river for two hours. A storm upstream had considerably narrowed the options for entering Mexico, as a five-foot rise had erased the gravel bars of the normally shallow crossing.

A small aluminum boat was chained to a post upstream from an old line shack now occupied by an old couple. After some discussion, the men decided to ferry the equipment, have one of them bring the boat back, and then swim the horses and mule over. The rain had slacked off, but the clay on the riverbank was slick and dangerous and would soon be marked with their tracks. Darkness would last another two hours, and either they hid out with the mosquitoes in the cane-brakes another day, or they went now. Crossing during daylight was not an option.

The rain clouds had appeared in late afternoon, with the distant booming of thunder clattering back and forth through the shallow canyons, and then seemingly shouting itself out north into the wastes of the desert. Winds shifted, first west, then east, and finally north. Dampened creosote and sage that had lain dormant in the shimmering heat emitted wafts of odor, changing the flat smell of finely ground dust into a bouquet celebrating a rare enough rebirth. The slightly acid smell of rain could mean a surge. There was no guarantee that the river wouldn't continue on a rise tomorrow, as well. The longer they suffered in the brush, the better the chance of being spotted. Desolate and isolated as it was, the area still had settlements near the river.

The unexpected rain decided them. The shorter of the two men knew this country. The storm could play out before there was a rise, giving only a cloudy respite from the heat and torpid conditions, or it could hammer them with a fierce and decidedly angry force.

Large cold drops slapped down on them suddenly, as re-built cumuli soared into the atmosphere and threw off frozen bomblets that had barely thawed by the time they thwacked painfully onto exposed skin, dampened bushes, and dimpled the river. This rain had come from upstream.

They untied the boat's small mooring rope from an old sucker rod driven into the ground. Their gear came off the mule and horses. Firearms, ammunition, and what they would need to accomplish the mission were packed into water-tight gear bags. They carefully loaded and lashed them down. Grabbing a nylon bow line, they dragged the boat upstream, sliding in the clay and quietly cursing. They got as far as an outcropping of metamorphized rock that blocked any further travel. This would be the start of the run across.

"You realize you'll head downstream fast, don't you?" the short dark-haired man said to the tall Anglo calling himself Smith. Smith was hardly his real name, and the short Hispanic didn't want to know it.

He pointed to the dim gravel bar on the south side of the flood waters. "If you don't hit that outcropping, there's no telling where you'll end up."

The man calling himself Smith was at least five inches over six feet, his shaved head under a boonie cap that kept some of the drizzle out of his eyes.

"Like you say, we'll have to chance it. It'll take me at least twenty minutes to drag that thing upstream to make a run back to this side. Once I flash the light, I'm in the water and you'd better be ready to grab me." He tied his boots onto the lashings inside the boat, pushing off with a powerful oar stroke.

The Hispanic watched apprehensively through a small night vision scope until he lost sight of the boat as it careened downriver and into the brush on the Mexican side. He then pushed up off his knees, returned the scope to its nylon and Velcro sheath, then followed the bank back to the grassy area around the boat landing. He then wound through the soaked brush and untied the two horses and the mule. Slickers had been laid over the top of the horses' saddles earlier in an attempt to keep the leather dry. The fording made that a wasted effort.

The Hispanic's bare arms stung with each raindrop. He unrolled his sleeves to cover them. The collared shirt now hid tattoos there. The shirt couldn't conceal tattoos emerging from his torso, onto his neck, and into his scalp. He rechecked cinches, gear straps, and the mule's pack lashings, and then led the animals quietly to the water's edge. He picked a spot that was gravelly enough to give the animals some sense of security as they picked their way off the cut bank to the water's edge. The sucking noise of water hitting rocks below the water's surface lent additional eeriness in the dark. He tied the animals to some overhanging mesquite limbs and returned his attention to the river.

With no way to help, the Hispanic reached into a breast pocket and pulled out a tin of Copenhagen. He didn't bother using two fingers, instead lowered his tongue inside, without looking, and lapped a dip that he shifted into the space below his lower gum. Lightning periodically showed the Anglo slowly pulling the emptied boat upstream and then past view.

A half hour later, a penlight flashed twice. The boat was coming back. The sound of a wooden paddle scraping furiously against the aluminum side showed the intensity of the fight against the current.

"Hey, you short Mexican fucker, you'd better catch me." There was a hint of panic in Smith's shout. The boat scraped mud and gravel, and then was swung back into the main stream by the flood current.

The short man spotted the boat almost too late, as a coil of sodden nylon rope flew by him. He grabbed the nylon and wrapped it quickly around the base of a small tree, but not before the river's pull gave him a nasty rope burn. The boat's forward momentum came to a halt, and it spun backward, banging into the slippery bank. The force knocked Smith off his feet and onto the boat's aluminum floor. Quiet curses and grunts indicated Smith's progress as he pulled his way up the rope, working his way back upriver into a small eddy.

"Everything's stashed. Let's get this thing back where it belongs and get the hell out of here."

They trundled the boat upside down to its usual resting place, then quickly re-wound its tethering rope to the sucker rod. They returned to the horses, mounted, and, kicking furiously, drove the animals into the dark frothy water. The pack mule tried sitting on its haunches, couldn't get a grip in the wet clay and gravel, gave up, and plunged in behind the horses. It snorted and whinnied as it pulled against the lead rope wrapped around the Hispanic's saddle horn.

The men kicked furiously at their horses' flanks, while trying not to get swept off. Wild-eyed, the horses' hooves met gravel, and scrambled up onto the narrow bank on the south side of the river.

They had 40 miles to cover, and it would have to be done at night. They avoided scattered jacals and pueblos that dotted the Mexican border. They pushed the animals hard to make higher ground before dawn.

Rain was a mixed blessing. It kept some noise down, but tracks would be obvious to anyone looking. Shod horses weren't that common, and locals' burro prints were considerably smaller than those of a horse or mule. Shod horse prints headed south would be highly unusual, and word would be passed. Fortunately, where they were headed was too parched and God-forsaken for running livestock, once away from the alluvial settlements.

Their chance of being noticed in the pre-dawn light was mitigated by a heavy, overcast sky, the remains of the night's deluge. The bleating of goats signaled that herders knew daylight meant it was safe to turn out flocks to forage in the brush. Hints of orange and purple appeared below the cloud cover. The two men followed a small knoll choked with brush, keeping off the ridgeline, heading up toward a spine of low hills that ran north and south.

"Up there." The Hispanic pointed toward a small indentation in the face of the cliff. He dismounted and led his horse up and over a ridgeback. "It's an old Apache camp."

The rough sands turned to gravel, then to loose rock, and finally to a kind of aggregate concreted into place by catclaw, huisache, and other desert growth. A small trail wandered through the brush and into columns of red sedimentary rock.

Yesterday's leftover clouds parted. The first shimmers of heat rose from the desert floor. The night smell of wet desert flora dissipated. Dawn broke as they walked their animals under an overhang of rock blackened by centuries of fires.

"Locals won't be up here. It's supposed to be haunted by a *brujo*," said the smaller man.

"What's a brew hoe? I don't speak your language."

The Hispanic was too tired to provide language lessons. "Evil spirit, ghost, male witch." The tension of crossing and traveling undetected, added to his fatigue. "We'll sleep here. You get first watch. I've got to get some sleep."

Smith unsaddled the horses. He tossed the sodden saddle blankets and grinned at the Hispanic.

"Hey, you remember that TV show, *Alias Smith and Jones?*"

The Hispanic shook his head but sat mute.

"Two guys on the lam; that's what this reminds me of. Since I don't know your name, from now on instead of 'short Mexican fucker,' I'll call you 'Jones.'" He slipped a hackamore over the first horse's nose as he removed the bridle and bit, not turning around to see the reaction.

"Christ," thought the newly dubbed Jones, "this skinhead looks like he's on steroids. I hope he is as good with a rifle as he with running his mouth. At least the asshole has some knowledge of horses and mules."

Jones knew he was as good as dead, but some deaths were worse than others. He did what he was told to do. And that meant getting Smith where the Anglo deep into Mexico. Jones threw a small sleeping bag into some dirt mixed with centuries of animal dung, crawled in, and fell asleep instantly.

ELEVEN

Smith And Jones

"Hey, rise and shine, buddy." A booted toe made sure Jones woke up.

Late afternoon sun had crossed over the small mountains. The rock undercut lay darkness. Both horses were already saddled. Smith turned and loaded a padded gun case on the mule, finishing its loading.

"Shit, you were supposed to wake me up hours ago. Did you pull watch this entire time?" Jones's guts roiled, and he felt a need to shit.

"Pretty much. Didn't see anything to be worried about. No one around. Moved the animals closer to us. We're okay." Smith's words came out like the staccato of automatic weapon fire.

Speed. He's hitting the speed too early. He could crash and burn if he's not careful.

Jones's worries welled up. "Any kid sees us, and we're fucked, *puto*." The angrier he got, the more pronounced his Latino accent became. "I don't know where you come from, but this is country I understand. I've got to get you in and out, or we're fucked. So, do me a favor. I may be a dumb *messkin* to you, but you don't know shit from frijoles about this part of the world. I've got you this far. Don't fuck it up for both of us."

I'm like a goddam animal treading water in a slick sided cenote, Jones thought. Far too late to turn back now. He would do his best not to get it his situation any more fucked up by some *gabacho* asshole. Smith's

51

technical skills aside, the guy was downright spooky. Jones's adrenalin pushed him to say more, but he held it back.

Smith cut a glance at Jones. He eyes squinted almost closed, giving him a feral look Jones had shown others. Now, it sent chills down his back. *Santa Muerte, me proteje.*

Smith got a small kick out of Jones's look, but there wasn't time to savor a sense of control. He paused, as if deciding whether to force a confrontation, blew out some air, then grunted and turned away. As far as he was concerned after Iraq, this kind of mission was like a back-country day hike. Or so he kept telling himself. *But the little shit is right—I'll give him his due. Tattooed gangbanger acts like he knows this place.*

Any settling up would have to wait. In the meantime, Smith'd play by Jones's rules, as long as they served his purposes.

The moment passed. The horses' cinches were rigged right, blankets and saddles secured. The mule, resentful of the pack frame, swelled up and fought against the cinch. Smith kicked the jenny twice in the ribs, and it settled down, allowing it to be tightened. Appreciative of Smith's unforeseen expertise with the animals, Jones wondered what other skills the tall man had.

The uneven terrain required another night to cover the 30 miles. They lay up during the day in arroyos, before carefully reconnoitering from over a mile away. From their position in the rocks and rubble they glassed a large compound. Jones looked through a range finder. Smith spotted through a Schmidt and Bender rifle scope.

The compound had once been part of a well-heeled but remote Mexican ranching headquarters. Forting up against renegade Indians, and later, Villistas and Orozquistas, had required the security of a walled compound by *hacendados* in the remote north of Mexico.

A 10-foot-high wall surrounded what appeared to be at least a five-acre compound of various buildings. The original whitewashed wall was made with adobe brick and in some places, rock. Recent repairs indicated concrete cinderblock had replaced adobe as the barrier of choice. There was enough exposed adobe under fallen away lathing to show that most of the walls still dated to a time when *narcotraficos* weren't able to buy and transport modern building materials from the encroaching outside world.

From their elevation and with the scopes, the men identified a large ranch house, swimming pool, garages, corrals, and tack rooms, and what were probably bunkhouses. In one corner was a *campo santo*, a burial ground for families who had owned or worked the place over the centuries. There were no changes to the satellite photo they'd studied at a ranch house where they'd been briefed. A Bell Ranger, its rotor blades lashed to anchor points, stood on a concrete pad. Four Humvees with pedestal mounted M-60s were parked at the front of the ranch house.

Armed men stood in four small guard towers built into the exterior corners of the walls. The occasional glint of sun on binoculars confirmed that whoever was in the towers wasn't asleep. Men in the compound, automatic weapons slung over their shoulders, lazily kicked at dust, while smoking cigarettes, or *mota*. They didn't look exactly bored, but then neither did they appear overly concerned. It was a relaxed look, almost casual, indicating that the object of security wasn't there to watch over, at least not yet.

Smith and Jones donned ghillies, sniper outfits procured for this mission. In the heat, they soon wished they hadn't had to. It was hot as hell, and air couldn't get through the heavy garb. Sweat stains appeared in the armpits and crotch of Jones's suit, and sweat ran down the middle of his back. He was tempted to roll over and rub around like a dog with a flea. A string of red ants wormed its way into Smith's pants leg, but he ignored them. Occasionally, he wrote something on a small notepad.

"What happens if we get caught?" Smith muttered as he continued scoping.

Jones didn't want that thought. "They torture us. They break our legs with boards. They smash our feet with rocks. They cut off our ears. And our balls."

"I heard about you people," Smith said in a low voice. "Your people do some weird shit."

"Don't you worry, little man. We'll either get out or die. We won't get caught." He acted unconcerned.

Smith used his digital watch to time the circuit of a Humvee winding through a bulldozed series of trails surrounding the compound.

"I need like to be within 1,000, but 800 is better." Smith dropped the scope and swept his eyes around the approaches to the buildings.

Careful not to make a sudden movement, he inched his hand out in front of him and pointed to a small hill with a side bulldozed away for the entrance road. The hill, really not much more than a hummock, had a crest that offered a down-angle toward the main entry to the ranch house.

"Hey, Jones. What's the range to the little hill?" He pointed toward a hummock the other side of the dirt road leading to the compound.

"Seven hundred-twenty-eight meters, according to this thing." "This thing" was a Newcom LRB 20,000A Range Finder, bells and whistles included. Smith's short course had given Jones the basics in sniper spotting, but Jones was still uneasy about his ability to make an accurate call

"And from there to the main house?"

"Looks like seven hundred-sixty-five, but you check it. I'm new at this."

Smith slid to his left, as Jones rolled out of his way, and re-checked the numbers given him. Rolling back, he quickly did some calculations, then grunted in confirmation.

"I can get him from there if I can see over the wall. I'll check it out tonight." He picked up the scope again.

The southeast guard tower displayed movement within the shadows of the adobe and rock cupola. A small parapet extended along both the connecting walls. One of the two guards walked out, holding a long tube-like object. At this distance, Smith and Jones couldn't hear what was being said, but it was clear the one with the tube was joking with the guard remaining inside the shadows of the cupola. He pointed the tube toward an imaginary aircraft, super-elevated and set the lead. He pretended to squeeze on its pistol grip.

"Holy shit, is that what I think it is?" Smith looked up, scoping in on a Humvee parked under a camouflage cover south of the compound. He continued to look through the scope. "Yessiree," he laughed. "They've got Stingers," he added. "God only knows where they picked up those beauties. No wonder they said *no aerial operations will work.*"

If they had Stingers, someone had raided an armory in the States, or bought them through arms dealers permitted by the U.S. to sell to "friendlies." That took connections. And those kinds of connections took lots and lots of money.

"I heard about these," Jones frowned.

Smith quickly retorted. "I *know* about these. Why weren't we told about all this extra shit? If they can shoot down planes, where does that leave us?"

Jones sat mute. *My people never said anything about missiles. What else are they not telling me?*

Shit, this puto *is as scared as I am. And he doesn't know shit about what* mis campesinos *are capable of.*

With the lengthening shadow of a cliff face directly behind them, the men eased off the hill's saddle without being backlit. They carefully crept down into a deep ravine, where a rock overhang made overflight observation impossible.

As they stripped off the camouflage suits, the fear that he had hidden in the pit of his stomach showed itself in Jones's face.

"Even if you pull this off, they are going to be on us like *mierda*. We either get out, or else they cut our balls off and stuff them down our throats. You forget Mister *norteamericano*—I know. I've seen it. I've done it." *I'd be a fucking captain now, posted somewhere near Guatemala, if I'd stayed in the ejército. Shitty pay, but I could be a grandfather someday.*

"I'm not planning on making this a kamikaze mission. Once I figure out where I can get a shot, we've got a way out. I was promised that when I took this job. Quit being a pussy." Smith bent over to pinch pus out of the ant bites on his lower legs.

A resigned fatalism washed over Jones. Invoking God instead of Santa Muerte, he wondered if he was asking for forgiveness, or just that he not be caught. Probably both.

Smith seemed to sense Jones's ambivalence. It amused him. He enjoyed making people squirm. He watched Jones and laughed aloud to himself.

"I've got enough on my mind without your bullshit, little man. Just do as you're told. Now, make the phone call."

Struggling to his feet, Jones quietly took a case containing an encrypted satellite phone, checked various LED readouts, and squatted on his haunches waiting for the sun to move so he could take advantage of the shadows of late afternoon. He crept back up the hill, staying below the skyline. Jones picked up the satellite phone, powered it up, and punched in a memorized number. A man's voice came on the line.

"*Estamos aquí.*" Jones didn't have to say where here was.

"The *puto* is coming. *Tu pinche* shooter – he's got to do it. We paid. He performs, *entiendes*?

Jones nodded as if his assent could be seen. "When, and how?" He needed this information for the *pinche* shooter to get the job done, and not threats.

The man on the phone gave Jones the information. Jones relaxed a bit. It was happening like it had been predicted.

"When can we expect you back?"

Really. So you think we'll make it? I hope so. "Dawn – two days. Pick us up. *No me dejas aquí.* Jones felt sweat run down his back. It wasn't all from exertion. "Where?"

A pause. "Where I told you. Nothing's changed. You're one of ours. We'll see you soon. Good luck, Paco."

"You don't leave us hanging in the breeze. You owe me that much." He knew he was pleading. He felt ashamed of his weakness.

"*No te preocupes carnal.* Later."

Don't worry? I'm so tense they couldn't drive a spike up my ass.

The line went dead. It was a short conversation, but it had lasted too long. Not good. Hopefully if and when the Defense Intelligence Agency picked this snippet out of the millions of calls, he'd be long gone.

Ten minutes later, he was back under the overhang. Cascading gravel signaled Jones's return down into the draw. "It's for sure. He's moving. He's flying into El Mosco, and his convoy will meet him there."

"When?"

"He's leaving noonish tomorrow from south of Nuevo Laredo. Puts him into El Mosco in about an hour and half, max. Then figure, two hours here. There's two Humvees and a Suburban waiting at the strip in El Mosco."

"Why doesn't he just fly here? It's a hell of lot safer." Smith's puzzlement was legitimate. It did make more sense to fly all the way in. And with a ground-hugging helicopter, there was little or no chance that any radar, either in Mexico or across the border, was going to detect the movement. Even the tethered balloons didn't have look-down capability this far inside Mexico. Drones? If someone had one of those up? Well, there wasn't anything they could do about it.

Jones sighed. This God-forsaken part of *la patria* he knew well—it was part of why he was here. "Like I said, he won't put his wife and kid in an aircraft of any kind. He doesn't show much fear but isn't going to put his *familia* in what he thinks is harm's way. Guess he figures that if he's got Stingers, so does someone else. It makes sense. His boys control all this territory, so a trip overland may be bumpy, but he's not too worried about anyone around here turning on him." *Except me, I guess.* "Best I can figure, what few folks scratching a living between this place and El Mosco are either kin to him or one of his *tenientes.*"

"You confirm they'll meet us?"

Jones paused. "They said it was all good."

"We going back the way we came?"

"Yeah, sort of. We'll meet them upriver from where we crossed."

"Why not go back at the same place? It's plenty isolated." Smith picked an ant off his arm and crushed it between this thumb and pinkie.

"Easier out. Trucks come right down to the water."

Smith shrugged. "Well, don't get killed. They get you, I ain't got a chance to get out if you die." He nodded once, and then tuned Jones out. "I've got tonight to get this figured then." He put on the sweat soaked cammies, grabbed both the scope and the range finder. Reaching into the mule's pannier, Smith withdrew several heavy rectangular objects, loading them into a rucksack. He then scuttled off into the arroyo.

TWELVE

Smith And Jones

A pair of Hummers, sandwiching a black Suburban, clabbered down the caliche road that headed into the compound, throwing gravel and dust in their wakes. Whoever was leading the small convoy didn't feel discretion was an issue. The front Humvee's horn started blowing a quarter mile from the gates of the compound. The turbine whine and *whop whop whop* of the helicopter signaled overhead security. The paramilitary types inside the compound scurried to open the two gates, and four Humvees moved out from inside the walls, stationing themselves in twos on either side of the opening. All were manned by a driver and machine gunner, who slouched over a pedestal-mounted M-60.

No one had reported heat sensors, but with all this security, the two men didn't chance it. They stayed put under the escarpment. As the chopper spooled down, they chanced quick glances over the scree at the top of their ridgeline. The road and gate-security vehicles had withdrawn inside the now closed gates. The Humvees were being lined up and their engines killed.

Small groups of underlings walked quickly to the main house and stood in rough attention as the doors to the Suburban opened, and two bodyguards escorted—what looked to be—a middle-aged man and a young woman holding a child. The woman held the child's hand as the trio moved leisurely into the main ranch house. Meanwhile, the chopper's rotors were tied down against wind gusts.

After that, things started settling down. Additional guards were posted on the parapets, and a couple of ATVs made cursory runs up and down the hills closest to the structures. None got within 200 meters of the concealed men.

Dusk came on within an hour of the arrival of whoever had been in the Suburban. Avoiding possible detection until dusk meant brief looks and had prevented getting good identification on who in the Suburban rated Humvee and overhead security. It really didn't matter. Both men knew whose place it was and who had been escorted into the compound with him. Too much time looking only would have shown unprofessional curiosity, which would get them killed.

"I'm going to get ready." Smith reached for a ghillie suit. "It's going to take me at least two hours to do what needs doing and get to that crest by the cut-back for the road."

"Okay, two hours over, but when this happens, how long back?" They'd rehearsed the scenario countless times in the past 12 hours, but Jones wanted to hear it again.

"Give me fifteen minutes, max. If what I think is going to happen, no one is going to notice me duck back over to here. Just have everything ready to go."

Jones nodded. It was going to be a long night and a hard ride to the border – if they lasted long enough to make it.

"Time for some stay-awake." Jones opened a plastic pouch, pinched powdered methamphetamine, and offered the pouch to Smith. Both took hits.

Smith cackled. "I think I can fly back north, amigo." He sneezed twice, and then loaded a pack with the spotter scope and other items Jones couldn't make out. Smith then slung the unsheathed sniper rifle over his shoulder and walked down the arroyo. Jones checked hooves and shoes, in anticipation of loading everything on the animals and being ready to scamper north.

Darkness and the chill that comes from dry desert air settled in. Jones had hunkered down while the mule and horses were deep into their oat bags, when he heard the distant echoing *craaaack* of a high-powered rifle. Tinkling of glass and a scream came from the compound, then—nothing, at least for the time it took for the shock to wear off. There was a flurry of pistol and rifle fire. Jones scurried up to the escarpment to watch the fireworks. Men ran around outside the various buildings, but he couldn't see if anyone or any thing was being fired at. It looked like most weapons were being discharged over the walls into distant hills, and not at anything in particular.

The coolness in the night air helped carry the sounds of running feet, ATVs being fired up, screaming orders, and the whine of a helicopter turbine. Men ran in various directions in what looked like a choreography of panic. The pilots, not bothering with any pre-flight, jumping in, screaming and pointing at the tie-downs, and fired up the turbine.

In the confusion, they were ignored. The rotor blades on the helicopter didn't get released from ground ties, and there was an incessant and ever-increasing whine as the helicopter turbine tried to compensate for its inability to make the rotors circulate. Finally, two men, hearing the whine, or perhaps the pilots' screaming from the cockpit, ran over and loosed the tie-downs. The blades immediately started rotating, along with the tie-down cables. A cable caught one of the men in the face. He fell to ground, roiling around in agony. He struggled to his knees, pressing his hand to what had been his left eye.

As the blades caught air and increased rpms, the tie-downs were flung off. The helicopter lifted, four men with automatic weapons seated with feet on the skids. Another muted boom hit Jones's ears, and he saw sparks fly off the tail rotor. The Bell Ranger continued to rise, and another boom echoed. This time the tail rotor threw fire off like a Fourth of July sparkler as the rotor blade disengaged and destroyed its housing. The Bell Ranger yawed, then began turning tightly on its axis. The pilots tried to get the machine on the ground.

They were partially successful. The chopper bounced, then settled, but the right skid missed its concrete pad, tilting the chopper over on its side. Rotor blades thrashed the ground as men tried desperately to avoid being eviscerated by the wild flinging of metal. Fire erupted near the exhaust. The pilot pushed open the left side door but couldn't get it to stay open. His hand would fling it up, but it would then bang back down on the inert form of the buckled-in co-pilot. Desperately, the pilot beckoned for someone to help him unbuckle the co-pilot, who was either dead or unconscious. Two men from the main house ran over to help, and with the pilot, got the man halfway out of the cockpit.

Suddenly, there was a large whoosh. The co-pilot's lower extremities were covered in flames, and one of the paramilitary types grabbed a poncho and smothered the fire. Everyone still able to move high-tailed it away from the pad. Four bodies lay in and around the heli-copter. They were soon engulfed in burning JP4 fuel.

So much for any aerial search. Jones caught himself grinning. *Oh, I wish I could tell someone what we've done someday. We fucking killed the pinche puto. Thought he could take over our fucking territory. No fucking way.*

The steel-plated front gate to the compound grated open, and Humvees and ATVs began to speed through it. There was a large graveled open area where they could spread out and head in different directions, but two Humvees never got the chance. As vehicles shifted from column to some sort of echelon, Jones saw a flash of light and micro-seconds later, the accompanying CRACK of a Claymore mine exploding.

"So that's what was in that pack." Jones thought.

Not the best anti-vehicle mine, but the lightly armored Humvees didn't slow down a sheet of ball bearings spread in a 140-degree arc. Both engines riddled, steam poured from the radiators, covering the vehicles in smoke. No one emerged from the cooling steam.

The remaining four Humvees paused, and then slowly inched out on different axes, M-60s firing long bursts in their general direction of travel. So far, no one was heading directly toward their ravine, but Jones knew it was a matter of minutes before the searchers would, by default if nothing else, stumble onto the place.

The roadside hummock became the focus of attention. A pair of two-seater Polarises, with men following behind, inched up the rise near the road cut. They may not have known exactly what type of ordinance had killed the Humvees, but the *narcotraficos* knew it wasn't something they wanted to run into. Spreading out, the small group rounded the reverse slope where Smith had set up. One Polaris stayed on the ridge, and the driver stepped out, talking into a radio. The other Polaris raced back to the compound. In a matter of minutes, the remaining Humvees had encircled the small hill. Men on foot slowly advanced toward where the Polaris remained parked, with automatic weapons at the ready.

Jones lowered his light gathering binoculars and checked his watch. Fifteen minutes. No Smith. It was time to head north. He quietly led the horses and mule up the wash, hoping to at least buy some time with his relative silence. Silence wasn't the only reason for the use of horses and a mule. Where they had come from, and their only hope of getting out wasn't accessible, even to ATVs. He had to get out of the lower scrub and up into the block-thrust mountains they'd traveled on the way south. It would have been easier with both men, but time had run out.

As Jones rose in elevation following the vee of the wash, he glanced back over the ridgeline that no longer shielded him from the compound. The main house was awash with lights and screaming came from inside. It was weird. He shouldn't be hearing anything from where he was, but the night air and bare hillsides created sweet spots where sound was funneled.

Moonrise wouldn't come until 4 a.m., and then only the sliver of a new crescent. The intense starlight provided some light to the desert floor. The searchers would be using spots and headlights to try to track in the dark. Glancing back to see if he was being followed, Jones saw a puff of smoke in the distance. It was followed by an echoing boom. Smith again. Compressed air wafted by, and there was a panicky nickering of his animals. The blast was much larger than the Claymores he'd seen go off. In the dark, he couldn't tell for sure, but it looked as if Smith's shooting site had been wiped clean of humanity and vegetation.

"Holy shit," he said quietly, then turned and continued north. Whatever happened was not going to stop an attempt at retribution. Jones knew there would be even greater pressure to produce the creators of the mayhem—or face death from the *narcotraficos'* bosses. He had few hours to try for the river, and there was no guarantee that he'd be safe even if he got there.

Jones heard a small spray of pebbles in front of him and froze. Still in his ghillie suit but without head cover, Smith crunched up the small arroyo. Sniper rifle at port arms, he carried a noticeably lightened rucksack.

"See you didn't wait on me. But then, I told you to hightail it. No time to talk now. Let's move. Which way, Jose?"

Smith shoved the rifle into its scabbard on the mule and grabbed the reins to his horse.

Jones knew animal hoof prints were easy to track, but it was a trade-off of riding the horses and using their speed to put distance between them and the pursuers, or abandoning the animals and hoping to leave less obvious tracks.

Jones saw that their pursuers had found the dry wash that trended north. Jerking the reins, he whispered hoarsely to Smith, "Follow me. We're going to head this way." He pointed back south toward an oncoming ATV.

"Where the hell you going? You're turning back toward them!"

It was Jones's turn to make the decisions. "You can go any way you want. I know what I'm doing. We keep this way, we're dead, with or without your firepower. It's too obvious. You wanna live, you follow me."

Smith cocked his head to one side, as if this would help him figure out what was happening. He grunted and pulled his horse in line behind the lead horse and mule. Like it or not, Jones knew this country. He'd proven that, getting them this far. If they rode into a trap, one 9 mm round would go in Jones's head before Smith bought it. ATVs whined up the draw, now less than 500 meters behind them. From the bouncing movement of the lights, it appeared that no one was seriously trying to track in the dark.

Jones leapt off the horse, leading it and the mule behind bushes into scree and small sandstone outcrops that continuously broke under the animals' weight. Balky to begin with, the jenny was now even more skittish. Letting out a bray, she planted all four feet and refused to move. Then she started backing down the scree, pulling Jones with her, and backing into Smith and his horse.

Suddenly, Jones pulled out his Beretta 9 mm and shot the mule between the eyes. The flash blinded him. Smith pulled his horse out of the way as the dying animal's front legs buckled. The mule fell downhill, doing a half roll before outstretched legs and a clump of cholla stopped her.

"Goddamn you. There's thousands of dollars' worth of equipment on that animal. What am I supposed to do now?"

"Hump it if you think you can." Jones eyes flashed angrily. "But I'm not having that mule get us killed. So, leave it here. Those bastards know this was a sniper hit anyway, and we don't have time to drag a fucking mule who doesn't want to go. We go now, or we aren't going at all."

A flash and *ka-whiiing* of a ricocheting bullet spanking off a boulder 10 meters to their left ended any further discussion. Scampering to the mule, Smith untied the rifle scabbard, which now lay across the dead animal's belly. The mule was lying on her right side, so there was no chance of getting the spotting scope stashed in that side's pannier. Smith pulled a rucksack with additional ammunition from the left pannier, throwing it over his shoulder. An AK-47 opened up again, but whoever was shooting wasn't sure where they were. Flashes like a welder's spark appeared on a small cliff face a hundred or so meters away.

"We've gotten all we can get. Let's go. *Now*, dammit." Jones tried to keep his voice down, but urgency raised the volume. The chatter of automatic rounds walked closer to the two, making pocking sounds as they disturbed gravel and dried mud. It appeared that the men working the draw were moving toward him and sweeping uphill.

Exchanging glances, Jones and Smith crab-walked to the remaining animals. Smith laid his rifle scabbard behind his saddle and began to rig a makeshift tie. Jones calmed his animal and threw Smith's rucksack straps over the saddle horn. Just then, what had been a continuous low whine of a four-wheeler got suddenly louder, and a spackling of white from the headlight appeared on nearby bushes.

"Get the hell out of here." Jones pulled his pistol out of its holster. "I'll slow them down."

The larger man didn't hesitate, pulling himself up into the saddle and wheeling the horse toward the north.

Jones stood there. *I must have shit for brains.* Any more introspection was cut off by the noise of the four-wheeler coming toward him in low gear. He heard two voices yelling, and when the headlight bounced off a large rock, he matched them to the two men in a Polaris. Jones tied the horse as low as he could to a greasewood bush. He prayed it would hold his horse if it spooked at the noise of gunfire.

Running toward the Polaris at a half crouch, he gave the horse some distance from what was about to happen. The four-wheeler stopped, and the driver killed the engine, listening for any movement. The passenger held a short-barreled rifle, and the two stepped out of each side of the open cab.

Jones rushed at them. The men looked up, trying to react to the unexpected movement. Jones's 9 mm went off two feet from the passenger. Unseen in the gloom, the bullet went in his left eye and exploded brain matter out the back of his head. Jones hit the man as he fell, mainly because he was in the way. By this time, the driver had swung an AK-47 over the small hood of the four-wheeler.

Too late, as Jones had pulled the trigger four times. Jones wasn't sure how many made contact, but as he reached the man, the driver sat down cross-legged on the ground, making a strange "oomph." The AK stayed cradled in his arms as he slumped over to one side.

Jones kicked the weapon away from the dying man, stooped and picked it up, and slung it over his shoulder. He reached down to the driver's chest, propping him up again so he could remove the loaded magazines stuffed in a bandolier draped over his shoulder.

Except for the ringing in his ears from the gunshots and explosives, sudden silence had descended. As he pulled the bandolier up and over the man's head, Jones sensed eyes watching him. In the gloom it was impossible for him to see.

"Madre de dios, Madre de dios," whooshed out of the dying man's mouth, and then his body went limp.

Jones mounted his horse and headed in the direction Smith had taken. In the distance, ATVs and Humvees came to life again, as if getting a second wind. Grinding transmissions indicated their climbs and descents from the hills near where Smith and Jones had once lain hidden. None was near the recently unmanned four-wheeler.

———

THIRTEEN

Smith And Jones

R ain caught up with them an hour into the ride. An overrun from a Pacific front coming up from the Sea of Cortez had made its way over the Sierra Madre Occidental and released the remains of its moisture on the border region where the two men traveled. The race back north was frantic, with no attempt at hiding tracks or staying in the high areas where there was less chance of being spotted. The sudden downpour was a surprise and a blessing, as rivulets of water washed tracks away almost as soon as they were made.

Periodically, the two men stopped and tried to determine whether they were being tracked. Neither had any doubts that anyone with half a brain would figure they were headed north. Jones was in his element.

Upstream 16 kilometers, as the crow flies, was a low-water crossing near a craphole of a village on the American side. They'd be picked up there, and his role in this nightmare would be over. *I'll turn this shooter over to those who will get* pinche *Smith out of the area, get back to* mi familia, *and lay low as the fight for control of the plaza heats up.*

One thing they could agree on—there was no time to rest. They moved further upstream toward the rendezvous. Jones half-expected another aircraft to come searching for them. It didn't happen. Either the shock of the attack or the bad weather kept aircraft on the ground. Rain, adrenaline, and fear wet their shirts, chilling them in the night air.

They quietly passed by the east side of a goat shed and corral called Manga de Lucio and watered the horses at a small stock tank at Los Perros. It was 3 a.m. when they heard dogs barking at a collection of *jacales* at Parrita.

The dogs stayed in the small village as they pushed toward the Herra Dura Crossing in a south-facing loop in the Rio Grande. The pick-up point on the United States side was a kilometer upriver from the American village of Lágrimas, north of when they started three days ago.

The false dawn and the cold that went with it arrived when the men let the horses blow one last time. They were half a kilometer from the Rio Grande.

"Is this the place?" Smith's voice was instinctively quiet.

"Yes. They'll have a trailer for the horses here." *At least that is what the boss told me. It couldn't be too soon to get rid of the shooter. Go back to New Jersey or Missouri, or wherever the hell he was from.*

"Stay put while I make sure everything is as it is supposed to be." Jones handed the AK-47 to Smith. "If something goes wrong, unload that thing on where the sound is coming from and cover me."

Jones had no confidence in Smith's willingness to help him, but self-interest and a desire to get back in an English-speaking country would probably guarantee Smith's assistance for a while longer.

Smith grunted his assent. Jones weaved through the salt cedar and mesquite down to the river's edge to scope out the crossing. Other than the gurgle of the river flow, there was nothing to see. A small dirt road ran down to a low-water crossing. Over the years, rocks had been placed across the river bottom to form a rough road for four-wheeled vehicles. The recent rains had washed some of the flooring downstream. It appeared that no one had placed additional rocks into the cavities left by the flood. No tire tracks on the Mexican side of the river either. No one in the crude brush shelters occasionally used by those waiting to cross or meet someone crossing south. All good signs.

The river's angry torrent seen earlier had abated, and apart from some moisture showing on the banks, there was nothing to indicate the extent of the storms at the time of the southward crossing. The rains upstream hadn't amounted to much, as far as continuous flow was concerned, and Jones breathed a sigh of relief. They wouldn't have to swim the animals.

The meth had long worn off. He needed a hit bad, if he was to keep his edge until this was over with. His nose running, Jones stayed in the brush line and worked his way closer to the crossing. The pick-up point on the other side of the Rio was at the base of an escarpment that ran for 500 meters or so on either side of a ravine. Salt cedar, an invasive growth, had choked off huge portions of the river from access. Usually, Jones cursed it. Tonight, its density was a blessing.

Jones didn't see anyone moving but spied a truck with hitched horse trailer pointing away from the river. The promise to retrieve them was being kept, *gracias a dios.* Downstream, he knew the poor families living in Lágrimas had lived along the river long enough to know when not knowing meant survival. All were related in some way to a scattering of kin that for the most part lived on the south side of the thin waterway dividing the haves from the have-nots. Faint noises upstream traveled far in the crisp air. No matter. It wasn't the village's business.

We load and head to the highway. La raza won't see or hear anything. We'll be gone like a gust of wind. The tire tracks...? If the Border Patrol even shows up here, there will be no one to tell them anything.

FOURTEEN

Smith

A penlight lit up on the north side and wove through the predawn darkness in the shape of a sideways eight. *Coast clear.* Jones took out his own light and waved back. *Time to get back to civilization.*

Smith was feeding bits of grass to the horses when Jones appeared out of the thicket.

"They're here. *Vamonos.*" For a moment, Jones almost felt a twinge of kindred spirit. It didn't last. Smith handed the assault rifle back to Jones, who looped its strap around his saddle horn. No need for this encumbrance while slipping and sliding across the river.

"'Bout fucking time. Thought you'd leave me here with the rest of the meskins." Smith laughed, as if this would mitigate the denigration. He safetied his Glock, stuck it in his boonie pants' leg pocket, and squeezed the Velcro seal shut.

The two led the horses along the gravel next to the river and headed toward the low-water crossing. No need to hide in the thickets now. Jones stepped into the water, walking slowly to allow his horse to check its footing. He was halfway across when he heard Smith and his horse splash into the river.

"*Donde esta la mula?*" A voice from the brush on the U.S. side reached them over the water.

"*Muerto.*" *Who gives a shit about a fucking mule? What kind of stupid question is this when we are trying to get home?*

71

Jones slogged up the muck that had accumulated on the cutback after the last rain. It made for slow going. He didn't recognize the voice but didn't expect to.

"*Ayudame con el caballo*," he said, trying to balance himself in the shin deep water as his boots sucked into the riverbank's mud.

"*Dame tu mano, carnal*." Jones grinned. It was almost over.

A figure stepped out of the brush and extended a calloused hand. Jones took it, pulling forward to step up on dry sand.

Jones felt something metallic brush his forehead and right eyebrow. There was a flash. The back of Jones's head exploded as the bullet blew skull and brain matter over the horse. Jones's body rocked back, then tipped forward, falling toward the bank. A hand pushed his body into the river.

"*No me ensucias, cabrón*." The shooter didn't want to dirty his pressed jeans.

Smith rolled his ankle on a smooth stone he had tried to avoid. He slipped forward as he heard the muffled pop and instinctively knew what had happened. In the gloom, he almost missed the muzzle flash because Jones's head was between him and the end of the weapon. Almost at the same instant, the crack of a rifle rang out. At a range of 30 meters, there was no way it should miss. The slip on the slick rock had saved his life. As he twisted in the water, a shot, aimed chest-center, went high over his shoulder.

Smith pushed himself behind the horse, which took the succeeding five shots in its neck and torso. He sensed rather than saw gunfire from the Mexican side, as two shots hit the horse on its flank. It let out a scream, thrashing in panic as Smith dived into the water, smacking his hands and forehead on the rocks in the shallow current. His only chance was to get downstream.

Smith crab-scrambled toward the deeper water below the crossing, grunting with fear. If he could get to the deeper water and faster current against the American side's cut bank, he might have a chance to put distance between himself and the shooters. Off to his right, someone was running along the Mexican side, and he could hear the crunching of boots against river sand and gravel as two men ran toward a large gravel bar on that side of the river.

He hit the smooth water showing depth in the darkness of the cut bank, as it swept around a curve. The problem was going to be when the water spit him out into the open as the current shifted to the Mexican side. There was another cut bank there, but also an intervening clear spot.

The shooters had already figured this out, and he spied two figures watching in his direction for the current to pass by the gravel bar where they stood. One had some sort of mini-mag, the other an AK-47. Desperate, he reached up and grabbed for anything that could hold him back. His hands found a limb hanging down into the river.

The limb held, but the current pulled his head under water. Smith fought to keep from sucking in water. He was only partially successful and came up choking on the muddy onrush. The cough caught the men's attention. They walked out further on the gravel bar, pointing their weapons toward the shadows looming over the opposite bank. Above Smith, dirt clods tumbled into the river, as someone working the American side slipped as the sand bank gave way, nearly putting the pursuer into the water.

A low curse emanated from the 10 or so feet above him, and then a flashlight beam started walking the darkness. If it spotted him, he was dead. If he waited too long, dawn would break, and he would be dead. If he floated downstream, the two men on the bar would see him. Smith moved closer into the bank, let one hand drop, and hoped the light wouldn't catch on the remaining hand as he ducked under water and held his breath. Something hairy brushed against his exposed hand. Rat! It was the only thing that made sense. A fucking rat had fallen into the river and was clinging to the back of his hand. And he couldn't let go.

No shots *pfffted* in the water, and he came up, trying not to be heard sucking in air. Slowly, he brought his other hand up out of the water to brush the animal off of him. He didn't want to get bitten, either. Careful not to splash, or to allow the whiteness of his flesh be seen moving against the contrast of the water's murk, he reached over, hitting the object hanging onto the back of his branch-grasping hand. It wasn't a rat, but a large chunk of Jones's skullcap—complete with matted hair. The curvature of the piece of cranium and the matted hair had caused the floating remains to wrap itself around the back of Smith's hand and wrist.

Smith was loopy from the shock and adrenaline sag. *Well, so much for the little shit's thinking cap.* Then he choked down hysterical laughter that unaccountably welled up inside him like some kind of stomach bromide. The hysteria passed, but without good effect. The water was cold, and Smith could feel his grip on the limb weakening.

The beam on the water played over the branch again as Smith ducked under the current. He held his breath as long as possible, expecting when he came up to feel a bullet hit him in the head. Instead, he heard jabbering in Spanish. The hunters were yelling at each other over the noise of the current. He didn't understand what was said. He didn't need too. The two sides were comparing notes on where he might be.

Upstream at the crossing, he heard the growl of a truck engine as the vehicle moved into the river, its tires rubbing river rocks together like dull castanets. The half-moon of the cut bank blocked his view, but Smith presumed that his horse's carcass and Jones's body were being removed, and the other animal loaded up, if it hadn't been shot up, too.

They—whoever *they* were—hadn't found him but didn't seem too concerned. The grey of the pre-dawn was breaking, and soon he'd be ripe for the picking. From what he'd heard of the Mexicans in the drug trade, he would be better off dying quickly.

Smith could make out the darker shadow of something floating downstream. The earlier rain had loosened vegetation upstream, and it looked to him as if a small tree next to the river's edge had let go. As the brushy limbs came by, Smith took a breath and holding onto a small limb, went under water, kicking furiously to stay down. He felt himself coming to the surface, and as a desperate measure, let out most of his air. The action kept him from bobbing to the surface, but drastically reduced his time hidden by the murky river.

No way would I let this bunch of vegetation pass by without checking it out. His prediction was justified, as the men on both shores began shooting at the tree with automatic weapons. Rounds hit the water, sounding like matches being put out in a sink. One hit the heel of his boot, knocking his leg down and numbing it up to the knee. Another hit the web between his thumb and first finger, and he bubbled a scream into the water. As the tree swept by the men on the gravel bar, someone splashed into the river, trying to wrestle the vegetation to the shallows. In doing so, the brushy tops did a 180 in the river, and Smith let go as the shooters were occupied pulling the trunk up into onto the gravel on the Mexican side.

"*Viste algo?*"

"*Todavia no.*"

"*Pues, donde fue ese puto?*"

"*Vallate al travesia en Lágrimas y miran para algo. Prisa!*"

Smith understood Lágrimas. Jones had said they were crossing above some town by that name. He hoped he could get below Lágrimas before they got there.

Dawn broke over the ridgelines of the border, as Smith pulled himself shivering into the thickets on the Mexican side. He had no idea where the hell he was. He only remembered crossing into this God-forsaken shit hole of a country just up from the Mexican couple's house.

As the dawn's warmth hit him, the shivering subsided. The adrenaline of the ambush had staved off the pain in his hand. Now it began to throb. He vomited into the sand and lurched back into the flow of the river.

FIFTEEN

Smith

FOUR DAYS BEFORE PRESENT–A WEDNESDAY

As the Rio Grande plods its usually sluggish way toward the Gulf, its banks exchange steepness between the two countries that it uneasily divides. A canebrake loomed in the early morning light and behind that, sheer rock. The rock edges were sharp as a razor and guarded by a legion of pitaya and Spanish dagger. His hand had dried at least partially, but there was no avoiding going back into the murky, polluted waters.

Smith hadn't seen or heard anyone since breaking free from the downed tree. There was no doubt that once they didn't find a body in a suck hole next to the American bank, they would head downstream. Whoever had bushwhacked him and the greaser would have to tie up loose ends. Either a body had to be fished out of the river, or the live one found and eliminated. Smith waded back into the river, finding daylight hadn't lessened the shock of its chill.

The remainder of the day was a blur of floating and shaking from the cold. Jones had said something about crossing upriver from the put-in point. Mother of Christ, it seemed so many lifetimes ago. At times, the process of just moving became excruciating. The fouled river water and hypothermia added to a sense of terror. Every small bluff held ambushers. The clacking of river rocks signaled a *narco* waiting to put a round in his head. Ambushers were swaying cane. Clacking rocks were beavers or other animals, panicking as Smith bobbed downstream.

Dusk came. *Where the hell am I?* The meanders all looked like the ones he'd seen near the crossing, and yet they weren't. Had he passed it? If so, where was he going to get out, and where was he to go when he did? The roadmaps he had looked at showed largely blank spots between the nearest Texas highway and river. No way was he going to make it bushwhacking across the desert without water.

Smith looked at his hands—his fingers were pruned and whitish gray. He looked up again and spotted it. A milk jug stuck upside down on a dead piece of cane. He remembered seeing something like that near the boat's sucker rod tie down. *I guess the old Mexican couple is probably not that much better than I am at trying to figure out the bends on this fucking river.* The jug would help them to spot the takeout point after a day of fishing or whatever it was they did on the river with their john boat.

It was dusk when he crawled out of the river and up the sand bank next to the boat, which was turned upside down and chained to the sucker rod. An ant mound had grown up the side of the gunnel. Smith stumbled against the aluminum, and a sea of red boiled out of the powdery mound.

What the fuck?

He hadn't seen ants like this before. Barely able to stand from the hours of cold water and fear, he instinctively skittered away from the voracious wave of mound defenders, falling against the hull. Grunting, Smith stumbled up the pathway toward the house that he remembered had been occupied by the old couple. *I'll hole up where I started from. Just a short time and I'm out of here for good.*

It was 300 yards or so through the salt cedar on a sand path toward the house. Grunting from the pain in his hand, Smith reached down toward the side pocket in the cammies. The Glock was still there. Would it still fire?

SIXTEEN

Smith

THREE DAYS BEFORE PRESENT TIME—A THURSDAY

Smith woke suddenly from a sweat-soaked sleep, filled with shapeless horrors and ill-defined fear. The sheets had the acrid smell of being in contact with someone not well, who had a corruption within. Whatever had awakened him was voiceless in the crispness of the South Texas night. Nonetheless, there was something there, no doubt about it.

The bed was an old steel framed tick-mattressed bed, with springs that spoke of any weight applied to them. Even without his bulk, the bed sagged of its own accord, as if age had gifted gravity in its deterioration. Smith moved carefully, trying not to startle the coiled metal beneath the mattress.

His Glock lay on the small nightstand near the left side of the bed. It had spent hours in the river. Would it work now? It may be too far away to grasp. He silently cursed himself at his indulgence in earlier moving the unyielding lump of its presence away from under the pillow.

He had rolled to the right during his sleep, carrying sheets and quilt with him. The gun was a continent away from him, on the far side of the bed.

An alien presence announced itself inside the house. Its presence was ponderous—a weightiness that meant only one thing—a human was here, intending to kill him.

Like a person drowning, Smith's brain split into two halves, one seized by the panic of the unknown, the other oddly detached and analytical. It cursed the apprehension that had gripped his every action for these last days, which he had allowed to slowly loosen its grip on him.

"You stupid bastard," it seemed to say, *"Did you think it would come to anything but this?"*

The slight creaking of center cut pine floors, shrunk from years of usage and dry weather, now made a presence a reality. The bedroom door was closed, but there were no locks, no deadbolts.

Reaching across the bed would betray an awareness of the danger. Instead, Smith slid off the bed. His knees hit the old rolled-rag rug. *If I can just crawl around the bed.* Not likely, with the foot of the bed not more than five feet from the bedroom door. Bile rose in his throat, as he realized that his presence was known to the stalker.

There was only a small slice of moon, but it and the Milky Way lit up the desert sand, which in turn threw reflected brilliance into the window of the bedroom. The door opened quietly. Smith froze in the shadow of the bed, his body performing a feral drawing up, the old ballet of survival that he knew was of no consequence.

Smith thought of himself as brave. Years of meting out force and pain had inured him to the prospect of something bad actually happening to him. Death wasn't an abstraction, but he had been its deliverer—not a recipient. Special Forces and CIA wet work in Central Asia had required him to kill both up close and from afar. Far, with a sniper shot, a puff of dust-like brain matter splaying from a well-placed head shot. Close enough to smell garlic on the breath and fecal release while watching his victims' eyes glaze over as he garroted them or cut their throats. Killings were choreographed set pieces he had directed, each with its own acts, scenes, and finally, the closing curtains.

What was happening now was anything but abstract. A fetid smell reached his nostrils. His bowels had let loose, its malevolence streaming down his backside onto his legs. Smith wasn't one for contemplative analysis of life. Brain chemistry or upbringing, his was a world of cause and effect, with little sense for anything remotely abstract. So, it was unexpected when shame welled up inside him at the way he was to die, and his inability to control his bodily functions. But there would be no beseeching God. If the Almighty existed,

Smith's ties to any mercy coming from that source had long been sundered. He had no right to beg for mercy.

The man in the doorway had done his homework well. He knew the layout of the house and the bedroom. His silhouette showed him holding either a rifle or shotgun. A shotgun, most likely, the one side of his brain said, as the barrel swung toward the darkness where he crouched

"Hey, *gringo*," he heard. "*Oye, compadre, 'stas aquí?*"

It was a mocking whisper like a bad bit from *Treasure of the Sierra Madre*. "Are you here?"

Smith said and did nothing.

Time stood still. The voice in the doorway asked, "Who hired you?"

Smith crawled and slid across the old rag rug, rounding the end of the bed, all the time watching the blackness of the open doorway.

"I said – who hired you?"

Anything Smith said would just prolong the inevitable.

"Fuck you."

The long gun swept toward him. The hope that whoever was in the doorway wouldn't see him was shattered as Smith lunged upward toward the Glock. A blast rang out. Smith's right hand, reaching forward, was shredded. *Shotgun-not a rifle.* He couldn't see in the darkness, but knew he had no fingers left. The bed lamp, hit by flying pieces of bone and flesh, spun and fell to the floor. The bulb popped softly, and the round lampshade and base rolled roll back and forth.

"They thought you might say that. I bet them you wouldn't, but I had to find out."

The initial shock wore off quickly. Waves of pain almost caused Smith to scream as nerve endings in his mangled hand began to spasm. He tucked the ruined hand under his armpit to try to stop the bleeding.

"Well, *amigo*, you hit *mi jefe* in the cheek. Blew half his teeth out on the patio. Looked like some street kid had dropped a box of Chiclets." The voice issued a rueful laugh, remembering the sight. "Left side of his head ended up going all over the furniture. The kid's Nintendo game got interrupted by his old man's brains messing up the computer screen. The new wife got glass and guts all in her eyes and face."

The voice paused as the door swung open fully. "How far away were you?"

Oddly, Smith felt a surge of pride. "Seven hundred-sixty-five meters, give or take." He gritted his teeth against the pain.

"No shit! No wonder we couldn't find where the shot came from at first. We were looking too close in. And then that BOOM from the hill. Was that you?" He didn't wait for a reply. "Some of *mis compadres* got blown to shit. Shit, we figured someone was with you. More than one, maybe? Maybe if you tell me who was that Mexican we killed at the river, I'll make this quick for you. Won't make you linger. Your fucking hand—I bet that hurts, eh? Damn, where did you learn that kind of shooting?"

No answer was expected, but there was a note of professional admiration. "Man, you created one hell of a mess. But now. Now we have to end this." The man at the door paused in his thoughts. "By the way, we saw your dead mule. You left a lot of good shit on there. Who shot my compadres in the ATV? Was it you? Or that fucker with you? You are a *pinche gabacho*. You don't know this place.

"I think one of ours led you in, *amigo*. How many others? I think the *puto* at the river was just a guide. We saw the horse prints, you know. Come on, be a stand-up guy. Either way, you're not leaving here, so why let some other *pendejo* walk. I mean, we'll eventually find out, you know."

Again, he paused, as if expecting an answer. "C'mon, mister *gringo*. I mean, you killed a big fucking *narcotraficante*, you know? You started some bad shit in my country."

The voice chuckled. "I mean, things are crazy now, you know? Lots of people already wondering if they're next. Maybe they will be, if they helped you. Like that old couple on the river. Who got them to help you? They wouldn't say. Just kept praying and praying. *Quidame, Jesus!*" The man laughed. "Jesus will help them in the next life, I guess."

In his agony, a thought went through Smith's mind. *How did they track me here? Why kill the old Mexican couple?* But that was beyond his ability to comprehend. Smith grabbed his right wrist, trying to squeeze the pain away. He looked up grinning. "I must be rusty. I was trying to take him through the ear. Who knows, maybe it would have taken out the kid or the bastard's whore." He wanted this over with.

Smith felt a huge fist of steel shot hit his right side. Sparks of spent gun wadding spiraled through the room. The impact of the 12-gauge double-ought buckshot threw him against the wall, turning him sideways as he caromed onto the bed. The impact of the steel pellets inadvertently gave Smith one chance at taking his killer with him. His body smashed and then slid toward the bed-stand where the Glock sat, round chambered.

The figure in the door never moved forward, choosing to swing the shotgun with his movement instead.

Blood, bone, viscera now played itself over a large swath of the wall behind the bed. Arterial blood misted the dark air. The pain of the two wounds finally caused a howl, eerie in its primal anger at impending death.

Smith tried to grab the gun. It lay convenient for right hand retrieval, though his grasp was upside down. The Glock dropped on the bed. He tried to turn it so he could aim. A blast was sensed, not heard, as the final shot blew off the top of his head. His body was driven into the bed ticking and the few pellets that didn't contact flesh ripped through the soft cotton of the mattress and imbedded themselves into the wall and floor under the bed.

There was no need to be sure of Smith's death. Nonetheless, a digital camera flashed. Confirmation of a job done was contained in the pixels of a Canon Sure Shot.

SEVENTEEN

Johnny Reagan

PRESENT DAY—A FRIDAY

Johnny Reagan had finally calmed Pete down enough to get a reasonably cogent version of what Pete knew, as he drove him into Santa Rosa in the Sheriff's Department cruiser. It was pretty simple and straightforward—he had tried to get hold of Papa Oto and Mama Raquel, as he had called them most of life. He hadn't heard from them in about five or six days but hadn't expected to. They were frugal, usually awaiting his call. Yes, they had a cell phone but rarely had it on, given the lack of coverage and Otabiano's attitude that "they were too complicated."

When Pete did call both numbers, the cell went to voice mail, and no one picked up the house phone. He got concerned, drove up from Laredo. He just felt something wasn't right.

Pete had some calls to make to some of his customers in San Antonio and justified the trip as a way to kill two birds with one stone. He'd have a good meal with the folks and take US 90 back through Del Rio and into Bexar County.

He reached the ranch entrance around 11:30. Skirting around the old headquarters buildings on the way down the river, he had seen the door on the main house's back porch standing open. Knowing that Otabiano kept the place locked up tight, Pete thought maybe he'd find his granddad doing maintenance on the place. Acknowledged he didn't see Otabiano's truck anywhere. He pulled up and honked. Not getting any response, he got out, thinking maybe a critter had pushed its way in, or an illegal had used the house as a sleepover spot on the run north.

He told Johnny he got as far as the screened porch before he knew something was wrong. He said he heard flies, lots of them, buzzing around inside. He smelled something "like meat starting to turn bad." Glancing into the bedroom, he ran back out of the house and got the dry heaves. He jumped in his truck and headed to the Vasquez house. Driving so fast, he nearly high-centered the truck as he fishtailed down to the cedar breaks surrounding the place. His grandfather's truck was parked in its usual spot. No one was there but he saw partially hung washing. That wasn't at all like his grandmother.

Now in a real panic, he used the Vasquez landline to call the Sheriff's Office, and then started combing the area for the old folks. He was still looking when everyone showed up—and that's when he found them, dead.

No, they didn't have any enemies. No, they had never complained of any recent unexplained river crossings, and no, they had never been concerned that they were in any danger. He had never seen the dead man before, from what he could tell from what was left of his face. And no, his grandparents had made no mention of anyone living permanently or otherwise at the place. He didn't think they knew the man with his face gone, as he described him.

Pete begged off giving a written statement. Given his condition, and the time, TJ agreed we'd get with him after he got some sleep. Reagan dropped Pete off at a cousin's house in Santa Rosa. Pete was too shaky to drive his car and left the keys for a deputy to drop it off at the Sheriff's Office.

Pete asked Reagan if he could make funeral plans. Yes, but there would be autopsies, and the bodies would have to be released before a date could be set. Pete said he would call Luther Beirne at the Hughes Funeral Home.

Johnny told him that would be best, as funeral homes were better at dealing with all the formalities. Privately he wondered if the county's only mortuary was prepared for this. Johnny shook Pete's hand, repeated his condolences, and said they would set a time to meet at the Sheriff's offices.

EIGHTEEN

Present Day – A Saturday

PURDY KENDRICKS

I t was nearly 4 a.m. before things wrapped up at both crime scenes. Betty was still in San Antonio. I drove up to our house and unlocked the door before realizing I had forgotten to pick up Forrest, or even call to let anyone know what was going on. I was too tired to worry about it.

Almost immediately, a fire truck's siren screamed outside the bedroom window, and I pulled the pillow tighter around my head. The sound got louder instead. The din of a three-alarm fire in my dream dissolved into my cell phone's relentless ring tone.

"Hello." I tried to sound pleasant, but it was seven in the morning. Paula's voice filled the receiver, and instantly I knew why she was calling.

"Purdy, we waited up, but Forrest got tired, and I put him to bed around ten. Do you want me to go ahead and feed him breakfast when the kids get up?" The unstated question of what I had been doing was dangling.

"God, I'm sorry, Paula. I got in at four." I was surprised she hadn't heard of the three murders. I filled her in, struggled to clear my head. It was time for my Saturday breakfast with Forrest. "I'll be by in half an hour." I figured that even with all the unfinished work, I still had to eat, and I couldn't think of any better distraction from the business at hand than spending some time with my son.

Paula's house was two blocks from her shop. I pulled up and did the "shave and a haircut six bits" honk. I saw four tow-headed kids hit the sofa in front of the large glass window in the living room. Spotting my county sedan, they turned and disappeared, reappearing at the front door a couple of seconds later.

Betty grabbed her kids, laughed at the antics, and waved as Forrest made it to the truck. I got the driver's door open and was hit in the chest by 50 pounds of gleeful five-year-old.

"Daddy, I'm hungry. Where are we going to eat breakfast?" He squirmed out of my grasp, crawled across the seat, and fastened his seatbelt.

I slid back in, slammed the door, and glanced at the tow-headed boy, who was already squirming in anticipation of a new adventure.

"Where would you like to go, rascal?" There would be no doubt as to the response, but it was his to make the first move.

"Hmm." He glanced at me, pretending to think about his choices. "How about Miss Beulah's?'

Trying to look like I had to think about it, I said, "Well, I'm not so sure." The truck was already headed in the general direction of the Cenizo Diner. "Possibly we could go some other place for a change. I'm getting really tired of going to the same place." I kept my head facing toward the windshield and glanced over at him.

He slowed his fidgeting. "Daddy, you know where I want to go. You do this *all* the time." He reached over, slapped me on the arm, and started giggling. That made me laugh.

We turned into the Cenizo Diner's gravel parking lot. It was too late for the early morning crowd. On occasion I would meet this mixed collection at some ungodly hour, often before official opening, as some of the retirees and ranchers in that group had their own key to the diner. Whoever got there first put on the coffee.

We arrived for the more sedate crowd of folks who ate after the sun rose in the east. I was relieved that it was only half-full. I killed the engine as Forrest bailed out of the passenger side and ran up the steps to the diner's wide front porch. He paused at the front door, checked to see if I was coming, and disappeared inside.

By the time I hit the front door, Forrest had ensconced himself into a booth. The boy's entrance drew a few glances and several smiles. Most of the breakfasters looked toward me. Things got quiet, and then the buzz of conversation picked up again. Waving at several ranchers I knew, I saw one of the waitresses starting a fresh pot of coffee in the Bunn.

Years before, an antique Bunn had given up its ghost. Beulah bought another drip coffee maker, got tired of the complaints—probably instigated by her many "regulars" who resented any change—and gave the thing away. A new Bunn showed up, and the bitching died down. There were a lot of grins from the conspirators. They were as pleased as if they were miners who had gotten a raise from the company after shutting down a coal mine.

I settled into the booth and waved us over a couple of coffees.

I had spent a lot of time just watching Forrest. He possessed such a rock-solid sense of who he was, that I envied him. He had a center core of calm I don't remember having as a child, much less as an adult. Both his mother and I realized that our muted troubles were probably being deciphered by a child who knew he was providing stability to a couple of adults who couldn't keep their own shit together. Tough and undeserved role for a kid.

He carefully dumped three tablespoons of sugar into his coffee from the dispenser. My small reverie was brought up short by Beulah. She was one of the few black residents of Kickapoo County. She had showed up, according to my dad, when she was kicked off a bus on its way to El Paso because this was as far as her fare money went. She had been here more than 30 years. She worked one menial job or another, scrimped and saved, and bought the Cenizo Diner. Beulah lived with a Mexican pipefitter whom she had never gotten around to marrying, raised three children, and sent all of them off to junior college or technical school.

"What's it gonna be today, little fella?" she asked. Beulah knew full well that Forrest would settle for nothing less than bacon and pancakes with enough syrup to put him in a sugar coma. I settled into the plastic chair and yawned. The lack of sleep had me feeling fuzzy-headed. Beulah looked at me, cocking her head questioningly.

"*Migas*, extra potatoes?"

"Extra frijoles, three tortillas." Her laughter was infectious as she mimicked me.

I grinned, and she slapped me on the shoulder.

"You look like you've been 'rode hard and put up wet,' Purdy. Take care of yourself, now, hmm?"

I knew the Cenizo Diner had a scanner, too. What news Beulah hadn't picked up from radio traffic had no doubt been supplemented by facts and surmise from the early shift. The killings had hit the internet editions of the *San Antonio Express-News,* and been picked up by CNN, Drudge, and a couple of other news outlets. While the *Kickapoo Kronicle's* weekly schedule wouldn't print the gory details until the middle of next week, by then it would be old news to everyone in the Cenizo. I looked around and saw few people who kept news apps on their cell phones, but Kickapoo County could give a Papua New Guinean tribe a run for its money in its ability to transmit and receive news magically.

Forrest paused between slurps of sugar-ladened coffee. "KayCee and me watched a movie, and Aunt Paula let us sleep on the floor. It was fun."

He stirred the coffee loudly. "Where did you go last night, Daddy?"

"Dad had some police business that just wouldn't get over with, and it's 'KayCee and I'."

I expected someone to come by the table and try prying something out of me, but Forrest's presence kept local news seekers at bay. The time passed peacefully.

We had discussed another catfishing expedition upriver from Lágrimas where I had fished since I was a kid. Forrest reminded me that this was supposed to happen today. "You promised."

Ouch.

I wanted to let it lie but knew I couldn't. Forrest deserved an answer.

"Son." I paused. "I want you to know something."

Forrest stopped pushing pancakes around in the syrup and looked up at me.

"I won't ever promise you something and then not follow through. I apologize to you for not going today." This was getting tough.

"But something very sad happened yesterday, and some nice people were hurt." I dared not say "important" because what was more important to a young kid than his dad's word?

"Do you understand this? I have to go be a policeman and catch the bad guys, and I can't take you today. But I will make it up to you, and you can hold me to that, okay?" I didn't know if I was making sense to my son, but knew I had to get through to him.

The kid let me off the hook easily. "Sure, Daddy. Mommy says that your word is as good as gold." He paused. "Is gold worth a lot?"

I almost broke into tears.

I dropped him off at Paula's and headed to the office.

NINETEEN

Present Day – A Saturday

PURDY KENDRICKS

The Kickapoo County Courthouse was built by the WPA in 1939 in what at the time was called the *moderne* style. It looked like crap when compared to the old mansard roofed beauty it had replaced. The ugly granite structure was surrounded by Confederate Generals—Lee Street on the east, Early Street on the South, Pickett Street on the west, and Beauregard Street on the north. These stalwarts of secession were in turn commanded by Davis Boulevard, otherwise known as US Highway 90, one block south. The town was too small to have attracted any attention for the *faux pas* of streets touting the Confederacy.

The Kickapoo County Sheriff's Office with its jail, was housed in the Courthouse Annex, across the street from the Courthouse on Lee Street. The box-like Annex was grudgingly built in the 1980s, when the Texas Jail Standards people forced the county commissioners to shut down the old, foul smelling, four-cell contraption built into the east side of the Courthouse basement.

Thankfully, the Courthouse was closed, so I didn't have to deal with one of the usual irksome hassles. I parked in the shade of a deputy district clerk's spot.

Diagonal parking spaces surrounded the Courthouse. The ones in the shade on Lee Street were highly coveted by the district and county clerks' office personnel. There was signage warning of this exclusivity. And the underpaid women working in those offices took this perk very seriously. There, the afternoon sun was blocked by pecan trees that someone had had the foresight to plant some 70 years ago. While there were trees scattered across the courthouse square, the rest didn't shade cars on the other three sides. Litigants and their lawyers, jail visitors, and prospective jurors had to park on Early Street, on the west side of the courthouse. Anyone looking for afternoon shade had to park a further walk from shelter.

Woe be unto any driver of any unauthorized vehicle parked on the shady side, especially if it was an out-of-town lawyer. The clerks had burned their hands often enough on hot steering wheels and brooked no transgression of their parking privilege. While cars were rarely towed for this breech of local decorum, the eagle-eyed courthouse workers knew which vehicles were owned by lawyers.

Legal papers got misplaced or failed to be brought to the judge's attention. It only took one time of parking in the afternoon shade for the errant lawyers to make amends, usually with flowers and cookies for the ladies behind the counters, who then would magically find misfiled pleadings, while professing complete lack of knowledge as to how things could have gotten so confused.

This rule applied to law enforcement, as well. If there weren't not enough spots in front of the Annex, you parked in the heat, or in front of some downtown store. You ignored the scowls of struggling retailers who were peeved about the space taken, and the gossip that a cop car parked in front of their business might cause.

I locked my cruiser and crossed the street. The Sheriff's truck and an unmarked sedan I recognized as that of Abner Selman were parked facing the front door, along with three patrol cars and a Border Patrol SUV.

The rising and falling drone of cicadas competed with the hum of an over-worked air conditioner unit, as it dribbled condensate into the empty flower beds.

Getting to the jail through the office door to the sheriff's offices played hob with security, particularly on Saturday prisoner visitations, but the design had been done on the cheap. Besides, it was rare that there were more than six prisoners, and usually those were sitting out misdemeanors. They had little incentive to break out. Real security risks were transported to Del Rio, where the Val Verde Sheriff's Office would house them for a hefty fee.

I pushed open the door to a gust of chilled air. Immediately in front of the door was a counter partitioning off the dispatch area. Jake Nichols sat in front of the radios, leaning back in a swivel chair, straining mightily to hold his weight. Age had settled in on Jake early. Never physically active, he looked and acted as if being sedentary was a worthy life's effort.

"I see you've been working out with twelve-ounce curls again," I walked around the counter toward the hallway. Empty Dr Pepper cans sat in front of a video monitor showing his latest effort at winning four-deck Spider.

"Ah, Mister Charm and Happiness arrives."

Since my return to our childhood home, Jake didn't pass up many chances to comment on my moroseness.

"Your audience awaits. And while you're at it, why don't you at least Bluetooth that iPod of yours? I'm tired of seeing wires hanging out of your breast pocket. Looks retarded. Just get you something not so obvious. Folks know when you aren't listening to them."

I pulled the iPod out, pretending to turn it off. "You say something? I wasn't listening. Had some good music on."

He shot me the bird and gestured toward the back end of the hallway, where offices and a conference room were located. The chair squealed as Jake shifted his weight forward to key the mic. One of the troopers had stopped a trucker for speeding and was asking for an operator's license check.

Jake had never married and lived in the small, asbestos-sided house his long-dead mother had moved into after Jake's father finally drank himself to death. He was not a loner by choice, but rather circumstances that had made him incapable of letting anyone get too close to him.

Jake had a face full of scars from years of teenage acne and was prematurely balding. In fact, he'd started balding in high school. "Chrome dome" and "Circ"—short for circumcised, I guess because the boys thought it would be funny to compare his bald head to an unsheathed penis—were two of many appellations he'd endured during that time. He played clarinet in the band, which didn't add to his cachet, either.

We had maintained a friendship for a variety of reasons. We had been the two Anglo kids in Lágrimas. On my side, he was my first real boyhood pal. No matter how obnoxious and undesirable he'd seemed to others, I had seen firsthand what he had grown up with and felt he was doing the best he could with the hand he had been dealt.

Our paths couldn't stray too far, as Kickapoo High School wasn't that big. Moreover, from time to time, the fact that Jake and I were tight helped fend off some of the more obvious bullying and harassment.

He had a first-class mind, and Jake's grades would have gotten him into college. But I think he was too afraid to take the chance. He settled into a half-life, living with his mom until she died and hiring on with the Sheriff's Office as a dispatcher. On my trips home from college or elsewhere to check on Mama, we had shared a beer or two at The Bar. After my sobriety became an issue, that changed to coffee. Jake didn't care. He just wanted the company of someone who had accepted him the way he was.

He once told me that I was his friend because I had never once called him by anything other than his Christian name. That floored me at the time. I remember thinking, if that was all it took to be looked on as a friend, then I had best not take Jake's feelings lightly. His internal equilibrium wasn't all that strong.

He tried to hide that by being overly gregarious, which caused people who didn't want to get involved in long discourses to avoid him. He had been dispatching for years, and he was good at what he did. It let him reach into other folks' lives without getting out of his chair, and without the chance of being spurned. He stayed up to date in computerese and saved the taxpayers some money by tweaking the outdated computer system and software package the County provided to its departments. Except for high school football and base-ball games, he rarely strayed from home. I suspected he pretty much lived his life through the Internet.

I waited him to run the check and sign off.

"How's it hanging, *amigo*?" I leaned over the counter to check my inbox, and in the process, lightly tapped him on the shoulder.

"Long and loose, and full of juice, and waiting for your use, Purdy."

Childish, but funny as hell for some reason.

"TJ's about to wet his pants over this election, and now he's got a three-for-one-killing that needs solving quick. Please don't make my life miserable by misbehaving. If he loses, I'll be looking for another job."

I laughed. I knew better. Dispatch pay was miserable, and TJ couldn't afford to can Jake. No one else would take the job, or work the extra hours he volunteered for when the other dispatchers were either sick or wanted off for their kids' baseball games. Besides, Jake had been here so long, he knew where all the skeletons were buried.

Recently, TJ spotted Jake talking to Livermore at a baseball game and had nearly come unglued. It turned out that the discussion was about Livermore's grandson's performance as first baseman. Since then TJ kept a weathered eye for any contact between the two of them. This had sparked some office wag to slip a "secret memo" addressed from Jake to Livermore onto the sheriff's desk. Its contents included "confidential" information about TJ's cross-dressing and propensity for trips on the q.t. to Ciudad Acuña's Boystown.

Word had gotten out on when to be around—but not too close—when this bit of artful imagination was discovered by our sheriff. I was in enough trouble at the time, so stayed the hell away. From all accounts, TJ could be heard gurgling with anger in his office. He was smart enough to figure it was a joke and didn't brace Jake over it, but occasionally his gimlet eyes would betray a fear that his chances at reelection were going to be scuttled by an overweight, acne-pocked recluse.

TWENTY

Present Day – A Saturday

PURDY KENDRICKS

After the pleasantries, I walked toward the nasal sound of TJ talking to someone on the phone. TJ's office wasn't the largest in the building. However, it was the furthest back from the entrance, which suited his aversion, at least until recently, to deal willingly with the public.

His office contained the usual trophy walls. The one facing the door was covered with signed, fading photos of mostly B list movie stars who had slipped in and out of the county during hunting season. Another wall held pictures of 4H and FFA show animals purchased, and Little League teams he had sponsored through the years.

The wall directly behind his credenza held head mounts of three white tail bucks he had bagged. He took pride that all held racks of at least 160 points or higher on the Boone and Crockett scale. Smaller kills had not been caped. Surrounding the three deer were plaque mounts of lesser victims' antlers.

My initial impression when seeing this monument to testosterone, was that the wall had grown spines. I had commented to Johnny Reagan, during one of my less tactful moments, that TJ's temper could result in some hapless victim who had pissed him off being thrown against the wall and impaled. Reagan had survived around TJ too long to appreciate my observation.

I'd wondered how, on a sheriff's salary, TJ paid the lease costs for the privilege of killing these monsters. That is, until I had seen his house. One look at the place told me he probably wasn't on the take. I guessed he spent what little he made on his one love—deer hunting.

The house hadn't had any maintenance on it in what looked to be years. The swamp cooler's water pan was rusted through and leaking around the various coatings of tar. Sun had bleached unpainted wood siding into a grey. The only thing good to say about the place was its location. It perched on a small overlook just north of Santa Rosa, where it caught breezes that sometimes died before they made it down into the town.

TJ and his wife, Erna, had two grown children, who had hit eighteen and skedaddled off out of state. Some say it was to get far away from their old man. I wasn't around, so didn't know. However, I could believe it. By all accounts TJ took seriously the admonition against sparing the rod.

The sheriff and chief deputy were drinking coffee with Abner Selman. Johnny Bonavita was chatting with someone in a Border Patrol uniform. He turned when I walked in, and I recognized him as Ignatius Gonsalvez, new to the region and already catching hell for the wrong spelling of his entire name. A couple of other deputies, who seemed fixated on a cell phone video game, were in an interview room. Given the county's refusal to pay overtime, I guessed TJ had promised the two some generous comp time.

TJ's cell rang. He glanced at the screen and took the call, grunted, and ended the call with a curt goodbye. He nodded, and we all exchanged pleasantries. Everyone looked haggard, except Selman, whose shirt was starched, pants creased, and boots shined. I had never seen him any other way and wondered whether the DPS had some huge slush fund for clothing for the Rangers, so they could keep the image up.

Trying to get a rise out of Gonsalvez, a Portuguese American from up-state New York, I asked, "*Hola Ignacio Gonzales, como estas?*"

Gonsalvez grinned. "Fuck you, *bolillo*." He was already fitting in quite well.

Even TJ laughed.

We compared notes and went to the squad bay's white board, writing out what had been done, what needed doing, and assigning responsibilities.

Reagan's account of the ride back with Pete created some back and forth. Some knew him or remembered him from childhood. His anguish seemed to leave everyone reluctant to delve into its depths.

However, the absence of a cell phone was a concrete issue that was more comfortable to discuss. It hadn't been on the bodies or in the house.

TJ glanced around. "Anyone look in his truck."

Bonavita nodded. "I did, Sheriff. And under and around it. I looked through the house some, too."

TJ eyed Bonavita approvingly, then looked around. "Do we know who they used as the carrier?"

Reagan poured another cup of coffee.

"I'll go through the house again. No disrespect, Johnny, but two sets of eyes and all that. And we need to find their bills. We should find something there. Before it gets hotter than hell, I'll take those two knotheads" —he pointed at two idling deputies— "and we'll walk the riverbank. Maybe we'll get lucky. Time to relieve the two reserve deputies we got down there, anyway."

I wasn't holding my breath on finding a phone, but maybe phone records could at least tell us something from calls in or out.

Selman sat quietly, and I wondered what he his role in all this was. After an hour, the meeting broke up. The Ranger touched my shoulder as I walked by.

"Give us a second, will you, deputy?"

I looked over at TJ and Reagan. I wasn't interested in doing anything without an okay. They caught the exchange, and TJ nodded. I guess I was cleared to talk.

"Sure."

TWENTY-ONE

Present Day – A Saturday

PURDY KENDRICKS

R eagan closed the door to TJ's office. Selman took off his Stetson,
wiped his forehead, and reached for a Tums.

What the hell is this all about?

"How well do you know Pete Vasquez?"

"I grew up with him, Ranger."

"Have you two had any contact recently?"

I had to think about that one. *What had happened to our friendship?*

"I think we've talked a few times since I moved back. He stays
busy making big bucks with some plumbing supply business of his in
Laredo. Mostly, I hear about him…" I caught myself and felt a sudden
tightness in my throat. "I *heard* about him from his grandparents."

Selman nodded. "That's what we figured, but just wanted to ask."

"What the hell is going on?"

Selman eased a butt cheek onto a corner of TJ's desk. I caught TJ
cringing and hoped Selman would fart. I bit my cheek to stifle a laugh.

"I'm not sure I know, Purdy. But one of his trucks crossing at
Bridge Number One in Laredo a few months ago was full of dope. No
one's been charged, but now this with his grandparents…"

"What? You think he's into the drug trade?" Stranger things had
happened, but I had serious doubts that someone raised as well as
Pete would be involved.

Selman eyed me. "Word out of Mexico is that Venustiano Huerta—
you heard of him?"

Who hadn't? La Familia Norteña boss who kicked the Zetas out of Nuevo Laredo. I nodded.

"Word is that he's dead. That someone blew his head off."

Huerta's thugs had decapitated, hung, disemboweled, and shot hundreds of their competitors in parts of Nuevo Leon and Tamaulipas. His cartel controlled the drug trade and border crossings in a large chunk of those two Mexican states.

"Where? Nuevo Laredo?"

"Nope. A ranch about sixty miles west of some shithole called El Mosco."

Holy shit.

This was starting to get awfully close to home.

"That would be what? Forty or fifty miles due south of the Griffin Ranch?" As I thought out loud, I tried to start putting pieces together. Nothing fit right. "What are you saying?"

Reagan chimed in. "We don't know, Purdy. Just that Pete's people get killed, as well as someone we have no idea who he is, and that bust in Laredo."

"So, why are you all having this discussion with me?"

TJ finally spoke. "You're my investigator. You need to *investigate. That's* why you're being told."

Selman waved a hand at TJ, signaling him to quit talking. "Actually, DEA is telling us that Nuevo Laredo just got hot again. Three killings in one night. The plaza has been calm for some time now. Makes us wonder if the intel we're getting isn't right. If it is, there is going to be hell to pay—some other cartel will move in. Maybe that was what the killing in Mexico was about. All I'm saying is keep your eyes and ears open."

Selman put his hat back on.

I wasn't finished. "Exactly what the hell is going on? Are you telling me that we"—I motioned toward TJ and Reagan "aren't running this show? What are you telling me? If all this involves Pete in some way, this little pipsqueak office and what we do isn't going to amount to much. Where did DEA get their info? If all this is connected, where is someone from that outfit this morning? Sounds like they're involved in some way already. You didn't come to this conclusion on your own—no disrespect."

"None taken. And DEA is *always* involved, whether we know it or not."

At the door, Selman paused. He spoke to TJ. "We'll give you all the support you need for this investigation—you know that. But there is no way this mess isn't connected some way with something bigger." He paused. "We'll maybe know more when we find out who had his head blowed off at the Griffin place."

Yeah, and you were in Kickapoo County before anyone knew about the killings on the Griffin place.

TWENTY-TWO

Present Day – A Saturday

PURDY KENDRICKS

I left the office feeling as if my head was going to explode. *What were we in the middle of? How much more wasn't Selman telling me?*

Jake glanced up as I walked outside for some air.

"You okay, *compadre?*"

I waved him off and scrolled through the iPod looking for something to take me away for a few minutes. I shook loose the ear bud wires, untying a knot in one of them. *Damn, I hate it when Jake's right —these wires are a pain.*

The hum of the air conditioners and sound of 18-wheelers on the highway made me feel as if I'd walked out into an alternate reality after what I had just heard. Like walking out of ICU to a Dairy Queen. Two different worlds. I felt detached from both of them.

I found Artie Shaw's *Nightmare* and punched play.

I had my list. I walked back into my office, which was not much bigger than a broom closet. I thumbed through my iPod play lists but couldn't find Carlos Santana's *Black Magic Woman*. Not that it was needed to bring back memories.

I called San Antonio and got Laura's AT&T landline answering machine. I didn't go into details but recited that Kickapoo County Sheriff's Office needed to talk with her pretty quickly. *I'll bet the messages won't be checked on that thing for weeks.*

The last address I had on Laura was in the upscale enclave of Alamo Heights, so I put in a call to the Alamo Heights PD and asked to speak with an investigator. I was passed through to Detective Glen Hohmeyer, and I told him briefly what was going on. I didn't want to waste a lot either of our time, so I asked if he could confirm that she still lived there.

"Oh, yeah, she's still there. Got the house free and clear in the divorce."

What divorce, or rather, which one? Alamo Heights was small enough for folks to know these kinds of things. I hadn't seen Laura Griffin in years. I decided to leave that alone for now.

"Uh, is she still going by Saenz?" I also recalled a Sandler somewhere in the marital chain but wasn't sure of its place.

"Oh, sure. Hell, she's on half the charity boards in S.A."

Hohmeyer agreed to track her down personally, "if she isn't gadding about out of state," and have her call me. He felt reasonably sure that he could get her cell phone number from someone who knew her.

Hohmeyer obviously knew his business. An hour later Laura left a message on my cell phone. She said she had "just gotten a call about the murders" from the owner of an adjoining ranch and was "about to pick up and call us" when she received my call.

Odd. The *San Antonio Express-News* electronic news had the Kickapoo County story in bold letters, mentioning "well-known socialite and charity fundraiser Ms. Laura Saenz" as the owner of the ranch where the murders were committed, with links to pieces on border violence, the upcoming Kickapoo County sheriff's race, life in the remoter regions of Texas, Arizona citizens' posses, and anything else it could tangentially tie in.

There was no way in hell that Laura Saenz had "just" heard about what had happened on her ranch.

I saved her cell number in my iPhone, typed it into the electronic report before I lost it in the shuffle, and called her back.

"Purdy, you old scamp, how are you?"

Whoo, boy. Her whiskey-aged voice flooded my senses. I think she knew it would.

TWENTY-THREE

Present Day – Sunday

PURDY KENDRICKS

Betty had called late on Saturday. She knew of my friendship with Pete and my relationship with the old couple. She offered to come home early. There was genuine sympathy and concern in her voice. The other women weren't married to cops, but everyone was feeling the shock of the killings. She and her friends had booked and paid for two nights of hotel rooms and couldn't get refunds, but she had reported they would follow her lead.

"We're all ready to drive back tonight, Purdy."

Betty meant it, too. I told her I didn't want her to ruin her time in San Antonio. Forrest was in good hands, and I suspected the case would make me less companionable than usual—and the usual level of our companionship wasn't very high right now. She whispered a "thank you," with relief in her voice.

She paused, uncomfortable with asking a favor. "Would you see that Forrest gets to church and Sunday School in the morning?"

I woke early enough to scramble some eggs put on a pot of coffee. I then called Paula to tell her I would pick up Forrest. Clipping on a tie and dusting off Tony Lamas worn for special occasions, I locked up the house and unlocked the county sedan. The summer heat was just now making its daily presence known. The desert dry coolness still hung on, keeping the shimmer of summer haze at bay. It was clear enough to see most of Santa Rosa from the carport, its structures spread out over the rough caliche hills a mile away.

I turned off our gravel road onto U.S. 90 and took in the quiet.

Sundays brought Santa Rosa's hardly robust existence to a crawl. Most retail businesses closed, with only a few exceptions.

The Mesa Tourist Court and the Stop Inn convenience store were owned and operated by Jagir Patel and his family, recently from India. Their failure to close was chalked up to the Patel's heathen upbringing, and thus excused. The two gas stations on U.S. 90 were doing a steady business. Paul Engelke's beer joint, known simply as The Bar, would open its doors at noon. Lydia Gonzales's place, Julio's Cantina, a block away, would open around 2:00 or 2:30. When the Bud Lite sign lit up, it was a sign that Lydia had changed out of her altar guild clothes and was ready for business. Nobody knew who Julio was, and it was rumored that Lydia didn't even own the place, although she'd run it since I was in high school. Supposedly, Faustino Reyes, married with five children, who worked off-shore for Halliburton, had set her up in business so she'd have something to do other than stir things up with his wife while he was on a platform in the Gulf.

There were six churches in Santa Rosa. Most Anglos went to either the Methodist or the Baptist Church. The Church of Christ had a small and rigid fold and offered services in English and Spanish. A defunct auto parts store housed a mixed group of evangelicals. The small Presbyterian Church barely clung to life. My Dad's death years ago had scattered his assorted congregants, and no trace remained of his following.

Santa Rosa was probably four-to-one Mexican over Anglo, and that meant the Catholic Church handled the largest number of worshippers.

I passed the Most Pure Heart of Mary Catholic Church, established 1946, with Father Joseph Levant as the current Priest in Charge. The parking lot had a smattering of parishioners' cars. Inside, their occupants were partaking of one of the three Sunday masses. Saturday evening mass had the largest attendance. Somewhere along the way the Catholics had figured out that if you went to church on Saturday, Sunday was free for doing what you wanted to do.

To confirm this, I slowed and rolled down both front windows. Off to my right was the lower end of Santa Rosa, where most Spanish speakers lived and, oddly enough, was known as "the Lower End," It was redolent with *conjunto* music and the beginnings of back yard barbeque fires. Meanwhile, the rest of the God-fearing portion of the county trudged its way to Sunday morning services elsewhere.

I parked the car in front of the First Methodist Church, and Forrest scampered into the classroom building. I had an hour to kill.

I wandered toward the coffee bar, hoping to avoid another invitation to an adult Sunday School class. A few other men doing the same came in, and we passed the time until the service.

The Methodist preacher had made a requisite home visit to encourage my attendance. I liked him, and I enjoyed his sermons. But I couldn't say I was anywhere regular in my attendance.

During the church announcements, the good reverend asked for prayers for the families of those killed. He looked in my direction, as if to let me know he had spotted me and was glad I was there. And I guess I was, too.

I begged off Sunday dinner with Paula and her family, changed into my uniform, and drove back to the office.

Glancing up from a Sudoku puzzle book, Jake nodded as I walked into the office.

"Kemosabe, looks like you're finally earning your keep around here. How was church?"

"What? You spying on me?"

"Nah. Better than that. Saw your car in the church parking lot as I drove in. I should be doing your job, I'm such a good detective."

"Not likely. You'd have to actually do something, instead of puzzles."

"Seriously," Jake looked me over. "Did you get some decent sleep?"

I appreciated his concern. "Actually, I did. The house was empty. I crashed and burned. Thanks."

Jake grinned. "By the way, got a new one for you. Three vampires walk into a bar. Bartender says to the first one, 'What'll you have?' The first vampire says, 'I want blood.' Bartender asks the second vampire, 'what'll it be for you?' Second one says, 'I want blood.' Bartender turns to the third vampire and asks him the same thing. This vampire says, 'I want plasma.' So, the bartender comes back with, 'Let me get these straight—that's two bloods and a blood lite.' Get it? 'Blood lite,' like Bud lite."

I groaned, "That sucked, Jake."

"Sucked. I get that. Pretty good, Purdy." He turned back to the puzzle.

I walked down the hall.

TJ, still in Baptist Sunday finery, motioned me into his office. Selman sat in a recliner in the corner. I guess he had spent the night at the Mesa Tourist Court. TJ tossed a folder across the table. The FBI logo was stamped on the front, as well as a warning about unauthorized usage or public dissemination. I raised an eyebrow and got a nod of permission to open it.

TJ didn't come by an FBI file through regular channels. Come to think of it, neither did most state law enforcement. It was beginning to look as if the Rangers had more pull than I had imagined, or that the Feds were already involved in something I wasn't privy to yet.

The folder had the usual NCIC criminal history printouts of someone named Robert Schivelli. Stapled to the left side was a color front and side mug shot of a male of the same name. He stood 6'4" according to the background reference measure. The shot was taken at Fort Leavenworth Disciplinary Barracks in 2008, according to the ID plate held by the subject.

Mug shots could be deceptive. Anyone in law enforcement would tell you that they can make the Pope look like a thug. The height bars, overalls, and a penal identifier plaque removed most semblances of respectability. The ravages of alcohol or drugs would often come through, but often as not, put the same person in a coat and tie and take the picture in front of a church, and most of us would probably think the person was leaving a deacon's meeting. I had long played a private game of guessing how an ex-con or scofflaw would be perceived, without the institutional accoutrements.

Shivelli's mug shot was, at first glance, no different from most others I'd seen. He had an aggressive looking buzz cut, and a full face, accentuated by a nose that looked like it had been broken and not reset. His ears were small and compact, on a large head set on a weightlifter's or football lineman's neck. But the eyes—even taking the photos' two-dimensional limitations—they were definitely different. The old saying is that eyes are the window to the soul. If that is case, Shivelli had no soul. I had seen killers who looked like school principals and college professors arrested for driving while intoxicated who looked like natural born killers. In a suit, Shivelli could have gone either way. But the eyes—they were lifeless.

"This who I think it is?"

TJ said, "He's your man in the ranch house."

"We didn't get to meet face-to-face."

My small attempt at graveyard humor was met by a groan from the recliner. Oblivious, TJ continued, "This was sent to us this morning. His prints got a hit. He served six years in the Army."

I flipped through the file as Selman chimed in. "Shivelli was a sniper. He had two tours in Iraq, the last one during the Surge in 2007. South of Baghdad, he killed at least eight bad guys, some from distances of over a thousand meters. Got crosswise a couple of times with higher-ups. Then went to United States Disciplinary Barracks at Fort Leavenworth, Kansas, for trying to frag a lieutenant."

Frag. I had read about this happening in Vietnam, but that was awhile back. "Didn't know anyone tried that anymore."

All this was interesting, but why was a disgraced Army sniper lying dead in an isolated ranch house in Kickapoo County? I started to ask, but Selman continued. "Shivelli was originally from the Youngstown, Ohio, area. He met up with someone while in the DB who put him in touch with the local wise guys. By all accounts, he was being used as a contractor by the mob."

I kept pawing through Shivelli's file. He had only received a two-year sentence. "How did he get away with a slap on the hand?"

Selman had read the whole file. "A couple of witnesses were in a firefight south of Baghdad. Their Humvee got blown up by an IED. Killed them. The military pled the case down."

"Lucky for this piece of work," I said.

Shivelli's file contained a lot of reports from various agencies, both federal and state, along with several "intelligence" reports of his reported involvement in mob-related hits, from Ohio to Toronto. There were also some references to South Florida and mentions of unsolved killings there.

As we continued talking, I noticed that all the deaths involved high-power, large-caliber, long-range kills to either the chest or head. Color glossies confirmed the accuracy and finality of the shots. The various hits included men in suits, black men with dreadlocks, and

Latinos with gang tattoos creeping up their necks. It certainly was an eclectic collection of dead men.

"This file sure seems to have a bunch more than the average NCIC/TCIC stuff. How'd we get all this so damned fast?"

Selman grinned. "Apparently what happened here got *someone's* attention besides us. FBI and DEA will probably be getting with us pretty quick. Their folks are asking some of the same questions you are."

"Do we get to keep this?" *Confidential* was stamped on various tabs. "Or is it going back where it came from?" There was no way I was going to absorb all the information and suppositions contained in the two inches of paper neatly clasped inside the file.

"I'm still trying to see any connection between all these dead folks and Mr. Shivelli." A quick glance had shown the usual intelligence reports that tried to put him in the area of each of the hits. But if they were like most intelligence reports I had seen, they contained a lot of supposition.

"Save me the trouble, Ranger." I kept flipping pages. "First, why does some rocket scientist with the Fibbies think he's connected? And second, why do we have some mob killer from up north and two old people dead here in Texas?"

"Hell, Purdy, none of us know. I guess someone better start by leaning on Pete Vasquez and Laura Saenz."

"Yeah," TJ chimed in, "sure as hell there was more going on at that ranch than raising *chivitos* for the Mexican's barbeque *pachangas*."

Jesus, TJ, you are such a dumbass.

He continued, "You and Pete were asshole buddies growing up. I want you to figure out what went on at that ranch."

I just hoped I could.

––––––––––

TWENTY-FOUR

Monday

PURDY KENDRICKS

P ete Vasquez showed up at the Sheriff's Office at 9 a.m. Five feet, seven inches tall, his fireplug body which had served him and Santa Rosa High School well when he played high school tackle, was now thicker by several inches around the waist. His dark black hair showed more than a little gray, and crow's feet marked the edges of his eyes. Just the normal aging process, I guess. What wasn't normal, at least to me, was the haunted look still carrying over from the Griffin Ranch deaths.

He stuck out his hand. "Purdy, it's been awhile."

If you don't count Saturday, it had. "I'd say I'm glad to see you, Pete. But I'm not. Not like this. Thanks for coming in."

"Any news on the autopsies? Luther said you hadn't called."

Hughes Funeral Home, Luther Beirne, proprietor, offered the only mortuary services in the county.

"I'll call Bexar County again this afternoon, Pete. I'll do what I can to get your folks' bodies released as quick as possible."

There was a little sleight of hand here, as the three autopsies were scheduled for later today. I was going to be there. It wasn't something I was looking forward to, but it was something that I had always done in suspected homicides. I had called the Bexar County Medical Examiner's Office and got cleared to be present.

Jake walked over from the dispatch area and shook hands with Pete, expressing his condolences. I motioned Pete into my office. Kick-

115

apoo County wasn't big enough or rich enough for anything like the interview rooms you see on TV shows. I had set up a digital audio and video recorder. Pete glanced at it.

"Jesus, Purdy. You going to record this?"

"Always do in cases like this, Pete." Of course, we hadn't *had* cases like this since I had moved back, and maybe not ever. "It's pretty routine to do it this way, and besides, Pete, I'm too lazy to write everything down." I snuck him a smile to ease the tension I was feeling. Pete wasn't buying it.

I motioned him to sit and turned on the recording equipment, reciting date, time, and reason for the interview. The preliminary questions were textbook where, what, why, when, and who. Pete's answers tracked what he told Reagan during the ride back to town on Saturday.

He saw the door open at the old ranch house and went inside. He assured me he hadn't touched anything other than maybe a door jamb going in or out. As I walked him through the arrival at the ranch, Pete's panic at seeing the body came through. I could see he was thinking about Papa Oto and Mama Raquel.

"Jesus Christ, the guy's face was blown to hell. Who was he anyway? You got any idea, Purdy? What the fuck is someone doing in that old ranch house? What the fuck was someone doing there?"

I didn't offer Shivelli's name. "We don't know who he is or why he was there."

"It looked like one of those videos the fucking towel-heads put out when they executed a bunch of prisoners."

We had all been subjected to the videos of ISIS and Al Qaeda executions. I had watched one of them. He had a point.

"I just knew. I just knew. Something bad had happened to the folks," he twisted in his chair and continued. "I ran out, puked my guts out, and drove down to the river."

I had a list of questions to ask but let him go on with the narrative.

"I got down to their house—there's no cell coverage, but I tried anyway. I don't know why. Oto wouldn't have had his phone on anyway. I ran through the house, saw the clothes still in the basket, and went absolutely apeshit. I used their phone to call you guys and went looking for them." Pete took a deep breath. "I guess you know the rest."

He started to cry. I was glad the video camera was behind me. My eyes welled up, and tears started running down my cheeks. I brushed them away and let Pete get it together. He settled down and shook his head, as if that would rid his memory of what he had seen.

"Sorry. I'll try to get through this."

"I'm sorry I'm having to do this. You know what they meant to me."

He nodded. "Yeah, you were like another son to them, Purdy. This has got to be tough on you, too."

I paused again. "About that cell phone. Did you ever find it?"

"No. Come to think of it, I didn't. Wasn't it with Oto?"

"Pete, this is a clusterfuck. Can you think of anything that might tell us why Oto and Raquel were killed? Had they seen something going on? Had they let anyone stay up at the old headquarters? We're fishing right now, and anything you can give us might help."

Pete said he couldn't think of anything. When they talked, Oto's conversations were short. He'd always let Raquel do most of the chatting with their grandson. Neither sounded afraid or worried. The couple rarely went to town, and then, only for supplies and to visit family.

Pete ran a plumbing supply company in Laredo. "I am doing fine, financially. I've tried to get Oto and Raquel to move there. I've got a big house I rattle around."

I guess what I had heard about a divorce awhile back is true.

"Big enough for all of us. Oto wouldn't have anything to do with it."

His grandparents were happy to live out their lives on the ranch. Yes, he worried about Mexico and them being right on the Rio Grande, but they both had family in and around Santa Rosa, and in Northern Mexico. They felt safe, and the narcos hadn't moved upriver, from what he'd been led to understand.

"Purdy, I gotta ask you. Do you think that dead guy killed them?"

"I don't know, Pete. But my guess is no. We'll know more, maybe, when we get autopsy reports, but it could be that all three were killed at the same time."

Finally, I got around to Laura. "Pete, what's Laura been up to lately? Did Oto or Raquel ever discuss her?"

"What do you mean, what's she been up to? Far as I know, she's not been up to anything!" Pete's face reddened.

Whoa. I had struck a nerve. It sure looked like he knew more about Laura than I was expecting. "Hey, *compadre,* I'm not saying anything bad about Laura. I'm trying to figure out if she would have allowed someone on the ranch without telling Oto. That's all."

Pete eased back into the chair, visibly relaxing. "Oto never said anything about that. He said she only called two or three times a year, just to see how things were. She trusted him to take care of the place. She kept an account open for him at the hardware store, and far as I know, never questioned anything he bought for the place."

I'd check that out, too, but didn't doubt it.

"You seen Laura lately?"

Pete tensed again. "No."

It may not have a thing to do with the killings, but Pete was lying through his teeth.

TWENTY-FIVE

Monday - Later

PURDY KENDRICKS

The interview finished before lunch. I told Pete I would be in touch, and we shook hands. I walked with him to the front door. He reached into his pocket and grabbed his truck keys. I was about to let the glass door close when he turned.

"I'm sorry we haven't not seen each other. I'm sorry I haven't kept in touch. Let's try to do better, okay?"

He stuck out his hand again and I shook it. He held my hand longer than necessary and pulled me to him in an *abrazo*.

"I mean it, Purdy." He walked toward the street.

I let the door close.

"What was that all about?" Jake asked. "Do you normally hug your witnesses?"

I just shook my head. "What, Jake? You didn't know I was gay?"

Jake's eyes widened.

"Gotcha."

"Asshole."

The drive east to San Antonio took three hours. I used the GPS to find the Bexar County Crime Lab, which housed the Medical Examiner's office. It sat across from a country club off Louis Pasteur Drive, northwest of Loop 410. I was escorted back to the autopsy labs.

The assistant ME, an eager beaver pathologist named Tim Villarreal, was waiting for me.

"Deputy Kendricks, right?" Already gloved up, he didn't offer a handshake.

We had met before. I reminded him of a drowning death I had attended a year ago.

"Oh yeah. The guy that fell out of the boat in a stock tank, right? Blood alcohol sky high?"

"Good memory, Doc."

"Hell, I can't remember my kids' names, but I can remember stiffs for some reason. I guess that's sort of strange, isn't it?"

I let that one pass. I thought *all* ME pathologists were strange, whether they could remember their kids' names or not.

I told him what we had found. His assistant wheeled in the first body. I could tell it was Raquel's. I braced for seeing her, at the same time taking up Villarreal's offer for Vicks VapoRub to put under my nostrils.

Mama Raquel's body bag was unzipped, and the assistant was ready with a digital camera.

The assistant washed Raquel's body, then fingerprinted her and took nail clippings. The bullet's exit wound above her left eye hadn't damaged as much of her face as I had expected. Raquel had been a shy woman, and I caught myself wondering what she would think of three men staring at her naked body.

"So, you knew this woman?"

"You might say that."

He glanced at me, nodded, and said, "Sorry, but what I've got to do isn't going to be easy for you."

The autopsy took less than two hours, fast by most standards. Villarreal kept up a running commentary into the hanging microphone. He noted arteriosclerosis consistent with someone her age. Her appendix had been removed, which I hadn't known. Her gallbladder had been removed, which I did remember. There was nothing medically remarkable otherwise, until the bone saw cut open her skull, and her brain was removed.

"Did you find any shell casings or bullets?"

"We've had metal detectors around where she and her husband were found, but nothing turned up."

"Come over here." He motioned me toward the shaved nape of Raquel's neck. "See this?"

"Stippling?"

"Looks like it. And fouling. We'll know more when we do all the toxicology, but I'd say this lady was shot from between six and 12 inches."

I had told him about the recovered Glock 9-mm near Shivelli. "If it's that close, any idea on caliber?"

"I doubt if it was done by that nine." He probed the entrance wound. "This is more consistent with what I've seen with a .45. No guarantee, but I'm fairly sure."

Villarreal called a time out after finishing up with Raquel's autopsy. It was nearly 5 p.m. "You in a hurry for all three to get done?"

I hesitated, not knowing if I would have to deal with Otabiano's autopsy the next day.

"Hey." He tossed the gloves in a bin and tapped me on my shoulder. "I just came on before you got here. If you're up to it, we'll get the other two done before you leave. But first, I'm hungry. There's a great Italian place about a mile from here. Okay with you?"

We drove there in his BMW. Surprisingly, I was hungry. Villarreal was in no mood for shop talk. The waitresses in the small restaurant knew him and brought out garlic, olive oil, and bread. I ordered eggplant parmesan. Villarreal ordered spaghetti Bolognese.

He was a Spurs fan. The fact that I didn't know shit about the team didn't faze him. He regaled me, between mouths of food, with statistics and trade reports for the upcoming season. He took particular delight in pulling a vacuum and getting a six-inch run of egg noodles sliding into his mouth.

Otabiano's autopsy took nearly three hours. There were two entry wounds, which I knew about already. There was an exit wound to the head shot. Rolling Otabiano's body over, Villarreal and his assistant couldn't find an exit wound for the gut shot.

"You might get lucky, Deputy. We may actually find you a bullet in the gentleman's body. If he was shot with the same caliber as the old lady, it would be surprising, given the punch of those things, but stranger things have happened."

He asked me to confirm there wasn't an exit wound noticeable on the exterior of the old man's body.

I then sat on a nearby stool, plugged in my ear buds, and punched play. I had heard enough pathologist chatter and needed a break. Chick Webb, that tragic band leader, hit it off with *Heebie Jeebies*, and a young Ella Fitzgerald tearing it up. Not as good a version as the Boswell Sisters, but it did fine. I almost felt completely separate from the reality of Otabiano's body being cut apart.

The Y incision and removal of ribcage, lungs and heart ensued. The bullet to Otabiano's gut had shredded his liver and spleen. His body cavity was full of clotted blood. No bullet was detected in the internal organs removed. Then Villarreal motioned me over. I stood up and pulled out the ear buds.

"Lookee here. I'll be damned. Somehow the round got stuck in the gentleman's vertebra." He pointed. "It's not in good shape, but you've got your murder weapon, and I'll bet you that's a .45 round."

Shivelli didn't kill the old couple.

TWENTY-SIX

Tuesday

PURDY KENDRICKS

I called home to tell Betty it would be late Tuesday before I would make it back. Santa Rosa was rife with rumors. She filled me in on some, then put Forrest on the phone.

"When are we going fishing, Dad?"

"I'm in San Antonio through tomorrow morning, at least son." I took a chance on making another promise I might have to break. "Get your pole ready. We'll go on Wednesday." He whooped and let out a yell.

"Dad's taking me fishing on Wednesday, Mom!"

I told him I loved him, to say his prayers, and I would see him soon. He handed the phone to Betty. I could hear him run out of our bedroom.

"Are you sure about that, Purdy?"

"I'll make it happen, Betty."

I checked into a Motel Six off Interstate 10 and crashed. I woke up at 6 a.m. and couldn't go back to sleep. I wasn't meeting Villarreal for Shivelli's autopsy until two. With time to kill, I took a deep breath and punched in Laura's cell phone number.

"What the hell, Purdy. It's oh dark thirty." She was trying to sound mad but didn't.

"You got time for breakfast?"

"Where are you?"

I told her and mentioned a Jim's Café near Alamo Heights.

"Purdy, I'm rich as shit. I got two maids. I won't bite you, and I'm not going to wait for a table to open up at that madhouse. Get your ass over here"—she gave me her address "and I'll feed you."

Why did I feel like a fly heading into a spider web?

The house was a 1920s Spanish colonial on a small street off Alamo Heights Boulevard. It sat on a huge lot, with live oaks, palms, and a circular driveway. I pulled up to the front door. Laura appeared, wearing tight-fitting shorts, a peasant blouse, and sandals that showed off a pedicure.

Time had been kind to her. Despite the years, I felt like a gawky teenager, weak in the knees. I worked on the Griffin Ranch during high school. She would come in from San Antonio during the summer. Like a lot of ranchers, the Griffins had a home in the city, in order to afford the offspring a place to get a decent education. Alamo Heights was three hours away, which in Texas terms wasn't all that far. The summer before I entered A&M, some cheap tequila, a full moon, and a blanket on the ground far enough away from the ranch headquarters had initiated me into the mysteries of sex. It had been wonderful and confusing. She was four years older than I was, and she knew a lot more about the subject than I did. She had finished undergrad studies at Baylor. She planned to make it in the fashion world in New York City.

I couldn't get enough of her or the sex, and fell in love, or at least in lust. Pete Vasquez knew what was going on, and he stayed pissed most of the time. He had a thing for her too, but then who wouldn't have? Laura, 5' 4" was unbelievably beautiful. Her body was lithe and taut from years of equestrian training. Smart as a whip, Laura had a streak of craziness that her old man couldn't control.

Mr. Griffin must have known what was going on between us but chose not to let it show. He knew his daughter well enough to count on Laura eventually doing what she figured was best for her, and that was going to New York. By the time I drove to College Station to enroll, we were through. Although she tried to let me down easy, I felt like I was going to die from a broken heart. I was convinced I would never have sex like that again. In short, I was miserable, and miserable to be around.

Mama finally had had enough of my moods. "Son," she said one day, "I'm sick of you moping around like some love-struck idiot. Go to college; amount to something. You may think you're miserable now, but I can guarantee that if the two of you stayed together, that gal would make your life a living hell." Kathryn Lea Kendricks did have a way with words.

I got over it. Time, geography, and good sense had kept me away from Laura. Later, of course, things got even more complicated.

Betty didn't want me to even mention her name, which I hadn't done when I told her I was going to San Antonio.

As I closed the car door, Laura was at my side. She turned me toward her and gave me a strong hug. "God, you're a sight for sore eyes, Purdy." She pushed me back and looked me over at arm's length. "You're still a fine-looking man. She eyeballed the length of a two-tone Lincoln Continental with wire wheels and welded chain steering wheel. "Where did you get the pimp-mobile?"

I looked at the car. It *was* pretty pathetic looking. "Dope seizure on U.S. 90. We arrested some guy muling cocaine from El Paso. Our illustrious district attorney filed a forfeiture, and the record owner never filed an answer. We got the car. The air conditioning works, which is more than I can say for the county sedan I'm usually stuck with. Give me credit. I *did* take the Jesus statue off the dash."

She shook her head and let out a laugh that began at the waist and moved up to her throat. It sounded wonderful. "Come on in."

The house was a Spanish colonial design, tile roof, stuccoed exterior, pastels. The terrazzo entryway opened into high-ceilinged rooms. Warm Southwestern hues, Western art, some by artists I recognized, Mata Ortiz pottery, Talavera inset tiles. The place was gentle on the eyes.

"Beautiful home."

"Thanks. I've gotten a lot of joy fixing it up. Come on. I'll give you a quick tour."

She seemed proud of the transformation that had been affected on "a 1920s beauty that was about to be torn down, it was in such bad shape," as it was described.

Walking behind Laura allowed me the chance to watch her without being noticed. She still had the light walk of a younger woman, comfortable in her own skin.

A majestic dining room, with seating for at least 20, showed off portraits of her father and mother, Laura, and her siblings. There was a gap between otherwise evenly spaced frames. A large portrait had occupied the space.

"Mr. Saenz," she offered, pointing to the empty space, "my dear former spouse, didn't fight me over who got the house, but wasn't about to let me keep his portrait." As she explained, the frown quickly disappeared. In its place was a mischievous look of a small child. "Actually, when we split the sheets, I told him that he needed to cart that ponderous looking thing out of here before something happened to it. Looked almost as bad as an Elvis painting on velvet."

She laughed again. It was infectious, and I joined in. It felt good.

I was relieved that Johnny Reagan hadn't come with me. If he saw how I was looking at the woman, and said anything about it in Kickapoo County, it would eventually get back to Betty. At the same time, I could have used extra protection from Laura's charm.

Breakfast was served on the inner patio, with migas, biscuits, fruit, and coffee brought out by one of the maids. Laura sat across from me at the glass table, kicking off her sandals, and swished around a Bloody Mary. She didn't offer me one. The smell of Worcestershire Sauce, Tabasco, and celery salt brought back good memories—and many more memories I would just as soon have forgotten.

She kept up the small talk while we ate, occasionally crossing and un-crossing her tanned, sculpted legs, swinging her bare feet back and forth. I moved my placemat a few inches to block out the sight under the table. I was having a hard time trying to ignore the tumescence in my pants. It was hell trying to concentrate. I knew she knew it. I found myself surreptitiously checking my wristwatch, as if I was due back at the ME's office. Time wasn't cooperating.

The table was cleared as I finished my third cup of coffee.

"Purdy, when's the funeral? I need to be there. And quit looking at your watch. Are you taking medicine?"

I reddened and decided it was time to start acting like a cop.

"Laura, you know I'm enjoying being with you and all that. But we're trying to figure out what happened at the ranch."

She suddenly teared up. "Those two old folks were Daddy's best friends in a way. I think he thought more of them than his own kids. But then, they weren't trying to figure a way to get more of his money." She smiled ruefully. "I didn't drive over when I heard. Figured I'd be in the way more than anything."

Left unsaid was Betty's discomfort with her being anywhere in the same county.

I opened my laptop, and two hours later, had a statement of what Laura said she knew. She didn't appear to be concealing any information. But then, this was Laura. The narrative was straight-forward, and there was only one surprise—Pete's plan to swing through San Antonio after checking on his grandparents had included an overnight stop in Alamo Heights.

I asked Laura if she had a printer. She did. I transferred the narrative to a flash drive and onto her desktop PC and printed it out. She signed it. Nearly noon, I passed on the offer of lunch and promised to let her know about funeral plans.

As I walked out, I asked about something I wasn't sure needed to be in my report or her statement.

"You and Pete? I thought that ended a long time ago." The question showed more interest than I had intended.

"He went through a nasty divorce two years ago. His wife brought two kids into the marriage. He was close to them, and he adopted them. When she left, the kids went with her. She moved back to Fort Worth. He thought of those kids as his, and it knocked him for a loop. Didn't you know about that?"

I ignored the question.

"We've seen each other now and then," she said

This was all news to me. I had never met Pete's wife, and I wasn't familiar with his personal issues. The old couple never talked about their grandson's life, out of respect for my feelings, I guess.

"I gotta ask you, Laura. Why did you and Pete hook back up?"

"We didn't 'hook back up,' as you call it." She reddened. "We've kept up with each other through the years."

I couldn't resist. "Did you two 'keep up' when *you* were married?"

That probably wasn't germane to anything to do with my investigation. It was childish and unnecessary, and it ended the discussion. Not answering, she gave me perfunctory hug, but didn't walk me to the car. As I climbed behind the wheel, I looked at her front door. She was closing it without looking back.

The drive back to the ME's office didn't go fast enough. The Lincoln's air conditioning came at a cost of a bunch of stares and honks from drivers on the northwest side of San Antonio. Welded chain steering wheels weren't *de rigueur* in this mostly Anglo area.

Pete's lying to me on something as benign as he and Laura playing the two-backed beast, married or not, didn't make much sense. San Antonio traffic kept me from spending too much time on what was an imponderable. I put in the ear buds, pushed shuffle on the iPod and hit play. Artie Shaw's 1938 version of *Nightmare* started up.

Well, yeah. With three dead people, a rocky marriage, and some not-so-good memories, I guess it is.

TWENTY-SEVEN

Tuesday (Continued)

PURDY KENDRICKS

I arrived back half an hour early and cooled my heels in the hallway. Dr. Villarreal met me and walked me into the lab.

"How did you sleep last night?" He didn't wait for an answer. "Where did you stay?"

"Motel 6. They left the lights on for me."

He kept walking, throwing talk over his shoulder as he went. "Okay mattresses? I always stay at Hiltons. Got a great deal on points with a Citibank Visa. Complimentary move-up to a suite. You ought to get one."

I guess he had never heard of Tom Bodett. He sure as hell didn't know anything about county salaries.

Shivelli was wheeled in, and his body bag unzipped. Villarreal and his assistant began the external inspection of his body.

"Geez, deputy, this one's a mess."

He went off on a story about seeing two gangbangers on the South Side who had been executed by shotgun, comparing the damage. His discourse sounded like a judge on *America's Got Talent,* comparing killers' skill levels.

The body was washed, and notes dictated on the extensive damage. It was hard visualizing the body on the table being the person in the FBI folder.

I stood off to one side, with Villarreal noting wounds that were consistent with double-aught buckshot. There were a couple of tattoos, both related to his time in the military. When he came to Shivelli's left hand, he motioned me over.

"See this?"

It was a large gash that had taken out most of the webbing between the thumb and first finger in the left hand.

"I'll look at this a little closer in a minute, but it looks like an older wound than the rest of the damage. Lots of infection and some scabbing. I wonder where this wound came from."

I told him about finding the smelly camouflage clothing we had submitted to DPS.

"I'll bet toxicology will find infection consistent with dirty river water. It could be a cut but," he probed the webbing, "this sure looks like a bullet tore through this part of his hand. You might want to try to find out about this one."

I planned on it.

Buckshot was recovered in several places in Shivelli's body.

"Besides the wound to the head, were there any other fatal wounds?"

It sounded like a silly question, but it was one that would be asked of the doctor on the witness stand if we were ever able to get Shivelli's killer into a courtroom.

Villarreal laughed. "Pick one. Liver, spleen, lungs, several arteries. Whoever did this didn't miss much."

Villarreal promised he would get the Vasquez's bodies released that afternoon, so Pete could finish funeral arrangements. The autopsy ended in time for me to get caught in evening rush-hour traffic. I was back in Santa Rosa by 8 p.m.

TWENTY-EIGHT

Wednesday

PURDY KENDRICKS

The Vasquez funeral was set for noon on Friday. Luther Beirne called the SO and asked Jake to pass the word, which he did immediately. Jake's email list was encyclopedic. Printed notices from the funeral home were passed around town by an old retired man. They would show up on business countertops, as was the custom, but would hardly be necessary this time.

Betty called in to work and said she'd be in late. After breakfast, she packed lunches for us. Forrest scurried around, pulling rods and reels out of the closet. He could hardly contain himself.

"What about the investigation, hon? I know it's big. How are you going to square this with TJ?"

"If he calls, I'm out investigating. We've got enough dead spots in this county that he won't be able to find me for a few hours anyway. "And," I paused as I took the lunch sacks out of her hand, "I promised the boy I would."

She suddenly grabbed me around the waist and hugged me close to her, burying her head in my chest. "Purdy, we gotta make this work. That boy needs us both."

A swarm of feelings washed over me, partly relief at not feeling like I had to be on guard, partly a sense of promise for the future, and more than a tinge of guilt for thinking about another woman while I held this one. I hugged Betty back, and we held each other for a good

15 seconds before Forrest came through the screen door and tugged on my shirt.

"Come on, Daddy. We gotta go, now!"

We broke into laughter. The moment was over. She pushed me out the door. "You men get going. I expect fish for supper tonight!"

A work order in place for a new air conditioner compressor had resulted in me swapping the sedan out for one of the county's maintenance department pickups. I had turned in "pimp mobile" the night before checked out the worn-out pickup. It needed realignment, but its AC worked.

"What say you and I go wet a line?" There were some deep holes gouged out of limestone on the river near Lágrimas, and channel and blue cats could get pretty big. Forrest reeling in a five-pound catfish was a sight to behold. I felt myself grinning as we turned west on U.S. 90.

"Daddy, I like it when you and Mama smile."

The kid had a keen eye, which made the times when Betty and I weren't smiling hurt me even more.

Forrest chatted away for the dozen or so miles to the turn off. "Dad, ya think I'll get a big one?" and "I bet mine is bigger than yours" being the two most often expressions of his excitement.

We pulled down through Lágrimas to the low-water crossing and parked the truck off the side of the road. I unloaded the rods and reels, stringer, and stink bait. I handed one rod to Forrest, and he took off upriver the quarter mile to our favorite fishing spot.

"Hurry up, Daddy."

Twenty yards or so down the river, the morning sunlight glinted off several things that didn't look like native rock. I walked over and stooped down, pulling a shell casing out of the gravel. It was a casing for a 7.62 AK 47. I looked around. There were dozens of the casings, scattered from about 10 yards above the water line down to the river.

What the hell? Forrest's yelling for me to "get going" brought me back to the fishing.

"I'll be there in a minute, son," I yelled back. I pulled out my cell phone and started taking pictures. I ran back to the truck and grabbed a metal container in the truck's bed and started loading up the shell casings. Forrest re-appeared.

"Dad, come *on!*"

"Son, I need your help for five minutes." A bribe was in order. "Five bucks if you pick up more of these than me." I showed him the 39-millimeter length shell casing.

That sealed the deal. It took 15 minutes, but Forrest wasn't keeping time at this point.

"How many did I get, Dad? Do I get the five bucks?"

Neither of us had kept count. "Son, you're the winner." I pulled out my wallet and gave him a 10.

"Daddy, this is more than five!'

"Yep, but you earned it, son."

By noon, we had caught six catfish, and while kneading stink bait onto Forrest's hook, I began to get an idea of where Shivelli had gone into the Rio Grande.

TWENTY-NINE

Wednesday Night

PURDY KENDRICKS

W e rolled into Santa Rosa as the sun dropped behind the hills. I turned up our street and pulled alongside Betty's Datsun pickup. The porch and carport lights offered a welcome glow.

Forrest hardly waited for the truck to stop rolling before leaping into its bed to retrieve a stringer of eight catfish, ranging from three to six pounds. I hooked most of them, but they belonged to him, by reason of the small boy's right to reel them in. Watching him was more fun than the fishing anyway.

The carport screen opened, and Forrest went screaming up the drive toward his mother. Betty's attention was one 100% on her son, so I hung back. She oohed and aahed, then helped lift the stringer into the outside sink used for cleaning game and fish.

"We'd better get your Dad some stuff to clean your fish with," she said, as they disappeared into the house. Kitchen drawers clanged opened and closed. Forrest came out with an electric knife, baggies, and a garbage bag for the guts. I plugged in the knife and filleted the cats, rinsing the white meat before placing it in baggies partially filled with water to prevent freezer burn. The gut bag went into the back of the truck to be deposited at the Sheriff's Office dumpster in the morning. I went into the house and washed off the knife, drying it and putting it in its storage box.

Forrest stripped down and headed to the bathroom. Betty came over and put her head on my shoulder. I put my arms around her.

"That boy loves you more than life, I think." She looked up at me.

I smiled. I enjoyed the moment. There hadn't been too many since my problems in Houston and the year we had been here. We sat down on the sofa.

"How was the trip?"

I gave a shorthand version of the fishing. This was Forrest's story to tell. Splashing and singing came from the tub. We looked at each other and laughed.

"TJ left several messages, but I told him you were out."

"Not far from wrong." Forrest couldn't keep his earlier reward quiet, so I decided to tell Betty what we had found in the sand at the Lágrimas crossing.

"The guy we found at the ranch had been in the river. I don't know how long, but the coroner in San Antonio said there was a wound that didn't fit with the ones that killed him. Looked infected. I'm wondering if those shell casings have something to do with it."

As I told her this, Betty's eyes widened. She wasn't happy with Forrest fishing where there was no cell coverage—and now this.

"Hon, I had no idea. If I had, we wouldn't have gone there. You know that."

She shook her head. "This place isn't safe, is it?" She didn't wait for an answer. "I don't remember growing up that we ever thought twice about the border. We swam and fished—never thought twice about crossing over. We'd sneak beer and drink it in Mexico, so the folks couldn't catch us. I couldn't wait to leave here, but there were some good times. But this at Lágrimas, and Pete's grandparents...."

The mention of the Vasquezes prodded my memory. "The funeral is going to be Friday. I'm supposed to be a pall bearer."

"That's an honor, Purdy. Did Pete ask you?"

"The funeral director passed the word for him, expressing Pete's 'appreciation.'"

The sense of loss, not just of the two old folks, but a long-ago friendship washed over me. I suddenly started bawling like a child. Betty grabbed me and pulled me against to her. She stroked the back of my head. I had seen her comfort Forrest that way when he was heartbroken over something. She just rocked me back and forth, quietly humming a mother's lullaby of comfort. There were no words, no discernable pattern of music, but I reacted to it like a child. I quieted to a whimper, and the spasms of agony eased little by little. Then there were only the sounds of small boy, obliviously splashing with his toys, and a woman imparting comfort in an ancient and unknowable language.

Regardless of where she and I stood with each other, I had never overlooked the fact that she was a damned fine woman. As she continued to hold me, I felt a familiar stirring in my groin, as one emotion began flip-flopping with another. Feeling a little guilty, I nuzzled her right breast, and felt the nipple harden inside the thin bra. Sex had been rare, but these few moments sometimes trumped our other problems. I reached up, and touched her left breast, and gently stroked it. I raised my head and put my mouth on hers. Her ferocity in meeting my lips and exploring with her tongue was almost frightening in its intensity.

We stayed like that until Forrest, naked as a jaybird, came running out of the bathroom and went to retrieve his pajamas. He had now begun the goodnight rituals that inevitably extended a 9 o'clock bedtime until closer to 10. I went over to the kitchen sink and ran cold water over my face. Betty finger-combed her hair and rose from the sofa.

"Time for bed, Sluggo." She pushed the boy toward his room, which also gave me some time to re-adjust myself. We tucked him in, said prayers, and promised to fry up the catfish the next day. Closing the door, Betty led the way into the bedroom. I prayed the recent feelings would be there after Forrest fell asleep.

And they were.

THIRTY

Friday

PURDY KENDRICKS

R osary was said on Thursday in the evening. I couldn't have gone if I had wanted to, given the amount of time required to deal with the paperwork on the case. Clete Morales told me the church had been packed for the Rosary recited for the souls of Otabiano and Raquel.

This was the preview of what I expected to be the largest funeral service in county history. The county's sense of outrage, combined with the large Vasquez clan, many friends, curiosity seekers, and the press, guaranteed that if I didn't get the family seated early, they would end up in the balcony or worse, standing. I had stood at a lot of funerals, but a full High Mass would be a grueling ordeal. I was lucky, if that was the right word, as I would serve as a pallbearer. I could hardly say no and wouldn't have. However, frankly, I had wanted to sit in the back of the church and watch folks. Now that wasn't possible.

Betty had taken off work for the funeral, as had a lot of others. Forrest came too, with surprisingly little fuss. He understood the solemnity of the occasion. It would make more sense to him somewhere along the way in his life. For now, all we wanted was for him not to squirm too much.

At 11:30, I walked from the office over to Most Pure Heart of Mary and got my boutonnière from Luther Beirne. Luther was about 10 years older than me, with a wicked sense of humor. He wasn't above telling funeral jokes to the pall bearers. I had seen several times when a casket was rolled out of a church when six pallbearers had to choke back laughs at some tasteless bit of humor. He seemed to know this wasn't going to be one of those times.

Paula met Betty and the boy earlier, and they staked out the end of a pew toward the back of the church, next to the Holy Water dispenser, which intrigued Forrest to no end. This was especially so, since Father Levant assured him on an earlier visit that for it to be Holy Water, he had to "boil the hell out of it."

The pallbearers included several Vasquez nephews, as well as Pete and me. As we assembled, I got stuck listening to a nephew who had returned from California and regaled me with tales of the good life in the L.A. area. Pete studiously ignored me.

The organist cranked up, which tamped the murmur of the crowd as the church filled. Father Levant gave us the high sign, and the pallbearers followed the priest and the pall-draped caskets into the nave. We sat on one of the front pews. After the pallbearers, the first four rows of pews were reserved for the Vasquez kin. Given the size of that family, there was no way all the kin could be shoe-horned into that limited space. There must have been some behind the scenes politicking to see who got to sit up front, and who was relegated further back.

The Catholic Liturgy for the Dead began.

The Kickapoo Settler's Cemetery had been declared desegregated years ago, but no Hispanic had been buried there. After the service, a motorcade made the short trip to the Guadalupe Cemetery. The bodies would be put to rest in the family plot in the old Mexican graveyard. In death, Santa Rosa was still divided between the brown and the white.

The ordeal finally finished, with the commendation of the bodies to the earth and their souls to God. Betty needed to be back at work, so I hugged her and Forrest and walked them to her car. After shaking hands with some of the family whom I hadn't seen in years, I went looking for Pete. It was time for us to have a talk.

Santa Rosa's only public meeting place of any size was the American Legion on the west side of town. The family had rented the place, and it soon filled up with well-wishers, mourners, and mounds of food. I parked across the street in a parking lot for a now defunct

Dollar Bill's Store and wandered into the front hallway of the Legion Hall.

Studiously avoiding me, Laura put in what was for her, a rather low-key appearance at the funeral and spent some time with the various branches of the extended Vasquez clan. I had to hand it to her. She had reached back into her childhood and dropped any "society" pretensions when she was in Santa Rosa. No entourage, no public grieving for the San Antonio TV stations covering the event, no clinging to a significant other. She had been around the border long enough to know that the Mexican culture expected a certain dignity and formality in grieving, and she did her part to honor that tradition.

The skirt-clad blonde sat with the various *tias* and *tios*, holding one of the *patron's* hands. And all this while speaking passable Spanish. I could tell it was noticed and appreciated. She hadn't lost her touch at working a crowd. And it hadn't hurt at all that she had paid for the tombstones and was covering the bar bill to the Legion.

Pete was in deep discussion with Oscar Saenz, an uncle on his mother's side, as I recalled. He occasionally took *abrazos* from folks offering condolences. I stood behind several men, and when my turn came, Pete seized the initiative, giving me a huge hug.

"Hey, buddy, thanks for being there for me and the family."

"No problem, Pete. It was an honor. Uh, you got a minute?"

Pete glanced at Oscar, and his uncle sidled away, probably after a cold beer. Funeral or no—the Legionnaires had to pay the bills, and the small bar was open for business.

"What can I do for you, Purdy?" No uncontrolled grieving here. Pete looked at me as if daring me to push any further discussion with him.

"Well, *amigo*, I'd like to get clear on a few things you and I overlooked."

"What are talking about? And why here, for God's sake?" Pete squinted his eyes at me. I felt his anger.

"I'm not trying to make you mad." I kept my voice low and as calm as I could make it. "I know you want to get this case solved, and I just have a few more things to go over before you head back to Laredo."

At this point, two small kids ran over for a hug from their often absent relative, and Pete swallowed his bile.

"Hey *chivitos*, how you two doing? Give your *tio* a big hug. You behavin' in school?"

It was obvious the boys had been told good things about this handsome kinsman. They lapped up his attention.

I stood there grinning, holding a Styrofoam cup of iced tea, pretending to be just another *bolillo* who had been made near-family by the old couple. But I wanted to see where this was heading, and I wasn't leaving Pete's side until I knew what he would do.

The boys scampered off, and Pete's response to me was muffled by the constant "mic—check, mic—check" of a local D.J. about to crank up some Tejano music on the stage.

"What makes you think I got anything more to say to you that would make one *pinche pedacito de mierda* of difference? And where do you get off bracing me like this?" He was almost choking, as he tried to keep his voice under control. A few folks nearby looked our way. Pete showed the rictus of a smile and said softly, "Well, okay, I'll meet you at the station in the morning, say nine?"

There wasn't much else to be said. I nodded yes and walked off.

I didn't stay much longer at the gathering.

THIRTY-ONE

Monday

PURDY KENDRICKS

I was played for a sucker. Pete never showed on Saturday. I called the numbers of his business in Laredo, only to be told by whoever answered that he was out of town at a funeral. On Monday, I dialed Laura in San Antonio. She didn't answer. I left a message. She didn't return the call.

Unanswered questions needed to be addressed, but right now I was stuck twiddling my thumbs, trying to find out where the rest of my week was going.

District Judge Sam McCullough sat at his desk in an empty office on the second floor of the Kickapoo County Courthouse that served as his chambers when he showed up in Santa Rosa. He didn't stand on ceremony. His Noconas were propped on the edge of an old roll-top desk. He was using a nail clipper to cut fuzz balls off an old polyester tie, while he half-listened to Josh Hinton and some defense lawyer I hadn't met trying to decide whether a venire panel was going to be put to work this week, or sent home.

Judge McCullough didn't think all that much of Hinton's prosecutorial fervor. He often hinted that some good lawyer needed to light a fire under Hinton's ass. The posted docket showed there were three cases on the jury trial docket, that one had already been dismissed, and the other had been continued to a later date. If this case got pled or dismissed, the good judge would have an entire week to tend to more important matters, like working cattle on his ranch in Val Verde County.

I had been subpoenaed in the remaining case, an aggravated assault. I had better things to do than to sit around the courthouse all day, and I tried to let the DA know I would be available to testify on a couple of hours' notice. Knowing Hinton's lack of interest in working too hard, I suspected that an 11th-hour deal would be offered to a Hispanic gang banger wanna-be from San Antonio who had stabbed a cousin in the ribs with a large toad sticker, which I had later relieved him of.

I had spotted him outside on one of the benches as I walked into the outer office. He gave me a vacant stare. The wanna-be had been drunk when he had decided that his *primo* was getting a little too friendly with a young female, tattoos indicating she was hooked in with some San Antonio street gang. Taking umbrage at a perceived lack of respect, he had coaxed the disrespecting party outside a friend's house and commenced to try to plunge the knife into his *primo's* chest. Thwarted by a rib that bent the blade, he was in the process of kicking his *primo* in the face when I relieved him of what was by Texas law a "deadly weapon," albeit a cheap one.

We didn't have many jury trial settings in Santa Rosa. Given the propensity of our illustrious D.A. to avoid going to trial, more often than not, those summoned to serve ended up, unless they were self-employed, with a free Monday off from work.

I stepped into the hallway after saying hello to the judge. Laughter and rustling of chairs soon confirmed my suspicion. The little scumbag outside the antechamber was going to get off with a light probation, despite his professed desire, shared with all in earshot at the time, that he wanted to "cut the *hijo de puta's* heart out."

Walking out of the judge's chambers, Hinton signaled me saying, "Hang loose until we get this plea done. It doesn't look like we're going to trial. Mister Defendant didn't want to take a chance with a jury."

Well, why would he? He was avoiding a jury trial for a couple of years on probation and a transfer of supervision to Bexar County. I bet he would quickly avoid reporting to his probation officer, and only get picked up after he and his *compadres* had done something far worse. From the gang banger's point of view, it was a no-brainer.

I shrugged my shoulders and said I would be over at the office doing some paperwork. Josh was from old ranching money and didn't need the job. That was a weakness to be sure, but it had on occasion turned out to be a strength. He wasn't going to work too hard, but he also wasn't susceptible to much outside pressure, either.

As I watched him head down toward his office on the first floor to get the plea forms, I was reminded of an old Army sergeant talking about young officers assigned to his company. "Purdy," he had said. "I've seen 'em come and I've seen 'em go."

Josh was like that. He had seen plenty of chest-thumping defense lawyers float through. He knew his constituency well enough to know what it would put up with and what it wouldn't, and just didn't let too much get to him.

Walking back to my office, I greeted several prospective jurors headed for the district courtroom on the first floor. Israel Sifuentes, the courthouse custodian, was slowly raising the American flag on a flag-pole, donated by the local American Legion, honoring the 11 boys from the county killed in World War II. Israel had been around since as long as I could remember; he pretended not to speak too much English.

Israel knew everything that went on in and around the courthouse. He was kin to virtually everyone of Hispanic lineage on this side of the border, and maybe to some Anglos who wouldn't admit to it. Born in Mexico, he still had family scattered up and down the brush country on that side of the river, as well. If I needed some information on a crime committed against or by any of his "people," as he called them, he would usually point me in the right direction, unless it was too close to home. It didn't stop there. Since Hispanics held down most of the menial jobs in the county, his "people" had access to bedroom, supper table, barroom, and deer camp talk that in some mysterious way filtered its way back to him. Taking Israel lightly was done at your own peril.

"*Hola, compadre. Como te sientas?*"

Israel was 5' 3" but a giant of a hypochondriac, who appreciated any chance to explain about his latest night sweats, swollen joints, and especially his theories about what made his bowels so windy.

"*Nada, Señor Purdy. Parece que hoy el cuerpo no me esta dando muchas problemas.*"

That was a switch. Not wanting to chance opening the door to any as yet undiscovered cancers, tumors, pustules, or the like, I dropped the subject, shook his hand, and walked off down the sidewalk. He stopped me with a low "*Oye...*"

"*Oye*" or "listen up" was Israel's way of indicating he wanted to pass along some information. He slowly tied off the lanyard, wiped his hands on his khakis, and shuffled over to where I'd come to a stop.

He continued in Spanish, "It sure is a shame about Oto and Raquel. Oto was my Mom's uncle's first cousin. Raquel, was a Palomo, so we were cousins down the line, too."

He paused, and I saw Paula wave as she walked up the courthouse steps. She was holding a jury card and acted like she wanted to walk over and say hello.

But Israel had something for me, and I wasn't about to break the mood. Looking over his shoulder as he decided which way to steer the conversation, I waved back. I pointed to my watch, as if I had an appointment, and cut my eyes off her, hoping she would stay away. As a beautician, she knew enough about Israel to respect a kindred spirit in the information gathering department. She nodded and left us alone. She proceeded up the stairs and went inside. I turned my attention back to Israel.

"Purdy, what happened was a shame," he repeated.

I nodded agreement, waiting for him to give me a hint as to where he was headed.

"The Palomos, now they're about gone from around here now. Most of the family headed out to San Diego and Los Angeles. Some went down toward Laredo, you know, where Pedrito has got his business now." He spat into the flowerbed. "It's bad losing your *abuelos* like that." He shook his head, then looked up at me. "Margie Palomo, she's old man Victor's widow. She was at the Rosary but didn't stay for the funeral. Victor had a bad heart, you know." He paused, as if to honor a fellow sufferer. "Victor sold out of the produce business a few years before he died. A fellow named Castruita bought it, I think."

I was wishing for pen and paper, so I could keep this flow chart straight.

"Anyway, Victor had a little shop down near La Posada. Why he kept it open there instead of getting some decent space, I don't know.

Who knows? I think maybe he made a little money with the *mojaditos*, and it was easier up against the river than somewheres else. I don't know. Anyway, Margie, she tells me, 'Israel, how did Pedrito get that big company so fast in Laredo?'"

I had given it some thought, but not much. Laredo was booming and would continue to do so as long as the *narcotraficos* stayed on their side of the river. Pete had never been lazy. I said as much to Israel.

"Well, perhaps you are right. But Margie, being around her is a *puro rollo*, my friend, and I tell her the same thing. She tells me that no *contractistas* in Laredo are using your friend. I know it's a big place, but it ain't that big, and Margie, she knows everything that's going on in that town."

"Hell, Israel. The town's not small anymore. It's growing like a weed. How can she know what's going on in Laredo, and what about the rest of Texas?"

My exasperation was spilling out, and I needed to reel it in.

"Sorry, *pero tu sabes* that we are getting nowhere. I thought Pete's company wholesaled all over. I'm up to my *nalgas* in guesses."

Speaking of *nalgas*, my ass was getting tired of standing, and I wanted badly to make a move toward the Sheriff's Office. I needed to sit on my tired ass, drink a cup of coffee, and try to catch up on the Vasquez case.

Israel shrugged and put his hand on my shoulder. It was light as a feather. *"Tu eres mi amigo. Cuidate, pero creo que tienes que verificar nuevamente de tu amigo, Pete."*

He switched to English. "You know what a *dedo* is?"

I nodded. *Dedo* meant finger, but an anatomical feature wasn't what Israel was talking about. *Dedo* was a slang term for an informant, a snitch.

"Are you saying Pete is mixed up with the narcos?"

Israel shrugged, repeating, *"Quidate, mi amigo."*

He was telling me something and he wasn't. Maybe he didn't know exactly what he was trying to say. But Israel's value was as a conduit for passing along feelings, vibrations, and the stuff. Almost like a medium. Any way I looked at it, I knew I couldn't ignore what he had just said. Old friend Pete was up to something. Israel was suggesting not only that Pete was dirty, but that he was someone's informant. Whether it had a damned thing to do with the killings, was still beyond me.

But I knew I had to take a hard look.

―――――――

THIRTY-TWO

Present Day

PURDY KENDRICKS

I came through the front door of the office. Jake was talking with TJ and Ranger Abner Selman. All three were drinking coffee.

Rangers occasionally dropped in casually on local law enforcement offices. However, it was apparent, not so much by what was said or done, but by subtle body language, that Abner didn't think much of TJ Johnson, as a lawman or as a person. If the Ranger was in the Sheriff's Office, it was an official visit, and not for a late morning chit chat.

The Rangers were putting out feelers, working their intelligence sources, and pushing DPS to finish the lab work. The reality, however, was that Abner and his folks could only do so much, constrained as they were by budget and understaffing. Judge McCullough had signed several subpoenas for phone records, but so far, the various carriers hadn't replied.

Abner put down his coffee cup and we shook hands. Since there was no one in the front office, we didn't go down the hallway. After Jake poured me a cup of coffee, he went back to the dispatch desk. He didn't bother to pretend not to listen.

Abner opened a folder, looked at it, and said, "Those shell casings you turned in from the crossing at Lágrimas—they're Russian. Not that this is any surprise. There's a lot of Russian ammo exported—a lot to the U.S. You can go on any ammunition dealer's Website and order all you want."

So far, he hadn't said anything I didn't know.

"But the manufacturer in question got shut down a few years back after the owner pissed off Putin. Apparently, he was someone who got too powerful for the Russian president. He ended up convicted of stealing from his company, and his assets were seized." Abner paused and showed me an enlarged photo of one of the shell casing's markings. "As far as we can tell, these casings are at least five years old."

"Hell, Ranger," I interjected. "There's old ammunition everywhere. I've got ammo at my house that probably is at least that old."

"No doubt, Purdy. It's just that we have intel that several hundred thousand rounds of this make of 7.62 were hijacked from a container terminal in Marseilles, France, just before Putin seized the company. Intel—and that's all it is—says several containers of this ammunition was off-loaded from a Russian freighter. Rumors are that the stuff somehow made it into Mexico through Veracruz. Since the Gulf Coast Cartel controlled that port, and since it also was shipping cocaine to a really nasty Italian crime family called 'Ndrangheta, it's not too much of a leap to guess that some Mexican bad guys used this stuff. Of course, someone could be stockpiling the shit out of these things in the States, but it's not much of a reach to conclude that the ammo fired at that Lágrimas crossing wasn't fired by Americans."

Abner hadn't driven here to drink coffee and shoot the breeze about some pretty vague topics relating to Mexican cartels or the 'Ndrangheta. I could read about most of this in *The Economist*, or in any of number of law enforcement bulletins.

He seemed to read my mind and handed me the folder with photos and scientific analyses. He didn't give it to TJ to give to me. Not a big thing, but he was making a point. He was cutting my boss out of the loop, but in a very subtle way. Abner had never discussed any of my law enforcement background with me. I had taken his silence on the matter as a token of respect. A few phone calls and my story with Houston PD would have been apparent. No doubt, he knew some stuff in my personnel jacket that wasn't supposed to be seen. The fact that this little discussion was going on now was his way of signaling me that I had passed some test. He expected me to solve the Vasquez's murders.

In that moment, TJ seemed to get the picture, too. As long as I didn't fuck up the investigation, my job was secure. Abner would see to it. I felt both gratified and afraid. My professionalism was acknowledged, but I was also being challenged.

THIRTY-THREE

Present Day

PURDY KENDRICKS

S elman helped himself to another cup of coffee, changing the subject, asking about the case, and talking about the latest round of gruesome killings in Nuevo Laredo. The control of the border town's distribution points, what the cartels called the "plaza," had been firmly in the hands of an off-shoot of the Gulf Coast cartel for a few years. The *Zetas*, a group of sociopathic killers recruited from the Mexican military, had made a move on their old employers, effectively wrecking the Gulf Coast cartel. The power vacuum had led to six years of gruesome, wholesale killings. Decapitations, torture, and countless innocent bystander deaths had finally ebbed when Venustiano Huerta's offshoot of the Gulf Cartel, dubbed *Familia Norteña*, with the help of other cartels, pushed the *Zetas* out and took control of the plaza. There was even talk of a "rebirth" of the tourist industry, at least by some optimists and Mexican politicians.

As we chatted, the dispatch phone rang. It looked like it killed him to do so, but Jake finally picked up the receiver.

"Kickapoo County Sheriff's Office. Can I help you?" Jake began writing in the phone log, and then on a yellow notepad.

TJ turned toward Selman. "You eaten breakfast yet? I'm buying. You, too, Deputy Kendricks."

The three of us engaged in small talk and walked toward the front door. Jake began snapping his fingers.

We turned, and he waved us back toward the dispatch area, continuing to talk on the phone.

"Yes, sir." He continued to scribble. "Where exactly did you say?"

He asked for more specifics. It was obvious whatever was going on was near the Rio Grande.

"Sir, do you mind if I get your name? No, it won't leave this office." A pause. "No, sir. But I sure would appreciate it."

Jake wasn't getting anywhere. He kept at it, trying to vector in on who was making the call by mentioning small stuff that might be familiar only to a local. The person on the other end of the line got impatient and probably knew calls were recorded.

"Fuck me? Fuck me? Sir, I'm trying to be polite here. C'mon...." Jake cradled the receiver. "He hung up."

"What was that all about, Jake?" asked TJ.

"This guy just said there's a body hung up in some bushes."

He stood and walked to the large county topographical map and pointed to a spot about five miles downriver from Lágrimas.

"Says some kids spotted it. Thought it was a dead pig. Went down to poke on it. Says when they stuck at stick in, guts came spooling out, and it started to sink. Didn't though. Still in some bushes on the Mex side of the river."

He looked at his notes and ran the recorder counter back until he found the beginning of the conversation.

Jack pushed play, and we all listened. The caller spoke with a thick Mexican accent. He sounded vaguely familiar. The caller sounded afraid, like he regretted making the call.

Neither Jake nor TJ recognized the voice. Dead bodies in the Rio Grande weren't that uncommon, but something in the voice told me whoever had spotted this one wasn't telling us all he had noticed.

"Protocol says we notify the Mex authorities if it's on their side," I said. I waited for the expected response.

"Fuck protocol." TJ warmed to the subject. "It'd take those fuckers a day to get here, and they couldn't find their asses with both hands."

I grinned and turned to Selman, "Want to go pull a rotten body out of the river?"

"You all got a boat and some equipment to retrieve the thing?"

We assured him we did.

As we started out, I paused and turned back toward the dispatch area. "Nothing over the radio, Jake. I don't want the body disappearing on us."

TJ phoned Johnny Reagan, who agreed to pick up Border Patrol Agent Gonsalvez and meet us at the location given. He called Bonavita off patrol and had him hitch up the county's flat-bottomed boat and trailer.

Selman rode with me to the put-in point near where the body was seen. TJ took his truck. As I drove up U.S. 90, I eyed Selman.

"Thanks."

"For what?"

"TJ isn't a fan of mine, as I'm sure you're aware."

He grunted.

"Anyway, the trust is appreciated."

"Purdy, I may not be doing you any favors. Something tells me that before this case is over with—if it ever is—you'll be wishing you hadn't touched it."

"Ranger, I'm already feeling that way."

"No doubt, but just be careful. You got a wife and child. They're more important than this goddamn case."

"You're the second person today who's told me to be careful."

Selman looked at me quizzically as I turned south of U.S. 90 onto a dimly marked dirt road. I told him about my discussion with Israel.

"Would Pete Vasquez be somehow involved in something that gets his grandparents killed? Not much to go on, but it does make one curious."

Selman grabbed the dash as the sedan bounced over a series of caliche outcroppings. "Old Israel may be almost as smart as I am," he guffawed.

"How's that?"

"We are both telling you to be careful. Always trust someone who tells you that."

"Neither of you is making me feel real comfortable right now."

We pulled over onto an outcropping that overlooked the Rio Grande. Bonavita slowly backed the trailer down a path between cane and salt cedar. Gonsalvez wasn't about to take a chance touching the Mexican side. He and TJ stayed on shore. Bonavita kept the boat steady as Reagan and I eased in. Gonsalvez handed down gloves, camera, and a plastic body bag. Firing up the outboard, Bonavita carefully pushed off into the muddy current. Within five minutes, we spotted the body.

No wonder the kids, if that's who actually found it, were spooked. A nearly featureless male corpse was pushed up against some fallen tree limbs, one colorless arm oddly erect, with the index finger pointing toward heaven. The body was completely naked, and it looked like fish or turtles had nibbled away at the genitals. Intestines wound out of an abdominal hole, probably the one made by the poking.

We tied in the brush just upriver, taking in the scene. Donning gloves, we opened the body bag. Careful not to upset the boat in a small eddy signifying deep water, we gently pulled the male corpse away from the bushes and alongside the boat.

A body that's been in water for a few days loses most distinguishing features. Critters can nibble on it, making guesswork of pre-death injuries. That was pretty much the case here—except for the corpse's cranium. The top and back of the skull was gone. There was no brain tissue left. Facial flesh was partly detached, and what looked like a small bullet entry hole was apparent at the top of the nose.

"You see that, Reagan?"

I nodded. "I doubt this guy drowned. I'm betting"—I pointed at what was left of the head "that was caused by an AK47 at the Lágrimas crossing."

Careful not to pull flesh and muscle that looked ready to slough off, we pulled the body into the rubber bag.

Bonavita gagged as we reeled in the intestines with a fish net. It was so macabre that we all started chuckling quietly.

"What are you giggling at, Johnny?"

"Shit, Purdy, what are *you* giggling at?"

Selman spoke up. "I'll tell you what *I'm* giggling at. Do you remember those trick cans that you give someone? They'd unscrew the top and a big old snake would spring out at them."

Bonavita nodded, nearly letting go of the outboard's tiller as he laughed.

Selman continued, "Can you imagine the looks on those kids' faces when they poked this belly? Ten or fifteen feet of intestine comes flying out at you like a carnival spoof. Must have scared the shit out of them."

. . .

TJ caught the rope as we pulled back to the put-in point. He noticed Bonavita's tear-streaked face.

"What are you crying about, Bonavita?"

Bonavita killed the outboard and failed to stifle almost hysterical laughter. The usually taciturn and seemingly humorless Ranger carefully stepped on shore, snorted, and turned his face away. Selman had taken several steps away, but I could hear him begin to chuckle, which got me going again.

Finally, Bonavita got control of himself. He tried to explain the imagined scenario to TJ and Gonsalvez. Neither seemed amused.

TJ shook his head. "Deputy Bonavita, you are one sick fuck."

That got me and Selman going again. Maybe we were all sick fucks, but I hadn't laughed like this in ages.

THIRTY-FOUR

Present Day

PURDY KENDRICKS

W e could easily get phone records. Since we weren't trying to find the content of calls, Texas courts allowed the police to see which calls were made to and from phone numbers. Pete told us that his grandparents had a cell phone, gave us its number and the carrier. The phone hadn't yet been located. My guess was that it never would be. We had at least one of Pete's cell numbers. Knowing who Otabiano or Raquel Vasquez had called around the time of their deaths, might prove useful. Nothing else was gelling right now. Pete's grief for his grandparents' deaths was real. Of that I was certain. There just seemed to be more to things than he was letting on.

It would be interesting to see what cell towers Pete activated in his increasingly frantic calls to his grandparents that he said were never answered.

Abner Selman offered to take the requests to Judge McCullough, who was holding court in an adjoining county.

"I've got two backhoes stolen off a construction site that the sheriff is working on. I've been putting off lending a hand, so this will kill two birds with one stone."

M y cell phone beeped. It was Selman.
"I got the return on those phone requests, Deputy. Meet me at the coffee shop and let's visit."

Odd.

He was sitting at a corner booth at the Cenizo Diner, stirring his coffee. Beulah brought me a sweet tea and left us alone.

"I had some help, but we got all the phone carriers served. Here's your signed acknowledgments." He handed them to me. "This can take sometimes a week or more to get any responses. The story AT&T and the others got from my people was that a local investigator would be mighty pissed if it took that long, that Kickapoo County's grand jury was meeting in three days, and that the Rangers had no control over the local DA serving a grand jury subpoena for the records custodian."

"Fat chance our D.A. would do that anytime soon. What else did you tell them?"

Selman took off his Stetson, pulled out a handkerchief and wiped his brow. "Well, I added that you were a horse's ass who had been known to present cases to the grand jury late into the afternoon, which would mean long drives back to the city, late at night, from a rather peculiar county on the border. That the Texas Rangers had been investigating you folks for years because you had a reputation for giving out traffic tickets for as little as one mile over the posted speed limit, and that your sheriff liked his men to work the highways at night."

I grinned at the taciturn lawman. "Ranger, a speeding ticket hasn't been given by the SO here since TJ was elected."

"Oh, well. I might be mistaken, at least about everything but the horse's ass stuff."

I was beginning to like this guy... "Thanks. Your help is appreciated."

"Well, since we are on the subject of appreciation—you'll appreciate this." He paused. "Your ol' sheriff doesn't exactly run an air-tight operation."

I cocked my head. Larger law enforcement agencies generally kept a tight lid on inner workings. Rural and small-town departments, however, could be leaky when it came to information getting out that shouldn't. Too many deputies with too many family ties, too many "friends of friends."

"What have you heard, Ranger?"

"Austin is getting questions from the DEA about this killing. Which makes sense; I'm surprised you haven't been contacted. It *is* the border, and no doubt it's drug-related." He paused. "But the questions, or at least a few of them, sure seem to indicate that the DEA knows a lot more about these killings than the reports being filed." He paused again. "Have you had any calls from those people?"

I hadn't—yet, and as far as I knew, neither had TJ or his deputies.

"Well, it's just a hunch, but I wouldn't be surprised if someone in y'all's office is feeding them information. Just from the nature of the questions asked. Purdy, you're pretty tight-lipped." It was a question phrased as a statement.

"I've been looking into some stuff." Still unsure of where we stood, I didn't offer anything else. "But it hasn't been shared, even with my boss."

Selman nodded. "Again, I'm just suggesting that you be real careful who you share information with. I'm not about to suggest TJ is bent. In fact, I don't think he's smart enough to be crooked. But the border has a way of turning good people bad. You got a wife and kid to look out for, too."

"Who do you think is talking out of school?"

TJ wanted a resolution to the killings. He would throw me under the bus if things didn't go right. But it was in his personal best interest in getting re-elected that the Kickapoo County Sheriff's Office got every bit of credit for solving the cases. I ran down the roster of deputies mentally. Nothing I had seen raised any red flags.

"What about your dispatcher buddy?"

Selman's question caught me flat footed. "Really?" I hadn't given it any thought, But now?

Selman pulled his hat off again. The handkerchief went to his forehead. I was getting the idea that this unconscious movement was a sign he was uncomfortable with the subject matter.

"Jake knows more about this office than anyone. He's here, but he's not, if you get my drift. He fades into the background at the dispatcher's desk. Volunteers a lot of extra hours. Takes up slack for the other two dispatchers."

"But why?" I was thinking out loud. "I've known him all his life. What did he have to gain? He's probably got fifty cents of every dollar he's earned. No family or love interest that I know of."

Selman took a sip, put the cup down on the saucer, and slowly turned the cup around and around.

"Who knows? He and TJ don't gee and haw. I don't even know it's him. Just keep an eye out. And lock up your files. Just some suggestions."

"Absolutely, although if he's doing this, he's hurting me more than TJ." I filed it away for a later time when I could sort through the implications.

Some of the phone records came in the next day. Maybe being described as a horse's ass made a difference.

The cell phone of the Vasquez couple had few calls, either in or out. Pete's cell phone had made repeated calls the day before we found them dead. Otabiano's reluctance to use the modern contraption was confirmed.

Only two calls came in from other sources. One of the calls was from a number registered to Southwest Airlines. As far as I knew, neither Oto nor Raquel had ever flown anywhere. I contacted Southwest Airlines' main office in the Dallas area, explained the situation, expressing confusion as to why the Vasquez phone number had been called. After confirming who I was to his satisfaction, the airline's security boss called me back.

"Deputy, the phone call was a standard 'to remind you of your flight' automated call we send to anyone with reservations."

"As far as I know, these two old folks had never flown anywhere."

"They were scheduled round trip out of San Antonio direct into John Wayne International Airport in California." He gave me the dates.

They were going to fly from San Antonio six days before they were found dead.

I could hear the click of keyboard entries. "Hmm. They didn't make the flight."

They were to return the day after we found their bodies.

"Who paid for those tickets?"

"Credit card purchase from a company card—Vasquez Plumbing Contractors." He gave me the address on the card. It matched Pete's business address in Laredo, Texas.

"No refund requested. No request for flight change. No request for future flight credit. Kind of unusual. Most folks don't like to waste money."

The airline would provide all this in writing. I thanked the security man and disconnected.

Things were getting weirder and weirder. Why would the old couple fly to California? I couldn't remember either of them discussing any relatives in the Los Angeles area that they would muster the effort to see. Concha, daughter of the Vasquezes, and Pete's mother, had moved there years ago. Concha died of diabetes complications, aggravated by booze and drugs. She had been estranged from her parents and was buried somewhere out there. The only time Otabiano had mentioned Concha, he had sworn that his daughter had succumbed to the evil ways of the big city. He thought it was best that they remember her the way she once was, and that as far as he was concerned, California could go to hell.

I punched in Pete's cell number.

"Purdy, what can I do for you?"

I was taken aback that the call hadn't gone to voice mail and didn't immediately answer.

"Hello? You there, Purdy?"

"Yes. Sorry to bother you again, but just a question."

Hesitation, then, "What?"

"What's with the Southwest Airline tickets to California for Oto and Raquel?"

Another hesitation. "How did you know about that?"

"Routine investigation." Pete had to know that his grandparents' phone records would be checked out, but I wasn't going to tell him that.

"Sorry I didn't mention it to you. You know my mother, Concha, she's buried out there. A long time ago, I promised my grandparents that if they ever wanted to go there, I would spring for the tickets. I was planning to buy a real nice headstone to replace the little one they put over her grave when she died. Oto said he and Raquel wanted to see it before they got too old to travel."

"Why didn't they go?"

"Got cold feet, I guess. I made the reservations. Even had a car rented and a motel for them to stay at out there. Mama Raquel called and said they had decided it was too much trouble. I was going to come and take them into San Antonio, make sure they caught the flight. Never happened."

Maybe it was my imagination, but the story sounded rehearsed.

"Why, is it important, Purdy? I apologize for not saying something about it. No big thing."

"Probably not."

I thanked him and was about to ring off.

"I know we had words, Purdy, but I appreciate what you are doing for Mama Raquel and Papa Oto. If there's anything I can do to help, I'll be here."

Bullshit.

THIRTY-FIVE

Present Day

PURDY KENDRICKS

The body in the river was taken to the Medical Examiner's office in Bexar County, and again I made the trek there for the autopsy. At least this time I was in a county sedan. Tim Villarreal was again the pathologist.

"Well, we meet again, Purdy," he said as he robed and gloved-up. I guess we were on a first-name basis. "The quality of the bodies you're collecting is going from bad to worse."

There were no surprises. Jose Doe, as we labeled him, was killed by a bullet that blew off the top of his head

"My initial external observation has been borne out by my internal organ examination. He lost his mind."

I figured this wasn't the first time he had used that tidbit of gallows humor. Dr. Villarreal grinned, seemingly pleased with his wit.

"Anything else you can tell me, Tim?" Using his first name felt weird to me, but what the hell.

"Well, besides the intestines you guys so clumsily re-attached," he pointed at the spool of guts he had set off to the side of the slab, "I didn't see anything special. The tattoo," he gestured toward a faint marking on the corpse's left shoulder, "we'll try to pull out more of it with UV lighting, and maybe some fancy photography..." His voice trailed off as plopped the corpse's hand back on the table. "We may get a fingerprint hit or DNA hit off the FBI systems." He lifted Jose's hand, showing me the nearly invisible fingerprints left in the skin of the long-submerged body. "Shouldn't take too long on both."

Still gloved-up, he offered me an elbow bump. I thanked him and headed to downtown San Antonio.

I spent the next four hours in various offices looking at digital filings of all kinds. Some of this could have been done on the Internet in Santa Rosa. I couldn't spend time on it at home, and there was no way to erase the computer history at the Sheriff's Office. I was here and felt I could do more good away from prying eyes on what I hoped was a wild goose chase.

Being a detective doesn't mean just pounding the streets tracking down witnesses or trying to get confessions from perpetrators. Often, homicide investigations meant grinding through tons of apparently meaningless documents. All the detectives knew how to do it. While not having much sex appeal, mind-numbing paper chases occasionally paid off.

Parking the sedan in an "official business only" spot, I escaped the heat and started with the county and district clerks' public computers. Laura Griffin had married a Sandler years back, divorced him, and later married a Saenz. I had heard he was a wealthy Mexican who had made money establishing *maquílas* on the border. After NAFTA, the number of American companies setting up cheap labor assembly plants in Mexico had increased to a flood. Supposedly, Saenz had done quite well as the go-to guy in the Mexican states of Tamaulipas and Coahuila for these land deals. All of this was third- or fourth-hand information that I hadn't had any reason to care about—until now.

Laura's Alamo Heights house was almost majestic. I had no reason not to believe that she had received it as part of a divorce settlement, as she had said. However, the more times I thought about her ranch's condition, some doubts were starting to gnaw on me. She had revered her old man. Out of respect for his memory, if nothing else, I had expected some semblance of care, but there wasn't any. The ranch's condition indicated either a lack of concern, or perhaps, the inability to keep it up. It wasn't clear to me what was the reason for the run-down fences and general look of abandonment.

Laura had lived in San Antonio for years, so it seemed reasonable to assume she and Saenz had applied for their marriage license here. The computer search was quick. Their license showed the date of marriage 11 years before. They were married by some shake-and-bake officiant, whose licensure to perform the ceremony, best guess, had come off the Internet. Just like Laura to say the hell with organized church procedural hassles. I caught myself smiling, imagining the wedding venue—no doubt in some garden with a string quartet and the guest list of movers and shakers. Mama didn't get an invitation, and probably no one else from Kickapoo County did, either.

Laura said she was divorced. The District Clerk's records showed that she and her husband, Emilio—I now had a first name—had filed for divorce two years before. There weren't any children—I knew that. Most couples cited "irreconcilable differences," as the reason for the breakup. That covered a host of possible reasons, but usually dirty laundry wasn't spelled out in court documents. Unless someone was abused, or financially defrauded, there just wasn't any reason to with Texas "no-fault" divorces.

Unless one of the spouses was *really* pissed off.

Evidently, Emilio had been *really* pissed off.

Emilio Saenz claimed what was called a "fault" ground in the divorce. The divorce petition alleged that my high school love had committed adultery during the marriage. Emilio's lawyer had even named a co-respondent: Peter Vasquez.

My two erstwhile friends had apparently been doing the two-backed beast, and their respective spouses had found out.

Marriages fail all the time because someone is stepping out. Most judges around here yawned when one side or the other claimed infidelity. Judge McCullough did more than that. He was reputed to have said to two lawyers about to go at it over the issue that "unless the fucker and the fuckee were caught doing it in the Walmart parking lot, and they had good color pictures of the action that would perk up an otherwise slow day on the bench," he didn't want to be bothered with it.

But Emilio Saenz was Hispanic, rich and—from the court's papers— oozed wronged *machismo.* The divorce petition did not attach a prenuptial agreement but made multiple mention of its contents. It was obvious that the agreement had been made to protect Emilio more than Laura. He was the one with most of the assets. It stipulated that, if she and Saenz divorced, she got a substantial, but set, sum of money—unless a fault ground was proved. Adultery was most definitely a fault ground. In that case, she got zip, nada, zero.

Emilio Saenz had come into the marriage "hoping for the best, but preparing for the worst," as one courthouse wag said.

Saenz wanted to drag Laura's name through the mud, even at the cost of his own manly reputation. Odd what some folks will do.

I scanned through the divorce decree. It looked like Saenz had cooled down some by the time it was signed a year later. Saenz's lawyer was prominent in matrimonial law. She must have charged by the page, because it ran to 55 pages. Emilio's assets consisted mostly of ownership interests in Mexican *sociedades anonimas*—corporations. Whatever was held in those companies' names wasn't disclosed. However, his interests were described as "separate" property. That is, something acquired before the marriage, or something protected by language in the pre-nup. Regardless, if Saenz's properties were in Mexico, she would have had hell finding them.

The lengthy decree, agreed to by all the parties and their lawyers, stated that the cuckolded husband waived any claim of adultery, agreed to a "no fault" divorce, and Laura got the property I had visited, and about half of what she would have gotten under the original pre-nuptial document. Most folks could live comfortably on that, but Laura wasn't most folks. There was no way she could keep up appearances, belong to charity boards, and live the lifestyle she'd become accustomed to on what she was getting. Not for long, given that her beautiful property also came with the debt owed on it. Unless Laura found a profession paying more than she could make with an undergraduate degree from Baylor in Interior Design, or unless she found another wealthy benefactor, she would be tapped out pretty quickly.

For a minute, I was pissed. It was reasonable, I guess, that Alamo Heights Detective Glen Hohmeyer hadn't aired dirty laundry when I inquired about Laura. She was local, good looking, did charity work, and probably contributed to the Department's equipment fund. I was an unknown hick cop from Bumfuck, Egypt. He didn't owe me anything, but it rankled anyway.

The county offices would close at five. I quit my musings and had enough time to check Bexar County Real Property Records. Laura's name, with surname Saenz, appeared on several deeds and financing instruments. Nothing unusual, until a foreclosure document on her house came up.

What the hell?

The deed in foreclosure to a local bank that held the note secured by a deed of trust, was dated nearly two and a half months before the slaughter at her ranch. Normally, the next step would be for the bank to tell the debtor to get out. Failing that, an eviction suit at a Justice of Peace Court would compel it.

Why was she still on the property?

A sick feeling began to form. I had loved this woman and still had feelings for her now. She was a part of my life. My hurt feelings and the continual low-grade "what if" fever I had lived with for years was, at times, almost a pleasurable ache of self-pity. Something was showing up on paper that seemed to indicate there was a dark side to her life I had never considered possible. The fabric of Laura, burnished in my memory, was beginning to fray.

I scrolled down through the computer hits. No *lis pendens,* or notice to the world that there were legal issues on the property. Then, two weeks after the foreclosure sale, up popped a warranty deed from the bank to Laura, for "10 dollars and other consideration." The document made no mention of another note or any security to the bank. The bank must have been paid with a certified or cashier's check, or a wire transfer.

Laura's Alamo Heights property was primo real estate. Banks were usually reluctant to foreclose and get stuck with collateral. It didn't look good to loan examiners. However, with the hot market for any "oh-niner" zip code property, the bank stood to make a quick buck on Laura's loan default. Its new asset was worth a hell of lot more than what she owed on it.

The bank wasn't under any obligation even to talk to her after she'd legally lost the place. Yet here was a document evidencing clear title, and no debt.

How did Laura Saenz come up with enough cash to pay off the bank? It must have been a bundle.

Laura had found a benefactor. Fear knotted my stomach, and sadness washed over me. I couldn't help but sense that her benefactor had wanted something in return.

THIRTY-SIX

Present Day

PURDY KENDRICKS

U sing an old personal credit card, I forked over a dollar a page for hundreds of pages of the computer images I had reviewed. Lugging the stack to the sedan, I wondered where I would go from here.

My first inclination was to drive to Alamo Heights and confront Laura. I turned west and headed down U.S. 90 instead. If she was in any way involved with the murders at her ranch, I would have to approach her as a cop would. And right now, that seemed almost like an act of betrayal on my part.

The drive back wasn't yielding any epiphanies, so I punched "play" on the iPod, hoping that, like a Ouija board, what I heard would point to a solution. No luck. Dinah Shore's version of *Blues in the Night* washed over me. Her voice was like dark Southern honey. The longing and sadness of the lyrics, expressed by this incredible singer, only led me into a deeper funk. As the sun set and darkness started filling in the canyons near the Rio Grande, I kept punching "replay" and howling over and over in a soul-wracked accompaniment.

Santa Rosa's lights came into view, and I passed by the Golden Horizons Residence Center. Too late to check on Mom. I promised myself I'd get by there the next day. Jake, for once, wasn't dispatching, and the bundle of legal documents was quickly stuffed and locked in my office file cabinet.

The dim glow of town receded as I turned up the dirt road to our house. Mail was still in the box near the carport door. The *Laredo Morning News* headline, above the fold, proclaimed *Border Calm Disrupted by New Round of Grisly Killings*. Skimming through the story by the dim carport light, I read that six more headless and prickless bodies, with letter Zs burned into their chests, had been put on display on an esplanade near one of the International Bridges. The severed heads, with presumably respective penises inserted in mouths, had been thrown at the entrance of the Nuevo Laredo municipal police station.

A bed sheet with crude lettering had been draped under a pedestrian walkway. It announced that Venustiano Huerta's second-in-command, Tico Borrego, no longer controlled the plaza, that the *Zetas* thought him nothing but—here the newspaper cleaned up the language—a "pansy." Anyone who could read gutter Spanish could see the sheet actually proclaimed that Borrego was a *pinche joto soplón*, fucking queer snitch, and his men would soon be made to *mamar nuestros vergas*—suck our dicks, before they were sent to hell. If it weren't for the horrific evidence confirming the threat, it almost read like a potty-mouthed schoolboy's blathering.

The relative peace was now a full-blown war for control of the lucrative Nuevo Laredo drug trade. The mention of Tico Borrego confirmed that Huerta *had* been killed. I reminded myself that where he had been taken out—near El Mosco—was almost due south of Laura's ranch on the Mexican border.

Betty was watching TV when I entered the house. Our recent reconciliation of a few days back had eased a lot of the tension, but my late hours and limited explanations were starting to chip away at our fragile mending. She glanced up from a game show.

"Glad you're back."

Her observation was weighted with nuances that I chose to ignore. The ball was in my court, and it was time I tried to smooth things over.

"I'm so glad to be back; more than you can imagine." It felt almost true. "Another autopsy in San Antonio. It went long. I'm sorry."

She nodded and turned the TV off.

"Forrest is spending the night at Paula's."

This was an opportunity to spend some time together, but without our son's presence as a buffer, I dreaded it.

"Do you mind if I run a couple of things by you? I'd appreciate your thoughts."

Betty hated my profession, or at least what I had let it do to me, but she had a keen mind and was a good listener. No doubt there were mixed motives in my asking. By appealing to her pride, I would mute the sullen anger she was showing. And I really did need someone to bounce ideas off of. There was no one in the Sheriff's Office now, including Jake, whom I dared confide in.

Nodding, she patted at the cushion next to her. Relief washed over me since I seemed to have avoided another fight.

An hour later, I stopped talking. Betty hadn't said a word, even to ask for a clarification. Nor had she stormed out when, taking a deep breath, I had confessed to meeting with Laura.

"So that, in a nutshell, is what I'm dealing with. I'm in over my head. TJ is expecting me to solve this. Either I do, or he probably won't get re-elected. Either way, I'm out of a job. Livermore has no use for me. I've got to resolve this thing, but there are too many moving pieces."

Wordlessly, she got up and went into the kitchen. For a moment, I thought she was walking away. She wasn't. Carrying two cups of coffee, Betty walked back, handing me one.

"Thanks."

"Jonathan Purdy Kendricks. You have screwed your life up, and in the process damned near lost me and your son. Now," she paused, "now, you're in a mess that could get you killed. And you got Forrest involved."

I started to apologize.

"Shut up. I'm not finished." She sipped on her coffee. Her head was cocked to one side, like it always was when she was thinking of something serious.

"You screwed up in Houston. The Department never said so, but your drinking damned near got you indicted. If it hadn't been for the Feds covering for you...." She left that unraveled thread dangling. "Then you let that bitch...." She choked back tears. My long-held desire for Laura, confessed while in the depths of the bottle, had nearly sealed our marriage's doom. "You tried to re-create something you never had. You wouldn't let it go."

Scared enough to say nothing, I sat there, heart pounding. Blood pounded in my ears, my stomach doing flip-flops.

Betty clearly had rehearsed this presentation. She wasn't about to be derailed. She was determined to get something out, without interruptions.

"I swore I'd never come back to this godforsaken place. Now I'm back, with a young son who loves his father fiercely. I took a low-paying job because on what you're getting paid, we'd be in the poorhouse."

Betty gasped. "Where are we going to go if you lose this job? Your Mama's nursing home bills are eating up what little there is of her estate. Not that I want a nickel of it, but we don't have a safety net."

Betty stood up, took two steps away from the sofa, and turned toward me. There was an opening, so I took a deep breath and asked the question. "Betty, do you want a divorce?"

"The question you'd better be asking yourself, big boy, is do *you*?"

Until a few days ago, I wouldn't have been able to answer honestly. There would have been equivocation. Betty would have sensed it—she knew me too well.

But now?

"No, I honestly do not. You are too important in my life. I don't want to lose you. What do I have to do keep us together? I can do something besides be a cop. Hell, I can get a teacher's certificate and teach school, or coach. I'll do what it takes."

Being a cop wasn't just what I did, it was who I was, or had become. But I said it, hoping I meant it.

Betty sat down on the far end of the couch.

"I wonder, Purdy. I wonder."

Her voice tailed off as if she was in some other place. Shaking her head as if to rid it of unpleasantness, she looked at me.

"So, tell me again how Pete may be involved in these killings?"

THIRTY-SEVEN

Laura Griffin Saenz

TWO MONTHS BEFORE PRESENT

The divorce and what led up to it rattled Laura's sense of her own invulnerability. Laura had always been able to handle situations where men were involved. But Saenz, whom she had professed to love just a few years before, was not willing to be controlled. The deck was stacked against her. Apart from the prenuptial agreement she never thought would come into play, there were videos of her's and Pete's trysts made by a private detective who had a penchant for all things electronic.

Laredo's La Posada Inn, snuggled up against the Rio Grande, hadn't been as discreet as the two had hoped. With the help of an assistant night manager, the love nest was wired for sound and color video. Pete was handsome. She was beautiful. Perhaps in some other context the contents of their time together would have been a moneymaker on the porno circuit. This was divorce.

Laura hired the second-best divorce lawyer in Bexar County. Saenz had already hired the best. It promised to be a nasty tell-all that would bankrupt her, and just as importantly, tarnish her hard-earned reputation as a do-gooder in Alamo Heights. Saenz decamped for Monterrey and seemed ready to let the District Court and the court of public opinion work to her detriment.

Then, as if he was tired of the squabbling, Saenz instructed his lawyer to offer a compromise. He kept everything he had brought into the marriage—he had made sure she would have hell getting any assets out of Mexico anyway—and dangled a reduced money settlement and the house in Alamo Heights, less his portrait, in front of her. Laura felt she had little choice.

Laura got the videos back. She also got the debt on the property. After the divorce settlement was worked out, she called Pete, "That son of a bitch. He got the elevator, honey. I got the shaft."

Pete couldn't help snickering. She had been getting his for some time.

"Well, lover, you can laugh all you want. But your good times are about to dry up."

Pete got cut off. The well went dry. No more rendezvous and sweaty sheets. For eight months, Laura kept up the note payments and taxes on her beloved Spanish Colonial. Then she ran out of money. The bank was unforgiving. Recently audited by the Feds, its board of directors was in no mood to cut her much slack—good deeds and better looks notwithstanding. The property went into foreclosure. Laura called Pete. It was time to beg for some help.

For Pete, it couldn't have come at a better time.

THIRTY-EIGHT

Pete Vasquez

TWO MONTHS BEFORE PRESENT

She called him on his cell phone. Still sulking and unaware of why Laura was calling, he didn't answer. After several attempts, Laura called Vasquez Plumbing Contractors. The receptionist knew of her boss's long-time involvement and his instructions not to take the call. Laura's response to being ignored was predictable.

"You tell that dark-skinned horn dog that if he doesn't take my call, I'm driving to Laredo for a personal visit. I don't want to, but if Pete doesn't call me back PDQ, I'll be glad to discuss with anyone who'll listen. And it will be personal stuff he may not want the Greater Laredo Chamber of Commerce to know."

Pete returned the call.

"I'm in a peck of financial trouble. You helped cause it, you studly rascal. I swore I'd never come begging to any man, but I need money."

"What is it you need, hon?"

"I've defaulted on the note, and the assholes at the bank finally cut me off. I've tried to refinance it, but the old goat bank president and his chump board of directors aren't buying it. Says the bank can't afford a bad audit with the Feds. I don't intend to lose my home." She told Pete the amount owed.

"Whew-wee. That's a lot of money."

"Hold on to your britches. It's going to take more than that to get the property free and clear. I need to offer the bank enough so they can square it with the regulators as to why it didn't end up with a listing agent to see what the market can bring. That's how it's normally done."

"Hell, I don't have that kind of money. What am I supposed to do? Shit it?"

Laura wasn't convinced. "You seem to be doing real well in the plumbing contractor business. You want me to turn the tap back on, you'll find a way. I *do not* want to lose this house. I love it."

"How much time do you have?"

"I have no idea but can't imagine it'll take the bank long to get it listed."

"I'll see what I can do."

The cocaine in the tractor trailer rig that tipped the dogs wasn't part of the original load of 200 kilos of contraband. Someone had set him up, or maybe his driver. It didn't matter. If he wanted to avoid dying, painfully and slowly, he owed Venustiano Huerta and the cartel several million for the lost product. And he didn't have the money, or anything close to it. To Huerta, it was beginning to look as if Pete was a cheat and not to be trusted. Pete Vasquez's services, while valuable, could be replaced.

For a month, Pete moved from motel to motel, always paying cash. "I'll be away from the office for a bit, but be checking in."

Pete did check in, but each time with a burner phone that he destroyed after each telephone call. He let subordinates run the plumbing contracting business, and Pete managed to stay alive. Huerta's *sicarios* scoured Webb County, without luck. That wouldn't last.

The DEA got to Pete first.

THIRTY-NINE

Pete Vasquez

TWO MONTHS BEFORE PRESENT TIME

T he knock on a Motel Six door in Del Rio wasn't room service.
Gut clenched in fear, clutching a .45-caliber Model 1911 Colt,
Pete peaked out from behind a frayed curtain. *I can at least kill some of
them before they get me.* Sheer bravado. Two Anglos stood at the motel
room door and continued to knock.

"Open up, Vasquez. It's hot out here."

Who are these guys? "What do you want?"

The rangy Anglo in jeans and a pearl snap shirt moved to the
curtained window and held up an official looking badge. It read
"Drug Enforcement Administration." The name on the ID stated its
holder was one Jack Eddleman.

"Open the fucking door, Pete. We're not here to cause a scene."

Pete almost felt relief, the DEA being the lesser of two evils at the
moment. He unhooked the door's flimsy privacy chain and let Jack
Eddleman, along with another man, whom Eddleman identified only
as Leroy, into the room.

"Put your gun away, please." Leroy's request came to Pete without
anyone shooting at him, or smashing him in the face, or handcuffing
him. It sounded almost apologetic.

"Sorry." He started to put the gun in his waistband, thought that
wouldn't be good enough, and hastily shoved the pistol in a nightstand drawer.

Feeling obligated to straighten up bedcovers, Pete tucked in pillows strewn around from another night of fitful sleep. He then turned toward the government agents, who had taken seats on two chairs around a small table.

Eddleman leaned forward. "Sit down, Pete."

Pete dropped onto the bed.

While Leroy played with his cell phone, Eddleman stared at Pete for 10 seconds that seemed more like 10 hours.

"I guess you've wondered why the U.S. Attorney hasn't indicted you yet, huh?"

"Not really," Pete replied. "Why would he? I haven't done anything wrong."

Eddleman pulled a toothpick out of his breast pocket and picked at something between his two front teeth, then put the toothpick back in the pocket. Finally, looking over at Pete, he said, "Because you've been hauling dope for *La Familia Norteña* for some time now."

"Bullshit." That sounded like a tough response, but Pete's mouth was getting very dry. Why didn't the fucking hotel room have a refrigerator with complimentary water bottles?

Eddleman let Pete wind down and gave another 10 seconds of his icy stare. It was getting downright disconcerting.

"Quit staring at me, man. You're creeping me out."

"The only reason you haven't been arrested before now, Mr. Vasquez, is because you have been a useful tool to your government."

"What are you talking about, man? I'm running a legitimate company."

That weird stare again.

"Before we leave this motel room, we are going to reach an agreement about your future. I will give you two choices."

Leroy was now clipping his fingernails with knockoff Swiss army knife scissors.

"Almost from the get-go, your business of hauling shitters and other plumbing supplies in from Monterrey has been providing you with cover. You think it's been pretty safe. It hasn't. I can produce for you wiretap transcripts, phone records, your faked manifests, videos of your deliveries, and financial records that, if brought into court, will guarantee you twenty to life in a federal super max penitentiary. You will live the rest of your life, or a good part of it, in a seventy-seven square foot cell, with a steel sink and shitter combo. You will get one hour of solo exercise a day. You will never see sunlight. You will be fed in your cell. The guards will not communicate with you. You will not talk to anyone. You will get no phone calls. You will get no visitors. The only sex you will have will be with Rosy Palm. You will slowly go insane." He paused. "Do I have your attention?"

Pete nodded. His mouth was dry as cotton. "You guys got any water on you?"

Eddleman ignored the question. "Good."

Puzzled, Pete asked, "If you have all this stuff you claim, why don't you just arrest me?"

"Because *La Familia Norteña* is about to be in a war with the *Zetas*. Because in a war, the normal business of *La Familia* gets disrupted. Too many politicians are concerned about the future of American cities. Because, frankly, your trucking operation has supplied a lot of high potency shit to dealers we've now identified, and who are about to be in for a surprise." He paused. "*La Familia Norteña* isn't happy with you. Your driver got popped four weeks ago with a lot of product. Your Mr. Huerta...."

Pete interjected, "My who?"

Eddleman looked at Leroy and snorted, "Are you believing this piece of shit?" He turned back to Pete. "If you play one more pretend game with me, we are walking out of this room. We'll be back with a warrant for your arrest. But it will take awhile. In the meantime, Venustiano Huerta may get to you first. 'Specially if his *sicarios* get a phone call from an anonymous source. Del Rio isn't as big as Laredo, and right now your vehicle has four flat tires. By the time Triple A or some other service shows up, I suspect your head may be removed from your body."

Now Pete was sweating through his undershirt. "What if I say I want a lawyer?"

Leroy was now pulling a tack out of the heel of one of his Tony Lama boots. He started laughing.

"Lawyer? Lawyer? Are you out of your fucking mind? We are past lawyers, *compadre*. We aren't even talking to you. This meeting never happened. What's it going to be? A slooooooow warrant and a phone call, or you play ball." He went back to gouging out the tack.

"Okay. What do you want?"

"Your government isn't happy with *La Familia Norteña*. Your government is not happy with the *Zetas*. Because of this rare opportunity, we are offering you a 'get out of jail free' card, but only if you cooperate with us."

"How?"

And Eddleman told him.

FORTY

Pete Vasquez

SIX WEEKS BEFORE PRESENT TIME

The *Zetas* got to Pete second.

Pete's new burner phone rang. *Who the hell knows this number?* He punched "answer."

"We hear your boss is trying to blame you, *esse*, for the shit that went down in Laredo."

"I'm sorry; you must have a wrong number."

Fuck me. Fuck me. Fuck me. He started to punch "end."

"Don't hang up, *carnal*. It would not be a good idea. *Tu sabes?*"

Where's the fucking DEA? How are they protecting me now?

"Okay, I'm still here."

Admitting to the *Zetas* that he was in any way associated with something they didn't control was a death sentence. Pete kept his mouth shut and listened.

"It's time for the plaza to come back to its rightful owners. And you are going to help us."

"How?" Pete's heart felt like it would explode out of his chest. He sat down suddenly. He felt as if he was going to throw up.

The Griffin Ranch was a perfect launching point for the killing of Venustiano Huerta.

"I can't. I don't own the place. I have no control over it."

Pues si, pero ai viven sus abuelitos. The *Zetas* made him aware that they knew his grandparents lived there. If some *acuerdo* wasn't reached, they would be the first to die.

"Besides, *esse*, you been fucking the white woman who owns the place, eh? You keep her away from there. That piece of shit part of *Tejas* is for us to use, if we need to, *comprendes*?"

"Yes."

"And you work for us now. Any product you haul, you haul for us from now on."

T hen Laura called, begging her ex-lover for money.

The *Zetas*, perhaps figuring that whatever they paid to keep the ranch owner happy was chump change to their bottom line, surprisingly agreed to give Pete enough money for Laura to get her house back. She didn't ask him where it came from.

"You need to make your *baturra's* place—she is your whore, isn't she? —available to us. If it works out, Huerta, you won't owe him. If it doesn't, *no vales verga*. Worthless, you get it?"

"*No, me manches*. Don't be mean." It sounded like a whine. He was going to do what he was told. But first, he had to get his grandparents out.

"I don't want to get popped while I'm helping you. Huerta has his *pinche sicarios* looking all over town for me."

"We'll keep an eye out, bro. You just do yours."

"I don't want my *abuelitos* to be involved."

"Tough shit. They stay there." The *Zetas* wanted added insurance that Pete wouldn't cross them. The old couple was to be additional protection.

Taking a chance, he rented a sedan and drove to the Griffin place for an unusual mid-week visit to the old couple's house on the river.

"*Abuelito*," Pete began, I need to ask you a favor."

They were sitting on the porch overlooking the Rio Grande.

"What is it, boy?"

"I know you lost your only daughter in California."

Otabiano snorted, "She was dead to us long before she died, *hijito*."

"But she was still my mother. I don't remember much about her. I was so small when she left. But I want there to be reconciliation."

Raquel spoke up, "What does that mean?"

Pete took a deep breath.

"You raised me as a son. I didn't want to dishonor you, but I purchased a new headstone for Concha's grave."

Well, maybe not yet, but he would buy one to make the plan work.

"I want you two to meet me in California. I have business, so I can't travel with you. But I want you to honor me and my mother's memory, as we place a new headstone on her grave."

Otabiano snorted, but Raquel stopped him from talking.

"Why do you feel this necessary, *Pedrito?*" she asked.

When Raquel used the diminutive for his name, he knew he had won.

"I have prayed much lately. I had a vision. *La Virgen* was telling me that for me to have something that the *norteamericanos* called 'closure,' I need this to come about."

Ultimately, to his great relief, the old couple came around.

"When do you want access to where my *abuelitos* live?"

"Write this down," an unknown voice said, and gave Pete a telephone number. "Call tomorrow. Use another phone. Get rid of the one you got."

The next day, the *Zetas* gave Pete the dates.

Two hours later, Pete purchased two-round trip airline tickets on Southwest Airlines.

"We'll make a small vacation, too," he told his grandparents.

Raquel demurred, but did allow as how she would like to see the Pacific Ocean before she died.

Pete ordered a fancy headstone for Concha, the mother he had no memory of, nor cared a whit about.

FORTY-ONE

Present Day

PURDY KENDRICKS

It was Sunday, and I had missed several visits. I drove down to U.S. 90 and then east, past Betty's office and two miles out of town to Golden Horizons Residence Center. Sunday was my day to spend time with Kathryn Lea Kendricks, age 71. After Daddy's death, Mama stayed in Kickapoo County, occasionally fending off the attention of widowers. She ascribed to the accepted local adage that older men were either interested in "a nurse or a purse."

Mama kept the drilling company going for a few years, appeared to lose interest and sold the equipment. She spent many of the years I was away as the assistant school librarian. Mama's love for the written word had always been a presence, and when I started getting calls in Houston of small things, such as misfiled books, I started to wonder what was going on. But I had my own issues to deal with and chose to pass it off as simple forgetfulness. All that changed when Mama left church and didn't show up at the house in Santa Rosa one Sunday. Clete found her car at one of Daddy's many old river crossings. A search by law enforcement turned up Mama standing knee deep in the Rio Grande carrying on a conversation with several KW hands, all of whom were long dead or retired.

CT scans and neuropsychologists confirmed early onset Alzheimer's. She was 65. We tried moving Mama in with us, but that was a disaster. Between worries about our young child and her propensity to wander off from our apartment complex, my attempt at

187

being a dutiful son lasted less than two months. Realistically, my good intentions really landed on Betty's shoulders. To her credit, Betty loved Mama and had given all the time and effort a young mother could spare. However, the reality was that regardless of where we lived, Mama was going to need to be institutionalized. My ties to Houston were getting more tenuous by the moment during that time, so one weekend I drove her back to Kickapoo County.

So, to end her years, Kathryn Lea Kendricks was housed in the "secure" wing of Golden Horizons.

I parked the cruiser in the small shade afforded by a trimmed mesquite tree that constituted a large part of what passed for landscaping. Several inmates, as I tended to see them, were sitting on benches lining the front door, smoking cigarettes.

"Hello, Mr. Purdy," said several of them in a singsong way reminiscent of elementary kids. Nicotine-stained fingers wagged in unison.

Lucas Peckall, Golden Horizon's administrator, tried to control cigarette consumption. But families tended to "forget" to turn in cigarettes to the nurses' station for rationing, instead slipping them into their kinfolk's cupboards. You can say what you want about the mentally challenged, but I've never seen any other subset of society, even inmates, who were better at rat-holing contraband smokes.

The nursing home was designed with four long corridors, crossing at a central phone and nurses' station. The station reminded me of a prison with a control picket, where a guard could control locked cell doors. I opened the glass front door and walked onto the linoleum entryway. Large Mexican clay pots filled with faux greenery were placed every few feet. If they were meant to cheer the place up, they failed.

Mama had lived (if that was the word) in the place for five years now, and I was known well enough that I didn't have to stop and get permission to go through the access-controlled doors into the Alzheimer's ward. A couple of nurses and aides nodded howdies as I walked by, but most were engrossed in the late afternoon seating maneuvers in the dining room. I dodged walkers and wheelchairs driven by residents hell-bent for Sunday night's chicken supper and punched in the code to let me into the lock-down wing.

The door clicked shut behind me. I left the aroma of cafeteria food, moving into the area of Lysol and urine. Lucas was a stickler for cleanliness, but there was only so much you could do to cover up mass incontinence. Mama's room hadn't changed in three years, nor had her roommate. She shared a relatively airy enclosure with Juana Campos.

Juana was an anomaly. She was in her late forties but wasn't the victim of a disease. Juana had earned her right to be warehoused because of a head injury incurred in a head-on collision between her boyfriend's car and a tractor trailer rig. A high school beauty queen, she was coming home from partying, when her boyfriend fell asleep on the long ride home from a dance hall in Ciudad Acuña.

She was well cared for by her family after a six-month stay in a San Antonio trauma center. Her bones had knitted, but a broken door column thrust through her forehead had left her with an IQ in the 40s and a propensity to wander off. She was picked up hitchhiking, raped, and left on the side of the road outside Uvalde. Her family finally had to acknowledge that they couldn't handle her.

Lucas had somehow gotten her some federal disability funds, and I always suspected he had allowed her to stay with some sort of discount. The place had been sold two or three times, and how Lucas got it by corporate and insurance bean counters was beyond me. However he had pulled it off, it had made him sort of a demi-god with the Campos family. It also set well with me, not just because of my long-standing feeling that insurance companies' corporate head-quarters should be housed in the seventh circle of Dante's Inferno, but also because Juana had been a fine roommate for Mama. She was perennially cheerful, neat, didn't steal, and guarded Mama from other residents like a hawk.

The onset of Alzheimer's is like a bad dream within a nightmare. When first detected, Kathryn Lea was, even in her late fifties, a woman whose very nature said, "I know who and what I am, and I'm proud of it." She had an almost regal bearing, a face of weathered country beauty that was a mirror to a steely inner resolve. She had a set of legs that would turn heads. She now sat, wearing a dingy housecoat and terrycloth slides, watching QVC on cable. Someone was selling cubic zirconia "gem sets," and she perched on the edge of her bed, engrossed. Juana knew I showed up on Sunday afternoons, so she was doing her best to groom Mama's raven hair. But Mama showed no interest.

"Hello, Mr. Purdy," Juana grinned, waving at me with the hairbrush in her hand. Mama glanced over, and then returned to the sales promotion. She had forgotten my name two years ago (about the time they caught her eating cigarette ashes), so I didn't expect a whole lot.

A commercial came on, and I took the opportunity to speak. "Hello, Mama. You doing all right?"

"Oh, hey, honey. How ya doing?" she said. "Constancio called and said he and the boys were at six hundred feet and hit good water sands." Her once clear speech was now slow and slurred; her physical outlines now turned blurry and indistinct.

"Great," I played along. I was her beloved Rupe, and Constancio his long dead Segundo. "What formation?"

"Why, the Wilcox, of course. You know that. When are you going to set pipe?"

We discussed completing a deep water well. I picked my memory for the right lingo, just to keep her going. Once the well was on-line and flowing water, I knew my Sunday with Mama was over.

"Should flow at least a hundred gallons a minute, and no sulfites, and low in iron. Sweet water, just the way you always brought wells in."

I gave Juana a goodbye hug and quietly closed the door to the room. I had forgotten to bring one of Betty's batches of cookies, but the dresser sported a small plate of *pan dulce*, brought in by someone in the Campos clan. There was nothing more I could do or say to maintain any semblance of relevance. Sunday visits had a lot to do with the years I had ignored her, but I knew it was too late to fix that.

FORTY-TWO

Luther Wellington—The Truck Driver

TWO MONTHS BEFORE PRESENT

L uther was fed up. The federal detention facility in Laredo was full of thugs, criminals, illegal aliens, and other riffraff. He had lost more than 15 pounds eating shitty food served on plastic trays three times a day. Take it or leave it. No cheeseburgers. No beer.

Bunking in the dormitory didn't allow for a great deal of restful sleep, seeing as how he had to keep one eye peeled for some queer who had blown him a kiss in the chow line. The dude had mentioned that—while a bit on the chubby side—Luther was "his type." Fuck that shit. He wasn't about to let a queer get friendly with him.

The federal magistrate had set Luther's bond at $100,000.00. He had about as much chance of posting that kind of money as the man in the moon. He had called his boss, Pete Vasquez, asking what the hell was going on and why there was dope in the trailer. Luther was just doing his job, and he didn't deserve to be in jail. After all, apart from a couple of public intoxication arrests when he was young, Luther had steered clear of the law. You couldn't keep a commercial driver's license in Texas if you didn't.

Pete had come to see him three days after the fiasco at the border.

"Luther, I'll try to get you out of here," Pete said. "But I gotta know —what made the Feds look in your trailer? You've crossed a thousand times, and I'm hearing the dogs alerted on the trailer."

"I swear, Mr. Vasquez. I have no idea. It was like they were waiting for me. Like it was a setup or something. I ain't done a damn thing wrong, and I want out of here, goddamit."

Luther gesticulated vigorously from behind the glass partition. It felt good to let out some righteous indignation.

Pete had taken it in stride.

"Luther, the Feds found a lot of dope in that trailer. They say some was near the back end, and then about two hundred kilos of cocaine in a front stash area. Do you know anything about that?"

Pete didn't figure Luther Wellington knew about the stash area, but he was damned curious about dogs alerting on the dope found in a toilet toward the back. Besides, right or wrong, Pete figured anything he and Luther discussed through the two-way was being listened to by someone. Better to be careful.

Pete had left the lock-up promising to see what he could do about getting Luther out on a bail bond. And sure enough, he had come through, although, dammit, it took three weeks.

A young woman who said she was a pre-trial release officer met with Luther and gave him a list of things he wasn't allowed to do. She didn't seem too impressed by Luther's promises that he wasn't guilty of anything. She acted like she heard that shit every day.

Luther walked out of the detention facility after getting fitted with a GPS ankle bracelet and promising to check in daily. Luther's wife was waiting outside the facility. They hadn't had the greatest of relationships, but right now she was looking mighty good to him.

"Hey, honey, thanks for coming." He really *was* glad to see her, but there was a Whataburger with fries sitting on the front seat of their Chevy sedan that was also mighty good. Luther was afraid his wife would see him salivating like a dog and would know that it wasn't because of her.

She drove them home while Luther greedily ate the cold burger. He immediately took a shower. The pre-trail release woman said his ankle monitor was waterproof. Luther hoped so, as the woman promised she would have him arrested if the Feds lost contact with the device.

The next morning, after a breakfast of three eggs, hash browns, sausage, and a pot of coffee, Luther almost felt human again.

"Honey, I'm going to be out in the back yard."

She was vacuuming and didn't hear him.

As Luther plopped down in a lawn chair, his cell phone rang. He didn't recognize the number, but it could be the pre-trial folks. Better not take a chance.

"Hello." He reached down and made sure the GPS monitor was still attached.

"A question for you, *señor*. Who did you let into the trailer in Monterrey?"

"Who's this?"

"Who did you let into the trailer in Monterrey before the seals were put on the doors, you piece of shit?"

The vacuum's soft hum back and forth echoed on the porch, as Luther's wife moved the Hoover toward the den. Luther's fresh scent from last night's shower turned sour as gut-clenching fear swept through him.

"I don't know anything about what you're talking about. Please." He was whining now. "Honest, I don't."

"We know better. You got five hundred *dolares* to leave that door open and let someone load one more toilet."

How did they know that?

"You stupid fucking *gringo*. Five hundred dollars? I pay more for pussy than five hundred *pinche* fucking *dolares*, you fucking piece of shit!"

The voice's staccato delivery was contemptuous.

"If you don't tell me who you let in, we are coming to cut your balls off and stuff them in your mouth. And rape your ugly wife, and make you watch. Now, once again, who was it?"

Luther disconnected and threw the phone down. He couldn't tell them who it was. An envelope with cash and a short note. He really didn't know. And he sure as hell couldn't tell Pete Vasquez. He ran by his wife, barely making it to the toilet before his bowels let go.

FORTY-THREE

Present Day

PURDY KENDRICKS

A s I walked by the front desk, Jake Nichols handed me a call slip. His handwriting was almost illegible.

"Shit, man, can't you print these things? I spend too much time trying to decipher your handwriting. The only folks who should get away with this hen scratching are medical doctors. And, Jake, I don't see you examining me any time soon."

"Penmanship wasn't required for this job, so blow me, Purdy. If I had to operate on you, it would be with a dull pocketknife. Anyway, some guy says call him. Says he knows you. Says it's related to some case you're handling. Didn't say which one."

I was too busy to deal with more than the Vasquez murders. Whoever was calling wasn't going to get a call back anytime soon.

"What's the name?" I pointed at the call slip.

"It says right there." He spoke in exaggerated slowness, as if he was interpreting for the mentally challenged. "Eddleman."

I closed the door to my office and used my cell phone to punch in the number on the call slip. Eddleman. I knew that name. I decided to call him.

"Jack Eddleman."

"Purdy Kendricks." I tried to keep it light. "To what do I owe the pleasure of this phone call out of the blue?"

"It's been awhile. I recognized your name from an NCIC request you made that dinged our computer. Didn't know you were anywhere around these parts. Must be an interesting story."

He knew more of that story than I wanted him to.

"Your computer? You still with DEA?"

"Yes." There was a pause. "Can we talk about one of your cases?"

I hadn't heard Eddleman's name in three years, and I wished it was thirty.

"Where are you? Last time we saw each other, you were stationed in Houston."

"Task force. Here, there, Laredo mostly."

"I'm jammed up on a murder case."

"That's why we need to talk. I'd like to visit with you—preferably outside your county."

I thought for a minute. "Why can't you come over here?" I felt like I was playing Twenty Questions.

"Come on, Deputy Kendricks. I'm not calling you to hear my gums flap. I don't want us to be seen together. You've got my number now, so call me. And," he paused, "don't take too long. Is the number you're calling from"—he recited it to me "a county phone?"

"It's a personal cell. Why?"

"I won't be using the county phone line again. You shouldn't, either, when talking with me. Let's talk, but privately. I think it's in your interest."

He disconnected. I looked at the "called ended" icon.

What the fuck?

I thought about it. If Eddleman was still DEA, he would know the location of several stash houses, safe houses, and the like. It didn't take a rocket scientist to figure out that any killing on the border had a good chance of being drug related. How did the Vasquez couple get tangled up in something like that? Wrong place and wrong time, or something more sinister. Whatever Eddleman had to say was going to be interesting, at the very least.

I called him back. "You're DEA. You call the shot on where to meet. There isn't a place in this county except on some lonely-assed county road where we wouldn't be spotted, and I can't guarantee even that."

Eddleman grunted and gave me an address in Laredo.

"You got a plain wrapper?"

"My county vehicle isn't marked, but it still looks like what it is—

police. I'll check out a county maintenance truck." It would be less obvious, and I sure as hell wasn't taking the seized gangbanger's car anywhere. We agreed on a time.

I sat at my desk and collected my thoughts. As I walked out, Jake asked, "That guy—you call him back?"

"Nope." I don't know if I fooled him, but at least my call didn't show on the switchboard.

"Where you going?" Jake asked.

"Home. Got some chores to take care of at the house."

After changing out of my uniform, I called Betty at her work.

"Sorry to do this to you, but I have to make a quick run to Laredo. I'll be back late."

After our talk, I was determined to tell her as much as I safely could about my whereabouts. It was a small thing to be sure, but it was something.

Betty paused, "Has something to do with the case, doesn't it?"

"Yeah, but to be honest with you, I'm not sure what. I'm meeting a federal agent who wants to talk, but not in Kickapoo County. I'll call you when I leave Laredo."

Another pause, then, "Purdy, thanks."

"For what?"

"Just thanks."

I dropped the sedan at the county barn and asked the mechanics to re-check the recently repaired air conditioner, even though it was working fine. I then checked out a county pickup that looked reasonably safe to drive. The drive took three hours. More than long enough for dread to build up at meeting Eddleman.

Heading southeast, I turned off U.S. 90 and onto U.S. 277. It followed the Texas border with Mexico. Kickapoo County's canyons and contours quickly disappeared. The green that marked the Rio Grande was almost lost in the haze of the hot afternoon. I reached down, hit "play" and shoved in my earbuds. Cannonball Adderley's *Autumn Leaves,* recorded in 1958, showed him, Miles Davis, Sam Jones, and Art Blakely at their best, and helped push away the monotony and dread.

The address was in a newish McMansion. I pulled into the driveway. Eddleman answered the door, and we shook hands. Eddleman was pushing 60 but looked in his 40s. His graying hair was cut high and tight. A pearl snap western shirt and jeans held a whippet-like body with a military bearing.

"Been awhile, Kendricks. Glad you came."

As if I had a choice.

We walked into a sparsely furnished living room. The house had the feel of a place not lived in and rarely visited. The DEA and other government agencies probably had many places like this scattered around Laredo. I looked around for cameras and recording devices, which was kind of silly. No doubt the place was wired with equipment that could pick up everything that was said, and every tic or facial expression I made. It was stupid to have agreed to this location. I had walked into a trap of my own making.

Before I could beat myself up anymore, Eddleman motioned me to a chair and sat across from me on a sofa. He leaned back and looked me over.

"You look well, Deputy."

I had to look better than the last he had seen me.

"I hate dragging you this far from home, and I appreciate you taking the time."

It was clear he didn't mean either statement.

"I'm here. What can I do for you?" No doubt that comment on an audio recording would sound like a whiney child.

"The old couple who got killed out your way—how is that investigation going? Word is that you don't have many leads."

"Are you here to tell me something you know on the case, or are you here to pick my brain on the case?"

"Both." He leaned back on the sofa.

He reminded me of a snake uncoiling.

"You seem to think that a local businessman here in Laredo had something to do with it?"

The penny dropped.

"Pete Vasquez. His grandparents. What's your connection with Vasquez? He with DEA? You owe him? You own him?"

I wanted to ask how the hell he knew about the investigation, but was guessing the Rangers were talking with him, or he had someone in the Kickapoo County Sheriff's Office keeping him informed.

Because the Vasquezes and the third person, later found to be Shivelli, had been killed on the border, and because of some educated guesswork that this was all connected somehow with a cartel king-pin's assassination in Mexico, I had forwarded some basic information to the DEA's El Paso Intelligence Center.

EPIC, as it was usually called, shared information on a need-to-know basis to various law enforcement agencies throughout the United States. It had been set up in the late 1980s after DEA Agent Enrique "Kiki" Camarena had been kidnapped, tortured, and killed by one of the cartels.

My EPIC report contained nothing on suspects. It never mentioned Pete Vasquez, nor related anything connecting Vasquez with the Griffin property. It made no mention of Pete at all.

Eddleman didn't respond to the questions thrown at him.

"Purdy, may I call you Purdy? I'm not trying to interfere with your investigation. I know this is personal to you."

So, he knows this too.

"I want to assure you that Mr. Vasquez had nothing to do with the unfortunate deaths of his grandparents. We want to provide you with any information at our disposal that would convince you of that."

I could feel the bile rising. I guess I expected something like this, but to hear it left me queasy. "What's going on? What are you going to 'provide me' that will convince me about anything?"

"We feel we have information that will show that Mr. Pete Vasquez did not and still does not have any information of importance on the tragic circumstances near Santa Rosa." He paused. "Of course, we want you to feel comfortable with what we provide you. We'll provide data, phone logs, and other documentation to show that there is no connection. Mr. Vasquez just wants to be left alone to grieve his loss."

This was almost comical.

"Since when is a senior DEA agent the lap dog for someone who may be perjuring himself, and who's been avoiding contact with local law enforcement? You're a little old to be toadying to a dope smug-gler." That was a shot in the dark. My suspicions were out.

Eddleman stood and walked to the back door, moving the floor-length curtain to one side, and looking out onto an empty swimming pool. He seemed to be in deep thought.

He turned and looked at me. He had made some decision.

"I covered your ass in Houston. You owe me a favor."

FORTY-FOUR

Jack Eddleman

TWO MONTHS BEFORE PRESENT

T he fear in Luther's voice was palpable. Eddleman wondered whether he'd thrown up, or shit in his pants. It was a toss-up, so to speak.

"Sounds like Familia Norteña is pissed off." He turned off the recording of Luther's phone call.

Another DEA agent nodded. "So, what happens now?"

Eddleman sat in the living room of a vacant building along with several other agents. "If it's going to happen, it'll start happening pretty quick."

The members of the team, three men and one woman, traded intel gathered from snitches and wire taps. *La Familia Norteña's* control of the plaza in Nuevo Laredo was about to be challenged by their old nemesis, the *Zetas*. Eddleman walked to a white board and began writing.

"Our Mr. Vasquez is in deep shit with Venustiano Huerta now. He is not trusted. That means that one way or the other, he's ours. Once we convince him of that, I think we can use him to speed up this little battle between those Mexican turds."

At least half the agents were Hispanic. No offense was meant, and none taken. After all, anyone connected to *La Familia Norteña* or the *Zetas was* a turd, and Eddleman's targets *were* Mexicans.

"What about Luther?" the woman asked. "Are we going to try to protect him." There wasn't too much concern in her voice, as Luther hadn't come clean with Eddleman that day on the border.

"We'll keep an eye on him and his old lady as best as possible. If we put him back in lock-up, someone will figure out we know something."

To Eddleman, Luther Wellington was possible collateral damage. Within the range of acceptable collateral damage, but to be avoided if reasonably possible.

———

FORTY-FIVE

Present Day

PURDY KENDRICKS

On Monday, campaign signs came out for the local elections. A couple of women were running for Kickapoo County Clerk, as the current occupant was retiring. Seth Roberts was running unopposed, again, for Justice of the Peace. For some reason he felt that the voters in Precinct Four needed to be reminded of his worth. A few of his signs were stuck in windows around the courthouse.

TJ had already printed up push cards that he had placed in businesses about a week before it was legal to do so, but no one had complained, so far.

Two big campaign signs were now glaringly present on Highway 90. They read "Elect Clarence Livermore for Kickapoo County Sheriff" in large red letters. Underneath, they told me that "He'll be Fair, Firm, and HONEST." One was near the right-of-way in the gravel parking lot of the Santa Rosa Livestock Auction Company. Bill Perry, the owner, had never allowed campaign signs on his property—until now. The other one hung between t-posts in front of Mildred Perez's second-hand store. Mildred wasn't even a registered voter, but her business made her popular with politicians at certain times. It was directly behind the city limits sign on the east side of Santa Rosa, just after the speed limit dropped from 70 to 45. The signs didn't bode well for TJ. They were, as political campaign signs go, eye-catching. But worse was where they were located. Santa Rosa's town marshal had called in some markers, or convinced Perry and Perez that he was the future of county law enforcement.

It was going to be an interesting few weeks.

I parked in the shade—no jury trials this week—and walked across to the Sheriff's Office. Jake Nichols handed me an email as I walked by.

"Looks like something on your case."

The Rio Grande floater had been identified by the Department of Public Safety's report from prints and DNA submitted by the Bexar County Medical Examiner's Office. Several photos from law enforcement showed his name to be Juan Gabriel Sosa. He was 41 when he was killed. Born in Coahuila State, Mexico, he received a green card as a youth, as his parents were naturalized citizens. He later became an American citizen. He had lived in Houston, San Antonio, and Laredo. A high school yearbook photo showed a small, wiry kid with a big smile who was the recording secretary for a South San Antonio high school 4H-FFA Club.

"Johnny," as he went by, had told the yearbook editor he "wanted to be a saddle bronc rider" and make it to the finals of the PRCA Rodeo in Las Vegas.

After graduating from high school, he took a few courses at a junior college and joined the Army. But something had gone sour in his life. He had been booted out of the Army with a dishonorable discharge.

Several arrests for small quantities of street drugs had resulted in a couple of probations. One had been revoked, and he had spent some time in a Texas state jail, a lockup for low-level felons. He had been discharged from the prison system about a year before the Vasquez killings to an address in Laredo. Laredo PD intelligence reports gave his street name as "Vaquerito" or "Little Cowboy." He had been a suspected low-level dealer with a street gang. That gang was connected to the *Zetas*.

At first, none of this made a huge impression on me—just another sad and wasted life. Then I re-read where Sosa was born: a town named Parrita. My mother and father used to take medical supplies into Mexico to help some of their workers' families during droughts. I knew where Parrita was. I had been there as a kid. It wasn't even a town. It was more a collection of *jacals* in an *ejido* where *campesinos* raised goats and tried to stay alive in the northern Mexican desert. Parrita was also 20 miles almost due south of Laura Griffin's ranch on the Rio Grande.

Some of this was starting to make sense. Shivelli had no connection with Texas. His claim to fame was as a sniper and hired killer. The FBI information on Shivelli didn't show any indication that he spoke Spanish, or that he'd ever lived in Texas, much less Mexico.

Juan Gabriel Sosa had been raised, partly, in the desolate Coahulian desert near where Venustiano Huerta had been killed. The only thing that made sense seemed to show Sosa had been Shivelli's guide into Mexico.

I needed to bounce some of this off someone, and that someone had become my wife.

But I was getting thirsty. I needed to make a meeting. That meant driving to Ozona, 150 miles away, and getting there for a 7:30 meeting of the Sojourners.

I made it with five minutes to spare. Stale coffee and cigarette smoke greeted me as I walked into the back room of a local café. I dropped a dollar in the kitty, shook hands with some of the dozen or so attendees, and bowed my head, reciting the Serenity Prayer.

It may not last long, but the one-hour meeting would get me through a few more days of sobriety—I hoped.

FORTY-SIX

Present Day

PURDY KENDRICKS

The AA meeting ended right at 8:30 p.m., and I headed home. The hour-long meeting cleared my mind some, and it felt good to be away from Santa Rosa. All of us at the meeting were fighting some of the same devils. None of the folks cared what I did for a living. I was just another recovering drunk. The one-name anonymity was a bit contrived—anyone at the meeting could, with little effort, figure out who the others were. But they didn't, or at least pretended they didn't.

The sun had dropped well below the horizon, leaving only a slight afterglow. Forrest would still be up. Betty and I were talking again, and the night air was purging itself of the day's heat. I pushed in the earbuds, punched *play* on the iPod, and the moment got even better. Nora Jones's *Come Away with Me* started. A mental massage.

Thirty miles out of Ozona, my cell phone flashed. I was surprised there was cell phone service. Selman was calling. I paused the music and pulled onto the gravel shoulder.

"Anytime you are calling me at this time of the day usually means that something bad has happened."

"Where are you?" Selman sounded concerned.

"On my way back home from Ozona." I didn't tell him why I was there, and Abner didn't ask.

"Damn, I'm surprised you have cell coverage." He paused. "Anyone with you?"

I assured him I was alone.

"You talked with any DEA folks lately?"

Uh oh. "Yes. Why?"

Abner paused again. "Purdy, I would appreciate you and me agreeing on something. I'm wanting to talk with you, but I sure would have a seriously hard time explaining what I'm about to discuss unless the two of us have an understanding."

I knew where this was going.

"This discussion never happened, Ranger. You just called me to see how the investigation is coming along, didn't you? I already don't recall you telling me a damned thing, seeing as how you Rangers are always so tight- lipped. That sound about right?"

"It'll do. DEA visits me yesterday. Guy by the name of Eddleman. You know him? And has he talked with you?"

"Yes, and yes."

A tractor-trailer rig hauling cattle rocked the car and spattered gravel on the windshield as it sped north in the gloaming. The scent of cow manure wafted through the vents.

"Mind sharing with me what you all talked about?"

I would share some, but not all.

"Eddleman told me to back off looking at Pete Vasquez as having anything to do with his grandparents' deaths. Said that Pete was an important person of some kind—didn't say what kind—just that he was 'important in an ongoing investigation.' Told me that putting pressure on Vasquez was bringing unwelcome attention to the man, that me probing Pete's business could get him killed and screw up a 'very important' investigation. Do you believe Eddleman?"

"Which part?" I responded. "That Pete is somehow involved with the DEA—yes. That he didn't have anything to do with his grandparents' deaths—no."

"Eddleman and one of the DEA higher-ups from D.C. met with the Colonel" —Selman meant the head of the Texas Department of Public Safety, of which the Rangers were a part— "and urged the Colonel to lean on us, and through us, on Kickapoo County, to let sleeping dogs lie."

This case was running my life, and now that I had sunk my teeth into it, I wasn't inclined to let go. I told Selman as much.

"Purdy, I'm not telling you anything, and if we, meaning the Rangers, come to talk to you about this, it won't be me doing the talking. That said, what have you got that Kickapoo County has jurisdiction over? So far, four dead people, all most likely killed by one or more Mexican cartels. You've got no one local that's been implicated, at least that you've told me about. Is Pete Vasquez involved? If you say so, I believe you. However, can you prove it? And exactly what did he do, if he is? There isn't anything that you're sharing with me, that shows dope coming in or money going out in your county."

His analysis was spot-on. Why *was* I trying to figure this one out? The opaque situation in Mexico had many losers and no winners. And me pretending that thin ribbon of water made much difference was proving a waste of time.

"Ranger, did you ever see the movie *Chinatown*?'

"Huh? Can't say as I have. What about it?"

"Without going into the plot too much, it's about a private detective who winds up over his head in about three or four bad things. Set in the 1940s. The show ends up in Los Angeles's Chinatown, where things aren't ever what they seem, and where there are no happy endings. The private detective has come close to saving his client, a beautiful woman, from the bad guys. He wants justice. He wants to punish the bad guys. Then it all goes to pieces. His client, who had also been his lover, is shot dead by the cops, accidentally it turns out. The PI is in shock. His cop friend pushes him away urgently. 'Forget it, Jake. This is Chinatown.' Movie over. Roll credits."

"Sounds like a lousy movie."

"No, actually, it's a hell of a picture. But the point is...."

Selman interrupted. "I know. I know. You want things clean and neat. This mess cleaned up with a neat bow tied around the case file. With convictions. With justice. And I'm telling you, it may not turn out that way. Hell, Purdy. You've been a cop for how long? Where in the world did you get the idea that's ever the case? And on the Mexican border? There's so much corruption in these parts, we can't even begin to comprehend it. Laredo's got houses where all the insulation in the walls are bundles of hundred-dollar bills. Wet-behind-the-ears Border Patrol agents are taking money and stashing it in duffel bags. And why wouldn't they? 'Turn the other way,' they're told, 'and we'll make you rich. If you don't, well, here's a picture of your wife and new child. Something will happen to them if you don't.' This whole part of the world is a cesspool. All you and I are doing is shoveling some of the turds out just fast enough so the whole country doesn't drown in shit."

Quite a speech.

There was a lot of truth in what he said, but hearing Selman say it was depressing.

"So, what are you saying? Walk away? Let it go? If I don't solve this thing, TJ loses and I'm out of a job. I'm not sure I'm caring that much about the job right now. But two old folks were killed and left lying on ant mounds. I can't let that go. So tell your Ranger bosses and anyone else to go fuck themselves."

Laughter wasn't what I expected to hear.

"Since you're hell-bent to press on, my friend, I'll try to get your back, but now you know. TJ is a boob, and he'll shed you fast if it suits his political future. Someone is talking in your department. Washington is leaning on us to lean on you. It's all a mess."

The tension went out of the air a little. Selman was telling me I had an ally, just one getting weaker by the day.

"I didn't know I was such an important person, Ranger."

"You aren't so important, Purdy. You aren't. You're just stepping on someone's toes you're not supposed to be stepping on."

"So why all this discussion?"

"I was taking your temperature. Be careful. And since you seem to persist in sticking your nose where it may not belong, you might want to do a little more digging on Pete Vasquez."

"What have I missed?"

"Three months ago, one of his trucks was inspected in Laredo. Two hundred kilos of pure cocaine in a stash hole. Dogs sniffed it out. He hasn't been indicted—yet. Driver, guy by the name of Luther Wellington, told the DEA that stuff had been loaded without him knowing anything about it. Which may or may not be true. Ol' Pete got the driver bailed out of jail. Nothing in the newspaper. Nothing on TV. I requested offense reports. Figured you might be interested. Got nowhere. DEA said they'd get it to me in due course. Then came the visit to the Colonel. It is curious."

I agreed it was.

"Be careful, Deputy. There isn't a case on earth that's worth getting killed over."

I pulled back onto the highway and plugged the iPod earbuds back in. Norah Jones was only half-way through *Come Away with Me*. I turned off the music. The only thing I heard the rest of the way home was the sound of the road and wind. I was on my own.

FORTY-SEVEN

Luther Wellington

PRESENT DAY

The pre-trial release agreement with the Feds required Luther to turn over any firearms he owned. He had complied, and now wished he hadn't. For two months he had been the best pre-trial release the Feds had. He was too scared to leave the house. No one had actually threatened him, but no one had to. The Laredo newspaper's headlines were featuring stories from Nuevo Laredo, Saltillo, and Monterrey attesting to a renewed bloodbath between rival cartels.

Luther wasn't a rocket scientist but figured whatever he had been involved with just might have had something to do with the increasing body count. Luther's Barcalounger usually rested near the front window of the living room. He contemplated moving it but figured that sitting there at least would give him a view of the street. What he intended to do if someone came for him, he had no idea.

Wellington's wife ended up mowing the yard. And edging the yard. And finally losing her temper.

"You've got that ankle monitor on. It doesn't mean you're helpless."

So much for the warm welcome home. Not allowed to drink alcohol, Luther had nothing to buffer the woman's carping.

To stop the whining, Wellington decided to take a chance. After all, it had been over two and a half months. If someone was going to hurt him, they surely could have done it by now.

After an afternoon nap, Luther went to the garage, pulled out the

Toro, and fired it up. The Wellington property wasn't much bigger than a postage stamp.

"I'll get this done *pronto,*" he thought.

Luther pushed the lawnmower out to the front yard and began mowing the area closest to the curb. A white four-door, crew-cab pickup pulled up.

"Hey!"

Luther glanced over, blanched, and killed the mower's engine. He looked at the truck. Three of the heavily tinted windows remained up. The "hey" came from the back seat driver's side. It originated from a heavily tattooed Mexican, who was now blowing Luther kisses.

"White boy, you remember me?"

It was the queer in the dormitory. What the hell was this tatted-up asshole doing in the neighborhood?

"Yeah, I do." Trying to be pleasant might give him some time to figure out how to get back inside the house. "What can I do for you?" Luther even smiled.

"Well, white bread, you fucked over *La Familia Norteña* for five hundred American dollars. Why'd you do that?"

Oh man, this wasn't looking good at all.

"I didn't do nothing to nobody, man. Why can't you leave me alone? I spent almost a month in lock-up for something I don't know anything about." He gestured to the ankle monitor. *Maybe it would be good if I could say I wouldn't even tell on anyone, not that I knew a lot anyway.* "I'm just a truck driver, and that's all."

The man in the back seat produced a shotgun. The barrel end looked like a cannon.

"Not a big deal, mister truck driver." He pronounced it *meester.*

Luther turned, or thought he did. Actually, he was in the process, but the double ought buck moved faster than Luther's thoughts, catching him in the chest. He was dead before he hit the swath of newly mowed grass.

FORTY-EIGHT

Present Day

PURDY KENDRICKS

As expected, nothing happened on the case. No new information. No leads. No tips. Nada. Not a damned thing. TJ was too distracted by his opposition's show of support to pay much attention to what was or wasn't happening with real police work. I called in a favor with Border Patrol and asked them to tell me if anything had ever happened with Vasquez Plumbing Contractors at border crossings, and got a hit. A friendly supervisor read me what he had over the phone.

"Almost four months ago. Truck got searched at a Laredo bridge crossing. Coming up from Monterrey. Found a bunch of cocaine. We turned in the paperwork to the AUSA in Laredo. Carted the driver off to jail. Anglo guy by the name of Luther Wellington. No criminal record of any kind, who swore up and down he didn't know anything about it."

"How much dope?"

I could hear him clacking away on a keyboard.

"Two hundred kilos. We've found more. We've found less. Only thing interesting was that the stuff was in two places."

Two places, four places, as long as they could stash it where it wasn't detected, what was the big deal with that?

"They've stashed dope in dozens of places. What's so significant about these two?"

"These cartels are smart as hell. They watch everything we do. If

215

they are going to bring stuff over in a commercial vehicle, it's going to be in a place where they are sure we can't find it, either with dogs, or sensors, or anything. Dogs alerted on something. Our guys broke the seals and found around half a kilo in a toilet in the back end of the load. That was all she wrote. We tore the whole rig apart. Found the main load in a stash hole. Pretty well hidden too. We wouldn't have found it, or even looked for it, if it hadn't been for the dogs."

"That doesn't make sense."

He agreed.

"No, it doesn't, unless someone was trying to make sure the load was taken down. Nothing on the border surprises me anymore. We're seeing more killings in and around Nuevo Laredo recently. We're hearing stuff about another war for control of the plaza. Who knows? Is any of this related? No way of knowing for sure."

We chitchatted for a bit, and I promised I'd reciprocate. As I was about to ring off, the supervisor added something.

"DEA was there at the bridge when it happened. Those spooks have their own rules, which we aren't privy to. Just interesting that they seemed to know something was going to happen."

"Any names?"

"His name is Eddleman. I've met him. He's some kind of honcho stationed here for a couple of years. He's one of the spookier of the spooks."

Eddleman. Son of a bitch.

It was time to take another trip to Laredo.

FORTY-NINE

Present Day

PURDY KENDRICKS

I was not sure exactly what I was going to do when I got there. I suspect I was heading to Laredo to stick my finger in Eddleman's eye. The investigation was going nowhere fast.

My first stop was at Vasquez Plumbing Contractors. Several tractor trailer rigs were parked up against loading docks. The place was locked up. Pete Vasquez was in the wind, or protected, or both. It was stupid to expect otherwise.

I drove to the Federal Pre-Trial Services offices for the Southern District of Texas. I hoped to find out something on Luther Wellington. The federal pre-trial folks told me that his employer had made a pretty hefty bond. After a bit of back and forth, they provided me with his home address. I was also politely informed that Wellington had been assigned a Federal Public Defender, so I shouldn't be talking with him without his lawyer's consent.

I had no plans on using anything Wellington told me against him, or sharing it with other agencies. I just wanted information. Eddleman's interference in the case had me at a low boil. Maybe I could wring some information from Pete's employee.

I found Wellington's neighborhood with the GPS. It looked like it had been developed in the 70s or 80s and was fighting a losing battle with respectability. Well-maintained lawns competed with yards populated by grass burrs. No junked cars on front yards, yet, but there were more than a few vehicles up on jacks in driveways.

The house address was in the middle of a long block. I drove by the place to see if there were any signs of life. A red-faced Anglo was cranking on a lawnmower. He matched Wellington's booking photo. I drove to the end of the block, passing a white pickup going the other way as I did. I pulled into a driveway, turned around, and headed back to Wellington's house. I hoped he could at least give me something to go on.

The white pickup rolled up to Wellington's house and braked. Shit. I wasn't interested in anyone being around when I tried to brace Luther about Pete. I pulled over to the curb at the adjacent house. Wellington seemed too focused on its occupants to notice me. I hoped Wellington's visitor would leave quickly. I killed the engine and watched as Wellington stopped mowing and walked toward the truck. He wasn't smiling. In fact, he looked scared to death. It hit all at once —this wasn't a friendly visit. Time slowed down as I uncaged the shotgun from its mount and stepped out of the unmarked sedan. I wanted to scream at Wellington to run, but suddenly there were too many things to do at the same time.

Before I fully unfolded from the seat, a firearm came out of the truck window. A low bark of a shotgun filled the air, and Wellington went down. The truck's occupants let out peals of laughter. Spent gun wadding floated in the air.

I was within 20 yards of the truck and still hadn't been noticed. The shooter stepped down from the back seat holding the shotgun. I knew instantly what he was going to do. He was going to make sure Wellington was dead by putting another load into him.

"Hey, stop. Stop, motherfucker! Put it down. Put it down!"

The shooter, an acne-pocked Mexican, looked up. His face registered shock and told me that no law enforcement officer was supposed to be anywhere around. The shotgun swung toward me, and I ducked behind the white pickup's bed as I pulled the trigger, pumping another shell in the chamber immediately.

The shooter screamed in pain, dropping his weapon and staggering toward the truck door. With the clarity that comes to a portion of the brain at times, I knew there was more than the driver inside the vehicle, and that they were armed.

Another Hispanic, screaming curse words in Spanish, jumped from the open rear door and rushed toward his injured *compadre*, intent on dragging him into the truck. I could hear the driver yelling, *"apurate! apurate!"* The truck began to move, and the front-seat passenger started screaming in Spanish for the driver to stop. The truck slowed, and the front passenger door flew open.

A thin Mexican with a semi-automatic jumped out and started shooting at me. Bullets punched through the tailgate's thin metal, as I threw myself on the ground. While all this was going on, I heard myself screaming at the top of my lungs. I think I was yelling for help from anyone who could hear me. It could just as easily have been a feral scream of fear. I don't know. I rolled behind a rear tire and fired at the shooter's unshielded legs. He dropped his pistol and fell to the tarmac. His right boot was shredded by buckshot, and the foot was turned at an awkward angle.

I chambered another round and shot him as he scrabbled toward the dropped gun. A "whoof" sound came out as he grabbed the front door and pulled himself inside. I rolled back toward the curb and got to my feet, covering the two Hispanics in the front yard. The one I had shot was motionless on the ground. His back-seat helper glanced at me, gave up on trying to lift the shooter into the truck, and dived through the driver's side back door as the truck sped up. I pumped two more rounds through the tinted back window.

Shattered glass scattered on the street as the truck jumped the curb and collided with a parked car in a driveway three houses down across the street from Wellington's house.

I glanced over at Wellington. An arm twitched spastically. His wife-beater was shredded in the upper chest area. A woman came running out of the house screaming, "They killed him! They killed him!"

"Get back inside, Mrs. Wellington!" It was a guess but by her look I figured she was his wife.

The white pickup wasn't moving. I kicked the shotgun in Wellington's yard away from the shooter and picked the front passenger's pistol off the street.

As I inched toward the wrecked truck, it suddenly dawned on me that I needed help—and fast. I reached for my cell phone. I couldn't find it, but a neighbor who had come outside to see what the hell was going on yelled, "I've called 911!"

I had a quick visual image of a man with military bearing. "Take this pistol and cover me." I threw the pistol into the grass at his feet. "Don't come any closer." I still needed to see if there was a threat from the front seat of the pickup. The Good Samaritan didn't hesitate.

Oh, please don't get yourself shot trying to help.

I came along side of the truck bed and slipped toward the front, afraid I'd get a bullet in the face.

I rushed the driver's door and pulled it open. The driver fell out onto the street, his feet remaining inside. The back of his head was covered with blood. At least one of the shotgun blasts into the rear window had struck home.

Shit!

I forgot about the guy in the back seat! I jumped back quickly and heard the POW, POW, POW of bullets going through the metal of the driver's side back door where I had been just a second before.

Oh shit, that motherfucker's got a gun.

I rounded the back of the truck and went to the passenger side. The front door swung open. My hands were shaking so badly I dropped a shotgun shell on the street, then shoved four more shells into the shotgun from the weapon's buttstock shell holder.

I fired two shots into the front seat area, hoping the buckshot would hit something. Shot Up Foot pushed his door open, yelling, *"muere, puto!"*

He had found another pistol somewhere inside the vehicle. He keened in pain as his butchered foot hit the ground, his shots going up into the air. I shot two more times, or three, and he fell to his knees. He attempted to crawl, and I shot again. He went flat on the driveway and didn't move.

Suddenly I couldn't breathe and felt faint. The adrenalin and fear were making my heart beat so fast, I was afraid I was having a heart attack. Sirens off in the distance indicated the Laredo Police Department was on its way. I slumped down near the driver's side rear fender well and reloaded again. Taking a deep breath, I yelled at the Good Samaritan. "You see anyone coming out of the truck?"

"No!" he yelled back.

I nodded rather than spoke. My mouth was filled with cotton.

Then the Samaritan screamed, "Back door's opening. Watch out!"

The downward angle of the truck allowed the rear door to fall open. An AK 47 flew out into the street, followed by an automatic.

"No me mates! No me mates!" The short Mexican who'd tried to pull the wounded killer back in the truck scuttled out and fell flat on his stomach, continuing to beg for his life. I wasn't going to kill him but wondered if the Samaritan would pull the trigger.

"Cover him, but don't shoot!"

I walked toward the prostrate Mexican, keeping my weapon pointed at his head. "I won't kill you, you piece of shit!" I kicked him in the ribs as hard as I could. I was still screaming at him and kicking him, as two Laredo PD cars roared up the street. I could hear the sirens of others coming, too.

The first officer stepped behind his car door and ordered me to drop my shotgun.

"Get down on your knees!"

My sedan was unmarked. My sheriff's uniform wasn't familiar to whoever was yelling at me, and I didn't want to chance getting shot by a fellow peace officer. I got down on my knees.

"I'm a cop!" I yelled. "I'm going to lie down in the street and extend my hands away from me. For God's sake, don't shoot me."

Suddenly, it was over. I began to shake uncontrollably.

FIFTY

Present Day

PURDY KENDRICKS

There were consequences—some expected, some that loomed later. By the time the six o'clock news hit the airwaves that evening, the Laredo shootings were, to mix metaphors, above the fold headlines. In Laredo, a man getting gunned down in his front yard wasn't necessarily a big deal, even if he had a GPS ankle monitor on at the time. After all, this was the border. Things along the border with Mexico were always a little rougher than most of the rest of the country.

What did Luther Wellington do to get killed? Piss off someone while in lockup? Not a big deal. Besides, Wellington wasn't a name associated with any of the large and interconnected families and *patrons* whose outrage might be of significance.

No, Luther's death wouldn't have rated much of a story. You might say his 15 minutes of fame would, in actuality, have been about 20 seconds of a news reader's mournful noting his passing, allowing the viewing public to tsk tsk about Laredo going to hell in a handbag.

Three Mexican thugs being killed at the same time might have, by itself, been a bit more salacious. The print and TV media wouldn't show close-ups, but it was guaranteed, this being Laredo and all, that someone would leak pictures of tatted-up *sicarios* strewn in the area of the killings. You Tube or Live Leak or some such outlet would upload the pictures, and the prurient interests of those intrigued by or enamored with the cartels' bloody history would hit the sites in a frenzy.

This would last a month or two, until bloodier pictures took their place.

That wasn't what happened. If I had been thinking clearly, maybe I would have left the shotgun caged and gotten the hell out of Laredo. But I didn't. The result was that by the end of the day, Fox, CNN, and all the major networks had a story that went something like this:

Voiceover: "Early this afternoon, four men, identified as members of a Northern Mexican drug cartel, are alleged to have killed a Laredo citizen, identified as Luther Wellington, as he was mowing his front yard on a quiet Laredo street.

"Laredo PD sources say that the men were surprised when an out-of-town peace officer who happened to be in the neighborhood, witnessed the event as it was transpiring and attempted to stop it. The officer, whose identity has not yet been released, produced a shotgun, killed three of the alleged assassins, and helped capture the fourth. A 911 call from a local citizen brought the local police to the scene. Richard Salazar, a neighbor who called 911, was there and saw things as they transpired."

"Mr. Salazar, what can you tell us?"

"I looked out my front window just as this white truck drove up to my neighbor's house."

"And your neighbor was Mr. Wellington?"

"Right. Nice guy. Heard he had a bit of trouble, but who hasn't? Anyway, I seen this cop car pull up in front of my house. It wasn't a marked cop car, but I mean, you can spot them a mile away, you know?"

"What happened then?"

"I hear this BOOM and Luther falls over. All of sudden, the *bolillo* —sorry—the police officer gets out of the cop car with a shotgun, and, man! I mean, I'm a veteran and member of the VFW. I was in some firefights in Afghanistan and all...."

(The reporter interrupted)

"Thank you for your service. Then what did you witness?"

"The cop shot the guy who shot Luther. Another dude jumps out to get that guy, and the cop shoots at him too. Then this guy in the front seat, he gets out and the cop, I think the cop blew that guy's foot off."

"Uh, how did he do that?"

"The guy in the front seat started plugging away, and the cop falls down and shoots the guy from under the truck. Under the [bleep] truck. I'm calling 911, you know, and run outside, and the truck took off. Then, BOOM, the cop takes out the rear window. Holy [bleep]! Un —[bleep] believable! In my neighborhood. I mean, this ain't the [bleep] 'hood.'"

(The reporter interrupted again)

"Yes, sir, I understand. Tell us what happened then."

"The truck ran up in my neighbor's driveway. The cop runs over there, and the driver falls out dead. That mo—[bleep]—er must have got him with the shot to the back window. Then the guy with the bad foot, he jumps out and tries to kill the cop. BOOM! Down he goes instead! The last guy starts throwing guns and stuff out into the street and yells at the cop not to shoot *him*! Then our local cops show up (sneering)."

"We understand you may have helped. Is that right?"

(Appearing reticent) "Not really. I mean the cop tossed a gun my way and asked for my help, but it was over with by then. He did it all, man.'

"What police department was the officer with, Mr. Salazar?"

"He had some uniform on, but it ain't Laredo or Webb County Sheriff, either. I didn't get close enough to talk to him. The cops put that crime tape all around the place. It wasn't too long after that, they whisked the cop outta there in an ambulance."

"Was he injured?"

"I don't think so, but, man, that dude was really shook up. I mean, it didn't look like that white dude was expecting this [bleep] any more than those *pendejos* in the truck."

"Thank you, Mr. Salazar."

"No problem. This bull [bleep] killing in this town's gotta stop."

(Interview ends and reporter turns to camera)

"Wellington, recently released on bail from a federal detention facility, had been accused of trafficking a large quantity of cocaine across a downtown Laredo border crossing four months ago. A Vasquez Plumbing Contractor tractor trailer he was operating was stopped and searched after Border Patrol drug dogs alerted on the trailer. Officials tell us that he recently posted a $100,000 bond.

"Whether his killing is in any way related to his recent arrest, is not known. Nor is it known whether this shooting is in any way related to the recent increase in killings in Nuevo Laredo, where, reportedly, two competing cartels are fighting for control of the lucrative drug trade."

The hospital stay lasted long enough to confirm that, apart from shock and an incipient case of post-traumatic stress disorder, I was okay to be released. I waived my right to an attorney and spent the next eight hours rehashing the shootings.

I bet my name would be out in public in less than a week. Stupid guess. It was out the next morning.

———————

FIFTY-ONE

Four Years Before Preesent

PURDY KENDRICKS AND EDDLEMAN

The process wasn't much different than what I had been through before, in Houston. Only this time, I wasn't drunk. Not intoxicated—that was too polite. In Houston, although "righteous," the shooting of a drug dealer had been badly timed.

I had been assigned to a joint task force comprised of Houston PD narcotics and homicide detectives, under the overall control of the DEA. We sat on a drug stash house off Airline Boulevard north of downtown, outside of Loop 610. Once a middle-class area, it now consisted of small auto body shops and sub-standard housing controlled by several gangs. Most had some affiliation with Mexican and Central American gangs and provided street-level distribution of methamphetamine, crack, and PCP.

The DEA wanted to take down one of the gangs' leader, Ignacius "Bootsie" Cardenas. Ignacius Cardenas was a colorful psychopath. His mother was African American. His father was from El Salvador. Ignacius got his sobriquet when a member of another gang was found with just the tip of his head showing above the waters of Little White Oak Bayou. Having seen one too many gangster movies, Ignacius had the guy snatched. After an afternoon of fun and games with a blow-torch, Bootsie's boys cemented the victim's feet in a Number 5 wash-tub. After it set up, the tub, with victim affixed, went into the bayou. Hence the name "Bootsie."

The DEA wanted this guy badly. Not so much because he was a

turd, which he was, but because he could lead that agency to bigger turds. We at HPD just wanted him off the streets. Whatever the DEA's labyrinthine plans were for finding Bootsie's suppliers, weren't at the top of our concerns. He was terrorizing decent folks. But federal task force involvement meant going by the DEA's playbook. Most of us locals would have preferred Bootsie doing hard state time, rather than in an air-conditioned Federal facility.

At someone's suggestion, after sitting in vans for hours and peeing in milk jugs, some of us on the stakeout adjourned to a nearby topless club on the access road of Interstate 45. Eddleman didn't give his okay, but he didn't object, either.

"One drink, gentlemen," was the only instruction, as the strange DEA agent said he would stay with one of the vans near the dope house. "No fuck-ups on this. My bosses want this guy taken down in one piece."

One of the DEA agents had used a dancer dubbed "Monique" as an informant and was "tight" with the club's manager. A few drinks, an inside restroom, some visual stimulation, a report that Bootsie was seen in an adjoining county conducting his business there and was not expected to return for hours. What could go wrong?

Bootsie came home early. Six gin and tonics, and a couple of tequila shots, and I was in no condition to stake out much of anything.

Truth to tell, all of us who had gone to the club had a snoot-full. But there were three SUVs full of cops wanting to take down a dope house on the near north side and snatch up one of the city's biggest turds. The adrenaline kicked in, trying mightily to counteract the alcohol in my blood stream.

There was an alleyway behind the suspected dope house. As planned, I was dropped off on one end of the garbage-strewn lane. Another cop was dropped at the alley's entrance on the adjoining side street. We were there as backup, intending to block any escape attempt through the backyard. The main team hoped to snatch Bootsie as he got out of his pimpmobile and before he made it to the front door. The search and arrest warrant allowed us to toss the entire property. The word was, there were several kilos of cocaine in the place. Some detectives waited on nearby streets, ready to search the premises once Bootsie was secure.

It didn't work out that way. Bootsie probably had an IQ of less than 80, but street smarts had kept him alive longer than many of his competitors. I began taking deep breaths, hoping the rush of fresh air would dilute the booze. As I staggered down the alley, my headset blew up with cops yelling that Bootsie had bolted. The Buick LeSabre with chrome hubcaps had made a sudden U-turn, trying to make it back to the Interstate. Blocked by an HPD van, it careened through a fence and into the alleyway behind the dope house, heading straight toward me. I jumped into a pile of rotting building material. The car missed me by inches. I could hear Bootsie in the passenger seat screaming at the LeSabre's driver, "Get the fuck outta here, motha fucka!" as the vehicle tried to escape.

The driver floored the heavy sedan, lost control, and the car plowed into a commercial refuse bin. Relieved that I was still alive, I ran toward the vehicle, weapon drawn.

The car went dark. Dogs, the LeSabre's horn, and police sirens filled the night air with yips and wails. Trying to catch my breath, I stopped a car-length from the passenger door, screaming at Bootsie and the driver to get their hands out of the windows where I could see them. Which was problematic, as the streetlights had long ago been shot out, I had lost my flashlight, and it was dark as hell.

"I'm coming out. Don't shoot! Don't shoot!"

"Stay in the car, Bootsie!"

He didn't. As I continued to scream, the dome light came on when both doors flew open, and shots rang out from somewhere near the trash bin.

I ducked and started firing.

"He's got a gun! He's got a gun! Put it down! Put it down!" My screaming was directed at the two leaving the car, and at the officers I prayed were heading my way.

In less than two seconds, I fired six rounds at the shadows where I had seen the flash and heard the shots.

In a matter of seconds, it seemed, Eddleman and others from the take-down team were there. Lights flooded the alleyway. Ignacius Cardenas's inert form splayed out over the mud and trash next to the LeSabre. He had taken one round in the middle of the forehead.

"Why didn't you call for backup?" Eddleman was in my face.

"No time." I bent over, trying to keep from fainting. "They took two shots at me."

"Who's 'they?'" The other occupant was nowhere around. Eddleman waved his hand like he was swatting gnats. "Christ. You're drunk as a skunk." He paused. "And you capped the motherfucker!"

"Yeah, but he tried to kill me. Tried to run over me. Tried to shoot me." *Didn't that count for something?*

They bagged Bootsie's hands. No gunshot residue. Bootsie hadn't fired a gun Tests showed he had not even been *around* one when it was fired. And the shooter? Never found him.

To his credit, Eddleman went to bat for me with his bosses and HPD. His version of events in his incident report didn't mention alcohol. It supported what I claimed I had witnessed. He claimed he had recovered a Jennings Bryco .380 automatic from the passenger-side floorboard with only three live rounds in the six-round magazine. As if any self-respecting thug would have ever touched such a piece of shit firearm.

The police department passed the shooting investigation to the DEA. The beauty of being part of a Federal task force was that a bad situation could be punted, where it didn't have to be looked at too closely. Besides, being assigned to a Feds had the advantage of immunity from prosecution in certain situations. It was a win-win, if such a thing exists, in what some saw as a questionable killing of a civilian.

But there was talk. I had a problem. I was a liability. It was suggested that I resign and sober up.

I resigned, went into rehab, and eventually got sober. So far, I had stayed that way.

But the DEA didn't get a chance at shoving a two-by-four up Bootsie's ass to flip him for higher-ups on the food chain.

Eddleman's bosses were pissed at him for allowing a fuck-up to screw things up. He had faced that heat, and hadn't blinked an eye when he "found" the gun he had sworn it must have been the deceased's, residue, or no residue.

Eddleman figured I owed him.

FIFTY-TWO

Pete Vasquez

PRESENT DAY

P ete Vasquez's phone call to Eddleman was curt, "Call me back, you son of a bitch. I need to know what's going on."

Eddleman called him back five minutes later. Ignoring the epithet, his voice feigned innocence. "What's up, Mr. Vasquez?"

"What's up? What's up? You assholes said you needed me. That you'd protect me. And what happens? My truck driver is snuffed on his front lawn! What the shit? What the shit?" Pete tried to catch his breath as he shouted over the DEA-provided burner.

"Calmate, pendejo!"

Of course, Eddleman spoke Spanish. He was a DEA agent on the border. Pete hadn't thought about it, and the barked phrase made him pause. "Calm down? What the fuck, Eddleman. The *Zetas* promised me if I helped them, they'd protect me—let me work for them. I'm supposed to help you guys. Huerta's dead, but his people are pissed off. They'll come after me next!"

Pete Vasquez was an asset. Nothing more. Eddleman was betting he would prove useful. The DEA agent wasn't feeling Vasquez's pain, but he had made a promise. If reasonably able, he was going to try to keep it.

"Pete, *La Familia Norteña* is sucking wind. You read the papers; you see the news. Your new employers are cleaning house in Nuevo Laredo right now." He paused. "Now, about your new employers, have you heard anything yet?"

231

Momentarily flummoxed by the shift in the discussion, Vasquez hesitated, "Er, no, I haven't. But…"

"You will. You know you will. They've invested in you. You're going to have to make good on that investment."

"How am I going to do that when I'm dead?"

"Think, Vasquez," Eddleman said. "The *Zetas* can read the label on your underwear if they want to. You need to take a deep breath. Head back to your plumbing business and get to hustling real business, so it doesn't do *el foldo*. Get your employees back on the road. Get your warehouse back on track and quit relying on someone else to do it for you."

Pete started to argue.

"Shut the fuck up, Vasquez," Eddleman barked. "You're only good to us if you do what you were doing. If not, we'll pick you up, and you can spend the rest of your short life getting sunshine pumped to you." He took a deep breath and calmed his voice. "You'll hire a new warehouseman tomorrow. He's one of ours."

"What's his name?"

Eddleman gave him the new employee's name.

"That's not his real name, is it, Eddleman?"

Eddleman ignored the question. "Just hire him. Like I said, the *Zetas* see you as useful. I'm betting you'll never need any extra assistance for personal safety from your new warehouseman. You can bet the *Zetas* will be keeping an even closer eye on you now."

There was silence. Eddleman could almost feel Pete squirming.

"I forgot to tell you something. I'm not so sure they trust me. I bought tickets for my grandparents to get them off the ranch. They never used them. The *Zetas* know about this. I'm not sure how much they trust me, you know?"

Since when did I start talking to Eddleman like my confessor? Pete turned his pinkie ring round and round, inwardly grimacing as he compared the DEA agent with Father Joseph Levant, his boyhood parish priest.

Eddleman didn't respond. The airline purchase was old news. No doubt there'd be more Vasquez would divulge. No one ever told the whole story at first. And sometimes, never.

Pete changed directions. "*La Familia Norteña* had places for me to deliver to. What makes you DEA guys think that the *Zetas* are going to use me, when the folks my trucks had gone to aren't getting regular deliveries? I mean, You guys gotta know the *Zetas* have their own delivery points I'm going to have to deal with."

Eddleman paused. He wasn't about to divulge anything of substance to Vasquez that couldn't be sussed out in a short time. There was virtually nothing about his business that he trusted Vasquez knowing.

"Vasquez, you don't need to know anything. All I'll say is..." Eddleman searched for how much information to convey. "What makes you think that the *Zetas* aren't in the process of taking over some of your old deliver points as we speak? You may even need to hire some new drivers. Vasquez Plumbing Contractors may be going to both old *and* new places."

Pete had a thousand more questions he had forgotten to ask in the motel room and later debriefing. He started to ask one of them, but Eddleman had already hung up.

After a few minutes of self-pity, Pete shrugged it off. More business? Hell, working for the government might make him even more money. Plumbing supplies going all over the continental United States. More trucks, more drivers. Not only would he be trafficking old and new locations, he was going to do it with the DEA's blessing ... assuming the *Zetas* didn't find out and kill him.

Pete felt like he had hit the lottery.

Sweet.

FIFTY-THREE

Present Day

PURDY KENDRICKS

L aredo Police Department's debriefing was not pleasant. The four
hitmen, three dead, and one arrested, and all resulting from the
actions of some Podunk County Mountie meant more paperwork and
a lot of questions from the public. I had to admit it was going to cause
a stir. I hunkered down and hoped I would come across as earnest,
forthright, and honest. I was on their turf.

Led by a hard-assed detective borrowed from Internal Affairs
named Cantu, the local's inquiry into how and why I was in Laredo
took center stage.

An Assistant Chief, a plainclothes Homicide detective, and Cantu
stared at me like I had farted in church.

"Let me get this straight, Deputy," Cantu said. "You show up from
a dipshit county, in uniform, in a plain wrapper, without notifying us
you're coming?"

A part of me was glad I wasn't in Cantu's shoes. My presence in
Laredo was out of bounds. "Yes."

"No warrant. No subpoena to serve. Just a friendly visit to our fair
city. Were you sent here by your boss, the sheriff? Did he even know
you were coming? Deputy Kendricks, how do I begin to untangle this
hairball?"

A knock on the interrogation room door interrupted Cantu. A
uniformed officer stuck his head in the door.

"Detective Cantu, there's a gentleman from DEA out here. Says he would appreciate talking with you for a minute."

Oh shit.

Cantu stepped out, and the fart-in-church description paled. The other two men eyeballed me as if I was a spore in a Petri dish.

These guys were starting to creep me out. "So, how 'bout them Cowboys?"

There was no response. "Don't tell me you're Texans fans?"

Again, nothing.

Cantu came back in and resumed his questioning. We went through the scenario several times. Occasionally, another officer would come in and hand him what looked like written statements. I presumed they were from Luther's wife and from the Good Samaritan who had helped me. Thankfully, whatever was on the statements seemed to corroborate my version of the facts.

Finally, the questioning wound down. "This isn't over with, not by a long shot, Deputy. But for now, we're kicking you. More than likely, this will be presented to a grand jury for screening. It's what we do in the big city when a cop shoots a civilian."

I couldn't resist. "Gee, Detective, we don't have those kinds of civilians in Kickapoo County. I hope we don't import any of yours."

He sneered. "Bullshit, *amigo.* You've had four people snuffed out lately, and you guys can't find your peckers with both hands. Stay out of my jurisdiction with your cowboy tactics." Point taken. But being nearly loopy from an adrenalin crash and lack of sleep, I couldn't resist. "Tell me, Cantu. What would have happened to the wife and the guy who called 911 if I hadn't been there?"

"Fuck you, Kendricks."

———

FIFTY-FOUR

Present Day

PURDY KENDRICKS

There was no way I was going to make it back to Santa Rosa without some sleep. Fortunately, there was a cot in a storage room used for investigators working long hours. I hoped I could get a few hours of rest before starting out. I had called Betty from Laredo PD headquarters before the debriefing, but only said I was tied up and would be back as soon as I could. She needed to hear about this from me personally, and not over the telephone.

Jake Nichols got to her first.

Somehow, I drifted off without reliving the shoot-out. Soon, I was trying to explain to Oto and Raquel why they needed to get out of an ant mound. I kept pleading with them to move, but they just stared at me. The ants were crawling in their mouths and eyes, but they refused to move. Then Pete Vasquez ran up, screaming, screaming, and screaming. He began to weep and began shaking me. He tried to tell me something, but I couldn't understand him. I tried to push him away, but he wouldn't let go.

"Deputy. Deputy. Your cell phone's been ringing. Wake up." It was the watch captain, shaking me. "It's rung several times now."

Relieved to be rid of the nightmare, I saw the call had gone to voice mail. I thanked the captain and sat up. The first 20 seconds of Lionel Hampton's vibraphone intro to *Flying Home* began again. The watch captain seemed like a nice guy, but Lionel Hampton's 1957 cover of that driving classic could never be described as "jangling." Idle and senseless musings. Betty.

"Hey, hon," I said, shaking out the cobwebs, as I reached for my boots.

"Purdy, are you all right? What happened? Are you in a hospital?" It all came out as one question. "I've tried calling you since I heard."

"I'm fine, Betty. What have you heard?"

"That there had been a shoot-out. That you'd killed some men who had assassinated someone."

"Who told you, honey? The sheriff?"

"No, Jake drove up to tell me. He said you were all right. He woke me up, beating on the door. Said he didn't want to call me. But he said he was sure you were okay."

"Betty, I'm okay. I'm at the PD in Laredo. After what happened, I was too tired to come home without some sleep. You didn't need to hear about what happened over the phone."

No, she didn't, not after Bootsie. Still half-drunk and fully witless, I had telephoned her. Left unsaid this time was my reasoning to tell her personally. No, no alcohol had been involved this time. Yes, bad men had been killed, but perhaps some decent folks had been spared because of it. I promised to tell her the whole story when I got home.

Betty sounded somewhat reassured.

"I love you both. Hug Forrest for me. I'll be home as fast as I can."

I finished dressing and quietly retrieved my car from the parking lot. The shotgun wasn't in its rack, and it took a few seconds to remember it would only be returned after ballistics test were conducted. Laredo PD had given me the sedan's keys after the debriefing, but not before they had rummaged through it. No doubt, Cantu would have loved to have found drugs or contraband. I just felt relieved he hadn't been mad enough to plant something. A rogue cop involved with a cartel was probably easier to deal with than my story.

My phone rang with incoming calls three times on the way upriver. TJ had a lot of questions but was almost gracious with his concerns for my safety. The second call was Abner Selman.

"Purdy, you okay?"

"Yeah, and thanks for asking, Ranger."

"Well, you lit up the scoreboard this time. I can't wait to hear about it, so give me a call when you come up for air." He didn't volunteer anything more, and we rang off.

The third ringtone was the foreboding first few seconds of *Nightmare*. Laura Griffin Saenz.

Need to change that ringtone. Artie Shaw deserves better.

I let it go to voicemail and listened to her message. Her whiskey-soaked concern washed over me like a small, warm Gulf wave, and my face flushed. Desire and shame competed as I replayed the message. After listening three times, I deleted it. It wasn't fair that I couldn't punch delete on her memory.

Forrest was up when I drove up to the house. It was Saturday, and Betty postponed any conversation we were going to have, so her "boys" could enjoy the Saturday breakfast together. I showered quickly and changed into jeans and a Saturday-chores shirt.

By then, news had spread that a Kickapoo County deputy, in uniform, but in an unmarked car, had shot three *sicarios*. It wasn't long before it became obvious that the stalled investigation of the killings on the Griffin place, and taking three bad guys down, was not getting me any attaboys from those who were remotely familiar with risks of living near Mexico.

Forrest jumped out of the car and ran up to the door of the Cenizo Diner. By the time I walked inside, he had scampered to our customary booth near a window, yelling greetings to customers and waitresses he knew by name. For a moment, there was nothing in my life except the exuberance of my young, beautiful son.

Taking stock, it was obvious that several discussions had been interrupted. From faces quickly turned away, and others nodding sheepishly, it was apparent the discussions involved me. Waving howdy, I made for the booth.

Lilly Pardo, one of Beulah's long-time waitresses, set down our cutlery and napkins, and handed me a mug of coffee. She fussed over Forrest as always, and they bantered a bit before she asked him if would have his "usual," pancakes and bacon. She turned to me, but her voice was decidedly less friendly. "What'll it be, Deputy?"

I tried unsuccessfully to make eye contact, but she averted her face. This wasn't what I had come to expect of one of the more outgoing servers in the Cenizo. "You okay?"

She turned without answering. *Uh oh.* It was dawning on me that something was amiss. Lilly served a couple on the other end of the restaurant. Beulah delivered the plates of food. As she re-filled my coffee, Beulah gave her usual caution to Forrest, "not to put too much syrup on those pancakes. You're too sweet as it is." Forrest grinned and then began cutting up his pancakes. She turned to me, as if trying to figure out who she was talking with.

"What?"

Forrest picked up a piece of bacon, gnawing the meat away from the fat. "Forrest, honey, can you sit here by yourself for a sec? Your daddy and me gotta talk for just a second, okay?"

Immersed in the joy of Saturday pancakes, Forrest merely nodded, continuing to whittle away on the second piece of bacon.

"Purdy, let's talk a bit, shall we?" She motioned to an empty booth. I grabbed my coffee and followed her. Beulah untied her apron and tossed it onto the seat, sliding in behind the table.

"Used to be able to fit into these spaces pretty easy. Not so easy anymore." She barked a rueful sounding laugh. "Purdy, when you came back here, we all knew you'd had some kind of trouble. Why else would a smart man like you, college educated and all, with the big city police" —she pronounced it po-LESE— "come back to this God-forsaken patch of earth?"

I started to say something, but she didn't let me interrupt.

"We know you are trying your damndest to figure out who killed that kind old couple. And everyone hears things. Things like maybe your best friend when you was in school has something to do with it."

There are few secrets in a small town. The more Beulah talked, the more it seemed that there were fewer in Santa Rosa than most.

"Now they's one dead fella at Laura's old place. We don't know, but we all hear he was no good. Some hired killer. We hear you and the Ranger and that worthless sheriff of ours fished another body out of the river with its head blowed off." She looked around, seemingly relieved that the breakfast crowd was thinning out—that no one appeared to be paying attention to our discussion. "But now? You gone and shot not one, not two, but three Mex killers in Laredo, Texas."

"Is that what's got Lilly's goat?"

"You damned right it is, boy." She slapped the table, then looked embarrassed by the outward display of anger, or frustration—I wasn't sure which. "Mexican folks in Santa Rosa are scared. Scared all this killing is going to bring more trouble thisaway. We've been, praise God, lucky so far. None of that head-cutting-off or other trashy stuff we see and read about in the news. But now...."

"Beulah, I'm only doing my job. You know that."

"Well, Purdy, I aint seen no one arrested for what happened to Oto or Raquel Vasquez, nor them other two either."

My face reddened. I felt anger for the first time toward a trusted friend. "I'm doing the best I can, Beulah."

She lowered her voice, grabbed both my hands in hers, and looked directly into my eyes. "I know you are. But lots of these folks" —she gestured toward Lilly— "have got relatives across the river. And that nasty smelling ditch hasn't ever stopped bad stuff from coming across it, neither. They're afraid that all that bad stuff is coming our way. And them and their families won't be able to get out of the way." She let go of my hands, seeming to sense my anger was fading. "And you need to be afraid, too. You got a fine boy there, and a fine wife. That badge won't protect you, or them, if bad things come to pass."

I looked over at Forrest pushing a forkful of pancake into his mouth. A cold chill ran through me.

FIFTY-FIVE

Laura Griffin Saenz and Pete Vasquez

PRESENT DAY

L aura settled into what had become an increasingly common Friday night at home. No gala scheduled. No supper with a 60-ish supplicant looking for a trophy wife. As she helped herself to 15-year-old Glenmorangie over ice, she almost convinced herself she was thankful for some time alone.

Since her divorce from Saenz was finalized, her social calendar had taken a hit. In the center of a population center of over a million and a half people, Alamo Heights, zip code 78209, was a small enclave. The 1600 hundred acres of Texas borderlands she had inherited gave her a *je ne sais quoi* that the newcomers would never have. No one really gave a rat's ass about her fooling around. Texans could be exceedingly tolerant in that regard. She wasn't the first oh-niner to have an affair. Occasionally, a good looking woman stepping out on an older husband even lent a bit of *cachet.*

However, Saenz had, in the words of her dear late daddy, "ripped her a new one." No self-respecting Texas woman, especially one with her looks, cheater or not, should have allowed herself to be taken to the cleaners. She was quietly being shunned, not because of any sense of moral outrage, but because she got caught. Laura realized that many of her acquaintances were less disapproving of her extramarital conduct than they were of her caving in to a settlement that damned near cost her the cherished Alamo Heights property.

The depth of her social demotion hit that morning. While shopping at the HEB Central Market, she overheard two women on the adjoining aisle.

"Honey," the husky-voiced one said, "she almost lost that house. My husband told me he heard at the country club that she begged the bank to give her some time to make good on the note...."

A higher-pitched female voice interrupted. "The bank president isn't married, for God's sake. She could have worked *something* out. If you know what I mean."

Embarrassment washed over Laura, as she heard the titter of the women's deliciously shared secret. She was certain she recognized the two confidantes' voices. She had served with them at several fundraising events. Alone next to the Specialty Meats and Cheeses display, she looked around furtively. She was relieved that a stocker taking inventory of Guatemalan coffee beans was too far away to overhear the conversation.

Thank God.

As the two women drifted away, Laura heard, "No telling where the money came from to pay off the note. I hear she's involved with a *plumber*, for heaven's sake!"

As she sipped on her scotch, she couldn't figure out which hurt more—the breach of confidentiality that had her neighbors talking about her, or the claim that she was involved with a plumber. Pete Vasquez wasn't a *plumber*, dammit. He was a plumbing contractor with a nationwide business. No plumber she had ever known would have been able to come up with the money to bail her out of the mess she was in.

Pete had come through for her, but his money only stretched so far. Unloading the ranch was starting to look like a way out.

Fortifying herself with another splash, she punched Pete Vasquez's speed-dial code on her cell phone.

He picked up on the third ring. "Hey, Laura," Pete sounded distracted.

"Pete, you've been a stranger around here. You doing okay?"

"Sorry. Been neglecting the business. Playing catch-up and putting in some hours."

"Are you coming to San Antonio any time soon?" A warmth spread over Laura, and she realized she wanted the physical contact with Pete. "Honey, I need a bed warmer, and there's no one here to take your place."

"Probably not for a few weeks. Sorry." He paused. "I miss you."

What? Why did he ignore my come-on? She let it go for the moment. "I miss you too. Can you talk?"

Another pause. "Sure. What about?"

She rattled the ice in the cut-crystal glass. "I'm going to sell the ranch."

Pete's response was unexpectedly sudden. "You can't do that."

God bless him. He's got more connections to the place than I ever had. Here I am talking business when his grandparents just got killed there. I should be more sensitive.

There was silence. "Just a sec. I'm still at work. We've got trucks going out. I'm going back to my office so we can talk."

She took another sip and heard a door close.

"What's this about selling your daddy's place? Are you serious? The ranch has been in your family for, I don't know how long. You grew up there. Are things that bad?"

She interrupted the string of questions. "Oh, honey. I'm sorry. I know the place means a lot to you. I shouldn't have sprung this on you. It's just that I'm short of funds again, and I can't keep coming to you to bail me out." Hoping to ease the tension, Laura giggled.

"Laura, listen. You can't sell the place."

"Pete, you're sweet. It's going to take a while to sell anyway, because of what happened. I need the money, and it's got bad memories now. It should for you, too. You'll have some time to get used to the idea."

There. His family was killed at the place. I've played the bad juju card.

"No, that's not it. You just can't sell the place."

"Why not?"

"You just can't."

Laura felt herself bridling. She put her drink down. "Well, *sure* I can, lover boy. I wasn't asking for permission." Her face flushed with anger. "I called to break it to you before I hunted up a farm and ranch real estate agent. I'm only wanting some idea from you on what you think it would sell for."

Pete's voice changed timbre. "Laura, you will *not* sell the ranch.

You will *not* list the ranch. You will *not* even talk to anyone about listing it."

The conversation wasn't going anywhere as she had intended. She almost punched disconnect on her cell phone but paused. "And why the hell not?" She was almost shouting now.

"Listen, and listen carefully," Pete pleaded. "Do you think that money to bail you out came from my checking account?"

Dumbstruck, Laura didn't answer. She hadn't given it that much thought.

"Do you? Do you?" Pete was almost yelling now. "Do you think my trucking company had some loose change lying around for me to sweep up and bring to your San Antonio lawyer?"

Laura responded quietly, "I... I... I'm not sure." *Oh, God. Why did I even call Pete?*

There was an almost eerie quiet. Pete's response was barely audible. "I owe people. I did you a favor. It cost me. Part of that cost is making sure your ranch is available when needed. Do you get it?"

Laura walked into the kitchen. Putting the scotch bottle up in the liquor cabinet, she noticed her hands were shaking. She went into the dining room and sat down.

Vague and dark shapes began to coalesce in her consciousness. Otabiano and Raquel Vasquez, Pete's beloved grandparents. The stranger whose blood and viscera sprayed over the walls in the old ranch house. An evil thing had invaded the land and forever changed what had been considered inviolable. She knew that from the first time she heard of the killings.

Now, Pete was hinting at something even darker—that he had some part in three horrific deaths. She held the phone away from her face and looked at it. Who was this person she was talking to? Pete Vasquez had been her schoolmate, her lover, confidante, and lately, her financial savior. Surely, he could not be the same person. Laura had an overwhelming sense of being tainted. "Oh, Pete. What have you gotten me into?"

"Babe, you didn't ask questions 'cause you didn't want answers. As long as you got your house back, you didn't care," Pete sneered.

"Pete—"

"Shut up, please, Laura. I gave you the money. You don't ever need to know where it came from. You just need to know that there were strings attached. I didn't expect I would ever have to let you know any of this. So, you just enjoy your life right now, and don't ever mention this to anyone, ever. Are we clear?"

Laura sat at the dining room table looking at the blank spot where Saenz's portrait had hung. "What's going to happen to me, Pete? What if I do mention it? What happens then?" She wasn't arguing with him now. Heart racing, she sensed that her insular life had just ended.

His humorless laughter sounded funereal. "I don't want you to die, girl. But if you so much as look cross-eyed about selling your border property, I'm a dead man—and you're a dead woman. I can't protect you. They" —he didn't say who, but she could guess— "they'll kill you. It makes absolutely no difference that you are living in San Antonio and not in Nuevo Laredo. They can reach you just as easily in either place."

Laura began to cry softly.

Pete's voice softened. "Laura, please listen to me. Please. I didn't start out to get you or anyone else into anything like this." He was almost pleading now. "I wasn't given any choice. Some things happened, and I wasn't given a choice. I wish I could take it back, but I can't."

"Pete, your grandparents. Did you have something to do with their killing? Did you? Those two folks raised you, for God's sake! Did you? Did you?"

He didn't respond.

She began to shout. "You fucking bastard! Did you?"

"I can't say any more. But you have to listen to me. No one was supposed to get hurt. You weren't supposed to have ever found out anything. Oto and Raquel were my *grandparents*. You think I would do anything that I thought would get them killed?"

Pete's volume matched Laura's, then grew ragged. "But something went wrong. I don't know what, but it did. I don't want anything to happen to you, or anyone else. And it will, if you do or say anything about your old man's place."

"Who else have you put in danger, Pete?"

He blew out a gust of air. "Just about anyone who looks too close."

"Like who?"

"Purdy Kendricks, for one. Maybe anyone associated with him. He's asking too many questions."

The line went dead.

The next morning, a recording of the intercepted phone conversation was hand-delivered to Eddleman. He loaded it into his office computer's drive and put on his headphones. When the conversation ended, he punched the intercom button. "Leroy, get everyone together." There was no need to say more.

The small group of agents running Pete Vasquez met in an unoccupied safe house.

"How can we expect the *Zetas* to keep using Vasquez?" one asked. "He seems to be getting in the headlines, whether we like it or not."

Another commented, "Laredo PD isn't happy about what's going on. It makes them look bad when some yokel comes in and takes out three shitbirds, and on a case that didn't even happen here."

Finally, Eddleman looked around. "Petey boy didn't tell us about paying off this Saenz woman's debts when we debriefed him. He's no different from anyone else. He only wanted to tell us enough for him to get by. Wanted to keep his squeeze out of this." He filled in the group on Laura Saenz, her divorce, and the sudden pay-off on the mortgage. "Better we found out about this now, rather than later." He turned to the agents. "You think the *Zetas* will take out Vasquez?"

No one was taking bets either way.

Unless things quieted down, all agreed that his usefulness to the DEA would be minimal.

"I'm guessing the *Zetas* still see him as a necessary link in the supply chain," Eddleman observed, smiling. "We've got someone who Pete will lie for. He's been dipping in that honey pot, and I'm sure he doesn't want her to die. You heard his voice. He was begging her." Holding up the CD of the phone intercept, Eddleman continued, "And I think we've found a way to stop Deputy Purdy Kendricks from straying off the reservation. Someone who'll convince Deputy Kendricks that he needs to back off."

"Who?"

"Deputy Kendricks's old love, Laura Griffin Saenz."

FIFTY-SIX

Present Day

PURDY KENDRICKS

After breakfast at the Cenizo Cafe, Forrest and I went fishing, but not in the Rio Grande. Betty's worries about her only child's welfare were open and raw, so there was no going back to the river crossing near Lágrimas, at least for now.

Paula had driven to San Antonio to buy beauty supplies the week before, and I asked her to swing by a sporting goods store. She came back with a new Shakespeare Ugly Stik Junior Spincast combination, now proudly displayed in a slot of the truck's rifle rack.

Clutching a $5 bill, Forrest ran into the Stop Inn to the refrigerator where the earthworms were cooled. I shut off the truck engine and rolled down the window, allowing the scent of curry to waft in from the next-door Mesa Tourist Court. The motel's room rate was reasonable, but I caught myself wondering whether any travelers complained about the no-extra-charge cooking odors and occasional sitar music that emanated from the manager's quarters.

I watched as Forrest plunked down his money, got his change, and waved goodbye to one of the Patels. That I didn't recognize the store clerk didn't surprise me. Jagir's family was large and seemed to add a new member on a regular basis.

"C'mon, Daddy. Let's go!" Forrest slammed the door and put the Styrofoam earthworm container in the console bin. "Where are we going today?"

One of the few perks of rural law enforcement is the generally good relations with landowners. To ensure access to ranch pastures, many provided the Sheriff's Office with gate keys. With this access came permission to fish in the ranches' earthen stock tanks. "We'll see. Let's stop by the office, and you can say hello to Mr. Jake, while I figure that out."

We pulled up in the shade of the courthouse trees, and Forrest ran for the door. Adjusting my eyes to the building's interior, I paused. Forrest and Jake were already in some kind of discussion. I walked down the hallway to the key locker, considering which rancher had recently stocked tanks with bass or catfish. I unlatched a key with a tag marked *Johnson* and walked back into the dispatch area. Forrest, just minutes earlier in a hurry to catch a fish, listened quietly as Jake took a radio call from a trooper working U.S. 90. The trooper had pulled over a Suburban traveling 85 in a 70, with an expired registration. Jake cleared the driver of any warrants, and the stop continued routinely.

"Let's go, Forrest."

Forrest listened to the radio traffic for a few more seconds, got a high-five from Jake, and skipped toward the glass door.

"Where y'all going to be, Purdy?"

"Bar LJ's east pasture. I think Lowell said they stocked the front tank with bass last year, and I've pulled some decent cats out of there."

Jake nodded. "Someone said they got a five-pounder a week ago. You guys have fun. You be back before dark?"

I nodded, and then thought of Abner Selman's comment about information leaking out of the department. "Jake, you remember the phone call from that guy named Eddleman?"

Jake paused, appearing to think about it. "Yeah, vaguely. Why?"

"I'm just trying to figure out where I've met him but can't seem to place his face. Do you ever recall anyone by that name around here?"

"Don't think so, Purdy, but I can go back through old phone and dispatch logs if you want me to. How far back would I have to look?" The sudden rush of color to his cheeks belied Jake's expressionless countenance.

I waved him off. "Nah, don't worry about it. Just wondering. No big deal. Will you be here when we get back?"

Jake looked relieved that the subject had changed. "No, I'm just subbing today, get off at six tonight."

Smiling, I turned and walked to the truck. I had just found Eddleman's source in the Sheriff's Office.

I turned off U.S. 90 and drove five miles on a dirt trail labeled as a "county road" to an entrance to the Bar LJ Ranch. Unlocking the gate, we drove the mile or so to the stock tank. The next three hours were spent helping bait hooks and stringing Forrest's several catfish and sun perch. While we watched the red plastic bobbers, I answered a volley of questions about fishing, which dogs made the best pets, and seemingly, anything else a five-year-old could think of.

"Daddy, you know what I want to be when I grow up?" Forrest asked as I untangled a tangled line.

"No, son. What do you want to be?"

He tipped his baseball cap up, then squeezed my arm. "I want to be a policeman, just like you."

I reached and hugged my son, tears welling up. My chest ached, as I tamped down a sudden and almost uncontrollable urge to cry. Forrest began squirming, so I opened my arms, trying to wipe my eyes.

"Are you alright, Daddy? Did I say something wrong?"

"No, son, you sure didn't. It's just that sometimes grownups cry when they're happy."

"Are you happy, Daddy?"

"Forrest, you always make your daddy happy. My love for you is bigger than...than, what?" It was a game we had played since he began to talk.

Forrest said, "As this stock tank!"

"Oh, no! Bigger."

He turned, looking at the low range of hills in the distance. "As those mountains!"

"No. Bigger!"

Pretending to be exasperated, Forrest demanded, "Then bigger than what?"

He knew what the answer would be but flew into my arms with glee as I shouted, "Bigger than this whole big world!"

We laughed and he went back to fishing. The thought of my son in harm's way sent a sense of dread through me,

As the sun dipped toward the distant hills, I began to wonder when my son would wind down. Throwing the fish in the ice chest, I drove to the gate. A dust trail indicated an approaching pickup, as I swung the metal gate closed. Responding to the darkening skies of early evening, the truck's headlights clicked on as it slowed. I reached under the front seat and slowly put my automatic in my pocket. It wasn't until he was right up on us that I saw the driver was Lowell Johnson, Jr.

Killing his engine, the ranch owner's son and publisher of the *Kickapoo County Register,* climbed out and shut the cab door. "Hey, Purdy. Betty said you guys were fishing." Lowell was still dressed in what he called his "publisher clothes," consisting of western cut pants, ropers, long sleeved shirt with bolo tie, and an unbuttoned vest.

I glanced at him quizzically and Lowell noticed. "She said you weren't headed to Lágrimas, so I figured you'd be on a tank somewhere. Stopped at the SO, and Jake let me know where you were." He spotted Forrest. "Hey, young man, you catch any?"

Forrest leaned out of the driver's window and assured Lowell that we were on our way to skin, scale, gut, and eat quite a few fish. Lowell laughed as we shook hands.

"What can I do for you, Lowell?"

Johnson was two years younger than me, and we had played high school football and baseball together. We had always been friends, but not especially close ones. Lowell was editor, publisher, reporter, and photographer for the county's weekly, which operated from a small office near the square in Santa Rosa.

'Some folks are wanting me to interview and write a story on you, Purdy."

I turned to Forrest. "I'm walking Mr. Johnson back to his truck. Sit tight, and we'll head home in a minute." I turned toward Lowell's truck, so he would have to follow me if he wanted to continue the conversation.

"Lowell, what do you want to interview me about?"

To this point, the coverage of the Griffin Ranch murders had only included quotes from TJ. There had been no coverage of the body in the river, nor the discovery of AK-47 shell casings at the Lágrimas crossing.

"Like it or not, Purdy, you're kind of a newsworthy character." Lowell looked down at his dust-covered boots, and polished one on the back of his pants leg. "I got a call from the Laredo newspaper suggesting that I write a 'personal interest' story on you. They would pick it up and re-print it. Said it could hit the wire services and help get the *Kickapoo County Register* on the map, so to speak."

That was the last thing I needed, especially after what had been relayed to me this morning at the Cenizo Café. "No way in hell, Lowell. First, TJ would have to approve it, which he won't, and second, I don't want the publicity."

Lowell didn't seem too upset by my refusal. "I figured you would say that."

"Christ, Lowell. I don't need this right now. I'm sorry." I paused, and taking a chance, decided to talk a bit more. "Lowell, I'm hearing at the Cenizo that folks, especially Mexican folks, aren't too happy with the way this whole thing is going right now. I'm getting a real bad feeling that some of them are worried the cartels and their evil is headed this way, if they're not already here." Lowell had his head down, so I squatted a bit to look under the brim of his Stetson. "This is between us, *amigo*. What are you hearing?"

He started buffing the other boot. "I'm hearing all sorts of stuff, Purdy. Most of which is third hand addle-minded bullshit. But some.... I don't know." He nodded. "You're right about *latinos* being edgy, though. I'm just a *bolillo* youngest son who's too stupid to help his daddy run a multi-million dollar ranch, and who wears a felt hat and a vest in the middle of summertime. But I've had this pissant newspaper up and running for seventeen years now, and I've learned to sense, you might say, Santa Rosa's vibrations. I drink coffee with Father Joe." He used Father Joseph Levant's nickname. "And, while not disclosing anything from the confessional, he's hinted that some of his parishioners are acting distracted and worried."

Lowell was talking to me, man-to-man, and not reporter to interviewee. I relaxed. "I'm distracted and worried too, *amigo*."

I caught myself looking down to see if Lowell would start buffing his boots again.

"Daddy, I'm hungry. Can we go now?"

We both looked over at Forrest. His interruption ended the conversation, at least for now. I stuck my hand out and Lowell shook it. "I'm worried, Purdy. It's not about our sheriff's race. There's not a nickel's worth of difference between TJ Johnson and Clarence Livermore. They're both boobs. They both proved the validity of the Peter Principle when they were elected to leadership positions in 4H." Lowell laughed at his witticism, then turned somber. "Kickapoo County has been spared a lot of what's gone on elsewhere on the border. I'm not so sure that's the case anymore. You be careful, Purdy."

"You're the second person today to tell me that, Lowell."

"Who's the first."

"'Beulah."

He snorted. "Shit. I must be in good company then. She's got a better sense about what's going on around here than anyone." Lowell waved at Forrest, who was leaning out of the driver's side window, making faces in the rear-view mirror. "That's a fine boy."

My throat tightened. "Yes, he is indeed."

"Take care, Purdy. If I hear anything, I'll pass it along. You catch the Vasquez's killers, but please be careful." He nodded at Forrest. "There's more to life than fixing that mess."

We pulled into the driveway after dark. Betty pushed open the carport's screen door, relief on her face. There was no denying that recent events were taking a toll on her. Forrest, blissfully unaware of the tension, quickly relayed the afternoon's events. Betty scaled the perch, while I filleted the catfish. Forrest kept up a running commentary.

"I got worried," she whispered. "I called. It went to voicemail."

"Bar LJ's east pasture. No cell coverage. By the time I got a bar, we were three miles from home."

The tightness in Betty's voice triggered my sense of guilt. The killings, investigation, and my involvement were taking a toll on her.

"I'm sorry, hon. I'll try to work something out where we're in phone range from now on."

Betty said, "Forrest, come take your fish to the kitchen sink and start rinsing them, please."

She turned as she went through the screen door. "Apology accepted, Purdy. Just remember, I've only got one husband and one son. I don't want to be worrying about either one of them any more than I have to." A small smile creased her face.

Supper was fried fish, hush puppies rolled by Forrest, and a salad. His engine finally began to run down, and the boy announced that he wanted to take a bath, brush his teeth, and go to bed. Betty tried to hide her look of pleased amazement at this sudden show of maturity.

"Where did that come from?" Betty beamed. "Did you and he have some man-to-man talk? I can't remember a time when our son voluntarily bathed."

"I can't take credit for that, Betty." I turned to her while drying the dishes. "Truth be told, he's got an incredible mother who does far more than I do to make sure he grows up right. He's just taking one of those steps you've taught him about."

Betty gave me a hug, then went to make sure Forrest washed behind his ears. I looked at the scratched finish of the cabinets, and the burned spots on the Formica countertop. At that moment, the lived-in kitchen in our rent house looked beautiful. I didn't want anything or anyone to endanger it.

FIFTY-SEVEN

Pete Vasquez

PRESENT DAY

The first Vasquez Plumbing Contractor's truck rolled out of Monterrey at 6:30 a.m. There were no Luthers; Pete's new bosses made sure of that. The semi's driver, unaware of the rig's additional contents, began its run north, clearing the border inspection before noon. Pulling into the company warehouse, the driver turned in his logbook, manifest, and import documents, and waved to Pete as he drove out of the yard.

The call came five minutes later. "Your *remolque*" —the caller gave Pete the trailer's license plate number— "it's going to Houston tomorrow."

Vasquez closed his office door. He held the encrypted cell phone—given to him by the *Zetas*—to his ear but didn't answer. Finally, he answered. "Sure, it is, but how...."

"You tell tomorrow's driver he's not deadheading back. He's picking up a load to bring back." The caller gave Vasquez the address —a warehouse district near the Houston Ship Channel.

"What's he bringing here? I didn't get any calls...." Pete suddenly felt stupid. It didn't matter what was being freighted back. His new employers were off-loading their product. Whatever was coming back to Laredo was a cover.

"You fuck this up, *carnal,* you won't be any good to us. So, let's get *nuestros negocios* up on the right foot, *comprendes*?"

Pete nodded, and then realized the Zeta couldn't see his reaction. "Yes."

"*Pues, bien. Oye*, you know this *pinche chereef*, Purdy Kendricks?"

Again, "Yes. We grew up together."

"He's asking around about you, *carnal*?"

"Not anymore, I don't think. Why?"

"He fucked up some of the fuckers with *La Familia Norteña*. Put three of them in hell, *carnal*. You know that. You watch TV. Lucky for you, those three dudes weren't any of ours. He was sniffing around Laredo, and it was all about you and *tus abuelitos*, man."

Eddleman hadn't told him the details. *Doesn't trust me, the shitbird.*

The Zeta spent more time on the phone than Pete expected, trusting in the Blackberry's encryption, he presumed. "What's this Purdy like, man? He got shit for brains—try to cause you trouble, eh?"

Pete's mind raced. His childhood companion could be doggedly stubborn. It would be a relief to back him off, but with the *Zetas*, that would mean killing Purdy. "No. He's not."

"Good. 'Cause if he makes trouble for you, that's trouble for us, and you become less than *mierda* to us, get it? And so does your *chica* in San Antonio, and so does he."

Pete's legs began to give out on him. His mouth was dry, heart pounding. "I can't do anything about Kendricks." He paused and added, "He'll give up, because I didn't do anything, anyway." *I don't want to even suggest that you bastards got me in the middle of a cartel killing. I won't make it through the night alive.*

"That's right, Señor Vasquez. You don't know nothing. You didn't do nothing. We get the idea you think otherwise, well…" The Zeta laughed and sang the first two lines of Jose Alfredo Jimenez Sandoval's *ranchera* classic, *Camino de Guanajuato*, then laughed and disconnected.

No vale nada la vida. La vida no vale nada.

Life is not worth anything. Life is worthless.

FIFTY-EIGHT

Present Day

PURDY KENDRICKS

We made love after Forrest fell asleep. Betty surprised me with the ferocity of her need. My appreciation for her almost raunchy quest for a climax was mingled with fear of this unexpected sexual aggressiveness. She drew me into her and, with eyes closed, urged me loudly not to come until she was finished. Teeth clenched, she demanded I suck her breasts as she rode me to a screaming finish. She collapsed onto my chest as I grabbed her buttocks and thrust into her, letting out an involuntary cry.

Her ragged breath huffed on my neck as she giggled. "Shhhh. You'll wake the boy."

"Look who's talking." I stroked her back, waiting for my heart to slow.

She raised her head, kissing me gently. "Cover us with a sheet. I'm getting cold up here."

I struggled to find the scattered bedcovers. We rolled onto our sides, and I pulled the sheet over us. She kissed my eyelids, cheeks, and forehead. Suddenly she thrust her tongue into my ear. Goosebumps ran down my arms, and I involuntarily pulled away, laughing. Betty held my neck and stuck her tongue in my mouth. I could feel myself hardening again.

"Hmm," she teased. "Did I just feel something get big down there? You think you might have enough for another round?"

Smiling in the near darkness, I said, "I'm having heart palpitations. Give me a few minutes and we'll see."

After round two, we talked until two in the morning.

"What's going to become of us, Purdy?"

We were in a better place than I could recall. "It's been a rough go, but I don't want to lose this." I stroked her flank. "I don't want to lose you."

I could feel her turn her face toward me.

"The only way you'll lose me is if you choose that option." She paused. "I've made my peace with being in Santa Rosa. We were together in Houston. But, Purdy, you weren't ever there, even when you there. You know what I mean?" She didn't wait for an answer. Betty was talking through something now, and I just needed to listen. "I lived with you when you crawled into a bottle, and I've cheered when you crawled back out. I'm real proud of you, husband. I just know neither I nor Forrest can go there again."

I shifted uncomfortably.

"I'm saying all this to let you know that I'm here for the long run, unless you choose otherwise."

"I've made my choice. I'm willing to move, do something else, if it makes you happy, Betty."

"I think what's going to really matter is what makes you happy. 'Cause we can move, but we bring us with us, if that makes sense."

I blew out a long gust of air. "I'm slow, but starting to get it. I'm good at being a cop. Used to love it, in fact. Now, all I want to do is get this mess at the Griffin place behind me, so I can think clearly about something else."

Betty rolled over, snuggling against me, then pulled my arm over to hold her breasts. "You think that's going to happen, hon? I mean, we all know one of the cartels killed the Vasquezes and that other fellow. Even if you wanted to, you'll probably never find, much less arrest, whoever did that. So, who's left?" She waited a beat. "Your old buddy, Pete Vasquez. So, he's somehow involved. As much as you have no use for Pete now, and I'm not sure what all that's about and you've never told me, you surely can't believe whatever he did was meant to kill the two folks who raised him."

I had chosen long ago not to share my reasons about why Pete's and my friendship had badly soured. I wasn't going to go there now with my wife. "No," I said, "I don't think he meant to get his grand-parents killed. I saw him when he found Oto and Raquel. I've never seen someone in that much anguish. But, something he's done caused those two good people to be murdered."

Betty pulled the sheet up higher. "Purdy, if you figure that out, then what? I suspect Pete's made his own hell on earth. What do you think anyone can do to make it worse?"

The longer the case dragged on, the more I had pondered the ques-tion. There were still no answers. "I don't know. I feel like I'm in over my head, and I don't know how to get out." Once spoken, the reality of the situation sank in further.

"I've always heard that if you're in over your head, quit digging."

Ouch.

Betty turned, kissed me, and said, "Let's get some sleep. You need your rest, you big stud." She rolled back, and within seconds was asleep.

S unday usually meant sipping coffee in the Parish Hall to avoid adult Sunday School, and later, making excuses for not having Sunday dinner with Paula and her family. Betty raised an eyebrow when I asked what her class was studying.

"Book of Acts. Why? You thinking about joining us?"

"Yes."

Betty turned away quickly, blushing. I felt a moment of shame at how little it took to make her happy, and how I had been avoiding making the effort. It would have taken so little to have put the attitude away and gone willingly on Sundays with her and our son.

A few folks gave me concealed startled looks when I sat down with the class. Within a few minutes, I felt welcomed—and relieved. Betty's poker-face belied her obvious pleasure. After the service, we headed to Paula's house.

"Did you tell your sister I'm coming? It's been awhile. Don't want to shock her." Paula was no stranger to our strained marriage, and I wondered if I was pushing my luck with Sunday appearances.

Paula greeted us at the door with hugs, and Forrest disappeared with his three cousins into the back yard. Paula's husband, a burly telephone lineman, turned on the TV, giving me some cover. The two women disappeared into the kitchen, while the NFL pre-season game allowed me to avoid much discussion, other than mumbling what I hoped were appropriate responses to comments about unknown football players and draft picks.

Dinner consisted of fried chicken, mashed potatoes, green beans, a store-bought cake for dessert, and incessant instructions on manners to four small hellions.

Paula, often gimlet-eyed around me, patted me tenderly on the shoulder, while setting a slice of cake in front of me. The sisters had obviously been talking, and my stock had risen, at least for the moment.

I left Betty and Forrest at Paula's, while the kids were having a great time building a fort out of cardboard boxes. I turned down a ride, needing to walk off the heavy meal. The five-block walk to the Sheriff's Office would do me good. I figured I'd have time for one or two songs on the way. I hit shuffle and play and pushed in the iPod's ear buds. Nina Simone's 1965 version of *Strange Fruit* came through. The anger in her voice as she sang of lynchings of African Americans in the South was palpable. The lyrics hardly matched my mood or the good weather, but I let the song run through. Billie Holliday's version was the best, but Nina nailed it.

Jake wasn't the dispatcher on duty. I was relieved. Closing the door to my office, I opened the Vasquez file on the computer, and for the hundredth time, reviewed my notes. Eddleman had warned me off of Pete Vasquez. My trip to Laredo to force the issue had been stupid. At least some of Kickapoo County's mostly Hispanic population was worried.

It was time to sit quietly and think.

FIFTY-NINE

Eddleman

PRESENT DAY

The DEA's drone was high enough and small enough that the Vasquez Plumbing Contractor's driver and the warehouse workers couldn't detect it. Eddleman sat in a parked van three blocks away, watching the live, high-resolution shots of the truck backing up to a large warehouse loading dock. A large commercial door rolled up, and three men came onto the dock. The truck shut down, and the Vasquez driver opened the trailer's rear doors. Soon pallets were set on the loading dock, but no one went into the back of the trailer. One man engaged the driver, and Eddleman watched as he appeared to urge the driver to get out of the sun.

"That son of a bitch wants Pete's driver the hell out of the way," said a bearded agent sporting a Houston Astros ball cap. "These assholes figured this guy would head inside and get out of this heat," Two other agents anxiously watched the large monitor. Eddleman punched in Pete Vasquez's number.

"Vasquez here," Pete whispered.

"Where are you, Pete?" asked Eddleman. "And why are you whispering?"

"In my office." Pete coughed, then said in a normal tone, "And I don't know why I'm whispering, other than I'm scared shitless. You know, seeing as how you're talking to me right now, and that can't be good."

Eddleman smirked, "You've been in this business for awhile.

You're just working for a different employer." Reminding Vasquez of the *Zetas* caused Vasquez to squirm. Eddleman enjoyed making Vasquez squirm. "Time to earn your keep with the good guys, buddy boy. You need to call the driver who took your shitters to Houston. Right now."

"Why?"

"Let's just say he needs to get out of the sun and have a nice conversation with his boss about how his truck is running, or his family, or the goddamned weather. You call him, right now. We need him occupied."

"I don't get it."

"Hold on." Eddelman punched mute and shook his head. He turned to the other agents. "The *Zetas* have got to get this load off the truck. I don't want them to kill Vasquez's driver. And they'll do it if he keeps hanging around that fucking trailer. Those homeboys have got orders, and if that driver smells a rat, they won't hesitate. They fuck this up, they're dead too. Any suggestions on what our boy Vasquez should tell him to get him away from the area?"

No one answered. Eddleman unmuted the DEA's encrypted cell and started to say something, then shut up, punching on the phone's speaker. The DEA agents all could hear Vasquez on the other cell phone.

"Hey, my driver's out there, and I'm having trouble getting through on his cell. Yeah. Name's Art Villegas. Yeah. No shit it's hot. Yeah. Hey, can you shout at him and have him call my cell on your land line?" Vasquez recited a phone number to whoever was on the other end. "Thanks. I've gotta talk to him about picking up another load. Can you make it quick?" Another pause. "Yeah, I appreciate your business. Tell your boss you guys are always welcome if you get down this way."

There was a pause. Vasquez's voice came over the speaker on the DEA's cell phone. "How'd I do?"

The agents watched as the drone's camera showed a man leaving the warehouse office and gesticulate toward the truck driver. The driver, presumably Villegas, walked toward the office, and the two men engaged in conversation. Villegas followed the man into the office.

The ball-capped agent said, "Look. The homeboys just got busy."

Eddleman watched as a forklift with an empty pallet drove inside the trailer. Several men coming out of the warehouse followed it. Suddenly, the forklift backed out of the supposedly empty trailer, this time with the pallet holding a large bundle wrapped in plastic.

"Bingo. They got their dope."

Eddleman unmuted the phone. "You did fine. What are you going to tell your driver?"

"Shit. I'll make up something."

The agents heard a cell phone ring.

"Gotta go. Not bad huh?" Pete disconnected.

"Cocky fucker," an agent snorted, obviously relieved.

Ten minutes later, the Vasquez Plumbing Contractors' driver left the office holding a sheath of papers.

"Manifest?" wondered Eddleman aloud. Then he snapped his fingers, drawing other agents' attention back to the monitor. "Oh, shit. This isn't good."

The driver was gesticulating to one of the warehousemen. His hand gesture was obvious: he made circles with one finger around the side of his head.

"He's telling one of the homeboys that his boss is crazy."

Eddleman shook his head.

The ball-capped agent said, "And that's bad, how?"

"'Cause I'm betting the Mexican side of this little operation will soon be wondering why, in the middle of an off-load, Pete Vasquez suddenly calls his driver on the phone, at the most critical time. How they got so damned lucky that the driver didn't have to be taken out."

"Shit."

Eddleman nodded. "Shit is right. The *Zetas* will kill anyone they even *think* might suspect something. If I was one of their *honchos*, I'd be saying to myself, 'Now our new transport flunky, who we don't trust anyway, he suddenly calls our warehouse office, and presto, his driver gets out of the way. Now how would he even know to do that? Could we have made a mistake? Is *Señor* Vasquez perhaps playing for another team? Could that team be the fucking *norteamericanos* and their fucking DEA?'"

Another agent chimed in. "We couldn't let them kill that driver, could we?"

"Probably not," said Eddleman. He wasn't so sure. "We may have just fucked up, boys. Let's get ahold of Vasquez quick. He's going to have to come up with a good story. In the meantime, some of us sit on this warehouse. If our eye in the sky shows a lot of activity, I'll bet someone is making arrangements to move the dope out of there quickly."

Eddleman called an Assistant U.S. Attorney, arranged for a search and arrest warrant for the warehouse, and put a take-down tactical team on stand-by. He called the DEA agent working at Vasquez Contractors and explained the latest turn of events.

"Keep a closer eye than usual on Vasquez. I don't want him to bolt, but I don't want him grabbed either."

Then he called the agent named Leroy.

"I'm stuck in Houston," he said, and explained the situation. "You need to face-to-face with Vasquez. He needs to know that the *Zetas* may have some questions, and if he doesn't answer right, he's dead."

SIXTY

Pete Vasquez and Laura Griffin Saenz

PRESENT DAY

"I'm *running* out of money." Laura rehearsed the line several times. "I'm running *out* of money. I'm running out of *money*." Where to put the emphasis? She settled on "*I'm* running out of money, motherfucker." Much better. She punched in Pete's cell number, silently practicing as she waited for him to connect.

Both the DEA and the *Zetas* used cutting-edge Sting Ray tracking devices, which pinpointed each of their cell phones with an accuracy of less than two meters. America's porous SS7 cell phone technology allowed both organizations to listen to what the two of them were saying.

"Hello?" Pete sounded distracted.

"*I'm* running out of money, motherfucker."

"What?"

Let's try again. "*I'm* running out of money, ***motherfucker!***" Emphasis with an exclamation mark. Much, much better.

It didn't have the reaction she expected.

"Laura, I'm busy right now. Can I call you back?"

"Pete, didn't you just hear what I said?" So, he wanted her to keep quiet and not sell the ranch. All well and good, but she was getting low on funds. Not critical, yet, but low enough to worry about.

"I'm having trouble making my bills, and the Bexar County Appraisal District just sent notice that property taxes are going up. I need your help."

Pete didn't have time to deal with Laura. Spending hours with the DEA agent he knew only as Leroy, had unnerved him. The guy was almost as spooky as Eddleman.

Pete had been practicing Leroy's suggested, and hopefully plausible, story if asked about his sudden phone call to his driver in Houston. *I don't need this shit right now.* "I've got problems of my own, hon. Big time."

She didn't ask what the problems were. He was relieved and simultaneously pissed. *Self-centered bitch.*

"You want more money? For what? I told you last time that wasn't my money." He thought a moment. "I'll tell you what, Laura. You get your old boyfriend off my ass, like I asked you to, and I'll see what I can do. Did you talk to Purdy yet?"

"No, but..."

Pete interrupted her. "No *buts*, Laura. Use your charms on that country boy. You're good at it. And you promised you would."

Suddenly, it dawned on Pete that he was no longer sure his phone was secure. "I can't talk right now. Really. I'll call you. I promise." It dawned on him that the DEA *and* the *Zetas* could be listening in.

"But Pete, it's important. I'm ..."

Pete paused and looked at the telephone number on his phone's LED. Laura *was* using her standard cell phone, and not the encrypted voice over internet (VOIP) he had bought for her on Amazon. *Oh, shit.*

"Shut up, Laura. I said I'll call you, and I will. I just can't talk right now." Pete's tone was getting through to her.

"Are you saying...?"

"Yes. Please shut up." Pete disconnected.

L aura's call came in while I was in my office. I hesitated and closed the door.

"Laura, what's going on?"

"Purdy, can we talk for a minute?" It sounded like she had been drinking, and I felt like kicking myself for taking her call.

"What has Pete ever done to you that you are causing him such grief?"

"What are you talking about?"

Ice cubes rattled in the background "You know what I mean. His grandparents are murdered, and you are telling everyone that Pete's involved in some way."

"Laura, I don't know where you're getting your information. I'm not telling anyone anything. I'm doing my job."

"Yeah, and that means trying to pin the killings on Pete."

"Who's telling you this? Pete?" I could feel myself getting angry, which was stupid and made me angry with myself. Arguing with a drunk wasn't going to get me anywhere. "I'm sorry. Let's start over. Why are you calling me?"

"I'm calling because I'm scared, and because you seem to hate Pete so much you are trying to pin a horrible crime on him." She paused. "And I want to know why. Why are you doing this to him?"

"I don't like Pete, Laura. Haven't for quite some time. But that's not what this is all about. There were three dead people at your ranch, and no one is walking into my office confessing to it. I'm just trying to find out who killed them."

"Maybe so, Purdy. But, you've got to know that Pete didn't kill his grandparents. No matter what you think of Pete, you've got to know that." Her voice was plaintive. "How can I convince you of that?"

"Do you know something about those killings, Laura? Something you haven't told me? Because, if you know something more than what you've said, I need to hear about it now!"

My demand was met with silence. Then, she asked quietly, "Are you still mad about what happened between us?"

"What are you talking about now?" But I knew.

"C'mon. It's been how many years now? Eighteen? Twenty? How many? You can't hold a grudge that long, can you?"

But I could. I took a deep breath. "You know what he did, Laura. To both of us."

She began to cry. "Oh, for God's sake. That's ancient history. Let it go! Let it go!"

I waited, not responding.

Laura didn't say anything, as if she was waiting for me to get myself together. "Pete didn't butcher anyone, Purdy. It just happened."

I stepped over and locked the door.

"You could have had the baby, Laura. You could have told me you were pregnant. We could have figured something out. We could have made a go of it. You didn't need to hide it from me."

Her voice sounded hard. "You were going off to A&M. You were a *boy*, Purdy. It would never have worked out. You know that."

"I loved you so much, Laura. I would have loved our child even more. And ..."

"And what? We get married, and everything is great, and we live happily ever after? Is that what you thought would happen? 'Cause it wouldn't have. We'd have hated each other soon enough." She laughed ruefully. "Hell, we can't see eye to eye on much even now."

Her words were becoming slurred. "Purdy, when you went off to college, it was over." As if to remind me, she screamed, "You and me —we were fucking over! Pete and I were already sleeping together. You knew that. You knew it because we both told you. I couldn't have your baby, Purdy. And Pete knew that, even if you didn't."

As I listened, I realized that the old unresolved pain was no longer there. "But the abortion! And you. Look what it did to you!"

"Oh, Purdy. It wasn't Pete's fault. At least, it wasn't all his fault."

I sighed, feeling drawn into long-ago events. "How can you say that? He found that abortionist in Piedras Negras. He paid for you to have it done. He didn't check out the guy or care. And this supposed doctor ruined you for childbirth as well! He knew he was putting you in harm's way and didn't care."

Laura's voice became quiet. "I forgave Pete a long time ago, if there was anything to forgive. We were young and stupid. And we made bad decisions. But Pete didn't cause that infection. He was there for me."

"Maybe so, but he wanted you. And aborting that baby ensured that I wouldn't be in the picture anymore." I was sounding like the spurned lover in a cheap soap opera. I had held it in for years, and the bile spilled out. "I think I could have lived with you having the baby and not wanting me. Raising him or her. You would have been a good mother. But Pete, he wanted that baby dead and gone. He found the cheapest way he could to abort that baby."

Laura began to argue. "How long have you carried this around? You would have blocked me out if you really loved your wife, Purdy. Truth is, you're still wishing for something that would have never happened."

It had taken a long time, but I realized much of what I was hearing was true. There was more to it, when it came to Pete Vasquez. I know how much he paid that butcher. The plain truth is that Pete, my former friend, didn't give a rat's ass. He got a Piedras Negras scam artist—not even a doctor—on the cheap."

I took a deep breath. "And you, are just too damned stubborn to admit that your lover of all these years ruined you. Your daddy would have paid for an abortion. He would have done anything for you. Always did. Abortions were legal and safe in Texas. You were so hung up on Pete that you let that snake in the grass sell you a bill of goods. And you still have your head up your ass."

She started to cry.

"That's an old trick, gal. I'm not buying it." As I said it, I knew that for the first time, I meant it. I also sensed that I had shattered her. I softened my tone. "I loved you more than life itself." No longer aching for a wished-for response, but just angry with myself for having wasted so much of my life in chasing something unattainable. "You've damned near cost me my marriage."

"What? How?"

"Just by being here. And being inaccessible. Betty has known about us from the get-go. She's taken second place in my heart since the start, and until now, I've let her do it. God help me."

Laura's phone call was bringing out the demons I had carried for years. She should have hung up, but she didn't.

"I'm so sorry, Purdy. I'm so sorry. I was happy when you married Betty. I hoped marrying a good woman would let you love a good woman and not obsess on me."

"I think you're a liar. I think you've enjoyed keeping me around in the background. You knew you could always pull my chain. I'd be there, in whatever form you needed. You loved it."

"I've been married and divorced four times. I haven't needed you."

"Oh yes you have. You need someone stupid like me who you can fall back on. That's over."

Most of what I had been saying was out of anger, or as a reaction to things from times long ago. Just now, I realized I was telling the truth. Laura no longer held sway in my heart. I felt that I had to go another step.

"Laura." No answer. "Are you listening?"

"Yes."

"I think Pete put you up to calling me. Hoping I'd react as I usually do when it comes to you. I think Pete's using you again."

She started to protest. "No one's using me, Purdy. You oughta know me by now."

"That's the problem. I do finally know you."

SIXTY-ONE

Present Day

PURDY KENDRICKS AND TJ JOHNSON

TJ Johnson, soon-to-be-former sheriff, if the case wasn't solved, called me into his office.

"Close the door, Purdy."

Not a good sign. I reached over and swung it closed.

"Grab a seat."

I made a point to sit in Ranger Selman's favorite chair, instead of one of the uncomfortable ones directly in front of TJ's desk. He reared back in his office chair and pulled his feet off the desk drawer that he kept pulled out as a footrest. A toothpick began to wander from one side of his mouth to the other.

"Anything gonna come of your visit to Laredo?"

If it did, he would use it as an excuse to fire me. Unfortunately, he would be justified in doing so.

"No. Word is that it's not even going to be presented to a grand jury for a No Bill."

Grand juries were often used to take the heat off prosecutors and police. A nameless group of citizens, meeting in secrecy, deciding *not* to indict someone, was enough of a rarity in Texas that those kinds of decisions were accorded a high degree of respect by the public.

"Laredo PD is pissed, but the reality is that those guys were professional killers. The DA isn't going to waste his time even going through the motions. Not enough public anger, despite the PD's hurt feelings."

TJ knew all this of course. The Rangers and God knows who else had kept him abreast of my ill-conceived escapade into Webb County.

"Good. Good." He nodded like a sagacious grandfather and feigned a sudden notion. "But speaking of Laredo, isn't there anything else you can do to prod Pete Vasquez?"

"Not unless you want me to kidnap him and shove bamboo under his fingernails to get him to confess." I smiled. "A grand jury subpoena isn't worth its weight in dog shit. You know that." I wasn't sure he did. "There's nothing much to take to a grand jury to indict." He knew that, too.

"I know. I know." There went the repeated response. "How about the Rangers? Abner says he's helping, but is it enough? I know our State Senator pretty well. He could jack 'em up some if we aren't getting enough help."

"Where are we going with this, TJ?"

He looked baffled. "What d'you mean, 'where are we going with this?' I'm just asking about the case."

"Sheriff, cut the shit." Maybe my renewed relationship with my wife was giving me some badly needed courage. "If you want to ask me something substantive about the investigation, ask me. But don't pull me into your office and play games."

TJ didn't even feign anger.

"All right. All right." Another double reply. "Purdy, we haven't gotten along. But I'll tell you, you've kept yourself sober—as far as I know—and have worked on this Vasquez mess as hard as anyone can." He paused, looking at a trophy mount as if the dead mule deer held some divine wisdom. "The local newspaper doesn't support me. My opponent has got some folks working against me. I think I may get beat this election."

Things must really be looking bleak for Johnson to admit this. He went on.

"Word is that if I'm gone, most of the deputies I've hired are gone, too." He shook his head. "I just want to protect my people. And I'm afraid if I'm gone, you'll be out of a job." He looked at the mule deer again.

TJ didn't give a shit about me and my job, but I played along. "Thanks for the concern, Sheriff. I know it's been rough. I'd like to wrap the case up, but I'm getting nowhere."

TJ veered again. "Abner tells me that he's getting no support. The Feds don't want us to look too closely at anything involving Pete Vasquez."

Again, old news.

"I know you thought well of the old couple, Purdy. And I mean no disrespect, but is it possible that those two had something to do with the drug trade?"

Where in hell was this coming from? "You're kidding, right? Oto and Raquel? Who's suggesting this story?"

TJ stirred uncomfortably and took the toothpick out of his mouth. "Calm down. I mean, think about it. They lived on the place for years. What do we know about them? Old Mexican couple. Mind their own business. Hardly ever see them in town. Isn't it possible that they just might have been doing something illegal?"

The bile rose in my throat. TJ had known the old couple for as long as I had. He knew what he was suggesting was beyond comprehension. I wanted to smash his face. Rather than lash out, I sat there watching him struggle as he tried to sell the theory.

"Think about it, Purdy. Griffin's old place is perfect for hiding stuff. That Shivelli character didn't just show up out there without them knowing about it. Maybe one of the drug cartels killed them because of what *they* were involved in, and they weren't just a nice old couple whom you and I knew forever and a day."

Quite a speech. I took a breath and played along. "So, what you're suggesting is that there could be an *alternative* theory, TJ? That Pete isn't involved. That, say Oto probably, was helping the bad guys and it came back and bit him and Raquel in the ass." I pretended I was thinking this through. "That would mean we could declare this case 'solved,' so to speak, and move onto other things."

"Exactly."

SIXTY-TWO

Present Day

PURDY KENDRICKS

The summer's heat sagged into Santa Rosa and felt as if it was not going to lift. TJ's desperate attempt at twisting the Vasquez's lives to enhance his reelection chances left me leaden inside.

Betty and I took Forrest and spent a night in a small motel in Junction. The rooms were clean, and it had access to the Llano River. I spent hours tossing a five-year-old, bunched into a cannonball, splashing into the water. Forrest's laughter was contagious.

After each toss, Forrest popped to the surface and immediately asked, "Was that the biggest one, Dad? How high was the splash?"

By the end of the afternoon, my left arm and shoulder ached.

Betty had splurged on a slightly revealing one-piece swimsuit and floated on an air mattress, usually avoiding the spray of Forrest's entries into the water. The sun brought out a spray of freckles on her sunburned face and shoulders. She looked stunning.

Returning to Santa Rosa, I avoided the sheriff, and spent some time on mundane matters. Two camp house burglaries didn't amount to much. Some canned goods and old clothing were stolen. Whoever had done them even closed the doors when they left. Since the structures were well off the highway, they were probably the work of desperate Mexicans traveling cross-country to avoid the Border Patrol. I was surprised the ranchers reported the break-ins. Most just left camp houses and line shacks unlocked with extra canned goods and plastic water jugs where they could be easily taken without someone tearing things up.

Betty and Paula had loaded up the kids and were spending two days in San Antonio visiting SeaWorld and Six Flags Fiesta Texas. The house felt lonely, so I spent long hours catching up on paperwork. I also relieved deputies who wanted to take some days off with their families.

On a Thursday afternoon, I checked to confirm that Jake wasn't at the dispatcher desk. I drove to his house. It was time to have the talk I had been putting off.

Some of the gray asbestos siding had broken off since I had last noticed. Pieces of the tiles lay where they had fallen. The front yard held no living thing other than grass burrs. In the chain link fence that divided Jake's property from its two neighbors, some of the metal ties had come undone. The mesh sagged, sometimes toward his house, sometimes away. The fence gate stood open with sand and gravel burying the lower few inches. Visible in the back yard was a mesquite tree. Oddly, it had been pruned and shaped, which had forced it to push upward. Now, its light green foliage provided some small shelter from the sun.

Jake's house squatted in the middle of the poorer part of Santa Rosa. Given the overall bleakness of our county seat, it wasn't much different from the more affluent areas. I glanced around. Working poor. Barbeque pits. Low slung, easy-to-assemble canvas and metal structures, which served as carports, oddly juxtaposed in a few of the driveways. I imagined an aerial photo would show nothing but a bleakness of browns and grays, small outbuildings, and rusting autos.

Mailboxes bore the names of Jake's neighbors. Armendariz. Lopez. Gutierrez. Poor but proud. Jake's lack of care for his mother's old house reflected badly on the neatness of the neighbors.

Jake's pickup sat facing the street, on the side under a dripping window swamp cooler. A quick glance showed this parking arrangement wasn't unusual. Santa Rosa's gypsum-ladened water had rusted a hole through the truck's bed. A cinderblock on the concrete porch propped open the screen door. The veneer was peeling off its wooden companion.

I tapped lightly. No answer. I knocked again, harder. Footsteps pounded from the back of the structure as Jake yelled, "I'm coming. Hold your water!"

He cracked the door open, a shocked look on his face. "Purdy! What are you doing here?" he stammered.

"Got a minute?" I didn't wait for a response; instead, I gently pushed the door open. He stepped out of the way, glanced outside as if to see if anyone else was nearby, and then quickly shut the door. Jake hurriedly turned on a pole lamp, relieving the darkness. The nearby desk held framed pictures of his mother, Sarah, and father, Elbert.

"Damn, Purdy, what's going on? You just come over without calling and barge in without a how-do-you-do." Jake was in his skivvies and an old t-shirt with a Curacao dive shop logo on the front. I momentarily wondered where he found the shirt, as he had never been farther than New Orleans.

Dirty dishes, computer magazines, and newspapers cluttered all the surfaces in the combination den and kitchen.

"Let's visit for a bit, shall we?" I shoved dirty clothes off a kitchen chair and sat down. Jake disappeared into what I remembered as a bedroom, reappearing with a folding chair. He pulled on a pair of jeans and arranged himself on the seat, then combed his hair with his hands and looked down at the floor.

"I remember your Mama with fondness, Jake." I nodded at her picture. "She was a good lady, and she was always kind to us kids." Elbert was a mean drunk, and Jake's long-suffering mother staggered from job to job around southwest Texas, trying to keep food on the table, while hiding any income in hidey holes around the house. In the midst of this sad odyssey Sarah had convinced a service station owner that she and Elbert could manage the place for him. An adjacent and dilapidated house went with the deal. Lágrimas, 20 miles from Santa Rosa, was dead bottom for the Nichols family. Sarah usually pumped gas, and Jake helped out around the station.

He barked a laugh. "She was. She was. Kept me in clothes and in school, which were miracles."

Jake, now soft and overweight, contrasted with the wiry kid I had grown up with. "You helped too, Jake. At eight, you could change a tire on an old, non-pneumatic tire changer. I can remember you pounding on a tire bar with both hands with a small sledgehammer, working a tire off a rim by yourself. You could patch a tube or tubeless tire and do a remount as fast as any adult by the age of ten."

"Had no choice. Daddy was usually passed out in the supply room, too drunk to help."

"Or beating on you 'til your mom got him to quit."

Jake's acne-scarred face showed rage at the memory. Then softened. "Purdy, your daddy helped put a stop to it a time or two, God bless his soul."

We sat quietly for a few minutes. I reached back in my memory of Jake's dad. Jake's darkened facial expression showed he was doing the same. Elbert Nichols worked off and on at the Santa Rosa Livestock Auction. Unless Sarah Nichols was there at 3 p.m. after the Thursday sales—or whenever Charlie Ross, the owner, paid out the hands—none of the money from that effort was converted into food from the Busy Bee Grocery Mart, or clothes from Mildred Perez's secondhand store, or Bill's Dollar Store on the main drag in Santa Rosa. That left the small income from selling gasoline, oil, and sundries like Cokes and Slim Jims to cover all the family's expenses. Thankfully, Elbert finally drank himself to death.

I broke the silence. "It was a tough go."

Jake looked around the room, absently rubbing his ravaged face. "I'm not sure Mama would be real proud of what I've become."

"Jake, we've known each other a long time, but this trip down memory lane isn't what I'm here for, you know?"

He hung his head. "Yeah, I think so." His voice was nearly inaudible.

I took a breath. "Who you been talking to about the Vasquez case, Jake?"

"I was told I can't tell, Purdy."

Suddenly angry, I grabbed a magazine and threw it at him. He flinched, putting up his hands to shield his face.

"I don't give a shit, Jake."

I reached over and threw an open cereal box. Raisin bran rained down on him as the box hit the wall over his head.

"I'm your friend, you asshole, and now you're fucking with me and my family! Tell me." I stood up and walked over to him. He cowered.

"I'm not going to hit you." I looked down at the top of a head of thinning hair. And was suddenly ashamed of myself.

I sat back down and waited. I didn't have to wait long. Jake seemed relieved to ease a burden he had been carrying.

"I got a visit about six months or so back," he said softly. "Late night knock on the door. I had just got in from a shift, so I was still up. Opened the door. There was this big guy asking to come in. Showed a badge. DEA. He said he needed to talk to me."

"Who was it?"

"Badge read Eddleman." He then described Jack Eddleman to a tee. "Said I could be a service to my country and law enforcement." Jake took a deep breath and slowly let it out. "Said they—I assumed DEA—was concerned about border drugs and such." Jake began to laugh. "He must have been reading my mail, Purdy. He knew I'm kind of a snoop, and that I know my way around a computer. Said that several federal agencies were 'worried about the integrity of sheriffs on the border with Mexico,' and my keeping him in the loop would" —at this point Jake made quote marks with his fingers "ensure that justice wasn't derailed."

"How?"

"Just report what's going on."

"What have you been telling him?"

"Not much of anything, 'cause there wasn't anything to tell. That is, until the killings on the Griffin place. Eddleman called, 'checking in' he said. Asked about the investigation."

Jake paused. "Purdy, I didn't think I had a choice."

"Of course, you had a choice, Jake."

He shook his head. "Purdy, I'm sorry. I truly am. But this Eddleman—he said I could help him get the goods on TJ. Asked me about the killings at the Griffin place. I told him he could call you or talk to the sheriff. That it wasn't something a dispatcher was going to know much about. Eddleman said that there was drugs involved. That the DEA's 'ongoing investigation' was to make sure that TJ wasn't covering up who did the killing."

"Don't tell me, Jake. You bought that?"

He shook his head. "At first, I sure did. Later, well, not so much. Seems like TJ just wants to get reelected is all. He's been a shitass with you 'cause no one's been arrested. But Eddleman's questions are always about you and Pete Vasquez." Jake began to cry silently.

"Christ. You must hate the sheriff more than I thought, Jake. Why did you even get involved?"

Wiping his eyes, he looked up dolefully. "TJ doesn't think I remember this, but after Daddy died, when TJ was a rookie sheriff's deputy, he'd come by this house and hit on Mama. And he was married. And we were broke. Mama was a decent woman, and proud." Jake straightened up, as if recalling his mother's fortitude. "The last time, I was around sixteen or so. I was outside and saw TJ's patrol car roll up. I slipped around the side of the house. I could hear the two of them. 'No, deputy. I've told you that before. Leave me alone.' That was Mama speaking. TJ got mad, and I heard him call Mama a bitch."

I didn't know what to say. He had never told me any of this before.

Jake's face grew red. "Mostly I remember him saying, 'You're tied down to that pock-faced creature you call a son. He'll grow up like his daddy, and you'll have struck out with everyone.'"

He stomped off and never came over again. But Mama saw me. She knew I'd heard what TJ had said to her, about her, and about me. I could see she had aged ten years." Jake picked up his mother's sepia photo, gently dusting it. "I remembered. I surely did."

I felt thoroughly soiled, and not because of Jake. He was a lonely, damaged soul. Eddleman had preyed on Jake and used both the good and the anger in Jake to make sure nothing about the Vasquez killings interfered with some scheme the DEA was involved in.

"How do you get in touch with Eddleman?"

"Mostly, he calls me to 'check in.' I've got his phone number, but I quit calling him lately."

"Jake." I stood up. "It's all right. From now on, let's have an agreement."

He peered up hopefully, as if I was going to throw him a life preserver in a raging storm. "What?"

"If you share stuff with the DEA, run it by me first. You and I both know TJ is too stupid to be corrupt. Or maybe not too stupid to be corrupt, but too stupid not to get caught. It's my investigation Eddleman's trying to derail."

"You? Why?"

"I can't say right now. Just don't talk with Eddleman anymore, at least without me knowing what's being said, okay?"

Suddenly, Jake rush at me, and pinning my arms to my side, hugged me. "Thanks, Purdy. Thanks."

"We're friends, Jake. This isn't going to change that." I broke his grip. My anger was long gone and, in its place, an aching sadness. I reach around his pudgy frame and hugged him fiercely.

SIXTY-THREE

Eddleman

PRESENT DAY

Things calmed down after the worries that the Vasquez phone call to his driver would force the cartel to move the drugs before they could be distributed. Other than workers' ins and outs in cars, nothing appeared to happen. No trucks. No large vans. The electronic tracking devices, imbedded by the DEA in the pallets, indicated no movement or relocation. It gave the agents some breathing room.

Several agents rented rooms at a Days Inn three miles from the warehouse. After three days of this, and with some of the tension easing, Eddleman took a break from the surveillance effort, hoping to catch some much-needed sleep.

Shortly after sunset on the third night after the *Zetas* off-loaded the contraband from the Vasquez Plumbing Contractors semi, the drone's infrared camera picked up a flurry of activity.

Wakened by the cell phone's ring, Eddleman groggily answered. "What?"

"We've got action at the warehouse."

"I'll be right there. Give me ten minutes." He made it to the surveillance van in six.

Eddleman and the three agents huddled around the monitor. "Anything from the trackers on the pallets?" he asked.

"Nope. And nothing on a pallet going out. But" —the agent indicated four large vans backed up to the loading dock— "these just came in."

"How many men in the vans?"

Another agent answered. "That's weird. Only one per van. The drivers."

The agents watched as cardboard boxes were loaded into each of the vans.

"Get ready to follow."

The vans departed, and DEA's cover teams picked them up as they entered Interstate 45, heading north.

Now comes the hard part, he thought. Eddleman contacted his superiors and explained what had been observed.

"We've got four vans moving. We don't have trackers on these vehicles. We couldn't get to them, but we should have enough people to keep them under observation." He was pleased. A chance was developing to take down distributors all over the United States.

Three hours later, he received a phone call from an agent following one of the vans. "Boss, we've got a problem."

Uh oh. "What?"

"Rain in Dallas. Like cats and dogs. The van I was following took the turn onto Loop 620, heading east. Lost control and flipped."

"Where are you?"

"Stuck in traffic. Emergency crews and police have got the ramp blocked, and we're behind it. We've got vehicles up on 620 running front cover, but they've pulled off."

"Wait one." Eddleman confirmed the three other vans were still on the road. Two toward Oklahoma City. One up U.S. 79, presumably toward Shreveport to pick up IH 20 inside the Louisiana border. "What about the contents?"

The agent could barely be heard over the driving rain. "I'm walking up there now. Other drivers are out trying to see what's going on, so I won't be too obvious." Three minutes later he called back.

"I'm not sure whether what I'm seeing will make sense. EMS is working on the driver. The boxes in the van are all over the road."

Eddleman quickly responded. "We've got to secure them. That's probably millions of dollars' worth of drugs."

"I'm not so sure. The boxes are soaked, and some have split open. I took a chance and IDed myself to a Dallas PD officer. Checked five or six of the boxes. The only thing in them was piñatas."

"What the fuck? Piñatas? Empty piñatas?"

"No, they're full of candy. It's all over the fucking place. The cop says that's all he's seen, too."

Eddleman rang off and turned to the surveillance crew. "Have DPS troopers pull over those other three vans. I don't care if they've got probable cause. Just tell them to do it. Now!"

Two vans were stopped north of Sherman, Texas. The third was pulled over outside of Jacksonville, Texas. The drivers, all Hispanics from Houston, professed to know nothing. Every box contained a piñata full of assorted candies.

DEA agents and Houston PD SWAT team members hit the Houston warehouse. Five local Hispanics sat, hands zip-tied, on the concrete outside the warehouse. A small cache of 9mm Glocks and several thousand rounds were found. Eddleman sat in the office. The search team came in.

"The trackers are still imbedded in the pallets." He indicated four empty pallets resting in the middle of the room. "We've run dogs through the entirety of the place. They've scented on the pallets and the area around them. We'll go back again to be sure, but we didn't find any narcotics."

Eddleman shook his head. "We were made. You won't find anything. They've used workers' vehicles to dribble the stuff out of there, under our noses. They must have known we were onto them."

The agents' faces told the story.

Eddleman muttered, "And if that's the case, our man Vasquez is made, too."

SIXTY-FOUR

The Zetas

PRESENT DAY

The DEA takedown at the warehouse was hardly a quiet thing. Within seconds of the property raid, phone calls were made. There were plenty of people living around the Houston Ship Channel willing to provide information on police activity.

Meantime, the live broadcast on a Metroplex TV station showed piñatas and candy strewn across an overpass south of downtown Dallas. The *Zetas* didn't receive an expected phone call from the van's driver. Since the wreck had broken his neck, it would have been difficult. There was much on-air conjecture as to why the driver of a rented, unmarked van, carrying a large number of piñatas, lost control in a fierce downpour.

The driver of the van heading to Shreveport was able to punch in a code on his cell phone as he was pulled over by Texas Highway Patrol.

At midnight, a meeting was called.

To the *Zetas*, the evidence was conclusive. Dubbed by the Mexican cops as "Cantinflas," Guillermo Blanco, the Zeta's Nuevo Laredo chief, looked like the long-dead Mexican actor. *"Matan los dos."* Kill them both.

"Porque la mujer?" asked a subordinate.

"Esa puta sabe demaciado." The whore knows too much.

Cantinflas continued in Spanish. "Our agreement with the *pocho*" —he meant a Hispanic posing as an Anglo— "was to get the product to where we wanted it. And the *pocho* was to guarantee us access to the river in the *condado de Kickapoo*. Does anyone believe we can be assured he's done either?" The question was rhetorical. Several at the table grunted angrily. The boss was mad and was working up a head of steam. The wise thing to do was to go along with what was being said.

Cantinflas looked at the dozen hard men sitting at the large table. "Perhaps Señor Vasquez is playing with us. More likely, the sanctimonious bastards in the *norteamericanos'* DEA have him by his short and curlies. That everything between him and us is *not* between him and us, but being shared with *nuestros enemigos.*"

Two bottles of mescal passed from hand to hand. Several *caguamas* —41-ounce returnable bottles—also made the rounds. The *Pacifico's* light lager made a good chaser. There was no fear of being overheard in the empty Nuevo Laredo restaurant. The business had closed during the first warfare over control of the plaza, 12 years before. At that time, American tourists decided that the possibility of good Mexican food wasn't worth the chance of getting caught in the daily crossfire of gang warfare. Nothing had changed since then.

Cantinflas continued, "We know Vasquez and the *blanquilla* talked too much."

Laughter erupted. Besides being a pejorative term for a female Anglo, *blanquilla* was a slang term for a hen's egg.

"We don't know everything he has told her." He sniffed, looked around. "Do any of you *pendejos* think this should not be done?"

Cantinflas didn't expect a response. "We know what must be done. To make a point to anyone on either side of the Rio Bravo that no one" —he slammed his fist on the table, startling several listeners *"no one* ever crosses the *Zetas.*"

Cantinflas sat back, trying to appear calm. "Cut his balls off. Stuff them in his mouth. The fucker's talking to the DEA. An example must be made."

The bottles made several more passes. Someone fired up a *mota.* It made the rounds. A small amount of calm settled in.

A Zeta commander muttered, *"Pues, parece que algunas veces, un poco sangre es necesario para dar vida a la tierra."*

Another broke into laughter. "As long as it's not my blood dripping on the ground, *carnal.* You ain't writing some dipshit *corrido.*"

"What about our men in the warehouse? All the product was gone. A few guns possibly, but that's all. Most are American citizens. *Fianzas* will be set. They will want to be bailed out." The speaker was a short man dubbed *Cuarenta-y-cinco* for his love of the Colt of the same caliber.

Blanco stared at the mescal bottle. "Arrange for their bonds. Get them out of jail. Question them. Then, kill them."

Cuarenta-y-cinco's face was ravaged by untreated acne, and a childhood ravaged by street fights. His broad, pock-marked face, fearful at the best of times, now formed into a rictus showing his displeasure. "All? *Hijo.* They are just *soldados.* They didn't even know enough to betray anyone. Why them?"

"Because it happened. And it shouldn't have. We all have agreed. When an arrangement is compromised, there is no 'soul searching.' The house is cleaned, and we move on."

Cuarente-y-cinco took another hit on the *mota* and shrugged. "*Y los oficiales? Los de la policia? Ese pinche sherife de la frontera?*" He touched the heavy automatic in his waistband. *I want to kill a fucking norteamericano cop,* he thought. *Maybe this is my chance.*

Blanco's bloodshot eyes looked like the insides of a furnace. He waved the bottle at the killer. He was one of few men who dared make Cuarenta-y-cinco feel like a cockroach.

"Let me think on that one. In the meantime, where's Vasquez?"

"Still at his business. Our watchers say he hasn't left for the day."

"Who's there?"

Cuarenta-y-cinco speed-dialed a number. In a few seconds, he responded. "They say three or four workers. No cops." He flashed Cantinflas a low-wattage smile.

Cantinflas grunted. "Get that *carbon,* Vasquez. If you can get him across the border, do it. If not, well, take care of business over there. But do it now." He pointed at Cuarenta-y-cinco. "Do it now!"

"*Y la puta?*" What about the *rubia* in San Antonio?

Cantinflas waved Cuarenta-y-cinco away. "Get going. Get your boys. Get him." He looked around the table. "I'll make sure she is taken care of. You got your orders. Get out of here. Get Vasquez before the sun comes up."

. . .

A vibration in his pocket indicated an incoming call. Punching the circuit open, the DEA man said simply, "What?"

"Eddleman here, Luke. Where are you?"

"Still hanging around Vasquez's business. He's working late, so I thought I'd stick around, too. He needed some of us to work late. Inventory, end of quarter, some shit like that."

"Good. Where's Vasquez?"

The Vasquez Plumbing Contractors' office was located inside one of the warehouses. Peering through one of its windows, Luke said, "He's at his desk. What's going on?"

"No time to go into it. You and he need to get gone from there. Grab Vasquez and go. Some of the team will fill you in when you are out of there."

Luke started walking toward the office while peering at the fenced yard, trying to see past it and into the gloom of the approaching darkness. "You gotta let me know something, goddamn it! How much time do I have?"

Eddleman briefly explained the situation. "Get to a safe house, but if you don't like what you see, just keep going. Let me know where you are later, once you feel safer. I'm sorry we got you in this. This isn't turning out like it was supposed to." He rang off.

Luke tapped of the office door. "Mr. Vasquez? Open up!"

Pete Vasquez glanced out the small window. "What do you want, Isidro?"

Luke began pounding on the locked door. "Name's not Isidro. It's Luke. You know who I work for. I've just got word we need to get the hell out of here, and pronto."

Pete stepped to the computer and began typing. "It'll take me a few minutes to shut down the computer and turn off the lights."

"Fuck that shit! You and I are dead meat unless we go—now." The normally taciturn agent's voice showed raw fear. "Your Mexican employers are coming for you!"

Vasquez stuttered, "I gotta kill this program. Won't take a sec." He inserted a thumb drive and punched several letters on the keyboard.

Suddenly, glass shattered as Luke shoved his automatic through the office window, pointing it Pete's head.

"Open up. Now. Or *I'll* kill you."

Shaken, Pete stood and unlocked the office door. Luke pushed into the room.

"What's so damned important that you're putting your life and mine in more danger, you fucking jerk? What did you do?"

"Crashed the computer. Scrambled it." He extracted the thumb drive and shoved it in his pants pocket.

Luke grabbed Pete's arm, hard, and led him out to Luke's pickup. Luke unlocked the passenger side door and pushed him in.

As the engine roared to life, Vasquez demanded, "You guys are supposed to be protecting me. What's going on? You mean the DE fucking A is afraid of the cartel? Where is my protection?"

"That so? What's on that thumb drive you shoved in your pocket, you fucker? You hiding stuff from us? Huh? Huh?" Luke screamed as he slammed the truck into reverse. "You cost us time—time we don't have, you shitbird. Luke slugged Pete in the jaw. "Give me that thumb drive."

Pete rubbed his face, grimacing as he tested to see if there were any broken bones. "Owwww, motherfucker! Why did you do that?"

"Now!"

What's on there is something I don't plan to share with the DEA, thought Pete.

Luke sped out of the parking lot, spraying dust and gravel as he went. "The thumb drive, or I'll toss your sorry ass out on the street."

No way I'll be able to talk my way out of this if they look at its files. What now?

"Okay, okay." Seeing he had no choice, Pete reached in and handed the object to Luke. "No big thing."

Luke dropped the thumb drive in his breast pocket. "Shut up." He kept checking the truck's rearview mirror for headlights, as they left the warehouse district.

Three sets of headlights appeared and kept pace. Making it to a safe house looked problematic. Luke decided to try and outrun the pursuers.

"We've got company." Luke handed Vasquez a small automatic.

Pete looked at the weapon now lying in his lap. "Why are you giving me a gun? I'm not supposed to have one, you know."

"It's got ten rounds. If we get hit, try to kill nine of the bastards."

"Why nine?"

"Use the last one on yourself. You don't want them to take you alive."

SIXTY-FIVE

Present Day

PURDY KENDRICKS

I t was good to have Betty and Forrest back. Forrest insisted that we play Candy Land three times before bedtime. Not surprisingly, the little fellow won every game. Of course, in the final game, Betty cheated, moving my pawn backward when I was closing in on the finish line.

As we lay in bed, I brought this up.

"And, I noticed you moved my pawn onto the Licorice Spot. I could have won that last game."

Suddenly, Betty's small fist hit me in the stomach.

"Ooff! What was that about?" As if I didn't know. The darkness hid my grin, as she kiddingly lit into me.

"You're a grown man, Purdy. For heaven's sake. I can't believe you are upset about your five-year-old son beating you at a kid's game!"

Enjoying the exchange, I determined to prolong it.

"It's the principle of the thing. I mean, how are you going to teach Forrest about life if he gets to win all the time? We've got to toughen him up." I knew that would evoke a response.

"Men. Nothing but overgrown little boys, with bigger toys. I can't believe we're having this discussion." Betty rolled onto her side, facing away from me.

I rolled toward her. Gently stroking her right shoulder and arm, I began to lick and kiss her neck.

"Listen, cowboy. It's late." Gooseflesh crept down her arms. "I need some sleep."

I reached around and lightly caressed a nipple through her night-shirt. "I'm just trying to relax you after that hard-fought Candy Land set."

She reached behind, touching me. "Hmm, well, it feels as if you *do* have a bigger toy back there." She sighed dramatically. "Well, it looks as if I'm not going to get any rest without relaxing something of yours." She then turned onto her back.

Fortunately, Forrest was a deep sleeper.

J ake's call came in while I was sipping coffee the next morning. I stepped outside into the carport. "What's up?"

"You seen the news?"

"No, which one, and why?"

"Piñatas and candy all over the highway up around Dallas. DEA raid on a warehouse in Houston."

"I'm not in the mood to be playing guessing games, Jake." I wasn't interested in playing forty questions in the carport.

"I know. I know. But Eddleman called me this morning. He's wanting to know if there's been any talk around here about Pete Vasquez."

"Did he tell you why he's asking?"

"I asked. He wouldn't say. Sounded un-Eddlemanly, though." He snorted at his phrasing. "Stressed out, kinda."

"Thanks, Jake." I wasn't sure what I was thanking him for, other than my sense that Jake was trying to make amends. "See you at the office." I started to hang up.

"Purdy!" It was a quiet shout, if there is such a thing. "Purdy! Don't hang up!"

"What is it, Jake?"

"Your buddy, the Ranger, just drove up. Gotta go." Jake disconnected.

Betty and Forrest pushed through the screen door as I hung up. "Give Daddy a hug and kiss. We gotta go, or I'll be late for work."

Betty opened the car door. As Forrest climbed in, she turned and stuck her tongue in my ear. Laughing, she backed the car out, winking at me as she turned toward the highway. It took a few minutes to get the shit-eating grin off my face.

SIXTY-SIX

Pete Vasquez

PRESENT DAY

L uke jammed on a headset and began talking into the mouthpiece, as he drove the truck. His aim was to get out of the industrial area and headed south on Interstate 35 toward downtown.

"I'm getting chased. Please advise, as I'm going to turn south on the Interstate."

There was a pause. Then, "No, it's faster this way. I'm afraid they are going to try to jam me up on city streets."

"You talking to me?" asked Pete. "How the fuck should I know?"

Luke ignored him, and Pete realized the conversation was over the headset with someone on the other end of a cell phone call. "Our snitch took precious time wiping a computer program. Had to put a gun to his head to get him to unlock the office door" Then, "Don't know, but I've got a thumb he was leaving with." Pete glanced at the truck's speedometer. Sixty-five miles an hour and a stop light coming up.

"Stop light!"

Luke ignored him and blew through the intersection, narrowly missing a north-bound sedan.

Fucker didn't even hit his horn! Shit! Pete suddenly realized he hadn't fastened his seat belt. *As if that'll do any good the way this truck is going!* He buckled up, pressed his feet to the floorboard, and clenched his butt.

Luke continued to talk with someone, glancing at the rear-view mirrors as he floored the accelerator.

"Coming to the on-ramp." A pause. "Shit! Blockers underneath it looks like. I don't think they're going to let me go south. I'll head north on 35."

In the distance, two dark utility vehicles straddled both directions of the underpass and slowly moved to angle off any attempts at the DEA agent's Ford looping under the Interstate and turning south toward the center of Laredo.

"I'm jumping on 35 northbound. You got someone coming?"

Luke quickly yelled, "I'm turning quick. I hope this thing doesn't roll on me. We'll be way too close to those guys when I do it!"

Pete realized the last comment was directed at him. He grabbed the door handle with his right hand and pushed against the dash with his left. As Luke suddenly braked, the Ford rocked up on its left side tires.

"Shit!" Luke let off the brake and turned into the near-roll. As the truck bounced back on all four wheels, he accelerated hard. The Ford shot up the on ramp and onto the northbound lanes of IH 35. Looking out the rear-view window, Pete saw tiny flashes blinking in one of the utility vehicles. This was followed by several metallic thwacks, coming from the tailgate area.

"What was that?" he yelled.

Luke continued to talk, almost eerily calm, on the cell phone. "Yeah. Entering now. They just sprayed us. No one hurt, I think." He turned to Pete, almost as an afterthought. "You hit?"

Instinctively, Pete touched his torso. "No. What was that?" A portion of his brain calmly noticed the pitch in his voice was near soprano range.

The Ford rocketed up the on ramp. One hundred and five miles an hour.

"I'm busy. Quit asking questions and tell me what you see. Otherwise, shut the fuck up." A pause.

"Tec 9 automatic, probably. Some hits on the back end, and this thing isn't even paid for, goddamn it!" Luke went back to talking into the headset's mouthpiece. "Webb County SO? Good. Where are our guys?"

One hundred-fifteen miles an hour. The truck suspension was starting to float. It wasn't designed for speeds like this.

"I've got to pay attention." A semi driver in the fast lane, apparently spotting the fast-moving headlights, signaled a move to the right. The tractor-trailer rig was half-way across the lane marker when Luke blew by him. The semi's horn dopplered.

"Whatta we got back there?"

This near Laredo, the north and southbound Interstate lanes were illuminated by highway lighting on tall poles. They allowed Pete to make out traffic behind them. He didn't like what he saw.

"Two Suburban types. Can't tell if they were what you called blockers, or the vehicles following out of the yard. Just went by that semi on both sides."

Pete looked over hopefully at Luke. "Can I take a shot at them?"

The cell phone conversation continued. "Thanks. Hopefully they'll get here first."

Luke yelled at Pete. "DPS and ICE coming south from Encinal. Webb County SO heading north. Should get here in time." He didn't sound convincing.

"Roll your window down."

Pete punched the Down button.

"Take the safety off and squeeze off five or six at either one of those vehicles. Can you do it?"

Not waiting for the answer, Luke aimed the truck around a Nissan Altima, swerving to avoid getting rear-ended. Pete turned and watched as its driver lost control. Luckily for its occupants, it spun in the wide median between the north and southbound Interstate lanes but didn't roll.

His attention snapped back to his own predicament, as Luke yelled, "Because I'm trying to save your worthless piece of shit life right now."

Pete had already figured that out. The wind almost pulled the gun out of his hand as he held it out the window, squeezing off rounds.

"Any luck?" Luke yelled over the wind noise.

"No." Pete paused. "Wait! I only see one truck now. I see dust in the median!" He grinned. "I got one of the trucks! I got one of the trucks!" He giggled loudly. "I'm not fucking believing this. I actually hit something." Pete punched the truck's roof.

"Where's the other one?"

Suddenly, there were two vehicles again. "Fuck, it's back with us. Where did it come from?"

"You didn't hit anything. The motherfucker turned off his headlights to fool us!" yelled Luke. The pursuers were now within a hundred feet of the Ford. The calm demeanor was now gone. Luke yelled into the mouthpiece, "We need help now, goddamnit. They're on my ass. Where are you?"

One vehicle, a Cadillac Escalade, tried to pull up on the driver's side. Luke twitched the steering wheel and nearly lost control, as the Ford sideswiped a small sedan. Caught by surprise, the Escalade's driver swerved off the tarmac and into the brush and cactus in the median before pulling back onto the highway. In the meantime, the second chase vehicle, a Chevrolet Suburban, rammed the Ford's bumper.

"Shit!" screamed Luke.

The vehicle began to fishtail, and he let off the accelerator as he fought for control. Ninety miles an hour. The Suburban hit the Ford again, which somehow stabilized it momentarily. A smattering of bullets whined off the passenger door, as they plowed into the sheet metal. Three rounds went through the back window, narrowly missing both the occupants, and starring the windshield as they exited. The Ford and Suburban closed on several motorists in the passing lane. Like the semi earlier, some of the drivers had seen the approaching headlights and started to move into the right lane.

Pete spotted what appeared to be a machine pistol pop out of the passenger side of the Suburban "Gun—out the window!"

Glancing back, Luke looked feverishly for anything that would block another spray of rounds that would be coming. He cut the Ford in front of a tractor trailer rig hauling oilfield equipment.

"Those shitbirds came loaded for bear!"

As he spoke, the machine pistol sprayed a 50-round magazine of 9 mm rounds. Bullets spanged off the steel of the semi's load and also punctured two passenger cars whose occupants had, until seconds before, been unaware of the deadly game around them. The sedans slewed as their drivers died instantly.

The Suburban struck the rear of one vehicle. The impact blew the small sedan into pieces, but also slowed that pursuer. The Escalade, running behind the Suburban, swept around the semi and came up on Luke's passenger side. Two men hung out of the passenger side windows with pistols and began firing into the body of the truck. Luke jerked the wheel of the Ford toward the Escalade. The gunmen ducked inside to avoid being crushed as the two vehicles banged together and veered apart.

All the while Luke yelled into the mouthpiece, "Where are you fuckers? They're on us!"

As the Escalade straightened up and approached again, Luke spotted a sign, "Next Exit—U.S. Highway 83/Carrizo Springs—One Mile."

"Hang on, Vasquez! I'm getting off at the next exit, but it's gotta be sudden!"

The howl of wind screaming through the perforated windshield made the command hard to understand. Pete looked up in time to see the Exit sign and pulled himself into a ball, as the truck suddenly jerked out of the outside lane, striking a breakaway sign, and raced down the ramp.

The Escalade, closing on the Ford's left side again, missed the exit, its tires chattering along rumble strips. Pete looked up and saw sparks flying as the Escalade scraped along the steel guard rail of the overpass. Suddenly, his head slammed into the dashboard, as Luke braked to pass left under the Interstate.

Unable to stop in time, the Ford slid past the intersection before coming to a halt.

"Fuck!" Luke put the truck in reverse and backed down to the entry of Highway 83. Suddenly, headlights flooded the Ford's interior. A vehicle was coming southbound down the northbound access road. The Escalade had passed the overpass and turned into the on ramp the wrong way.

Pete glanced toward the south and screamed, "Someone's coming! Someone's coming! We're boxed in!"

Luke accelerated onto U.S. 83, as the already damaged Suburban blew two tires trying to make the turn. It ran up the concrete overpass revetment and slowly rolled onto its side, blocking the Escalade momentarily.

Zetas crawled out of the Suburban and fired at the receding Ford.

"Way to go, Luke. One truck down!" Pete began pounding on the

DEA agent's shoulder. "Way to go!" Then, "Why are we slowing down? Let's go!"

The Ford began to drift onto the two-lane highway's right-side rumble strips. Luke's hands slid off the steering wheel and gently dropped into his lap.

Pete began to scream. "What the fuck, man! What the fuck!"

He shook the agent's shoulder, and Luke's head lolled against the driver's door frame. In the dark, the blood wasn't visible. Its warmth and metallic smell were all Pete needed, however, to know the agent was hurt badly, possibly dead.

Pete looked back and saw headlights approaching. The Escalade was back in pursuit of the DEA's agent's slowing truck. Pete unbuckled the seat belt and moved onto the center console. Grabbing the steering wheel, he kicked the inert agent's foot away from the gas pedal, desperately trying to steer the truck onto the main highway surface and stop the unnerving chatter of the rumble strips. His left foot found the gas petal, and he accelerated the Ford onto the highway. The headlights were gaining, and the pitch of Pete's voice climbed upward.

"They are going to kill me. Oh, shit!"

Regaining a small degree on consciousness, Luke raised his right hand and slapped at Pete. With his head still canted toward the window, he tried to say something.

"What? What? What are you saying?" Pete screamed at Luke, at the same time trying to keep on the road surface. He could feel the wetness in his crotch. He'd lost control of his bladder.

"Get... out." Luke's right hand weakly pushed at Pete. Looking at the approaching lights, Pete let off the accelerator.

"What about you?" There was no answer. *Fuck this. I'm outta here.* As the truck rolled off the highway shoulder and into the South Texas brush, Pete reached into the wounded agent's pocket.

I need that thumb drive back.

Nothing! Luke's left hand was hidden in the darkness next to the driver's door. With no time to search, Pete pushed open the passenger door and dived into the darkness.

The battered Escalade pulled alongside the idling Ford. *Zetas* swarmed out. Two pulled the wounded DEA agent out of the driver's seat. Others began firing into the darkness of South Texas brush, where they suspected Pete had fled.

"*Paretes, carbones!*" Cuarenta-y-cinco fired a .45 round into the air.

The indiscriminate firing slowed to a halt. The Zeta shined a flashlight at the inert DEA agent and kicked him in the ribs. Luke grunted.

Cuarenta-y-cinco commanded two men in Spanish, "Roll him onto his back."

Kneeling down, Cuarenta-y-cinco grabbed Luke's face and threw off the headset. "Meester DEA asshole. Can you hear me? Where is your *puto* friend? Where were you taking him?"

Barely breathing, Luke muttered something.

"What? I can't hear you, Meester DEA." Cuarenta-y-cinco leaned closer.

"Your mother is a whore," the agent whispered and spat blood into the *sicario's* face.

"Fucking son of a bitch!" Quarenta-y-cinco placed his .45 to the agent's forehead and pulled the trigger.

The .45's loud report rang in his ears.

"*Jefe!*" A Zeta gunman grabbed Cuarenta-y-cinco. "*Vieneiene la policia!*"

In the distance, police sirens wailed.

"*Vamonos, muchachos!*"

The killers ran for the Escalade, and Cuarenta-y-cinco yelled in Spanish into the darkness where he presumed Pete Vasquez had fled. "You are a dead man!"

The Escalade sped off into the darkness.

SIXTY-SEVEN

Laura Griffin Saenz

PRESENT DAY

Another fundraiser. I can't keep this up.

A It was nearly midnight when Laura kicked off her Christian Louboutins, as she shut her front door and re-armed the security system. Sighing, she reached down and picked up the red-sole heels.

Hell, these cost me nine hundred dollars. I'll be reduced to wearing cheap-shit pumps that'll break off. Hell, maybe even Sketchers. Bitches. Serve them right if I showed up wearing sneakers! The thought amused her, and she laughed loudly as she envisioned downsizing her lifestyle.

Tonight's soiree, a fundraiser for a new shelter for abandoned pets, had turned a bit boozy. She had bought two tickets several months ago, but after the blow-up with Pete, wasn't inclined to ask anyone to accompany her.

After making the obligatory loop pretending to consider the silent auction items, Laura was seated at a table with five other people, only one of whom she knew well. Another of the five, the owner of the Ace Hardware Store in Knippa, introduced himself and confided that he was recently separated and thinking about selling his business and moving to San Antonio.

When he isn't trying to get a glimpse of my tits, which was about fifty percent of the time, he seems okay, even if he does have a comb-over.

The hardware store owner produced a pocket flask of clear liquid, telling Laura that both the white and red wines being served were "pretty weak stuff, if you know what I mean."

Trying to be circumspect, Laura nodded toward the flask, "What's in there?"

"It's a type of Mexican liquor."

"Buddy," —that was his name— "I was raised on the border. I know what tequila is." She almost felt insulted.

"No. No. No. This is better. Here, take a sip," he urged.

She looked around. Dinner plates were being placed on the tables, as the emcee and volunteers set up for the live auction. No one seemed to be paying attention, so Laura drained her water glass and handed it to Buddy. He splashed three fingers of the clear liquid in it and handed it back.

Laura took a swallow and tried to catch her breath. "Jesus Christ, Buddy!"

That got the rest of the table's attention. Red-faced, she apologized.

"Sorry, my new friend was telling me a very sad story, and, well, I just overreacted." As if to confirm this, she dabbed at the corners of her eyes with her dinner napkin.

Buddy held the flask below table height, trying to look somber. "I truly am sorry for upsetting you, Miss Lura."

Fortunately, the servers showed up with some sort of rubber chicken in gravy, with a side of the never-tuneful "vegetable medley." The chatter restarted, as everyone pretended what was being served was "just delicious." Servers worked the tables, as a string quartet sawed away.

Quietly, Laura asked Buddy, "Okay, what did I just drink? It tastes like gasoline."

"Mescal, ma'am. It's the in thing with the younger generation in Mexico now. I'm surprised you haven't ever tried it. This stuff is aged, too. Actually, I've grown fond of it."

As if to prove his point, Buddy poured his wine into his water glass and surreptitiously splashed at least four fingers into the now-empty stemware.

"*Salud!*"

The liquor slowly spread warmth through her body. Laura glanced around at the roomful of tables. Most were closer to the dais than the one she was at. *I'm like an untouchable in India*, she thought. *Well, what the hell?*

"*Salud* back at you, Buddy."

They clinked glasses. Soon they were swapping stories about South Texas deer leases and Garner State Park, a perennial favorite with Texas teens wanting to party far away from their parents.

Thirty minutes later, servers began clearing tables. The emcee announced the beginning of the live auction. The auctioneer, who normally handled livestock sales, reminded everyone that "the money goes to a wonderful cause, so please don't be afraid to spend generously."

An open bar and the table wine loosened up the crowd. The mescal started to take on a previously undetected bouquet for Laura. One of the first items up for bid was a foot massage at some Vietnamese place off Broadway.

"The only foot massage my wife's ever given me was when she booted my ass out of the house," said Buddy.

Well into her second three-fingers of mescal, Laura found this exceedingly funny and promptly out-bid another bidder.

"Buddy, this is my gift to you," she giggled

The hypnotic auction chant with its filler words, and the charity's celebrity ringmen with their good-natured goading of potential bidders, had their effect. By the end of the evening, Laura had bid on several items. Eyebrows were raised when she got into a bidding war with Buddy and ended up the proud owner of an "All-expense-paid, five-day trip for two to Cozumel!"

Moon-eyed, Buddy offered to pay for that prize and accompany her on what he knew would be his ticket to paradise.

"Of course, it'll have to be after my divorce hearing." The trial date was three months away.

Suddenly, the venue's ceiling lights came on. The time had come for the winning bidders to pay, collect personal belongings, blow air kisses and give quick hugs to departing attendees.

Laura realized she was drunk.

"Buddy, would you be a dear and take this check to the auction desk for me?"

I'm going broke, and I'm buying crap at an auction! Cozumel! Cozumel? Of all the places in Mexico, why would I want to spend five days with anyone in that tourist trap?

Now alone at the table, Laura realized she needed something to dilute the fiery booze in her system. She managed to reach three half-empty glasses of water and downed them quickly. Focusing her eyes with difficulty, she gave Buddy another once-over. His comb-over had done a 90-degree turn, and strands hung down his over his forehead. When he smiled, a yellow canine confirmed the remaining teeth she could see were capped.

Oh shit, this has gone too far. I've got to get out of here.

"Honey," she said as she stuffed the prize receipts into her purse, "I'm not feeling well. I can't wait for us to see each other again, but I'm Ubering home before I get sick."

Re-adjusting the comb-over and unable to hide his disappointment at not being allowed to drive Laura home, Buddy nodded, wrote down his cell number on the back of his business card— "don't call the store, please. My wife still does the books there" —and escorted her outside.

SIXTY-EIGHT

Eddleman

PRESENT DAY

A Texas Highway Patrolman beat other law enforcement to Luke's pickup. Eddleman pulled up within seconds and pushed by the trooper toward his DEA agent's body. The flashing red, blue, and white lighting added an other-worldly touch to the macabre scene. Luke lay splayed out on the Texas asphalt, brain and viscera spread around his head.

Sirens and lights accumulated as others rolled up on the scene. Eddleman was left alone with Luke as cops spread out to secure the area. The dead agent's face appeared oddly serene, except for the stippled bullet hole centered in his forehead.

Where is that thumb drive that may have cost you your life, Luke?

Eddleman's eyes settled on the dead agent's clenched left hand. He gently opened it and saw the thumb drive there. With his body shielding his actions from view, Eddleman palmed the device and slipped it into his pocket. Until Eddleman knew what the drive contained, he was ensuring it would not be inventoried as part of the crime scene evidence.

E ddleman's next 24 hours were sleepless. Reinforcements poured into the area. The search for Luke's killers turned up nothing but an abandoned SUV in the South Texas brush country near the border. Had the *sicarios* grabbed Pete Vasquez? Eddleman didn't think so, but there was no way to be sure. With a dead DEA agent to answer for and the guarantee of being killed while "resisting arrest," the *sicarios* weren't going to waste time dragging along a captive. More likely, tracking dogs or a swirl of buzzards would turn up Vasquez's body.

Eddleman unlocked the door to his rented apartment in Laredo, woke up his personal computer, and inserted the thumb drive. To his relief, it didn't require a password, so he opened its only file, entitled "Stuff."

Thirty-five lines of text and numbers.

That's it? This gibberish is what cost Luke his life. What the hell is this?

Hackamore tree - 375k

Diablo chico - 1.2

Oto's bench - 823k

East vega notch - 228k

Sunset Y - 1.7

The list went on and on, with arcane names, such as *tinaja*, and numbers with a *k* attached, or more startlingly, no *k* beside the numbers.

Suddenly, he understood. Eddleman smashed his hand down on the table.

"That bastard has stashed cash all over the Grifffin place."

When he had flipped Pete, Eddleman had given him no choice. Divulge any hidden funds, in banks or elsewhere, in any way related to the drug trade. In the hurry to turn Pete for use against the *Zetas*, he had ignored his agency's regulations on the scrutiny needed to ensure compliance, and he had failed to discover a substantial cache of currency—American money, easily retrievable.

He stood up, knocking over the desk chair. Pacing, Eddleman muttered, "These are his hidey holes for dope money. I'll be goddamned. That little bastard held out on us."

Then another thought hit Eddleman—disclosing Pete Vasquez's duplicity now, given Luke's death, would assure the end of his career in federal law enforcement.

Who else knows about this, he wondered. *If Pete Vasquez is alive and gets arrested, chances are he'll end up telling someone how he put one over on me. I've got to find out what these file entries mean and get the money off that ranch. Even better, if he dies, no one knows about it. If Vasquez isn't dead, I'm going to make sure he ends up that way.* He righted the desk chair, sat back down, and began to plan.

SIXTY-NINE

Pete Vasquez

PRESENT DAY

He almost made it away from the *Zetas* unscathed. The DEA agent's command to *run* kicked Pete's body into overdrive. He bailed out when the truck slowed. The darkness was a welcome shield for his movements. An old four-strand barbed wire fence hardly slowed him down, and Pete cleared it quickly. He tripped several times as he frantically reached for distance and cover from what his terrified mind knew was occurring on the road.

Dozens of shots rang out, and rounds whined in the distance.

They're not shooting toward me.

His relief lasted only a few steps. A new series of shots from what must have been machine pistols and the whizz of several rounds, passed within feet. A mott of trees loomed in the dark.

Almost safe!

Twenty feet from the stand of small trees, something spun Pete to the ground. Had a Zeta bullet knocked him over? He struggled to his feet and continued to run for the small shelter. He slammed into the growth under the trees and threw himself flat. Pete looked back toward the highway and tried to catch his breath. Now that he was some 250 yards off the road, he looked back toward the highway and dimly saw men milling around the agent's truck. Suddenly, the activity ceased, an SUV sped away. Silence and darkness enveloped the highway.

Why did they leave? Thank you, Jesus!

Pete took stock. He checked his pockets—private cell phone, wallet, ring of keys. No thumb-drive, though. He hoped that in the darkness, no one would become aware of its existence. Fat chance, but there was nothing he could do about it now.

Something wet near his midriff. Sweat? Opening the cell phone, Pete held his left hand up to its light. Blood! *Where did that come from?* Then he remembered being slammed to the ground minutes before. The cell phone's light showed a spot of blood on the front of his shirt. *Did I scratch myself?*

He lifted the shirt. A jagged hole wept a slow but continuous stream of blood, soaking into the waistband of his khakis.

"Oh, God. Oh, God." Gingerly, he felt around his back, and his index finger found a small hole. "Ouch. Goddammit, I've been shot!" Pete stood in the dark, trying to process this information. As he did so, his eyes and ears adjusted to the darkness and quiet.

Pete smelled the sweet resin of creosote bushes. *God, it's beautiful. I'm alive. I can't believe it! Fucking DEA agent got my thumb drive though.*

Pete tried to feel sadness for the murdered agent but couldn't muster up any.

Suddenly, Pete's legs felt wobbly, and he almost fainted. Then he began to retch uncontrollably. He shivered from a sudden chill in the air.

What the hell? It's hot as hell out here! He sat down suddenly and rolled onto his left side. The depth and intensity of the sudden pain of the action scared him. Rolling onto his uninjured right side, Pete coughed up sour vomit and spat it into the low foliage.

The adrenalin of the chase was wearing off, and with it, the protective shield it provided against pain and fear disappeared. The void was replaced with a dull throb of pain from Pete's flank. Terror gripped him. *Am I gut shot?* He spat again and checked the spit's contents with the cell phone's light. No blood. He coughed, nearly fainting with the pain in the process. Then spat out the phlegm. No blood there.

Maybe it's not too bad.

I've got to get far away from here, he thought. *I've got to get out of the country. The DEA is going to get me convicted. I'm not going to be safe in jail or prison. The Zetas will get me inside prison, unless it's a Supermax, which is worse than death. I'm dead on the outside if I'm anywhere the Zetas can find me.*

Since discovering his grandparents' bodies, Pete hadn't returned to the Griffin Ranch. And since Purdy Kendricks had turned on him, coming damned close to outright accusing him of killing them, he had avoided going anywhere near Kickapoo County. That had to change. Pressing a hand to the exit wound, Pete moved away from the flashing emergency lights in the distance.

Three hours and several miles later, Pete woke up his cell phone and punched in a number.

Answer, you bitch.

SEVENTY

Laura Griffin Saenz

PRESENT DAY

A t 6:30 a.m., The Destroyers' *Bad to the Bone* began pounding in her head. Pete Vasquez.

Why is that bastard calling me at this ungodly hour?

She refused the call and tried to go back to sleep. It didn't work.

Sorry son-of-bitch threatened me.

It didn't work. Heart pounding from a mix of anxiety and hangover, Laura reached for the cellphone in her purse.

What the hell?

Then she remembered that the call came in on the encrypted phone Pete had given her. Puzzled, she tried to focus.

I thought I had gotten rid of that thing. Reaching into the night table's drawer, she pulled that phone out.

Still mostly charged up.

Pete didn't leave a message. She speed dialed him. Pete picked up after four rings.

"Why are you calling me at oh-dark-thirty, Pete? What's going on?"

"They tried ...me! ...uckers tried to kill..."

"Pete, where are you? What's going on? You're breaking up."

There was a pause—then, "Is this better?"

The connection was still weak, but she could make out the panic in Pete Vasquez's voice. "I hear you, Pete. What's going on?"

"They came and tried to kill me, Laura! They came and... Oh, Jesus Christ! They..." He began to sob.

Fully awake now, Laura got out of bed and slipped on some jeans, putting the phone on speaker mode as she headed toward the kitchen. Her head pounded. She needed coffee and she needed to concentrate.

"Who are 'they,' baby? Who are 'they?'"

The sobs continued. Then, like a child confessing, in a small voice, Pete said, "The *Zetas*."

She thought she had misheard. "What? You mean the Mexican cartel *Zetas*?" Laura's voice rose in volume. Now she knew. His warning. Thoughts ran behind the words coming out of her mouth, as if her brain needed additional confirmation of what was already evident. "Are you involved with the *Zetas*? Was that what the threat to me was about?"

"Yes." Simple. No further explanation needed.

"Mother of God." Laura could smell the fear coming off her body. "Mother of God," she repeated. Pulling at her ponytail, she walked around the kitchen island, again and again. When Pete didn't offer any further information, she asked, "What just happened? Where are you that I can hardly hear you?"

Pete began to cry again.

"Quit crying, you pussy!" she screamed. "Answer my fucking questions!"

Pete's words tumbled over the phone, and she had to ask him twice to slow down. Finally, he did. The DEA agent, the chase, the bullets. Lastly, the sound of a large-caliber bullet and *Zetas* fleeing.

"Where are you?" Laura asked again, giving each word of the question several seconds of its own.

"I'm in some creosote bushes, looking across the highway at an RV park. I think I'm about ten miles north of IH 35 on U.S. 83, but I'm not for sure where. I'm near a sign that says *Carrizo Springs—56 miles*. I've been hiding here for a couple hours."

Laura tried to place Pete on her mental map of South Texas. *Jeez fucking Louise. He's in the middle of East Jesus.*

"Who are you hiding from, Pete. Talk to me and tell me what's going on!" The phone connection nearly broke again. Laura held her phone out and screamed into it, "Move to a better location, Pete. I can't understand you!"

A pause—then, "I moved, but not much. I got shot, and I'm bleeding. I don't want anyone to see me. There are cop cars everywhere. A helicopter came over a few minutes ago." He paused again. "I'll figure something out, but that's not why I'm calling. Do you remember me warning you about the danger?" He didn't wait for an answer. "You gotta get out of San Antonio, right now. The same guys who tried to kill me may come after you, too."

What bullshit. She interrupted, exasperated. "Pete, for God's sake— wave down a cop car. Why haven't you done it before now?"

"The only way I was going to stay out of prison was by helping the DEA, Laura. I'm no good to them now. I'll go away for a long time. I don't want to go to prison for the rest of my life."

This was more news. "Why would you do that, Pete? Are you a drug dealer? What?"

"They say my company trucks were transporting it. For a long time. The narcs finally got wind of it. They threatened me. Either I helped them take down a Zeta operation or I was toast." He began giggling hysterically. "Hell, I'm toast now!"

They say, my ass. You sorry shit, she thought. *Purdy's right.* She caught her reflection in the glass patio door as she paced. *Hell, I'm not much better. How did I end up in this mess?*

Laura felt mentally and physically drained. "Oh, Pete, I am so sorry I ever met you." There was no anger in her voice. There was...nothing.

"Listen, I'm down to two bars on my phone, so I've gotta go now. You need to get out of there right now!" He paused. "We can lay low and figure out what to do next."

"What's this 'we' shit, Pete? This is total bullshit. You've got yourself into this mess. Now, you need to get yourself out of it."

Pete's voice took on a menacing tone. "Listen, lover. You think you are some kind of squeaky-clean white chick? You're not. You got bailed out on your house in Alamo Heights. You come help me now, or I'll dime you out to the Feds. I'll be glad to tell them where the money came from. I'll tell them that you knew all along the *Zetas* or *La Familia Norteña* were providing money to keep you afloat. It sure as hell won't be hard to do."

Silence, then Pete began again. "Are you hearing me now, Laura? *Honey?* I warned you. And there won't be a damned thing you can say or do that'll keep your sweet, blonde ass out of the slammer. It may not be a lot of time, but you'll do some." He paused. "They like white chicks. You'll be switch-hitting before you know it, bitch."

Instinctively, Laura interjected a denial. "I had no idea, Pete. I thought you were helping me because you were my friend...."

Pete snarled. "Your nice life is about to go down the crapper, babe. There's not going to be a single person in your beloved Alamo Heights that'll have a damned thing to do with you, *when* all this comes out."

"I hope the *Zetas* cut your balls off, Pete. I truly do."

"That's if they catch me. And they won't, if you get here and get me away. If the Feds catch me first, I promise you, Laura..."

She caught her breath. *Oh, God. Oh, God. I need to think.* She played for time. "I've got to figure out how to get to you without someone seeing me. How do I do that?" Her stomach's curdled contents welled up, and Laura fought a sudden urge to vomit.

Pete wasn't fooled. "You're thinking about calling the cops. I know it."

She started to protest, but Pete ignored the interruption. "You're short of money, aren't you?"

What's that got to do with anything right now? However, the question kept her on the line.

"I'm listening." She grabbed a kitchen towel, biting down on it as another wave of nausea hit.

"You want to go to the cops. Go ahead, but first I'll make it worth your while to hold off, and to help me. How much you got in the bank right now?"

She told him.

"Chump change, lady. I've stashed cash on your ranch for years. I'll give you half if you'll help me get it and get out of the country."

"Where is it?" She was suddenly intrigued.

Pete's laugh was short and bitter. "You're kidding, right? It's a big place, Laura. Sixteen thousand acres, as I recall. It's stashed all over the place, and I'm not about to tell you where any of it's hidden. Only way you get any of it is by helping me. You get me to the ranch and help me disappear. Then you get your cash."

I'm being reeled in like a big old catfish. But.... "Pete, you can't go anywhere without a passport."

"You think I'm some high school dumbshit? I've been running

drugs for the fucking cartel. Don't you think I can get a couple of clean passports?" Pete bragged. "I could have got them in Tepito" —Mexico City's most dangerous flea market was known to house several sellers of identification papers— "but I didn't. You just do what I ask. Get me out of the U.S., and you'll never see me again. And, you won't need to find some sweetheart to keep you flush."

"How much money did you hide, Pete?"

He told her.

Holy Mother of God!

Laura decided she would go get Pete.

T he oak floor on the second floor creaked—then creaked again. This time it sounded closer to the stairs leading down to the living room. What were her maids doing up there? Then she remembered. She had let one go, and today was Adela's day off.

Oh, my God. Are killers coming after me?

Heart beating like a trip hammer, she remembered her Glock was in the drawer of her nightstand. There was no way she was going upstairs to get it.

Laura quietly walked to the gun cabinet in the den. Retrieving the key hidden in a Lalique vase, she unlocked the glass front doors and pulled out her daddy's favorite hunting rifle. She had used the Fabrique Nationale .270 with Weatherby stock and Zeiss 3.5-10x50 riflescope to take an elk in Alaska at 250 yards. She figured the 150-grain bullet, suited to the rifle's tight barrel twist, would do just fine to kill a man.

The hangover suddenly cleared by adrenalin, Laura quietly released the safety, opening the bolt just enough to ensure a round was properly seated in the chamber, and below it, rounds in the internal magazine. Closing the cabinet door, she tiptoed back to the kitchen and retrieved her cell phone.

Why didn't I just call 911 first?

As she thumbed in the code to unlock the phone, a voice called out.

"Señora, where are you? Are you home?

What in hell?

"Adela, is that you? What are you doing here?"

Adela Campos, her long-time employee, trod heavily on the steps, her varicose veins making the descent painful.

"You told me to come in today, señora." Adela rounded the stairwell and stopped abruptly. "What are you doing with that rifle, señora?"

Laura set the cell phone on the kitchen counter and carefully thumbed on the weapon's safety.

"I forgot, Adela. I didn't hear you come in." Tears began to flow.

I could have killed her. It could have happened so quickly. Oh, God.

She walked over to the gun case and placed the .270 in its rack, then locked the door.

"What's wrong, Mrs. Saenz? Are you okay?"

As the tension eased, the hangover roared back. Still shaking, Laura hugged Adela.

"I was just remembering my daddy and making sure his favorite rifle was in good shape. I'm going upstairs to get cleaned up. I'm going out for awhile. Be sure to lock up when you leave, Adela." Trying to act casual, she turned to the woman she had known for decades. "I'm sorry if I scared you, Adela. I apologize. The rifle wasn't loaded, though."

As Laura shakily walked up the stairs, Adela retrieved the gun case key, unlocked the cabinet, and carefully took out the .270. She hated firearms. She had lost a son in Iraq. Somewhat imprecisely, she opened the bolt and glanced in.

Laura had lied to her. Mentally retracing what had just happened, Adela quickly put the rifle back. She had smelled the stale odor of alcohol on her employer's breath and wondered just how close she had come to being killed.

SEVENTY-ONE

Present Day

PURDY KENDRICKS

Not in any hurry, as Diana Krall's exquisitely sultry *Temptation* had another two minutes to keep me somewhere else mentally, I was almost disappointed when there was no traffic on U.S. 90 to slow down my getting to the office. My playlist moved to Abbey Lincoln's deeply sad *Throw It Away*. Remembering that as one of my "four-scotch songs," I shut off the iPod. Today was starting well, and I didn't want to ruin it

My cell phone showed an incoming call—Eddleman. I rolled up the wires to the ear buds and stuffed them in my breast pocket. *So much for the pleasant day.*

"What?"

"We need to talk."

I wanted to start with a quick "Fuck you," but his four words contained a sense of desperation. I took a deep breath. "Can this wait? I'm driving to the office right now."

"Kendricks, I've got a problem. No. *We've* got a problem."

I turned off U.S. 90 and pulled up to the Stop Inn. One of Jagir Patel's extended family stuck his head out of the front door and waved cheerily. I waved back, although I didn't have a clue as to who it was.

"Okay, what's up?"

"Your friend, Pete."

"What about him?"

"Have you heard from him, or seen him?"

"You're shitting me, right? You've been warning me to stay away from him, and now you're asking me if I've heard from him?"

Eddleman paused. "Where are you right now?"

"In front of the Stop Inn at Santa Rosa."

"Pete Vasquez has been working for us. The *Zetas* got wind of it and tried to kill him. We're trying to reel him in before they succeed. I was hoping he had maybe reach out to you. We aren't aware of any other family or close personal friends he has, other than that woman in Alamo Heights."

I was getting a summary, without any details. "Working for you? What are you talking about? Is he DEA?"

"Not exactly."

I did a quick inventory of feelings. Pete was my best friend once. Did I care? Should I care? I was convinced he had something to do with his own grandparents' deaths. All that belief had gotten me was a lot of problems—and no solutions.

"Eddleman, I don't want to talk to you unless it helps me wrap up the Griffin ranch killings. I don't want to have anything to do with you or the DEA. I'm about to hang up unless I get a lot more about what's going on than what I've just heard."

Eddleman came back quickly. "Don't hang up. Pete Vasquez was dirty. He was using his trucks to haul dope for *La Familia Norteña*. The *Zetas* took over and started to use him. We got wind of what was going on and suggested that it would be in his best interests to help us —which he was doing."

"But something's gone wrong." It wasn't a question.

"Have you listened to the news this morning?" He didn't wait for a response. "No, I didn't think so, or you'd start putting some stuff together. We lost a good agent early this morning north of Laredo. *Zetas* came for Vasquez at his business. He and one my best men made a run for it. My agent—one of my best—he's dead. Your pal got away. It's on all the Laredo and San Antonio TV stations. Two civilians also died in a chase up 35. We've kept my man and Pete out of the news, but I don't know for how long." Eddleman sounded rattled.

Sweet Jesus. Remembering the South Texas landscape, I asked, "How did he get away?

As much as I disliked Eddleman, it wasn't pleasant hearing the uncertainty in his voice.

"We've got drones and helicopters out looking but no luck so far. Border Patrol found an abandoned Caddy Escalade in the brush ten miles from the river. It looks like a bunch of the bastards made it across into Indian country." He used an anachronistic term for Mexico and enemy territory. "A Chevy Suburban rolled under the Interstate a few miles from where the *Zetas* caught up with my man and Vasquez. There were two dead *sicarios* in the vehicle. Looks like they were crushed when it went over."

I asked about the DEA agent. I shouldn't have.

"He caught a round through the lung during the chase. He was still alive when the *Zetas* caught up with him and Pete." His voice cracked. "Someone blew his brains all over the pavement."

"They kill your agent and let Pete get away? That doesn't sound likely, Eddleman. He's probably dead under a bush somewhere."

"We had DEA, DPS, Webb County, and Laredo PD rolling trying to get into play. We didn't make it in time. But our folks came up on my agent's pick-up truck, apparently right after he was killed. No blood on the passenger side. Door open. Tracks went off the shoulder and across the Border Patrol drag area."

He was referring to the loose soil next to South Texas highways tilled frequently, so footprints of illegal aliens could be seen.

"Then off into the brush. No blood, though. We don't think they got Vasquez. Our people got there too fast."

As I listened to the narrative, I kept asking myself why I was being brought into Eddleman's confidence. What did this have to do with Pete's grandparents' deaths? And even if there was a connection, why was he telling me a damned thing? Then it started to come together.

I put it into words. "That killing of the head of *La Familia*, south of the Vasquez place—did Pete have something to do with that? And the shooter, Shivelli, found on the Griffin place. This is all somehow mixed up together isn't it?"

One of Jagir's family members witnessed my angry gestures through the Stop Inn's glass door. He poked his head out the door, giving me a look of concern. I waved him back inside. I didn't recognize that family member, either.

"That bastard got his grandparents killed, didn't he? And the fucking DEA probably had something to do with it." I didn't know what, or if what I was screaming was connected, but the sudden anger overrode any plan for calm discussion.

"You piece of shit, Eddleman. You sanctimonious piece of shit. You people got two old folks killed because of your little war."

A customer pulled up next to the patrol car. The driver looked over at me as I pounded on the steering wheel. He looked shocked. Instead of going into the store, he backed out and drove off. I wasn't doing the Stop Inn's business any good.

"We didn't have anything to do with that assassination. That was a done deal before we found out about Pete Vasquez."

I didn't believe him but kept quiet. Jagir Patel, the patriarch, I did recognize, and he was coming out the store's entrance. He tapped on the windshield and made a gesture. I rolled down the window. Hitting the mute button on the phone, I apologized.

"Sorry, Jagir. I'm leaving."

"Purdy."

He had once tried to show me how Hindi language speakers roll their tongues up into the top of their mouths to create a distinct English accent.

"Purdy. Sir. Please. I am a poor immigrant, and you are having an attack of temper in my parking lot. Please, go."

I apologized again and backed out onto Highway 90, un-muting the phone as I did so.

"Pete's on the lam. Why didn't he turn himself in to you guys? You can protect him, can't you? Seems like this is an easy choice for him to make. You keep telling me he had nothing to do with his grandparents' deaths. I don't believe you, but you've been protecting him."

I could almost see Eddleman shaking his head. "We've told him he was no good to us unless he produced on the *Zetas*. That there was enough on him to ensure that he would spend the rest of his life in a Super Max, where he would never see sunlight. Maybe that's why. I don't know."

"Eddleman, I'm a pissant deputy in a pissant county in the middle of nowhere. You've made that clear. So, what has this got to do with me?"

"He's got nowhere to go. He's got some kin in your county. He may be trying to head there. I'd like to make sure he doesn't get killed before we can catch up to him."

He had been seen at least 150 miles from Kickapoo County. Half of the free world's law enforcement was probably looking for him.

"No way he'll come here. Too few people. Too close to the border." As I said it, I wasn't so sure.

"So, who do I confide in, Eddleman? You don't trust our sheriff. You don't want anyone to know you guys are involved in this area. What am I supposed to do? Go look under bushes for him? Maybe rent a local DJ's sound system and put it on a pickup truck and drive around the county? What?"

Eddleman was quiet for a moment. "You're from Kickapoo County. You grew up with the Hispanics. You know the people there. Some of them may talk to you. In the meantime, I'd think on it." He paused. "Kendricks, we don't know who's dirty and who isn't. It is imperative that the DEA get to Pete before *anyone* else does. *Anyone*. I mean anyone in law enforcement, too. We just don't know. Another pause. "If you hear anything, call me personally."

"The only reason I'll help you find Pete Vasquez is if the DEA gives me what I need to get him indicted."

I had wasted my breath. Eddleman had disconnected.

Judge Sam McCullough was holding court, so parking was at a premium. Frustrated drivers circled the courthouse, trying to find a parking spot with shade.

I cut off another driver and pulled into an open space, ignoring her single-digit salute. I opened the sedan door.

"Señor Purdy! Señor Purdy!" Israel Sifuentes's old-fashioned formality usually prevented him from raising his voice. His raised volume got my attention. I had spotted Ranger Selman's sedan and needed to talk with him, but it would wait.

I gave Israel a nod and crossed to where he was rewinding a garden hose. He looked relieved that he had been noticed but walked away from me after getting my attention. Whatever he was about to share, he didn't want it done in the open. Israel disappeared around the west side of the courthouse. I knew he was headed to a small room under the exterior concrete stairs where janitorial and gardening supplies were kept.

Rather than going around the outside, I walked up the stairs to the first floor on the east side, greeting the few lawyers gathered there with their clients. The building had no attorney conference rooms, so most discussions were in hushed tones in the hallway. Walking out the west side and down the exterior stairs, I rounded the corner and pushed open the small room's steel door. "Israel?"

"Here, *mi amigo*." Israel's voice echoed from behind some shelving. "*Entres, y cierra la puerta*."

I closed the door. My eyes adjusted to the single light bulb, as I wondered what all the secrecy was about. "Israel, what's going on?"

He grabbed a pair of hedge trimmers and tested the action. "*Hijole*, with my arthritis, working with these old things causes me a lot of pain." He rubbed a shoulder tenderly. "I wish you people would spend some money for electric trimmers."

"You people?" What's that shit, Israel? Tell some of *tus hermanos* about the cheap shit you have to use." Still I cracked a smile to let him know I was kidding—sort of. Three of the four County Commissioners of Kickapoo County were Hispanics, and Israel's "you people" occasionally got tiresome.

He wasn't about to let that go by without getting the last word. "*Pues*, Purdy, they're just trying to be part of the *sistema*." A half-smile told me he was trying to get my goat. I was too rattled by Eddleman's call to respond.

"*Perdoname, mi amigo*, I don't want to seem rude, but have you got anything to tell me?"

He slipped into the border custom of seesawing between Spanish and English, and I followed suit.

"You remember me warning you to be careful?"

I nodded. "Yes, and thanks. It is much appreciated."

Israel sat down on an ancient wooden chair with broken spindles. He took a deep breath and looked up.

"Your friend, Pete Vasquez. He's in trouble with the law."

Where was this going? Eddleman had assured me that no names had been released on the early-morning DEA agent's killing, or Pete's presence.

"In what way, Israel?"

I waited as Israel meandered toward the point of his story. I remembered a college class on Greek mythology I once eked through. I felt I was being held hostage by an aging Spanish-speaking Cassandra. There was no sense in trying to prod him along. The more important he deemed the information, the slower he got.

"My people tell me, Pete" —he spat on the floor— "*los malditos*, the bad ones, are trying to kill him. That he was a *narcotraficante*. That he is working for the *nortemamericanos*. That *los malditos* say he is a *chaquetero*."

I searched mentally for the translation. "You mean he was supposed to be working for a cartel and is now" —I found what I thought was the right word— "a turncoat? That American law enforcement has him *volteado*—flipped?"

Nodding, Israel motioned toward the exit. "The Ranger is there. You need to go." He rose from the chair and stuck out his hand for me to shake.

I grasped his callused hand with both of mine and gave him an *abrazo*. "Israel, where are you hearing this?"

"We are not so far from Laredo and," he paused, "'other places,' that one does not hear things. As I told you the last time, *mi gente* are afraid that the killings in Mexico will come here. I am telling you this for two reasons. First, because you are *mi compadre*. But more importantly, because my people on *ambos lados de la frontera* don't want the infection caused by *las drogas* to come here. If it does, it will never leave. You know that. You worked in the big city as a policeman. Santa Rosa will become like a sewer pipe for the filth of the north and the south. There are already bad men we don't know near Lágrimas. Their type has already been here, as you know."

Remembering the dead body downriver from the crossing, and my fishing trip with Forrest and the trove of expended ammunition at the Lágrimas crossing, I nodded.

"My family and friends in Mexico—they will either have to become whores for *los malditos* or die." He squeezed my hand hard. "There will be no other way."

Israel's look was not one of a friend. His rheumy eyes held an anger and a determination I had never sensed before. This old man was showing me that he was much more than a janitor. I felt shame that I had sometimes treated this man with condescension. And I was suddenly afraid of his steely determination. He was letting me know that I was the intruder, the outsider, in a world I only partly under-stood, or could understand. I was being told what needed to be done, so I could remain welcome in my own county.

SEVENTY-TWO

Adela Campos

PRESENT DAY

A Range Rover pulled into the Alamo Heights driveway. Only one occupant got out. He went to the recessed front door, rang the doorbell, and when there was no answer, looked back toward the driver. He shrugged his shoulders, as if asking what he was to do next. Getting a response, he turned and began banging on the heavy-timbered entry.

Adela looked through the front window and noticed the high-end vehicle. That put her somewhat at ease, or at least lessened the tension she had been feeling since the episode with Mrs. Saenz, earlier in the morning. A Land Rover was an expected sight in 78209. Thugs didn't drive that type of vehicle.

Responding to the continual banging on the door, she cracked it open. "Yes?" She realized her mistake immediately. Vehicle doors opened and slammed shut as a young man with a tear drop tattoo below the left eye and neck tats above the shirt line, pushed through the front door. Her first thought was that *cholos*—the low class trash no decent person would have anything to do with in the *barrio*—were here to burglarize.

Even as this thought raced through her mind, she knew she was wrong. The tattoos on the face and neck. The teardrop. The scum who wore those markings were either prison whores—men who had been raped in jail—or killers. As his hand went over her mouth, she looked

333

into his eyes and smelled the grime on his hand. She knew the intruder was a killer.

"*Donde está la señora?*" Three more dark-complected men walked quickly inside, shutting the door. The tattooed man took his hand away, expecting an answer. The others moved through the downstairs, checking each room.

Tears welled in her eyes, and she closed them. *I am afraid. God forgive my weakness.* Adela began to mentally recite the Rosary. *Hail Mary full of Grace, the Lord is with thee. Blessed are thou among women and blessed is the fruit of thy womb, Jesus. Holy Mary Mother of God, pray for us sinners now and at the hour of our death.*

Other voices echoed through the empty house, as at least two went up the stairs to the bedrooms.

"*Donde 'stas, puta?*" Where are you, whore?

The speaker had a high-pitched voice, almost like a girl. He repeated himself, giggling. Adela kept her eyes closed. Shaking, she felt herself sliding down the wall. She couldn't stop.

A door slammed. Garden door. Then, in Spanish, "Not here."

Another door slammed. From the walkway to the garage and its roof garden. "The bitch isn't here."

Halfway to a seated position on the floor, two sets of hands roughly lifted Adela. "Open your eyes and look at us, *señora!*"

Adela shook her head "no." *If I don't know what they look like, maybe they won't kill me,* she thought.

"Open your eyes, *viejita*. We're not going to hurt you!" The scum with the teardrop on his face again.

She didn't believe them. *Where did I leave off?*

Pray for me, O holy Mother of God....

No! No! She had skipped so much. *Father God, forgive me.* Where had she left off?

Glory be to the Father, and to the Son, and to the Holy Spirit....

Fingers opened her eyelids. "Look at me! Look at me!"

She blinked away the tears, suddenly shamed as urine ran down her legs.

Hail, holy Queen. Mother of mercy, hail, our life, our sweetness and our hope. To thee we cry....

Another man walked up to her. "*Mamacita*, where is the *dueña*? Just tell us and we will go."

But I don't know where she is. And I don't know where she went. She didn't want these evil men to kill *Señora* Saenz. "I don't know. She is not here!"

The man with the girl's voice grabbed Adela's face. "But you know where she is, don't you, *mamacita*?"

Shaking her head violently, Adela wept. "No. No. NO! She is not here. I don't know where she went. I don't know when she will be back. She didn't tell me!" She began to cry again. "I have a husband. And children. And *nietos*, grandchildren. All I do is work for the *señora*. And she is not here."

The girl-voiced man guided her to a nearby chair. Others rummaged through the *señora's* belongings.

Scum.

"You must understand, *viejita*. We are not here to harm you."

I don't believe you.

He shook his head as if reading her mind. "No, we will not harm you, if you tell us where she is."

"I don't know. I swear to you. I don't know. She left three hours ago..." *Oh, I have said too much. They will find her and they will kill her.*

The man smiled. "What was she driving?"

"She has three. I can't tell them apart. I didn't see her go. She left while I was cleaning."

He struck her face suddenly with the back of his hand. Adela's head snapped backward and she nearly lost consciousness.

"You're lying, *señora*. Please. I don't want to hit you again. You are much like my mother."

Your mother shit you out of her asshole, you scum. Adela tasted blood in her mouth. Snot poured out of her injured nose.

"I know you think badly of me, *señora*. But I promise you, we will not hurt you. What was the vehicle she was driving? And its license plate number? We know you have worked for this Laura *puta* for many years."

Adela told him the vehicle Laura had driven off in.

"And the license plates?"

"How would I know that?" She looked at him angrily. He struck her face again, from the left side.

She told the man where the filing cabinet was that held auto papers.

"Thank you, *señora*."

He yelled at the others. As they left, the man turned to Adela and told her the name of the school where two of her grandchildren attended.

"They don't live here in this cocoon for the Anglos, *señora*. As you can see, even here, you aren't safe. Please, do not call the police. You, of course, want them to have long lives."

The door shut behind them. Adela sobbed in relief, in shame, and in fear. She did not call the police.

————————

SEVENTY-THREE

Present Day

PURDY KENDRICKS

The chill of the Sheriff's Office lobby put it in a different world from the small space under the courthouse stairway. I had stepped from one reality into an alien world. I shook it off and waved at Jake. He motioned in the direction of TJ's office. I walked down the hall and tapped on the open door. Ranger Abner Selman sat perched on the edge of TJ's desk. He looked up and nodded.

"Come in, Purdy. The Ranger just dropped by for a visit and was asking about your case."

I shook hands with Ranger Selman and reached over the desk to do the same with TJ. The sheriff rocked forward in his desk chair to reach my hand but didn't get up.

Something wasn't adding up. Abner Selman wasn't dropping by to discuss my case. He could do that on the phone. If there was anything of consequence, Abner wouldn't be asking me about it in front of TJ. Abner had never liked or trusted TJ, and that wasn't going to change.

"Not much going on at all, as you know, Sheriff. Kind of at a stopping point, whether I like it or not. Still running down some loose ends, but like you said, this may be one of those cases."

I left it at that. I wasn't going to bring up Eddleman's phone call. Selman? I was having trouble figuring his play here. I played along.

"Ranger, you haven't heard anything that would help, have you?"

"No, Purdy. I'm just stopping by. I spent the night at my fishing camp in Pandale. Unfortunately for me, they've got good cell coverage

337

out there now. I was hoping to have a couple of days without being bothered."

Pandale was a town, sort of, near a ford in the Pecos River, south of Ozona. I knew Selman occasionally went there to fish. It was a good three-hour drive from Santa Rosa.

Selman continued, "An officer was shot over near Laredo, and they've called in everyone and his dog trying to find out who did it. Some DEA agent. I guess you saw it on the news."

Nodding, I asked, "Any chance that whoever did this is coming our way?"

"No. In fact it looks like the shooters hightailed it back across the border. Border Patrol found the vehicle. Governor authorized us to use our helicopters to see if anyone else is hiding in the brush. But I doubt it."

Abner stood as if to leave. Pandale's cell coverage was spotty at best. Selman had lied about that. It was nine in the morning. I wasn't buying he had just driven three hours. No mention of Pete Vasquez.

I shook hands with Abner. "Safe travels, Ranger. I've got some work to do, unless you've got something else, Sheriff?"

TJ waved me off, officiously. "Thanks, Deputy." He stood and grabbed his hat off an antler. "Heading out to do some campaigning. I'll walk you out, Ranger."

I stepped into my office as the two men walked by.

Selman stopped suddenly. "Damn it, Sheriff. I've got those DNA reports."

He told TJ, "It's old stuff y'all have asked for and been provided. I just forgot the hard copies out of the sedan. S'cuse me. I'll walk out and get 'em and bring back to your investigator before I head out."

TJ walked out with Selman chatting about the weather. Selman was back five minutes later. "You got time, Deputy?" He motioned toward the outside.

"Sure." I locked my office and waved at Jake. I could tell his curiosity was killing him, as Selman and I walked into the day's heat.

"Follow me, will you, Purdy?" Not waiting for an answer, Selman stepped into his sedan. I followed the Ranger out of town toward the Shell gas plant. Thirty minutes later, he pulled up to a non-descript pickup truck. A scruffy, tall, dark-complected stranger stood beside it. Scruffy or not, he had cop written all over him.

"Purdy, this here's Leroy Breaux. He's with the DEA."

I shook hands with the man. He attempted a smile. "Heard about you, Deputy. Glad to meet you at last."

If he had heard about me, it was from Eddleman. "You fellas want to tell me what's going on?"

Abner spit on the ground. "I'm getting too old to be standing in this heat. Let's sit in the air conditioning."

I got in the back seat. Breaux turned. "My boss call you?"

I nodded.

"We can't find Pete Vasquez. We can't find Laura Saenz, either."

Oh shit.

SEVENTY-FOUR

Later That Day

PURDY KENDRICKS

Betty had supper fixed when I arrived. The dual aromas of chicken frying and biscuits baking created a fragrance that shouted "home." Betty smiled as she hummed at the time-worn gas stove. I must have done something to deserve this kind of treat. The days' ominous beginnings melted away.

I nuzzled the back of Betty's neck, grinning as the gooseflesh appeared, and she ducked away with a playful protest.

"Forrest, your daddy's home." Betty turned a cheek to kiss as she announced my arrival.

No response from my boy. Not the usual yelling and joy to see me. I walked to his room. Forrest sat cross-legged on the floor, assembling Legos, and having a discussion with a small toy soldier.

"No, you can't. No, you can't."

"What can't he do?" Forrest looked up, smiled, and ran and gave me a hug. I repeated the question.

"I didn't hear you come in, Daddy. I was telling my soldier that I wasn't going to let him into his castle until I get it builded."

"Built."

"Yeah. Builded."

"Well, why not?"

"'Cause I've gotta make his castle just right, so the bad guys won't get to him. I'm going to build the walls big and strong. Then he can live there with his mommy and daddy and his wife and his little boy.

And he can protect it better. But if it's not builded right, he won't be able to do that."

Made sense, and I told him so. "You're like a Prince Galahad."

"Galalaham?"

I laughed. "No, Galahad."

"Who's that, Daddy."

I shoved some coloring books out of the way and sat down on Forrest's bed, searching my mind for the tiny bit of *Morte d'Arthur* I remembered from a college English literature course.

I said, "He was a strong and fierce knight who saved ladies and little boys from bad people."

"I like him." He picked up the soldier. "I'll call him Sir Gala... Sir Galaham."

I laughed. With hair bleached by the sun and a smattering of freckles across the ridge of his nose, my son was the most beautiful thing in the world at that moment. I decided that Sir Galaham was a fine name for Forrest's soldier.

"Let's go to supper, little man. Mama's got fried chicken."

Forrest jumped up, and Sir Galaham, noble though he may be, was unceremoniously dumped on the floor.

"Yay!" He pulled me up from the bed. "Let's go, Daddy!"

He stopped in the doorway, a quizzical look on his face. "Daddy, do we have a good castle here for you and me and mommy?"

Whoa. Involuntarily, I glance at the small room's walls, popcorn ceiling, and interior hollow-core door. "Of course, we do, son. But we don't need a castle, do we?"

Mentally moving on to other things, Forrest hugged me and said, "I guess not, Daddy. Mom! I'm hungry!"

Later, as Betty helped Forrest with his bath and bedtime, I walked outside. The heat of the day was abating, the sun's rays now broken by the distant small mountains. What about my family's castle? It wasn't much. The small rented house perched on some gravel a mile west of Santa Rosa. Three bedrooms, two bathrooms, and a carport. Small front porch that held a couple of beat up lawn chairs, faced east, away from the afternoon sun. Propane tank. Small storage shed full of camping gear and a lawnmower for the small yard that Betty somehow kept green. Some garden tools and Forrest's bicycle. No walls. No portcullis.

Remembering Israel's warnings, I gazed south. I couldn't see the Rio Grande. Two miles of intervening hills hid it. Through the heat haze I could glimpse Mexico, as its part of the alluvial plain crept up toward distant hills. For the first time since living in Kickapoo County, I felt the menace to me and my family emanating from Mexico's close presence.

After tucking Forrest in, Betty put on a pot of coffee. She sat on the sofa, her legs curled under her, while I sat across from her in my old recliner. I told Betty what little I knew and what I suspected about Pete, the DEA, Mexican drug runners, and about Jake and his machinations. She rarely interrupted. Her expressions alternated between anger, shock, concern, and curiosity.

Betty got up and poured a third mug of coffee for me. She handed it to me and sat back down.

"Has any of this latest stuff changed anyone's—the DEA, the Rangers—*anyone's* mind about you trying to piece together the Vasquez murders?"

I didn't know the answer.

Betty pushed further. "If Pete is dirty, and it sounds like he is—big time—do you really think he had something to do with his grandparents' deaths?" She didn't wait for an answer. "From what you tell me, he's guilty of something, but I doubt he intended for that to happen, do you?"

Pete was many things, but I didn't think him capable of killing his family. I said so.

"Well, Purdy, do you believe in your heart of hearts that anyone's going to be brought to justice over what happened? Because I don't. You may 'solve this thing,' but no one who deserves punishing is going to pay."

My anger flashed quickly. Betty stopped and shook her head. "Don't be angry with me, hon. These are the cards you've been dealt. It's a bad hand. I love you because you're trying to do what's right. But I think you know I'm stating facts."

"I am angry, dammit, but not at you. At least not mostly. Killers cross the border and brutally kill an old couple. The grandson probably got them killed because of what he was up to with the cartels. I can't get anyone to even acknowledge this, and now the bastard's on the run. I feel like I've wasted a whole lot of my life on this."

Betty came over, bent down, and held my face in her hands. "Time wasn't wasted, Purdy. This has turned out to be the best thing for you and me in a long, long time." She kissed me, on the lips, the eyelids, forehead, cheeks.

I opened my eyes. Tears glistened from hers. "I love you, big man."

SEVENTY-FIVE

The Next Day

PURDY KENDRICKS AND DEA AGENT LEROY BREAUX

Jake met me at the outside office door at 8 a.m.

"Headed home?" With his wrinkled shirt and stained uniform pants, Jake looked like a stereotypical hick deputy in a Grade D movie.

"Double shift, Purdy. Yes, I'm pooped. You doing alright?"

I acknowledged things were okay. Then asked, "Heard anything interesting?"

"Lots of BOLOs down along the border south of us, for bad Mexicans. 'Course not phrased quite like that. But everyone knows some bad boys from down there shot up a bunch of vehicles" —he pronounced it VEE-hickulls— "and high- tailed it back across the border. Nothing this far upriver that I've seen."

"You heard anymore from Eddleman?" He winced when I mentioned the DEA agent's name.

"No, Purdy. I promised I'd tell you if I did." Jake's sly grin appeared. "I couldn't help noticing that you and the Ranger left out of here yesterday in an all-fired hurry. Where were you going?"

"Hell, Jake, you had to get up and walk outside to see us leave like that." I laughed at his discomfort. "Curiosity killed the cat."

"I can't help myself. But you still haven't told me where you guys went. Sure seemed like ole TJ was left out of the loop of what was going on between the two of you."

I didn't answer.

Jake kept on, seemingly oblivious to my ignoring his prying.

"Damned interesting that the reports talk about the shootings on IH 35, and U.S. 83, but that sure seems like a lot of manpower for someone who just killed two civilians. Don't get me wrong. That's bad and all, but there were enough DPS, county, and city cops, it makes me wonder if there was more to it than that. Like a manhunt for a cop killer or something."

I waved Jake off. As if sensing my arrival, my cell phone rang.

"Meow, Purdy. Meow. Curiosity's killing this old tomcat."

My cell phone rang just as I closed the door to my office.

Selman.

"Ranger, what's up?"

"Got you on speaker. I've got Breaux with me. I'll let Agent Breaux fill you in."

Breaux spoke up. "We finally got Ms. Saenz's maid to talk to us. Adela, last name Campos, has worked for Ms. Saenz for years. Tracked her down at her house. Laura Saenz took off in her Mercedes two days ago, as you know. Interestingly, she left her cell phone in its charger at the house. A quick check shows no calls to or from Vasquez on any phone we knew either of them had. No one was able to find her. The house was in a mess, but Alamo Heights says they've seen worse. Anyway, we tried to talk with Adela, the maid. She wouldn't say a damned thing. Then we went back to the maid's home after her husband called us. Turns out that his wife had had the shit scared out of her by some men who sound like *sicarios*. Why they didn't kill her, I don't know. But they didn't."

I interrupted. "I think I know who she is. I saw her at the house when I went to interview Laura." It seemed a lifetime ago.

"Anyway," he continued. "Mrs. Campos claims that Laura Saenz left in her Mercedes." He recited the Texas license plate number. "Apparently, she left in a hurry the morning after our DEA agent was killed. Sometime later, some shitbirds, no doubt associated with the *Zetas*, show up at her house looking for her. The maid, Adela, answers the door and ends up getting slapped around and threatened."

"Why are you guys just now hearing about this?"

"Good question. The answer is that they scared her damned near to death. There were four or five of them—she's not exactly sure how many. Showed up in a Range Rover if you can believe it. Clearly extremely interested in the whereabouts of Laura Saenz. Damned lucky for Saenz, she wasn't there. Searched the house, wanting to know where the woman was. Then told Mrs. Campos which school a couple of the Campos grandkids attended. She went home and tried to cover the bruises on her face with makeup, where she was slapped around. Her hubby wasn't buying it. Confronted her, and she finally broke down and told him. Mr. Campos is old school. He called Alamo Heights PD, who called us."

"Where was Laura? Did the *Zetas* find her?"

"Mrs. Campos, she's calmer now. Made of stern stuff. Seems more ashamed than she is scared. The *Zetas* made her to tell them which vehicle her boss was driving, and the license plate number. Mrs. Campos, on account of working there forever, apparently knew where to find the paperwork."

Sensing my impatience, the Ranger took over the narrative and finally got to the point. "Purdy, about your last question. We don't know. Ms. Saenz's Mercedes was found about two hours ago at the airport near Freer. The Fixed Base Operator, FBO for the place, one of his mechanics spotted it, sitting near the airport ramp. The place is pretty small. Some private planes in and out of there. It's one of the few paved strips in Duval County. Used mostly by ranchers and, occasionally, student pilots. The Mercedes caught his attention. The mechanic didn't recognize it as anyone's who has an aircraft hangered at Freer. Covered in dust and scratched all to heck. It was unlocked, so he looked inside, where he spotted bloody bandages on the floorboard passenger side. A Duval County deputy sheriff responded to the call. He says there appears to be some smeared blood on the leather seat and door handles. Also, possible blood on both seats in drips and smears. Won't know for sure until we get it towed and the forensics folks go over it."

Things were getting weird. I searched my mental map of the area. Freer is due south of San Antonio. It is also about 50 miles *east* of Interstate 35.

Had Laura actually been able to drive into the sparsely settled brush country and escape with Pete Vasquez?

I expressed my amazement. "Sounds like Pete and Laura had other cell phones the DEA wasn't aware of, doesn't it? How else could he get in contact with her without you knowing about it?"

Breaux grunted something unintelligible.

I went on. "Are you saying that with all the law enforcement running around after your agent got killed, somehow Laura sneaked by all of you, picked up Pete Vasquez, and got as far as Freer?"

Breaux sounded uncomfortable. "Don't know yet."

"Knowing Laura Saenz"—if I really did know her— "she didn't drive directly from her house in Alamo Heights to an airport almost a hundred miles away in a dirty and scratched up vehicle. A lot of things don't make sense. Why in God's name would she be in Freer, Texas?"

I had only passed through there a few times, and the place made Santa Rosa look like a metropolis.

Breaux came to the point. "Our sources aren't picking up anything out of Mexico, but it's awfully early to hear any intel from there. All we know for sure is that the *Zetas* are after both of them. We don't have them. We don't know where they are, and we're worried. If we don't find them, Vasquez and Saenz are in for a very unhappy ending."

No shit.

Abner Selman picked up the narrative. "Just guessing, but it looks like Vasquez was wounded, despite no one seeing any blood going off into the bushes after Mr. Breaux's agent was murdered."

Selman and Breaux weren't tag-teaming me to give me a weather update. "If the car was near an airport in Freer, Texas, why are you calling me?"

Abner spoke again. "You know, or knew, them both. We're letting you know that the DEA doesn't have Pete Vasquez. If anyone grabbed him, it's the cartel. We're just reaching out, asking if you have any sources that can help us."

He paused. "We have no idea what's happened to them."

"Since you've pulled me into this, why don't you tell me how Laura Saenz and Vasquez are connected. They've been lovers off and on for years, but why did he go to her, and why did she help him. If she did?"

"Eddleman can fill you in on most of it, but the bottom line is, Pete Vasquez bailed out Laura Saenz when she was broke. And he did it with dope money."

"That's why we're calling you." Selman again. "Everyone has

come up with a goose egg on finding either one of them. No aircraft stolen in Freer. Of course, no one's at the airport at night. It's not in controlled airspace. If the cartel snatched them and flew them to Mexico, it would be hell to track, even with all the radar along the border. We're not sure why Mrs. Saenz's vehicle is there. The two of them might have been trying to make it to Corpus Christi. It's on the coast. It's got a commercial airport. It's a pretty big port city."

He sighed and continued. "I think that's a pipe dream, of course. There's a good chance some coyote or wild dog will dig up the bodies months from now. Either way, maybe someone in your county will get wind of it. Pete's got some family in Kickapoo County. Is there any way you can sniff around, without raising too many eyebrows? If, by some chance, Vasquez and Mrs. Saenz are in the wind, we'd like to have a chance of reeling them in before the *Zetas* do."

Breaux finished the conversation. "My boss sure wants to find Pete Vasquez. It has gotten personal with him."

SEVENTY-SIX

The Same Day – Afternoon

PURDY KENDRICKS

I left the car windows down after lunch at the Cenizo Diner. There was a small sense of impending autumn in the air, and it was enjoyable to pretend the summer's heat was losing its grip.

I could almost see Edith Piaf's tearful gestures, as her amazing *Non, Je ne Regrette Rien* played on the iPod. I drove west out of town for a few minutes, so I could replay her song of defiance. Sure, I could push the Pause or Stop button and listen later, but I felt the selection was perfect. *Non, rien de rien. Non, je ne regrette rien.* No, absolutely nothing. No, I regret nothing. The song's dedication to the French Foreign Legion in 1960 foretold a losing cause in Algeria. I hoped my love of its challenge to fate didn't foretell the same result in Kickapoo County.

As the song ended, I made a U-turn and headed back to the office. During the lunch hour, Clarence Livermore had put up another large campaign sign. This one was on the side of a downtown building adjacent to the Courthouse square. Clarence's countenance, topped by the obligatory Stetson, leered out. His bulging eyes looked directly at the Kickapoo County Sheriff's Office. His promise of HONEST law enforcement was seemingly an accusation of malfeasance directed at TJ Johnson.

As dense as Livermore was, he showed a bit of genius in the sign's placement. Pulling the iPod's ear buds off, I stopped Sinatra's early recording of *Night and Day* and started to laugh. Chief Deputy Johnny

Reagan pulled alongside me and parked. There was no way he missed my reaction.

Reagan had for the most part steered clear of the Vasquez murder investigation, other than occasional progress updates. After my shootout with cartel members in Laredo and the ensuing dust-up, I had noticed the Laredo PD incident report and witness statements lying on his desk one afternoon. Various parts were highlighted in pink, blue, and yellow. He never discussed the shootings with me, other than to say, "Nice work." He had made no recriminations about being out of my jurisdiction. Just, "Nice work."

After Eddleman's warning, I had also steered clear of discussing the Vasquez case with Reagan, primarily because he *was* Sheriff TJ Johnson's Chief Deputy, which possibly required a personal allegiance to someone whom I didn't respect or trust.

"Purdy, that sign over there," he pointed at Livermore's jowly face, "I think Livermore is trying to harelip our sheriff."

Usually taciturn, Reagan showed me a small smile. I began to re-think his guilt by association.

At 3 p.m. my cell phone rang. It was Lucas Peckall.
Uh oh. What has happened to Mama?
"Lucas, what's up?" I had seen Mama four days ago. She had seemed fine. It was rare to get a phone call from Lucas. My voice was tight.

"First, Purdy, nothing is wrong with Kathryn."

I breathed a sigh of relief. "Sorry, Lucas. It's just that I don't get calls from you, usually, unless something bad is happening."

"Kathryn is doing fine. Or at least as fine as we can wish for."

Relieved, I quickly responded, "Good."

"But I was curious, Purdy. Did you or Betty, or anyone you know, send your mom flowers lately?"

Mama's birthday was five months away. "I haven't. Betty would have told me if she did. So, no, I don't think so. Why?"

Lucas said, "Someone did. It's a large bouquet. Cost some money, I'm telling you. Came in one of those chilled containers. UPS delivered it. The driver got one of the aides to sign for it and left."

My heart began to beat faster. "Was there a card?"

"Just a second." I could hear Lucas asking someone. He came back. "It says, 'To a wonderful lady who has a very nosy son.' That's what it says— 'nosy.' That's a heck of a greeting, Purdy. I guess you *didn't* send it."

Blood sang in my ears. I sat down, trying to stay calm. "Lucas, do you think Mama or Juana are going to miss that arrangement if I borrow it for awhile?"

"No, of course not. We were going to put it in the dining room, anyway. I'm afraid one of them would accidentally knock the vase over and make a mess." Lucas paused. "What's going on, Purdy?"

"Probably a bad joke. Lucas, one of us from the Sheriff's Office will be over there to pick up those flowers and that note in a few minutes. Just leave the flowers where they are and put the note in a plastic bag, will you?"

I rang off before there were any more questions and speed-dialed Ranger Selman. I explained the note at the nursing home.

"You're not here. I need to retrieve all those flowers, the vase, and the note. I doubt seriously there's anything we can learn, but I'm an 'interested party,' so I've got to trust someone around here. I'm not sure whether the flowers have anything to do with Vasquez, but I'm worried."

Oh, hell, yeah, I'm worried.

I walked into Johnny Reagan's office. "I need your help, Johnny. We need to go out to Golden Horizons."

"Why?"

"Mama just got a bunch of flowers with a card attached. We need to see if we can find where they came from. I think I've just been threatened."

I n pondering Betty's wisdom about "solving" the murders, I felt a guilty sense of relief that perhaps the saga was ending—that somehow I could put it all behind me. The pleasant sensation didn't last long. I realized I was already mourning the loss of two people who had been important in my life. Now, the cryptic note on flowers sent to an old lady in the Alzheimer's lock-down wing of a nursing home, made me afraid. Even if the two were dead, I may have already crossed someone's invisible point of no return.

Forrest's innocent questions about my family's castle kept coming to my mind. Two competing forces gripped me: fear, because my investigation could, and maybe already had, put my wife and child in danger, and shame for being afraid.

I felt nauseous.

I drove home. Betty was at work, and Forrest was at his cousins' house. Sitting in one of the lawn chairs in the shade of the east-facing porch, I called Eddleman and explained about the flowers and the note.

"You guys are pulling strings to get the Rangers to help you out of a ditch. At least you've decided to trust Ranger Selman. What am I supposed to do in Santa Rosa that's going to help you, without hanging myself out to dry?"

"Purdy," began Eddleman.

I interrupted. "I'm not on a first-name basis with you, Eddleman. Haven't been for years. Don't start now."

"Calm down, Deputy. I apologize." He sounded like he meant it. "My best guess is that Laura Griffin Saenz pulled a fast one on us. Somehow, she found Pete Vasquez and tried to get him some help. Given where her car was found, it's possible the two were heading to Corpus Christi hoping to get to a doctor, or just get out of the area, and didn't make it."

"No one trusts our sheriff." I caught myself nervously running a hand across my face and scalp. "If I do something behind his back, and it gets back to him, he'll want to know what's going on. What am I supposed to tell him?" I didn't wait for a response. "Even scarier, if I ask the wrong person, someone will track me and put a target on my back. Or, just as likely, I'll put someone I love in danger, if I haven't already done it. I'm not about to help you with this mess. I'm scared, Eddleman. I'm not going to deny it. I've got a wife and a five-year-old son. My house is two miles from the Rio Grande. Can you protect me? More important, can you protect my family?"

I saw Forrest's tricycle next to the back door. I could hear the desperation and fear in my voice. *Sweet Jesus, I hope Laura and Pete are dead or far, far way.*

The old urge to numb unpleasant sensations hit me. Without realizing it, I had walked around the house while on the phone. *God, a few shots of Stoli or Jose Cuervo Añejo would sure help right now.*

"Kendricks, you still there? Didn't you hear what I said?"

I hadn't. "No, sorry. Bad connection. What did you say?"

"You're right. We can't protect you in Kickapoo County. Your family is important. We'll leave you out of this one."

"Appreciate it." I rang off and began to cry.

SEVENTY-SEVEN

Laura Saenz

THE SAME DAY

The 1993 Ford F-150 pickup truck's odometer read 201,126. Sixty miles further west, it still read 201,126.

Laura glanced at the instrument panel. "Shit." She laughed at herself. What can you expect when you buy a guy's truck on the spur of the moment?

Hell, I would have paid the old drunk four times as much, if he had asked. Glad I spotted him coming out of the bar. Hope the extra five hundred keeps him from talking, at least for a while. Hope he doesn't start bragging about getting a butt-load of money to drive a car to the airport, especially after I paid him for his shitty old truck and his silence.

"What did you say?"

Laura glanced to her right. "Nothing, Pete. Just talking to myself. You hang in there. We're still a long way from San Antonio."

"San Antonio? You aren't listening! We're going to your ranch."

Damn. She acknowledged to herself that attempting to sneak back to Alamo Heights wouldn't work anyway.

Pete moaned. "Why couldn't you get us something with air conditioning? I'm burning up." He shifted uncomfortably, his chin nearly touching his chest.

She ignored the question. It was hard to hear with the truck's windows down. Besides, it wasn't the late summer heat that Pete needed to worry about. He was burning up with fever.

"Honey, you've been shot, and I think the wound may be getting infected."

The late afternoon sun bore through the sand-pitted windshield, creating starred patterns. Laura searched for a place to turn off, hoping to find some shade. Between the hell of driving into a setting sun and the approach of the small border city of Del Rio, it was time to lay low until after dark. A small road, no doubt leading to a ranch, cut off to the right. The truck's brakes juttered as it slowed. She wondered when any of the vehicle's parts had been replaced, or even checked by a mechanic.

C'mon. I just need you for a few more miles. I just hope Otabiano's truck is still at the ranch, 'cause this thing isn't going much further.

Turning off the tarmac, the truck swayed dangerously, its worn-out suspension reacting to the uneven caliche of the road's surface. A lone cottonwood in the distance grew over a source of underground water, its sparse foliage offering some shade. No dust trails showed on the horizon, so Laura decided they were probably safe from anyone's view for a couple of hours.

I need to walk off the day's tension. And see to Pete. I'm betting my ass on his promise. He can't die on me now.

Dust drifted in the open windows as the truck came to a halt. "Wake up, Pete. We're going to rest here while the sun goes down. I need to check your wound." Laura pushed the driver's door open and walked around the hood, its surface pinging as the metal cooled. Pete pushed open his door and swung his feet off the rocker panel.

"Whoa! Let me help you." Laura pulled his right arm over her shoulder and eased his feet to the ground.

"I'm thirsty."

"I bet you are." She pulled another disposable water bottle off the floorboard, cracked its seal, and handed it to Pete. "Drink all of it." She was glad she had paid the old drunk to buy a bottle of aspirin and a case of water at a convenience store in Freer. "Take four or five of these, too." She handed Pete the aspirin. "I need to check your side."

Pete swallowed a handful of aspirin and guzzled the water as Laura lifted his bloody shirt. The makeshift bandage—two sanitary napkins affixed to his abdomen and back with wide packing tape, was soaked through.

"Oh, honey. We've got to get this cleaned up." The wound's stench caught her off guard, and she nearly retched.

Pete looked at her with glazed eyes. "You can't let me die. You won't get the money." He chuckled, and then winced in pain. "How bad is it?"

Laura pulled the tape off and exposed the wound. An inch-wide exit hole with ragged edges showed on Pete's flank about four inches below the ribcage.

"I'm no doctor, but you it looks like you were hit on an angle. The entry hole is little-bitty. If we're lucky, you may be okay, as long as we can keep the infection away."

Growing up on a ranch, she had killed and gutted deer. It gave her a rudimentary knowledge of where an animal's internal organs were. She presumed Pete's injury didn't involve anything inside the peritoneum.

"I hope you're right. I don't want to die gut shot. I've read it's a horrible way to go."

Laura grabbed a small tube of topical antiseptic ointment out of a shopping bag. "Ol' Sancho, or whatever his name is, came through for us. The store clerk had to be wondering why the old guy was buying this stuff." She squirted the ointment into the exit hole. "Turn around, Pete."

He winced at the ointment's astringency. Laura repeated the process on the small entry wound, and then taped new sanitary napkins around his midriff.

This will help, but we need some real medicine.

An idea came to her. "Pete, as many years as your granddaddy worked on the ranch, I know he kept veterinary supplies around for sick and hurt cattle. Do you think there's any still around?"

Pete gingerly walked to the back of the truck and tried to drop the tailgate. He looked at her, and Laura did it for him.

"I don't know. It's been awhile since the livestock were sold off. If Oto had any left, it would be in his house. Assuming no one has ransacked it since he and Grandma died." He paused and looked off into the distance. "For a minute, I thought of them as still alive." Shaking his head, Pete eased onto the tailgate. "I need to lie down for a while."

Laura nodded in sympathy. Then raised the issue that had precipitated the mess she felt she had been dropped into.

"How exactly did they get killed, Pete? I'd like to know."

He raised up on his right side and looked at her. Through clenched teeth Pete hissed, "I did not kill my grandparents!" The outburst over, he lay back on the ridged bed of the truck.

Laura inwardly shook her head. *Yeah, but you had something to do with it. If the infection doesn't kill you, your conscience probably will.*

In less than three days, she had gone from an Alamo Heights socialite to a fugitive from God knows how many different groups of dangerous people.

Almost wistfully, Laura ignored the highway sign indicating the turn back east led to Alamo Heights. Then she shrugged. *In for a penny...* At about 8:00, she spotted a large grocery store on the west side of Del Rio, busy with shoppers.

"Stay here, Pete."

He nodded, his eyes bloodshot and watery.

"I'm going in to see what I can get us. Food, medicine, you name it." Laura pulled out a credit card, and then laughed. "This isn't going to do me any good. How much cash you got left on you?"

Pete pulled out a wad of twenties. She raised an eyebrow. "Dope money?" She was only partly joking.

Pete gave her a wounded look. "An ATM three days before I got myself shot."

She grabbed the bills and slammed the door. She couldn't help herself. "If I'm not back in thirty minutes, call the cops." Erupting into laughter, she walked through the parking lot and grabbed a shopping basket.

The occasional looks of other shoppers, all Hispanic, kicked Laura's paranoia into high gear. She went down the narrow aisles quickly. She checked out and pushed a full cart back into a lane two rows over from the rusty Ford. Cars on both sides of the old truck had left. Pete's head was barely visible above the dash. Confirming that nothing looked out of the ordinary, Laura pushed the cart up the side of the truck.

"Hey, it's me."

Pete lurched awake, eyes darting frantically. "Fuck! Don't scare me like that!"

"If you are up to it, start unloading the cart into the bed of the truck. I've got another full cart they're watching for me at the checkout area." Without waiting for an answer, Laura turned back to the store.

She soon returned. Pete was still slowly stowing grocery bags into the bed of the truck. The blood on his shirt and pants was clearly visible in the parking lot lighting. She glanced around. No one seemed to be paying attention.

"Christ, woman. What did you get?"

"We may be at the ranch for a while. You want to eat while we're there, or are you going to go hunt your food?"

She had kept the electricity service paid up but had no idea what they would find. "If the refrigerators haven't been stolen, we've got a place to chill things. Otherwise, we'll need this ice." She showed him three bags with ice blocks. "No decent ice chests for sale, but these will mostly keep until we get there." She began to help Pete.

"Shit!" A Del Rio police car pulled into the parking lot. Laura glanced down at Pete's bloody shirt. "Get back in the cab. I'll finish this." She pushed him toward the passenger door.

Only one officer was in the car. The cruiser eased down a lane two over, and Laura frantically finished loading bags of ice and six one-gallon jugs of water. She then latched the tailgate and climbed behind the wheel.

The police car, now one parking lane over, suddenly stopped. The officer left the engine running and stepped out of the car. The parking lot's lights showed him to be a young Anglo.

Laura started the truck's engine, hoping the cop's attention wasn't focused on the old F-150.

Holy Jesus, I hope this truck's lights all work. Glancing at the front windshield, Laura realized the Texas inspection sticker was five months out of date. Backing out, she nearly hit a group of shoppers pushing grocery carts.

"Wachale!"

She waved an apology and turned out onto the highway. *This town is damned near one hundred percent Mexican-American. I'm a blonde woman driving a piece of shit truck, and I stand out like a sore thumb.*

"Pete, look behind us. Do you see a cop car following us?"

Pete leaned slightly out of the passenger window. "Nope. The cop's shooting the shit with someone across from where you parked."

She wiped sweat off her forehead. The armpits of her shirt were soaked. "Pete, you smell bad. And I smell worse."

The gasoline pumps at the grocery store had been the next planned stop. Instead, she found a small filling station next to a liquor store on the edge of town. Eight forty-eight. She had 12 minutes to buy liquor before mandatory closing time. "What kind of booze do you want?"

Pete seemed not to hear.

"Stay here." She parked the truck at the gas pumps and ran to the liquor store entrance. As the store's doors locked and the Closed sign came on, she returned with three fifths of Jose Cuervo. Inside the convenience store, Laura took one of the last twenties and had the attendant turn on the pump.

J ust before 11 p.m., Laura spotted the Kickapoo County sign on U.S. 90. *Thank God. Four miles to the cut-off.* To the south and west, she could see flashes of lightning. The night air sent signals that rain was coming. *If the rain will hold off until I get onto the ranch.... No tracks to be seen. We'll at least have made it without being spotted. I hope.*

She got her wish.

———

SEVENTY-EIGHT

Present Day

PURDY KENDRICKS

I called Abner Selman. "Ranger, I've been threatened, or at least I think I have been." I described the flower delivery to Mama and mentioned the janitor's comments about "bad people" near Lágrimas.

"Where are you now?"

"At the office, but not for long. Forrest is fine. He's at Paula's. Betty's at work." I was coming unraveled. "I need some help, but I'm not sure exactly what for."

Abner Selman's voice dropped an octave. It got that way when he was deadly serious. "Purdy, let's see what we can do for you. I'm calling my Captain. I'll get back to you within fifteen minutes. In the meantime, hang tight." For a moment, his calm and slow delivery tamped down my fear.

He called back less than 10 minutes later.

"I've talked with Eddleman. He says he's not involving you in helping trace Vasquez or Laura Griffin Saenz. Is he telling me the truth?"

"That's what he says, Ranger. I guess I believe him. I'm not sure at this point that it makes much difference."

Selman agreed to meet me at the Sheriff's office.

"In the meantime, Clete Morales is going to help provide some security for your family."

"Clete? He's a DPS trooper." Clete hadn't been involved in the Vasquez investigation. I saw no reason to involve him now. "You can't expect a highway patrolman to take on that job, can you?" I began to feel like a kid crying "wolf." My face flushed with embarrassment. "That's not his job."

"He'll be in the marked DPS cruiser. That should get someone to thinking about bothering you or your family."

Selman rang off. I had no idea how to explain this to Betty and Forrest. I drove to the Kickapoo Valley Electric Cooperative.

The three of us ate a subdued supper. Betty had taken the news better than expected. When we explained the situation to Forrest, it didn't seem to faze him. As he ran off to his room, I looked over at Betty. I saw clearly a dimension of her being I had been too self-absorbed to notice. Her steely countenance said it all: Forrest was her child. Short of someone killing her, she would allow no one to harm him.

The tension was interrupted by a knock on the kitchen door. Startled, I reached for my service weapon. Betty flinched, and her eyes darted from the door to my hand unsnapping the weapon's holster strap.

"Purdy, you here?"

My face flushed. I knew that by reaching for my weapon I had confirmed in Betty's mind my own deepest fears.

"Clete's here. I'll let him in."

Betty nodded, saying nothing.

"Hey, Purdy." Clete nodded at Betty. "I'm sorry I have to do this."

Betty stared at the trooper, appearing lost in thought. Clete sensed he had walked into a tough situation.

"I'll just be outside, Betty."

Betty stood, and then took a breath.

"You'll have some coffee with us first, Clete." She walked to the kitchen and poured water in the Bunn. Smiling unconvincingly, she said, "This is just a scare. We'll get through it. Thank you for keeping an eye on us."

Relieved by the break in the tension, Clete smiled.

"Hell, folks. They're going to pay me overtime for just sitting in my car. I'm just sorry for the problem."

Clete wasn't married and had no children. Betty appreciated his courtly manners toward her and other women. She hugged him. Clete looked at me and blushed.

"Thanks, from all of us, Clete. We didn't expect this from DPS, but we're honored that you're here." I shook his hand as Betty kissed him on the cheek.

After putting Forrest to bed, I turned to Betty. "You get some rest. I'll be up awhile."

"Purdy, I'm scared."

"Nothing to worry about. DEA and the cartel are after Pete Vasquez and Laura. Not us. This will blow over."

Betty nodded. She didn't believe what I was saying. Neither did I.

I nodded off to sleep in my recliner. I woke with a start at four a.m., clutching my 9 mm. The cruiser sat in the driveway. I walked outside and quietly called to Clete. "You awake?"

"Sure, Purdy."

Climbing into the front seat with the trooper, I handed him another cup of coffee. "I'm embarrassed that you've been ordered to do this, Clete."

"What's this all about, Purdy?"

We sat sipping coffee as I told what him what I knew. I slipped back into the house at dawn.

SEVENTY-NINE

Pete Vasquez And Laura Griffin Saenz

PRESENT DAY

After closing and locking the ranch's entrance gate, Laura drove the Ford past the old headquarter structures.

"I'm worried about staying too close to the river, Pete, but if Otabiano has any vet supplies, they're probably there."

Laura had hired people from Santa Rosa to clean up the gore left after Shivelli's body had been removed and had them secure the outside door. She had not been back, even when she attended Otabiano's and Raquel's funerals. Now, the empty, dark windows of the house seemed to stare at her as the truck moved past the lone oak.

"Besides, I don't want to sleep in a bedroom where someone had his head blown off."

Pete leaned forward and looked up.

"Half moon. There's enough light. Kill the headlights."

Laura punched off the headlights, and the truck crept down the hard-packed caliche and sand toward Pete's grandparent's home.

Leaning back, Pete grunted.

"Hurts like hell. Hurts no matter what I do." Staring straight ahead, he continued. "Hope my grandparents' house isn't haunted. What do you think?"

She didn't answer. Ten minutes later, Laura eased through the arroyo, and pulled into the darkness of a shadow cast by the Vasquez house. The gentle susurration of the eddies in the Rio Grande competed with the pinging of the truck's cooling metal.

"Can you get out on your own?"

Pete nodded.

"I'm going to move the truck over there." Laura pointed toward a large copse of mesquite, white thorn, and salt cedar whitened by the moonlight. "Let's get this thing unloaded first."

Thirty minutes later, with the drapes drawn and only an old kerosene lantern lit, she examined Pete's wound.

"This tetracycline is long out of date. Lucky the electricity is still on, and your granddad kept it refrigerated."

Laura plunged a needle into the ampoule, drawing out the viscous solution.

"This needle is for cattle. It's going hurt like hell. Pull down your pants."

Handing Pete a dishtowel to bite on, she jammed the syringe into his buttocks.

Pete's scream was muffled in the cloth. She pushed the plunger. He began to shake with pain and passed out.

P ete slept until 10 a.m. The sheets on the old couple's bed were soaked through with his sweat.

"Laura?"

She walked in the room.

"You don't look so good." Not waiting for a response, he continued. "I'm hungry."

Laura touched his forehead.

"You tossed and moaned most of the night. I tried sleeping in a chair. Fever's broken, maybe. You just might live long enough to follow through on your promise."

"Did I say anything bad, Laura?" *I'm trying to remember all thirty-five of my stashes. If I say anything that makes sense to that woman, she might grab what she can and be gone. C'mon, stay focused. My memory of where the money's hidden is the only thing that's gonna help keep her around until I can leave this place.*

The sunrise brought the day's heat with it.

"I'd like to turn on the air conditioner," Laura said, pointing at the small window unit. "But I'm afraid to. Someone could hear it."

Pete gingerly rose from the bed, and the two of them took turns peeking through the windows. Neither saw any activity except vultures riding updrafts over the Rio Grande.

---

EIGHTY

Present Day

PURDY KENDRICKS

L illy Pardo ignored me as I walked into the café. My eyes felt gritty from the lack of sleep. Settling into a booth, I smiled thanks as Beulah set a mug of coffee on the table, momentarily enjoying the aroma of bacon grease and biscuits.

"I heard the DPS was guarding your house last night. What's going on?"

"I don't want you to chew me out, Beulah. I'm still smarting from our last conversation. And, no, I haven't done a damned thing of consequence since we talked."

Beulah took the hint. Snorting a retort, she turned and walked to the cashier booth where a customer waited to pay.

Uh-oh! I didn't want to do that. I didn't need to lose any friends, especially one like Beulah. It seemed as if I was already on my way to doing that, before the outburst. Embarrassed, I put my head down and noticed no one had wiped the last customer's coffee stains and crumbs.

I ate quickly. Beulah ignored my hand signals for a coffee refill. She waved me off when I signaled for the check. I left money for the meal, along with a large tip, on the table. It was starting to be a long, sorry day.

. . .

J ake nodded as I passed by the front desk and went back to reading the *Kickapoo County Register*.

I closed the door to my office, sat down, and shut my eyes. Startled awake by my cell phone buzzing, I discovered I had dozed for over an hour.

Abner Selman.

"Things go okay?"

I tried to keep from yawning.

"Thanks, Ranger. Clete was there all night. No problems."

"They're still looking for Vasquez and the woman. The two were seen in Corpus Christi boarding a Greyhound bus going to Houston. Someone's visiting with the bus driver and showing him some pictures. We'll see." He sounded doubtful. "DEA has its sources. Some of them are saying the two were killed, and the bodies were dumped in Mexico."

It seemed that, if that was the case, there would be no need for a peace officer to be threatened. I told Selman that.

"This whole sorry affair should be over with. My family and I shouldn't be in any danger. Can you give me any assurance on that one?"

I didn't expect an answer, and none was given.

"DEA hasn't found their man, or at least they aren't telling me if they did. Eddleman is a prick, but with as many state law enforcement folks involved at DEA's behest, he'd be crazy not to tell us. It'd cost him his job. Those drug boys from D.C. need us. In the meantime, let's keep your family safe. I'll arrange a place for Betty and Forrest to stay in San Antonio for a few days. Where is your family right now, Purdy?"

"Forrest is with his cousins at Paula's house. Betty went into work. I figured during the day, we're okay. Besides, I'm trying to keep this as low-key as possible. Sounds like you're suggesting otherwise."

"For a while. Just to be on the safe side." Selman rang off.

Betty wasn't going to like this one bit. I punched in her cell number.

"No, I'm not going. We'll see this through together, Purdy. Her voice was raised, so I knew she had stepped out of the office to talk. "We're a family. I'm not going to run."

I felt gut twisting fear, mixed with pride in Betty's determination.

"I can't take a chance on you staying here right now. I think this whole thing is going to blow over, Betty. They're thinking they are either dead, or in Mexico, or escaped through Corpus Christi."

"So why do we have to go anywhere, if that's the case?"

"No one knows a damned thing for sure, is why." My worries about her and our son's safety were turning into anger at Betty's refusal to cooperate. "Dammit! Think of our son, Betty! I can't do my job. I can't even think clearly if the two of you are in danger. Please!" No sound. "Are you still there?"

"Lower your voice, Purdy. I'm your wife. Don't talk to me in that tone of voice."

"I'm scared. I admit it. I apologize."

Silence. Then, "You're rubbing your face and forehead with your hand right now, aren't you?"

"How did you know that?" I took my free hand away from my forehead and put it down in my lap.

"You always do when you're stressing out. Might want to quit doing that. Your hairline is receding as it is."

Suddenly, we were both laughing.

"God, I love you, Betty. I truly do. But I wish you'd quit making me laugh. This is some serious stuff." Which only got us laughing again.

Ultimately, she agreed to pack a few clothes, pick up Forrest, and meet me at the Sheriff's Office. The Rangers would take her and our son out of the area. I apologized again for my anger and went back to work.

A t 5:15, Selman knocked on my office door. "What time did you tell Betty to be here?"

Shit. I had let the afternoon pass by, temporarily pushing my concerns to the back of my mind.

"Five o'clock. Hold on." I punched in Betty's phone number. It went to voicemail. No answer on the office phone at the Cooperative —after five and closed. I punched in Paula's cell number and took several breaths, trying to keep my voice calm.

"Hey, Purdy. What's up?"

"I'm trying to track down Betty. We've probably got cell tower problems, and all I'm getting is voicemail." *Breathe. Breathe. Breathe deeply.* "Have you seen her in the last hour or so?"

"She picked up Forrest, and they were heading home. That was about two hours ago. She said something about taking a trip. What's going on, Purdy?" Paula continued without pausing, "They were coming by here afterward, but I haven't heard from her. She told me about Clete parked all night in his patrol car at your house. Is my only sister in danger?" Her voice was taking on a hysterical edge.

"Of course not. No big deal. Gotta go." Paula's voice had grown several decibels when I disconnected, cutting off further questions.

Jake was regaling Johnny Reagan and Deputy Bonavita with some humorous story when we came down the hallway. They looked up, startled, as Selman and I hurried toward the exit. I stopped long enough to explain what was going on.

"Someone may have taken Betty and Forrest."

Reagan tapped Bonavita on the shoulder.

"Let's go!"

The young deputy looked confused.

"The killings on the Griffin place. Maybe something to do with that. I don't know. Don't have time to talk right now."

Bonavita's face told me he was re-seeing the viscera and dead body of Shivelli in the bedroom of the old ranch house.

As the four of us pushed through the door, Jake yelled out, "What do you want me to do?"

I couldn't think of a thing and shook my head. Selman insisted on riding with me and unlocked the trunk of his State car, extracting a short-barreled assault shotgun. I uncaged my vehicle's shotgun from its rack, and he and I climbed into my tired Sheriff's Office patrol car.

Jake came running out, waving his arms frantically.

"Purdy, I need to help. What can I do?"

I was about to tell him how little his need to help meant right now. Thinking the better of it, I told him to call Eddleman and have the DEA agent call me.

With a clearer head than mine, Selman waved at Reagan and Bonavita, backing out in Reagan's cruiser. Leaning over me, he said, "No sirens or lights."

Sheriff TJ Johnson drove up as we were clambering into the two cars and waved me down.

"What's going on Deputy?"

I looked at the two yard-sized political signs he was clutching.

"Sheriff, my family may be in trouble. I'll tell you later."

"But, I need to know...."

I rolled up the cruiser's window and shoved the transmission into drive. In my rearview mirror I could see TJ showered with gravel and dirt as the tires spun. *Fuck him.*

"Calm down, Purdy. Your family's going to be fine."

Jesus Christ. I swung around a tractor trailer rig doing the speed limit. Two eastbound cars swerved to avoid getting hit. Selman gripped the dash and gasped.

"Purdy, slow the hell down! You shouldn't even be involved at this point. If I had a lick of sense, or the power to do anything about it, I'd make you cool your heels back downtown."

I eased off the accelerator, but not much.

"You couldn't stop me, so don't try."

Thankfully, Abner didn't say anything the remaining mile to the turn-off. With Reagan directly behind us, I pulled over halfway to our home and stopped. Reagan pulled alongside and rolled down the passenger window.

I explained the layout of the house—kitchen, living room and dining room combination, hallway, small guest bathroom used by Forrest, the big bedroom with Betty's and my bathroom. Quick questions from the other three. Was there an attic? No. Which way did doors swing? I couldn't remember, but guessed. Entrances and exits. Just two—the carport door, used almost exclusively, and a front door in the hallway facing east, toward Santa Rosa.

Selman said nothing when I made the decision on how to enter. "We'll take the carport entrance. You two cover the northeast and southeast corners."

Reagan nodded. Before his cruiser sped past me, he yelled, "You know your house better than I do, Purdy. I'll let you check things out, but you gotta promise me you won't go charging in and get yourself shot."

I nodded and pulled up to the carport. Betty's car sat nose in. Abner and I approached the back door after getting the high sign from

Reagan, who had stationed Bonavita behind some caliche outcroppings about 20 yards from the northeast corner of the house. Reagan knelt behind the flimsy storage shed. *That's not going to stop a bullet, dammit.*

The late afternoon sun made the back end of Betty's car hot to the touch. The hood, in the carport's shade, was barely warm. The car had been there for a while. Abner, shotgun in hand, took the house's southeast corner, where he could see our small front yard and cover me as I edged toward the carport door. Forrest's tricycle lay on its side, no doubt where my son had left it. A little draft of air swung the seat on our child's swing set. The forlorn sadness of the toys not again being touched by my five-year-old momentarily swept my thoughts away from the immediacy of our possible danger.

Abner tapped me on the shoulder, hard. He whispered, "Get your goddamned head in the game."

Nodding, I banged on the outside door with my pistol, while standing off to one side where brick wall could provide some protection. Nothing. I rapped on the wood again. Nothing. The door was unlocked. Normally that wouldn't have concerned me. We often didn't lock it when we were home. However, with the threats, I knew Betty would have secured the house after she was inside. Especially with Forrest there. My internal alarms were clanging.

I pushed the door open and quickly glanced into the gloom. No lights were on in the living room and kitchen. Except the microwave oven. Its door open, a coffee cup sat on the turntable. The digital readout flashed End...End...End.

No movement. No noise. "Betty! Are you here? Forrest! Son! Are you here?" I prayed to hear something benign. Something to free me from the gut-clenching fear that something had happened to the two people I loved most in the world. Nothing. I called again. "Betty! Are you here? It's me, Purdy. Hon, there's four of us here. You're in no danger!" Again, nothing.

I backed out.

"Ranger, there's nothing that I can hear in there."

Despite the cool interior of the house, sweat poured down my face. Suddenly, my arms felt too heavy to lift. I moved outside, lowered my weapon, bent over, and took a deep breath.

"Before we go in, let your two deputies know what we're going to do." He paused. "Did you see any signs of...." Abner stopped. He didn't need to finish the sentence.

I shook my head, and Selman gripped my upper arm and squeezed.

"Purdy, it'll be okay."

From the cover of the brick wall, I called Reagan on his cellphone.

"What is it, Purdy?"

"We're going in to check." I filled him in on what little I knew.

"Before you go in, Bonavita says there's broken glass scattered around outside of the master bathroom. I looked at it. There may be blood on the windowsill."

Gorge rose in my throat, and I swallowed to keep from vomiting.

"If someone comes out other than the two of us or my family, kill them." I could sense his nod.

Abner and I entered quickly. As he went to the refrigerator on one wall, I could hear his labored breathing from the danger and stress. The Ranger wasn't a young man anymore. He nodded, and I went past the kitchen to the hall doorway. Nothing. Abner, pointing the shotgun, moved toward the door to my son's room. Forrest's small suitcase lay open on his bed.

The door to Forrest's bathroom off the hallway was open. Forrest's toothbrush stood mutely in his plastic Ninja Turtle cup. No blood anywhere so far. Two more rooms. Our bedroom and the adjoining bathroom.

Selman signaled me to cover him. I tried to push past, and he pushed back, shaking his head. This wasn't about proper police procedure. This was the Ranger hoping to spare me if something had happened to my family that I shouldn't see. I crouched, leveled my pistol, and nodded. Abner gripped the doorknob and pushed.

The door swung inward, squeaking as it did. *Betty asked me to spray the hinges with WD-40 last week, and I forgot. Need to get that done.* Idiotic thoughts, as I prayed Abner and I wouldn't die in a hail of bullets.

No movement. Abner flipped on the light switch and backed out, glancing at me. I couldn't take it anymore. Squeezing past the Ranger, I dived into the room, trying to cover all points of the compass with my pistol as I rolled toward our bed. Abner ran toward the bi-fold closet doors, pulling one off its tracks as he shoved his shotgun inside. Again, nothing.

"Fuck!" The oath exploded from both of us as we lurched toward the closed bathroom door. Selman pointed at four small holes patterned waist high, and shrugged, as if to ask if the door had suffered the damage before. Shaking my head "no," I noticed there was no splintering into the bedroom through the door's cheap luan panel. I looked toward the nightstand on Betty's side of the bed. Its drawer was pulled open and clearly, the snub-nosed 9 mm pistol was missing. What the hell had happened?

The door handle was nearest me. The Ranger handed me the shotgun, and I holstered my automatic. He reached for the door handle, and I pointed the shotgun at the wall. If shots came from the bathroom, the shotgun's double-ought buckshot would blow holes through the wall and into anyone on the other side.

Abner counted silently, "One, two, three," He pulled the door open. I crouched, ready to return fire.

Nothing. From my angle, I could see myself in the vanity mirror, and instinctively ducked.

Abner finally said, "I'm looking inside toward the shower and a small window, Purdy. No one is in there."

Handing him the shotgun, I wiped the cold sweat from my eyes. No one was in the bathroom, but someone had been there. Small spatters of blood made a pattern on the wall away from the bedroom. Blood smeared the tile under the small bathroom window. What remained of the glass and the window frame were pushed out. Heavier, blackened streaks of blood smeared the shower wall and the frame's surfaces.

"Purdy, someone got shot here."

"And Betty's automatic isn't in the nightstand drawer." *O Sweet Jesus. Where were my wife and child?*

Instead of answering, Abner yelled, "Deputies, we're coming out. Don't shoot us." His wheezing seemed to lessen.

Both Reagan and Bonavita acknowledged they had heard. We opened the front door and stepped into the yard.

I had allowed the adrenalin to momentarily take my mind off Betty and Forrest. The frantic fear rushed back, and I began to hyperventilate. *Where is my family?*

Bonavita yelled out, "Hey, I found something. Come here!"

I leaned forward to keep from passing out, and Abner steadied me.

The young deputy had left his spot behind the caliche outcropping and scrabbled downhill. Still cautious, the three of us approached. Bonavita stood over a man's body, his automatic trained at the inert form.

Reaching him within seconds, we stared at a dead Hispanic, blood pooling around his body. Both arms were under him, as if clutching his abdomen. A Colt .45, heavily plated with silver designs, lay out of reach.

Abner pulled the dead man's hands out where we could see them and rolled the body over.

Eyes, already turning milky in death, stared into space. The dead man had been gut shot and died after escaping out the bathroom window.

Reagan checked the body for identification.

"Nothing on him. But that is one ugly fucker."

Pockmarked and scarred, even in death the corpse seemed to exude evil. A black rage swept over me, and I began to kick at the body, screaming, "Where is my family, motherfucker!"

As I pulled back to kick again, someone threw me to the ground. The Ranger stood over me. As I scrambled to stand, he pushed me down again.

"Knock it off, dammit! The man's dead! He's not going to tell you a damned thing!"

My rage changed to shame. Turning away to avoid Abner's eyes, I began to sob.

Reagan called the Sheriff's Office.

"Jake, get an ambulance out here and bring crime scene tape." He paused. "No, we've got a body, but we haven't found Betty or the boy."

By this time, I was running up the hill away from the house. The sun's rays now cut by the hills, cast shadows that crept toward the east. Soon, it would be dark.

I started screaming, "Betty, Forrest, where you?"

My howls echoed in the bare hills and gullies. In the background, Abner was calling the Department of Public Safety, requesting a helicopter and additional assistance.

Bonavita appeared beside me and yelled, "Mrs. Kendricks. It's me, Johnny Bonavita. If you're out there, call out!"

I ran out of breath and motioned Bonavita to quiet down. In the distance, flashing lights heralded an ambulance and other law enforcement heading west from Santa Rosa.

As I took a breath to scream Betty's name again, I heard a woman's voice faintly in the distance. "We're here! We're here!"

I ran toward Betty's voice, at the same time screaming, "Where are you?"

My wife and son appeared from a small ravine a football field's distance from our house. *Oh, Sweet Jesus Christ, they're alive!*

Forrest's eyes were wild, and he clung to his mother. Betty, jeans covered in dirt, slowly walked toward me, shoving her small automatic into her pants pocket. As I reached them, she fell toward me. I held her up.

"Oh, Daddy! I'm glad you're here." Forrest clutched my leg.

Betty reached down and slipped me the small automatic.

"I don't want to see this again, Purdy," she whispered. "I saw one man outside and then heard someone in the bathroom. They were waiting for me and Forrest." Tears streamed down her cheeks. "I think I killed a man."

I began to cry, and I held my family tightly as several patrol cars and an ambulance arrived with wailing sirens and flashing lights.

EIGHTY-ONE

Present Day

PURDY KENDRICKS

E van Smithers had been a family doctor for decades. He had given tetanus shots each school year to every Santa Rosa football player. He had mended broken bones, treated chicken pox, and written prescriptions for the aches and pains of our county's small population in a small remodeled house near the courthouse. He never advertised it, but Doc, as he was called, had attended a first-rate medical school in the Northeast. Rumor had it that a failed marriage and a weakness for the bottle had ruined a burgeoning practice somewhere in Kansas. He had licked the booze problem years ago, obviously something I admired, and at times, envied. Whatever the reason, he had opened a family practice in Santa Rosa.

Doc splinted my broken arm in the seventh grade and treated me for tonsillitis in high school. Now nearly 80, he gently examined my wide-eyed son, asking him quietly about any physical injuries he might have suffered.

Forrest's responses were all negative until the doctor rolled the boy's thin arms outward. Red, rapidly bruising marks showed on each upper arm, clearly indicating four splayed finger marks. Doc paused, glanced at me, and made no comment. He unwound his stethoscope and checked Forrest's heart and lungs.

I stood by the door, quietly watching the small boy's trust in the old man. Doc's examination room hadn't changed a bit over the years.

The Norman Rockwell prints still hung, a bit faded, but just as askew as I remembered.

Forrest sat perched on the edge of the tired-looking exam table, swinging his tennis shoe-clad feet back and forth.

"Doc, can I ask you a question, sir?"

"Mmm?" Doc pulled the stethoscope earpieces off. "What's that, young man?"

"Will you check on my mom, please? She was real upset and was crying a lot. I want to be sure she's okay."

"Sure, Forrest." If Doc had looked right at me then, I would have lost it. "I guess she and you had to run pretty quick, didn't you?"

"Yessir. My mom, she grabbed me, and she said, 'Forrest, we need to run.' She was screaming, and she ran so fast I couldn't keep up. Then she grabbed me again and carried me. I kept telling her I'd be okay, and to put me down, but she wouldn't. And then we slid down a hill and she got all dirty, and I guess I did, too. And we waited, and she wouldn't let me say anything and told me to hush. She promised if I did, we were going to be okay, and my daddy was coming, and...."

The words seemed endless. I became aware that Doc hadn't turned on the air conditioning. The five-year-old's recitation of his experience and the cloistered heat of the tiny room were too much. In a panic, I reached for the doorknob to escape the claustrophobia sweeping over me.

I opened the door, and a small waft of cooler air stopped me.

"Purdy."

"Yes, Doc?"

"Forrest is doing just fine. Just some bruising." He turned to my son. "Your Mama isn't hurt. I checked her out, too. You don't have anything to worry about now." Forrest didn't look convinced. Doc tousled his hair and smiled. "Your Mama is just fine. Why don't you hop off that table, put your shirt back on, and go see her?"

Forrest jumped off the table and ran down the hall toward the reception area.

"Mama, Doc says you're okay!"

Doc closed the door to the examination room. "Good, sweet child there, Purdy. You and Betty should be proud."

I opened my mouth to respond, and my throat closed up. Tears suddenly streamed down my face. Snot leaked from my nose as I tried to control my weeping.

Doc handed me a wad of tissues.

"I'll prescribe a sedative for sleep for all of you. They may need it. Looks to me as if you probably will too, Purdy. I'll get them to open the pharmacy tonight." Doc grasped my shoulder. "Boy, they have been through the wringer. But they came through it. Take a couple of deep breaths and get yourself together. They need you to be strong. You go have yourself one hell of a cry, or two, or three. But later, and away from them. Okay?"

I blew my nose and wiped my eyes, then headed to my family.

Doc's reception area held more people than it was designed for. I handed the prescription slip to Johnny Bonavita, who agreed to head to the pharmacy. Law enforcement and well-wishers crowded the small space. TJ Johnson stood by an old gumball dispenser, wringing the brim on his weathered Stetson. He looked genuinely concerned.

I nodded in gratitude at everyone.

"Thanks for coming. We're all okay."

We weren't, but that's what people say. I looked at Betty's haggard, pinched expression, and got us the hell out of there as fast as I could.

I took Betty and Forrest to Paula's house and returned home, accompanied by Abner, to pick up some clothing and personal items. Pushing several strips of crime scene tape aside at the carport door, I tried to crack a joke.

"Looks like someone was trying to wrap this place up as a present."

The Ranger merely grunted.

Paula Richardson answered my knock and quickly took the small suitcases I had brought.

"I gave both of them Doc's prescription. They've both conked out."

Her facial expression confirmed that whatever yardage I had gained recently with her had been erased by penalties.

"You're welcome here, Purdy. Whenever you get done with what-ever it is you need to do tonight, come on back." She handed me a key. "Your wife will be needing you near her when she wakes up."

She closed the front door. I heard the deadbolt slide shut with a sharp thwack.

. . .

I couldn't recall the Sheriff's Office ever having this much activity at one in the morning. Its parking spots were full, and more vehicles were parked at the courthouse. The smell of coffee perking hit me as I came through the glass doors. The subdued chatter stopped as we filed into the conference room for an informal debriefing. I spotted Eddleman leaning against a wall in the far corner. Abner introduced the DEA agent. TJ tried unsuccessfully to pretend he was aware of what had been going on. I felt a momentary sense of sadness at the man's confusion. It passed.

In the next hour, Eddleman described the assassination in Mexico of *La Familia Norteña's* Venustiano Huerta, *Los Zetas'* takeover of the Nuevo Laredo drug routes, the deaths of the Vasquez couple in Kickapoo County, and the disappearance of Pete Vasquez and Laura Griffin.

Nothing was said about Pete's involvement with the DEA, or of him muling drugs for two different cartels. *Odd*. Eddleman still didn't trust TJ, or claimed to. He was disclosing a lot, but not everything. Maybe he was embarrassed. I was too tired to care. I sat quietly, watching the reactions of the men. Several had quizzical looks.

Behind me, someone spoke up.

"Yes?"

"You're telling us that Pete Vasquez and Ms. Saenz were heading toward Corpus Christi, and they may be dead, or captured."

I turned. Clete Morales was referring to a notepad he had apparently been taking notes.

"I know Deputy Kendricks has been investigating the killings at the Griffin place. I'm not clear what Pete Vasquez has to do with that. I'm not clear why they're after the Griffin lady, either. Mostly, I'm wondering what any of this has to do with Purdy at this point—and his family."

There was a murmur of agreement. Several men patted me on the back. Abner looked in my direction and waved at Eddleman, who didn't respond.

"It's one in the morning. Deputy Kendricks needs to see his family, and we all need some sleep. Let's continue this in the morning." Almost as an afterthought, he turned to TJ. "Is that all right with you, Sheriff?"

Shaking off his lethargy, TJ nodded. We'd all meet at nine in the morning. In the meantime, two deputies volunteered to guard Paula's house in Santa Rosa. I remained seated as everyone filed out.

"Ranger. Eddleman. What about my family? You got any ideas on why there were two of them at my house? They could have killed my wife and child. Where's the one who got away? If they were grabbing Betty and Forrest, that means someone thinks they're tradable. What is it that makes them valuable?"

The DEA agent paused.

"We haven't found Pete or the woman. Maybe someone thinks you might know more than you do."

Befuddled with exhaustion, I shook my head. Abner ended the discussion.

"Purdy, you look like shit. I *feel* like shit. It has been a long day. Let's pick this up in the morning. I've got some criminalistics folks coming from Austin in the morning to go over your house. The man your wife shot is on his way to the Bexar County Medical Examiner. No doubt I've got a luxury suite at your dot-Indian buddy's Mesa Tourist Court. Assuming there are no bedbugs, I'll get some rest."

I nodded and headed to my car. It was only three blocks to Paula's house. I parked in the driveway, waved to the deputies and killed the engine. I jammed the iPod ear buds in and punched *play*, hoping for a few minutes of escape from Santa Rosa. I closed my eyes.

A live recording of the Johnny Pizzarelli and Jessica Molaskey duet of *They Can't Take That Away From Me* started. Pizzarelli's seven-string guitar riffs were magical. I glanced in the rearview mirror and caught myself smiling.

The song ended to the Luca Jazz Center crowd's applause. *Man, I'd love to be there right now. A Glenmorangie in a heavy glass tumbler. Just one....*

My cell phone screen lit up. *Lowell Johnson.*

"Hey, Lowell. I'm not in the mood to talk right now."

"Not looking for a story at this late hour, Purdy. I didn't expect to get to talk to you at Doc's office. I was tempted to walk into the SO. Looked like a convention being held there. I've been driving around and saw you sitting in the car. You look out of it. Didn't even notice me. You doing okay?"

"Yeah. Thanks, Lowell. I appreciate it."

"Sure, but I do expect a story from you on this before someone from San Antonio or Laredo news outlets get to you. Promise you'll talk to me first? I'm just a weekly, and I can't beat anyone to the public, but who knows. Maybe I'll do an in-depth series of stories on Kickapoo County's sometimes errant deputy sheriff, and land a Pulitzer." He cackled with laughter and rang off.

My body screamed at me as I opened the car door. Muscles that had tensed from fear earlier now started to cramp.

"Shit." I took several deep breaths and did a few quick deep knee bends. My cell phone lit up again. *Israel Sifuentes.* I didn't realize I had him in my contact list.

"Yes?"

"*Señor* Purdy?"

"Is that you, Israel?"

"*Si. La gente*, we've heard about what happened. There were two *malditos*, weren't there?"

I started to ask him how he knew there was more than one, but he interrupted me.

"I need you to see and hear something."

"Now? It's almost two in the morning. Can it wait until I get some sleep?"

"*Señor* Purdy, everyone heard what happened. That is why I want you to meet with me. Please. Trust me. And please, *señor*. Don't bring nobody with you."

EIGHTY-TWO

Present Day

PURDY KENDRICKS

The 20 miles to the border hamlet of Lágrimas seemed to take forever. *I should have told Israel it would have to wait.* I suddenly realized no one knew where I was heading, I pulled off the highway. For some reason, I called Jake Nichols.

"What? Purdy? Is this a butt dial? You okay?" Jake yawned loudly into the receiver. "I had to clean up everyone's coffee cups after you guys left. Not supposed to be a dispatcher's job. I'm not paid enough...."

I cut him off. "I'm heading to Lágrimas, Jake. Israel Sifuentes called and asked me to come. I wanted to...."

"Jeez, Purdy. You want me to call some folks to meet you? I'll come out there. Jesus Christ. That's in the middle of Bumfuck, Egypt! Do you know what you're doing? Jeez, oh jeez, Purdy."

I cut him off and explained that I just wanted someone to know where I was.

"Okay, Purdy. But, Christ! Isn't that upriver from where you found the dead guy in the river? And all those spent AK47 rounds?"

Uh, yeah. It was.

"Jake, please. I don't want anyone coming out here. Israel made it clear that I'm to come alone. Whatever he's got to show me isn't going to happen if I show up with the cavalry."

Jake was still muttering about me being a damned fool when I rang off.

Heeding Sifuentes's instructions, I looked for an abandoned adobe structure near the low water crossing. I pulled the car off the gravel road 30 yards from the ruin. As I opened the car door, I instinctively unsnapped the holster strap and eased the safety off my automatic. I waited for my eyes to adjust to the dark.

A quarter-moon washed the area in pale luster. No lights shone in the few occupied buildings uphill from the abandoned adobe. A dog began barking. It suddenly grunted and went quiet. Its owner had kicked it. A man's voice shushed the animal as it was dragged inside, and a door was slammed. Except for the susurration of the Rio Grande's waters, the quiet resumed.

This is crazy.

"*Señor* Purdy. *Vente pa ca.*" The beam of an electric lantern shone through a paneless window. I stepped over pieces of scrap wood and adobe brick dissolving back into the earth and through an open doorway. Lilly Pardo stood next to Israel Sifuentes.

"Lilly, what the hell?"

Lilly's countenance showed fear and determination. I quit talking. As I moved closer, an old man appeared from behind Israel. Speaking in Spanish, Israel introduced me.

"This man is *el jefe* of an *ejido* called Parritas."

The old man shyly put out his hand. It felt like a tortoise's shell. I glanced down. Huarache sandals, not shoes or boots.

"Teofilo Ramirez, at your service."

Parritas. Where Juan Gabriel Sosa, el Vaquerito, was from. The man we found in the river with intestines streaming out into the Rio Grande and his head blown off.

The three moved to one side as in a choreographed movement. Israel held the lantern in front of him, illuminating a man lying on his side. Duct tape trussed his wrists and arms. Insulated electrical wire bound his shoulders to his side. A rag stuffed in his mouth gagged muffled grunts as his eyes moved in my direction.

"Who is he?"

Lilly Pardo answered. "He is one of the men who tried to take your wife and child."

"Are you sure? How do you know this?"

"After your wife shot his *compadre*, he drove here to cross the river. Someone saw him when his truck broke down near Lágrimas."

"Thanks, Lilly. Thanks, Israel. We need to get him to the sheriff, where I can ask him some questions." The inanity of my response hit me almost as soon as I said it.

"No!" Israel rebuked. He continued in Spanish. "You ask your questions here. Besides, you need to hear what he has to say before anyone else does."

He reached down and pulled the rag out the man's mouth. Then he pulled the heavily tattooed man onto his haunches. Whoever he was, the captive had the marking of a *sicario*.

Squatting, I looked at the man's swollen face. Someone had worked him over.

"Were you at my house today?"

There was no answer. Israel aimed a kick at the man's ribs.

"Answer the man, *cabrón!*" Grabbing the electrical wire wrapped around the *sicario's* shoulders, Lilly kept him sitting erect. Israel drove another kick into the man's ribs.

"*Contestale, hijo de puta!*"

My stomach lurched as the man groaned in pain.

"Goddamit! Stop, Israel." I leaned in. "Were you at my house today?"

Nodding, the *sicario* mumbled something.

"What?"

"You know where the *soplón* and the *puta* ran to. We were told to take your son and wife, so you would tell us."

This made no sense at first.

"Who are you talking about?"

"Vasquez and the blonde woman."

I looked up at the three.

"I don't know where they are. Why would I?" I turned back to the *sicario*. "Who sent you?"

"*Mi jefe.* Some call him 'Cantinflas.'"

Christ almighty. I had heard that name before. Almost anyone in law enforcement anywhere near the border was aware of the *Zetas'* top lieutenant. Northern Mexico, and especially border towns, were littered with his handiwork—mainly decapitated bodies and garbage bags of severed heads.

"Guillermo Blanco?"

He nodded.

"So you're a Zeta?" No answer. "Who was the other man with you?"

"We call him *Cuarenta-y-cinco*." Forty-five. *The dead man with the Colt automatic clutching his guts behind my house.*

I was still confused.

"Don't you have Vasquez? Don't you have the blonde woman?"

The man shook his head.

"We cannot find them."

I stood up.

"I need to get this man to the sheriff, Israel."

"No, *señor*. There is more." Turning to the captive, Israel rattled off something too fast for me to grasp. The man mumbled something in return. The sparse light prevented me reading facial expressions to help with my Spanish.

"What else, Israel?"

"This *cabrón* isn't just some *pinche* cowboy. He knows things." He nudged the man. "*Dile lo mas.*" Then to me. "Ask him about the American drug cops."

"You mean the DEA?"

He nodded. I squatted next to the Zeta.

"What's your name?"

"Jose. Jose Escarate."

The dust rose in motes as I repositioned myself next to the trussed man. Israel handed me the lantern, which I set on a piece of lumber lying on the floor. Other than an unexpected shoot-out in Laredo, I couldn't remember if I had ever been this close to a living Zeta.

"Jose, you know something about the DEA?"

It sounded like a stupid question. Of course the *Zetas* knew something about the DEA. The DEA was the *narcos'* nemesis. I didn't know how to start the questioning that Israel wanted to pursue.

Escarate nodded. The whorls of adobe dust caused him to sneeze. With the sneeze came several gasps of pain from the broken ribs and whatever else had been damaged.

Escalante spat a gobbet of phlegm against the wall to his right, and then turned back to me. "Tu amigo, Vasquez. He's a dead man, *gabacho.*"

"If you get him first, for sure."

Escarate huffed a mocking laugh.

"You *norteamericanos* think your *policia* is always doing what is right, eh?"

When I didn't respond, he continued. "We will kill Vasquez for sure. If *La Familia Norteña* has any *soldados* left when we finish with their *joto* asses, they will try to kill him for sure."

Escarate went silent and looked up at his three captors.

"But?"

Escarate's look told me he was holding onto one bit of information that he could trade for his life. "I tell you—I have nothing else. They kill me." He spat again, this time in the direction of Israel, Lilly, and Teofilo Ramirez.

I doubted it—and told him so. Escarate closed his eyes. He seemed to be making a sort of internal computation.

Ramirez, of obvious indigenous blood, had stood passively, his face displaying little emotion. Suddenly, he leaned down and quickly stabbed Escarate in his cheek. Ramirez's motion was quick and totally unexpected, at least by me.

Not sure of what I'd just witnessed, I saw him tuck a small knife into a pocket. Escarate's face sprouted redness as blood welled to the surface and quickly began streaming into his clothes.

"Jesus Christ!" I pushed up. Israel shoved the village elder away and turned back to me. Lilly screamed at the two men to back off and spoke soothingly to Escarate.

"*Por favor*, tell this *norteamericano* what you know. He is not DEA."

Escarate spat more phlegm, this time ruby red. The knife wound had pierced his mouth. Now, more rapidly, he said, "*Los* DEAs" —he pronounced it deh-ee-ahs— "they don't want Vasquez to be arrested. Their *jefe*, the tall *pinche*" —he described Eddleman— "he wants to make an example." Another grunted laugh and another gobbet of blood. "Just like us. What you think of that?"

"Where did you hear that? Why?"

"His man—*Cuarenta-y-cinco* killed him when he tried to escape with the Vasquez piece of shit. Put a bullet through the *puto* cop's head with his forty-five. *Tu amigo*, he doesn't have any choices." Another gobbet of fresh blood sprayed into a dusty corner. "We kill him and his *puta*, or your *narco policias* kill him. "

"*Sin duda*," I said. "But how do you know the DEA intends to kill him and the woman."

"*Esos pinches*, the fucking DEA *jefe*, the tall one in Laredo, maybe he thinks Vasquez turned on him." Escarate grunted a small, painful laugh. "That Vasquez *puto*, we turned him against *La Familia Norteña*. *Los* DEAs, they turned him against us. Who's to say he didn't turn again? *Los* DEA. They will kill Vasquez. If they find out where he is, their boss, he'll be there for sure. The *narco* cop's boss, *ese* DEA *puto, he* will kill Vasquez... If we get to Vasquez first, that would be better for him. Either way, Vasquez never makes it into the safety of a fucking American penitentiary. We will cut his balls off and stuff them in his mouth. We will break his bones with a baseball bat. We will rape his woman. Many times. Then we will kill them. The *norteamericano* DEA *jefe*, he will just kill him and perhaps the woman. They'd better hope they die that way. It will be a better way to die."

Any sympathy for the *sicario* disappeared.

"I am asking you, one more time, *cabrón*. How do you know the DEA *jefe*" —I didn't use Eddleman's name— "wants Pete Vasquez and *la rubia* dead?

Escarate sneered at me.

"As you say in *los estados unidos*, 'this is the *frontera*.' You think *los* Zetas don't hear things and see things, in Laredo, *Tejas?* You don't think a *gabacho* can be bought, just like one of the *raza?* And there are fucking few *gabachos* in Laredo, anyway. You think *los Zetas* don't have many, many contacts on your side of the river?"

"Who?"

"I don't know, and I wouldn't tell you, anyway, *puto*."

Sickened by what I had witnessed and heard, I stood. Israel stuffed the rag back into the Zeta's mouth and duct taped it into place.

"We brought you here so you could get answers that might help you. But this piece of shit isn't going with you."

The light came on in my head.

"Christ. You can't take justice into your own hands. It's not right!" As I said it, I realized just how stupid I sounded.

As the *sicario* had reminded me, this was the border. I reminded myself that I was armed. As if reading my thoughts, Israel shook his head and pointed a rusty revolver at my head.

"Please, *Señor* Purdy. There is nothing more for you to see here. Please leave now."

Lilly touched my arm.

"Mr. Purdy. If he goes with you, the *sicarios* find out how he was found. The people here" —she gestured toward the hamlet— "they will be killed." She pointed at Teofilo Ramirez. "He will be killed."

Teofilo nodded. "The people in my *ejido*. None of us wants this scum near us. We cannot let him go. *Los Zetas* or another cartel—they used Juan Gabriel. Then they spit him out."

Lilly tugged at my arm. "Please, Mr. Purdy. Please leave."

"And him?" As I nodded toward Escarate, the *sicario's* eyes widened in fear.

Teofilo Ramirez shook his head. Israel lowered the pistol.

"You know what would happen. No matter what you promised. The *Zetas*, they have eyes and ears everywhere." He gestured toward Escarate. "You heard this scum. Someone would tell. We, and our families, we would be killed. You know."

I did know. I left the man with them, stepped outside the adobe, and got into my vehicle. I pulled up to the highway, stopped, and turned off the ignition.

The small pop of a pistol shot disturbed the night air. A dog barked. I opened the door and vomited, then drove away.

EIGHTY-THREE

Present Day

PURDY KENDRICKS

I slipped into Paula's house at 5 a.m., showered, and slid into bed next to my wife. Thankfully, she was asleep. Sensing my weight on the bed, she moved close, and I held her, listening to her breathing. I did not sleep. With the brightening of the room by the morning sun, I carefully untangled myself and dressed.

Paula was in the kitchen frying bacon.

"I thought you were going to be right back last night. You didn't show until nearly five a.m. Long meeting?"

"Yes." I reached for a coffee mug. The consequences of what I had heard and of the soft *pop* of Israel's rusty pistol in the night's stillness haunted my thoughts. "Hope I didn't disturb anyone."

Paula cocked her head and looked at me quizzically.

"You look like hell, Purdy. Did you sleep at all?"

"Some." I sat down, and she set a plate of scrambled eggs and bacon in front of me. She busied herself at the range. Thankfully, there were no more questions.

I left my sedan parked in Paula's driveway and walked the three blocks to the courthouse square. Outside the Kickapoo County Sheriff's Office, two media crews, from Laredo and San Antonio, stood near vans with satellite uplinks. Santa Rosa was making headlines.

Clarence Livermore, festooned with political campaign buttons, held forth with the San Antonio TV crew about TJ's "inability to protect his own deputies and their families."

Kickapoo County's rarely present District Attorney, Josh Hinton, looked around, as the Laredo news crew hooked a mic to his shirt collar. He had never had an opponent, but that didn't mean he was going to miss a shot at good publicity.

A woman in a news crew spotted me, and I saw her make gestures to others standing near a van. She yelled out, "Deputy Hendricks! could we have a moment of your time?"

I ducked behind the Sheriff's Office and beat on its back door. A deputy shoved the inside panic bar abruptly. The irritation on his face disappeared as he recognized me and the media approaching for an interview.

"Good move, Purdy. But you just missed your fifteen minutes of fame."

I rolled my eyes, then thanked him and stepped into the conference room.

The Sheriff's Office conference room quickly filled with an assortment of law enforcement folks. Two Rangers had come from Austin. Reagan had apparently been given the nod by TJ and had taken it upon himself to call in all the full-time deputies. He had also pulled in three or four citizens who carried Texas peace officer certifications through the Sheriff, who usually were used for crowd control at high school football games. Quiet but conspicuous, Eddleman and two DEA agents stood by a wall. Someone had turned down the office air conditioning, but it couldn't compensate for the crush of bodies.

"A real clusterfuck outside, Purdy."

Groggy from sleep deprivation, I didn't recognize the voice at first. I turned, and Border Patrol agent Ignatius Gonsalvez shook my hand.

"It is that, Ignatius."

Nodding toward the front of the room, Gonsalvez laughed quietly and said, "I wonder if this is one, too."

Chief Deputy Reagan introduced Ranger Selman. Still haggard looking, Selman related what had occurred to Betty and Forrest. After that, Abner introduced Eddleman, who gave a very brief overview of cartel internal warfare in and around Nuevo Laredo.

"The *Zetas* are the worst of the worst in Mexico. They've got *La Familia Norteña* on the run and now control the plaza there."

And so it went. The Vasquez deaths. The hit man found on the property. The unanswered questions remained: why was tiny Santa

Rosa involved in Nuevo Laredo's issues? Eddleman finally came around to an explanation. It wasn't what I expected.

"Someone in the Vasquez family, knowingly or not, allowed the *Zetas* to use the Griffin ranch as a launching point for a kill team that took out *La Familia's* chief about thirty miles inside Mexico."

Someone? The old couple didn't have a damned thing to do with it. That's why they're dead!

Eddleman studiously avoided looking my direction, as I screwed up my face in ill-hidden contempt of his blaming Oto and his wife.

"Pete Vasquez has a trucking company in Laredo, and he's been hauling dope for the *Zetas*. He also became a confidential informant for the government. The *Zetas* were tipped to this and tried to kill him. He escaped, but as you all heard, one of my best agents was killed trying to protect him. Vasquez is in the wind. We think the *Zetas* missed him. We're pretty sure he's with the Griffin ranch's owner, Laura Griffin Saenz. We don't know is she's been kidnapped or is with him of her own volition. We are aware of a prior relationship between Vasquez and Ms. Saenz. We have reason to believe that he has taken advantage of this situation to induce or coerce Ms. Saenz to assist him in his attempts to escape justice. And there is a remote possibility that Vasquez set us up. Either way, a good man was shot between the eyes on a Texas highway."

Eddleman cleared his throat and swallowed rarely displayed human emotion. "After our man was killed, for whatever reason, Vasquez refused to go with the killers. Our informants tell us that he may owe money on past dope shipments and was afraid that if he ran to Mexico, he would be killed there.

"The *Zetas* probably tried to grab Deputy Kendricks's family as bargaining chips, in case the deputy or anyone he could influence knew Vasquez's whereabouts." Eddleman continued. "We are assured that Deputy Kendricks does not have any contact with either of the two individuals. We're contacting law enforcement across South Texas, as well as in major cities in the state. We regret to see a law enforcement officer of Deputy Kendricks's caliber having his family endangered because of this issue."

Eddleman, Reagan, and Abner fielded questions from the reporters. The meeting ended with Eddleman apologizing to Kickapoo County law enforcement for what had occurred.

"We appreciate Ranger Selman, your sheriff, Deputy Kendricks, and the rest of you. I personally apologize that Laredo's troubles came your way. We think the cartel has made a mistake and realizes it." He paused for several seconds, as what he was about to say was of greater gravity. "If anyone hears, from some of Vasquez's kin, anything on this situation, call me personally. The DEA needs to get to Vasquez before the bad guys do. For his sake and the woman's." He wrote his cell number on the white board.

The meeting broke up. I sat there as the men filed out. I then walked to the front of the conference room. Eddleman started to extend a handshake. I ignored it.

"You guys in the DEA play by your own rules, don't you?"

Eddleman looked at me quizzically. Abner, looking equally as puzzled, quietly closed the conference room door.

"You're going to kill Vasquez, aren't you? Or get someone to do it for you."

Eddleman shook his head as if to deny my accusation and retorted, "Who gave you that idea? We're trying to *keep* him from getting killed."

Maybe it was imagined, but a flicker of panic seemed to mix with the scent of his deodorant and aftershave.

"Fuck you, Eddleman."

Eddleman picked up his briefing notebook and walked out of the room. Turning at the doorway, he said, "We're heading back to Laredo. I promised you, Kendricks, that I would not involve you in the search for Pete Vasquez. Sorry it happened. Kickapoo County is a backwater and I've got limited resources that'll be used better elsewhere."

Abner asked quietly, "You want to tell me what that was all about, Purdy?"

"I don't think the DEA wants to arrest Pete. I think at least Eddleman wants him dead."

"Why would they do that, Purdy? He's their snitch."

Still trying to make sense of the Zeta's information, I replied, "One of Eddleman's best agents was killed trying to protect Pete. Something went wrong. I don't know exactly what. Maybe Pete got cold feet and told the *Zetas* he had been flipped. That's asking for a bullet. Whatever happened, a DEA agent got his head blown off."

"Where are you getting this, Purdy?"

I could tell Abner was taking me seriously, but there was no way I could tell him what I had witnessed just a few hours before.

"Can't say, Ranger."

"Can't, or won't?"

"Maybe both. But trust me on this. If Eddleman has his way, Pete Vasquez is dead, regardless of who gets to him first. And that means Laura is in the line of fire, too."

I took a deep breath, realizing how desperately I needed to get more rest. "I never thought I'd say this, Ranger, but I hope Pete and Laura are far, far away from Texas right now."

EIGHTY-FOUR

Present Day

PURDY KENDRICKS

Boxed in by TV newscasters, I hid in my office for several hours. Finally, the reporters grew tired of waiting around for someone willing to give a cogent interview, or were pulled off to cover a newer story. They began packing up. Because I had walked from Paula's house, I avoided them by taking a circuitous route away from the courthouse. This also allowed me to avoid bumping into Israel, if he was at work today.

Two different deputies stood next to a cruiser outside Paula's house. After thanking them, I tapped on the front door. Betty peered out between the curtains, smiled wanly, and unlocked the door.

"You look like I feel," she said with a brief smile. Her pinched face and smudges under her eyes spoke of exhaustion and sadness. She reached for my hand and led me inside. Closing the door, Betty leaned against me and rested her head on my chest.

I held her and stroked her hair as she wept silently. After several minutes, she leaned away from me, wiping her eyes.

"I'm a mess." She shook her head, as if in disbelief. "We'll get through this, won't we?"

I pulled her to my chest again. "No doubt about it, babe. No doubt about it." I prayed we would.

We sat at the kitchen table, sipping coffee, not saying anything. The silence was comfortable.

Finally, I asked, "Where's Forrest?"

"Paula took a bunch of kids fishing." Sensing my apprehension, she continued, "No, don't say anything. Several parents know what happened and decided this would be a good 'kid-fish' day at one of the tanks. I think every adult was armed."

The remainder of the day seemed almost normal—except that we weren't in our own home. And there were bullet holes that needed patching. And blood and viscera to wipe up. And bad memories that needed erasing.

The Methodist minister dropped by Paula's house for a blessedly short visit and offered the church's prayers and assistance. Father Joseph Levant called. True to his Catholic tradition, he offered to perform a house blessing, ensuring us that the Holy Spirit's presence would go far in exorcising the evil that had invaded our home.

Betty was going to say no to that, but I asked her to hold off on a decision. Something about that spiritual mumbo jumbo appealed to me. Certainly, there were "powers and principalities" I had witnessed that made me feel the reality of evil. Hard to say for sure, but much of humanity hadn't shown its best side to me lately.

The next day, much of the excitement had died down. Betty and I spent the morning in Paula's back yard playing catch with Forrest. At noon he insisted on a hamburger. Betty thought a trip to the Cenizo Diner was just the thing. Beulah's anger and Lilly Pardo's presence loomed darkly. I hadn't shared my confrontation with Beulah. I sure as hell hadn't mentioned Lilly Pardo and Lágrimas.

Thankfully, Beulah was all smiles, and Lilly had called in sick. Several of the coffee drinkers dropped by to offer words of support, but mostly we were left alone.

While Forrest chattered about enrolling in T-ball in the fall, and I listened to dishes being loudly bussed, a distant memory hit me. A fellow police officer in Houston had been diagnosed with a rare and virulent form of cancer. It metastasized, and he became terminal less than a month after his diagnosis.

I had parked my car in one of the cavernous lots near a hospital in the sprawling Medical Center south of downtown Houston. Like many other officers, I visited him in the oncology ward. He lay withering away in the hospital bed. His wife sat beside him, promising him, and herself perhaps, that he "was getting better and would be out of this damned place soon." Everyone in the hospital room re-enforced the lie, perhaps afraid that one of us could just as easily be the one wasting away, as chemicals did their futile dance with the disease.

Leaving my friend's looming death, I walked out of the hospital and drove to a burger joint a couple of blocks away. As I ate a burger, I watched people of all descriptions come and go. The reality of the oncology ward was as divorced from the reality of people grabbing a quick meal and returning to an office or blue-collar job, as night from day.

And so it was now. My wife and child sopped up ketchup with French fries, as Beulah and her staff took orders and laughed with the customers. A small distance and a few hours separated the three of us from a different, darker reality. This reality that I had accepted as mine to deal with, was, at least in part, shared with my wife. Lágrimas's addition to that reality was mine alone. I did not intend to ever share it with my wife, and for now, not with anyone in law enforcement. Physically, I was in one place, but my thoughts shifted into a much bleaker one.

"Purdy. Hey, hon. You okay?" Betty shook my arm.

"Yeah, Dad. Mom was asking you if we could go on a vacation before school starts."

"Sorry. Just got distracted watching all those dishes you're gonna have to wash, son. Mom and I didn't bring any money to pay for your lunch!"

Betty gave out a small, forced laugh, and Beulah saved the situation.

"Move your skinny little behind over, Forrest," she laughed, as she shoved into the booth next to him. "Are you giving your mom and dad trouble?" It was if she had picked up an actor's dropped line and saved a scene from unraveling in front of the audience.

Forrest chimed in, "Daddy said we forgot our money, and I have to wash the dishes to pay for the meal."

"Forrest, honey, your daddy is full of baloney. Ain't that right?"

He beamed and turned to me. "That's right, Dad. You're full of baloney!"

For a moment, a reality of a happy child pushed away the darkness. It felt good.

A fter dropping Betty and Forrest off at Paula's house, I went to the office. Any intentions of getting work accomplished went up in smoke. It was a slow day. Too distracted to do anything, I spent a couple of hours talking with Jake at the dispatcher's desk. Somewhere in the discussion, he confirmed that Eddleman hadn't left for Laredo yet.

"Thought I heard he and his agents were leaving?"

"Where did you hear that, Jake?'

He shrugged.

"Maybe I didn't hear it. Just assumed they would clear out of here and go where the action is, I guess."

Eddleman had said something of the sort, but Jake hadn't been in the conference room when that happened. I wondered where he had picked this up. Sensing my curiosity, Jake changed directions.

"You didn't spot him, I guess, but he and a couple of his guys are still over at the Mesa Tourist Court. You aren't solving any crimes right now, Purdy, but you're sure helping the Patels' bottom line. Between the motel stays, gas, and soda waters everyone's buying, I'm sure you're appreciated. Dead or alive."

"Har-de-har, Jake. You ought to take it on the road."

I left the office at three, just wanting to clear my head. Driving east on U.S. 90, the late summer sun created a shimmery mirror on its surface. The sedan's speedometer sat on a sedate 55 miles-an-hour, 15 miles-an-hour under the speed limit. I was in no hurry.

About a mile behind me, what looked like two SUVs seemed to keep pace rather than close the distance. I checked the shotgun in its mount and radioed Jake.

"I'm heading east on U.S. 90, just patrolling, Jake. I've got a couple of SUVs about a mile behind me."

"You want someone heading your way?"

"No. I'll turn around at the county line. If I don't call back in five, send someone, but I don't think it's anything."

I felt better that someone knew where I was. Diana Krall's album, *The Girl in the Other Room,* pushed aside the road noise, keeping my mind off issues I didn't want to face—like leaving Santa Rosa for good, and Betty's and Forrest's well-being. And where the hell I was heading in life.

I hit the east end of Kickapoo County and wondered what it would be like to just keep driving. I pulled well off the road surface and faced back west, so the sedan's body would provide some cover. I unracked the shotgun, checked that there was a shell in the chamber, and stood by the driver's door, shotgun down by my side. I watched the SUVs pass. Bicycles were secured in rear-mounted racks, and what looked like camping gear was lashed down on the roofs. One driver honked, and a hand came out of the passenger side front window and waved.

I'm getting fucking paranoid.

Relieved, I radioed my location to Jake and gave him an all-clear. Two miles later I pulled onto the cutoff for the county road that led to the Griffin Ranch. I hadn't been back since the days after Pete found his grandparents' bodies next to the Rio Grande. It seemed lifetimes ago.

It looked as if a rainstorm had hit the area within the last couple of days. Several ranchers used the unpaved and rarely maintained road, and vehicle tracks wended south, disturbing the recently rain-dimpled surface. Evidence of the storm ended three miles from the highway, and dust boiled out from my tires from the road not blessed with the recent moisture.

Boogie woogie piano kicked off *Love Me Like a Man.* Tapping my left foot on the floorboard, I topped a small hill. *Oh, Mary Lou Williams can tear it up.*

At the bottom of the small descent, the county road made a shallow turn to the east, as it meandered through the badlands to various ranch holdings. A smaller track teed off toward the Griffin place. Diane Krall's bluesy joy suddenly didn't belong in my head.

One set of tire marks led to the property's gate.

EIGHTY-FIVE

Pete Vasquez And Laura Saenz

PRESENT DAY

A shallow well, drilled years ago by Rupert Kendricks, still provided water to the old couple's rock house.

"I remember Daddy telling me when this well was drilled. As old as it is, I'm surprised it hasn't silted up," Laura flipped the switch that engaged the pump pushing water into a cistern next to the house.

"Oh, it has, several times," Pete replied. Tetracycline had stopped the infection, at least temporarily. Pete's wound started to close, and its smell abated. "I guess he never bothered you with it, but Oto would borrow one of Rupert Kendricks's old pulling rigs and do a workover by himself, after I left. Oto tried to rent the rig from Purdy's mom, but she wouldn't take any money."

Laura's brow knitted when the Kendricks name was mentioned. *I don't need to hear anything about Purdy Kendricks's old man right now. I sure as hell don't want to be reminded of anything to do with Purdy Kendricks.*

Pete had avoided discussions about his grandparents, and his mention of Otabiano revealed his discomfort.

Laura wanted to goad Pete. It was easy. Whatever had happened to Otabiano and Raquel, he had had something to do with it. She thought about it and decided stirring things up wasn't worth the effort. It would only provoke screaming denials.

The son of bitch may try to cheat me out of the money he's got hidden on this fucking place.

She stuck a lit match over the small stove's burners and turned on the propane. With a soft whoosh the burner lit, and she placed a large pot of water on to boil. Then she lowered small pieces of torn sheet into the water to sterilize them. Laura's resolve to let things lay weakened as her temperature rose with the water's.

"This is pure dee shit. How long do you plan on staying here, Pete? We've pushed our luck being here. I want to go away from here."

Pete didn't answer. Instead, he stared into Mexico from the south-facing window. The day's heat was building, and he re-opened the glass to allow air in.

"Pete, I asked you a question. How long are we going to have to stay in this place?"

Angrily, he turned and barked, "Unless you've got some surefire way of getting out of here without us both being killed, keep your fucking mouth shut, Laura. I'm still thinking about it."

"Thinking about it? What the fuck have you been doing all the time you've hid dope money out here—while your grandparents took care of this place." The words spewed like venom. "You act guilty for whatever you had to do with their murders." Laura turned off the propane and stabbed her index finger into Pete's wound. "But you could have gotten them killed every time you stashed dope money out here."

Pete grimaced with pain, then reached over and slapped Laura hard across the face, knocking her into the small kitchen table. She slumped to the floor.

"You rotten bitch. That 'dope money' you refer to kept you in high cotton with your snooty, artsy-fartsy, white bread crowd in Alamo Heights." His face turned nearly purple with rage. "If I didn't need you, I'd throw your ass in the river." He turned and sat heavily in a chair. Blood began to dapple his shirt where Laura had punched the wound.

Laura struggled to her feet. Her left cheek showed the shape of Pete's hand. She gave a small laugh.

"You must be addled in the head. Are you sure your fever hasn't messed with your brain? You need me, you bastard. I could drive that old truck to Santa Rosa and leave you to the cartels, or the law, whichever came first."

Pete leaned back in the chair and reached into a front pocket. He pulled out the pickup's ignition key and waved it around.

"You'll have to walk."

"As B.B. King says, 'the thrill is gone.' And it has. Fish your own damned bandages out of this water once it cools. I'm going to take a walk. I don't want to be around you right now."

"Good riddance. Just remember, if I don't get out of here in one piece, you aren't getting one fucking dime of the money I've got stashed."

Laura moved outside and let the screen door slap shut. She walked toward the river.

"Goddamn. Goddamn. Goddamn!" She screamed. She could hear Pete laughing at her inside the house.

I'm not going anywhere without some indication of where Pete's money is hidden.

She reached an opening in the catclaw and salt cedar and sat down in the Bermuda grass. Otabiano's boat still lay upside down, tied to its mooring pin.

Laura wondered out loud, "How in hell did I end up back here, and how in hell am I ever going to get out of here?"

There was no one to hear her or give her a satisfactory response, so she lay back in the grass and closed her eyes. *I am so damned tired. Just let this be over.* Somewhere in her dream, she heard a car's engine. Then she heard the popping and crunch of gravel.

She woke with a start. *How long have I been asleep?* The sun had moved across the sky. *Fuck.* Rubbing her eyes, she sprang up and started moving through the brush toward the house. She stopped and held her breath. *That's not a dream! Someone's on the ranch, and they're heading this way!*

EIGHTY-SIX

Present Day

PURDY KENDRICKS

Diana Krall would have to wait. I pulled up to the steel gate at the Griffin place and walked onto the disused cattle guard. Time, rain, and winds had filled the spaces between the pipes. At some point, rather than digging out the cattle guard, someone, probably Otabiano Vasquez, had put up a steel gate. It made it more of a hassle for Otabiano and Raquel to enter and leave, but old man Griffin, and later, Laura, had gone cheap. Besides, the cattle had been sold off, and a gate kept out trespassers wanting to poach deer, mostly.

A small chain wrapped the gate to the creosote post. The lock was secured. The road went straight through caliche outcroppings, and I knew less than a mile later sat the ranch's old headquarters building. Three miles further and hard up against the Rio Grande was the small house, where Oto and Raquel had lived for so many years.

The single vehicle tracks disappeared over the small rise. Whoever had entered the Griffin place had a key to the gate and hadn't come back out.

My last contact with Laura Griffin Saenz had been when I had been able to finally come to terms with our long-ago relationship. Other than concern for her safety, I hadn't given my feelings for her much, if any, thought. Someone's presence on her property changed that. I didn't like it. Betty and I had made our peace. We were dealing with life together. Laura's memory was a distraction I had been well rid of. Now her damn presence was with me again.

Who was on the Griffin Ranch? I thought of Laura and Pete, but dismissed it almost immediately. No way in hell those two would come anywhere near this part of the world. The hardscrabble acreage butting up against Mexico was a dead end. I reached into the Dodge sedan and depressed the transmit button on the mic.

"Jake, you copy?"

His voice came back barely intelligible. "Yeah. Pur...y...at's your...cation?"

The cracking and static confirmed the lack of radio coverage in this part of the county. I started to respond, but I didn't.

Who's out here? What are they doing on the Griffin place? And why? Then it hit me. Eddleman and half the law enforcement in South and Southwest Texas hadn't found Pete and Laura. I began to think out loud. "Are you two in here? Why in the hell would you come back to this Godforsaken place? This is a death trap."

Hoping for cell coverage, I checked my phone. No luck. The nearest phone was a land line connection at the Vasquez house on the ridge above the Rio Grande. *I need to find some coverage and get someone out here to help me check this place out.* I turned and headed the sedan back toward U.S. 90 and radio and cell coverage.

Two miles from the highway, I stopped the car and killed the engine. If Pete Vasquez was in Kickapoo County, and if Israel was right, then Pete's life was forfeit.

I mulled over how much I wanted to disclose; then I tried Abner's cell phone. It went to voicemail. I didn't leave a message. I called Jake.

"Have you seen Selman today, Jake?"

"He came by this morning. Said he had some other things to take care of a couple of counties west of here."

I thanked him and rang off. Jake had promised me he would no longer assist Eddleman. I had told him I trusted him. Now, I wasn't so sure. After 30 minutes, I called Abner again. Again, voicemail. This time, I left a message.

Back at the entrance gate, I checked the lock, then opened the sedan's trunk. I grabbed a pair of bolt cutters.

This isn't real smart. You could have gotten yourself killed in Lágrimas. And now you're going to break a chain and go onto someone's private property.

No, it wasn't too smart, but I did it anyway. After driving onto the ranch property, I closed the gate, then took some bailing wire and secured the chain back together. As long as someone didn't look too closely, it would be hard to see that the gate wasn't secured.

Staying in the ruts left by whoever had driven onto the place, I drove the mile to the ranch headquarters. The tire tracks continued past the place. With shotgun in hand, I walked around the buildings. As dumb as it was to be out there by myself, I wanted to make sure that whoever I would meet further on hadn't left someone who could block my exit.

The old ranch house was locked up. A dried mop and bucket sat outside the screened porch door. Two empty bleach bottles lay on their sides. A new hasp and padlock hung on the main door into the screened porch.

Laura must have hired someone to clean up the mess Shivelli's brains and blood left in the bedroom.

Ten minutes later, and satisfied that apart from a cleaning crew, the place hadn't been disturbed, I crawled back into the sedan and started for the river.

EIGHTY-SEVEN

Present Day

PURDY KENDRICKS, PETE VASQUEZ AND LAURA GRIFFIN

After Laura stormed out of the house, Pete lay back in the chair. At first, he felt some remorse for smacking her across the face. As his pain grew and the bloodstain on the front of his shirt blossomed, he changed his mind. Suddenly tired from the exertion of the argument, Pete carefully stood and walked into the bedroom. He lay down, trying to get his mind off the oozing wound.

"We should have sewed up these holes." Realizing he was talking to himself, Pete barked a painful laugh. "Oh yeah, my friend. They would a'heard me twenty miles into Mexico if she had used a needle and thread on me."

As he drifted off to sleep, he realized he had left the water boiling on the stove.

"Fuck!" he yelled. "Hey, Laura!"

Then he realized she probably hadn't returned to the house, was possibly nowhere near, and wasn't going to fish out sterilized bandages from the boiling water.

Grunting with pain, he swung his legs off his grandparents' bed and stood. He started to black out and sat down quickly.

"Stood up too fast, dammit," he muttered. As he shuffled the few steps into the kitchen, Pete laughed. "She'd probably pour this boiling water all over me anyway, the greedy bitch."

Pete turned off the propane and fished out the bandages with one of his grandmother's wooden spoons. Placing the wet fabric on a dinner plate, he pushed through the screen door and stepped to his grandmother's clothesline. A frayed, sun-bleached cloth bag full of clothespins hung near one steel T. He reached for it with his left arm. The movement re-opened the bullet's wound further. The pain caused him to instinctively clutch his side, and the dinner plate with sodden bandages fell from his right hand.

"Fuck me. Oh, fuck me!" The wet pieces of torn sheet were now coated with dirt. Distraught and increasingly worried about the suppurating wound, Pete realized he needed Laura's help.

"Laura!"

No answer, and shouting aggravated the bleeding and pain near his abdomen. Pete went back inside and grabbed a dish towel. He then started down the path in the salt cedar, hoping Laura had gone toward the Bermuda grass near the banks of the Rio Grande. He noticed he felt unusually hot, when a chill ran through him. *Fever. I think the infection's back.*

In the afternoon shadows of the brush, he paused for a moment to press the dish towel more firmly against his side. Catching his breath, he looked up between the salt cedar branches. Vultures wheeled in the updrafts, and small clouds scudded northward. Small birds flitted from branch to branch, avoiding the occasional hawks in search of prey. Momentarily, his nerves were soothed by the familiar smells and sights.

Suddenly, Pete heard fast moving footsteps and rasping breath. Laura appeared at a bend in the thicket. She yelped with surprise.

"Didn't you hear it?"

"What are you talking about?"

"Jesus," Laura rasped, barely above a whisper. "I heard a car or truck coming toward the river!"

He started to reply when she shushed him angrily.

"Listen." She pointed in the general direction of the old headquarters building.

They stood there, hearing only their breathing for several seconds. Even the birds' twittering and flitting in the brush seemed to have stopped. Then, the sound of tires on caliche reached into the bushes and grabbed Pete by the balls. Nausea coursed through him, and he dry heaved, spittle dribbling onto the ground. He almost blacked out again. Pete pointed toward the house. "Where's that gun you said you brought with you? We need it!"

Laura ran up the path. As she came out of the bushes, a vehicle's dust trail floated above the ranch road leading toward the river. She ran to the bedroom and grabbed a heavy revolver from a small canvas bag. She peered through the north-facing window. Evidence of the vehicle's approach disappeared as it dropped into the small arroyo a quarter mile away. It would reappear in seconds. She sprinted back into the brush line.

"Can you tell who it is?"

Pete wiped sweat from his face as another onset of chills ran through him. He shook his head.

"My eyes aren't focusing too good right now."

Still breathing heavily, Laura spied the reappearing dust blossom. Pete took the pistol and broke open the cylinder. The old Colt Python's six cylinders were loaded.

"Where did you get this thing?" He didn't wait for an answer, knowing Laura's gun case and safe in Alamo Heights mostly held her dead father's firearms. "Did you bring any extra ammo with you?"

"Jesus, Pete. No, I didn't. What do we do?"

Pete clutched his side and grunted with pain. It was difficult to tell whether what he was feeling was from a spreading infection or raw fear.

"If it's cartel, I'm dead. If it's not, it's probably some kind of cop. If I kill one of them, they'll give me the needle. Stay here." He edged toward the opening in the heavy riverine growth.

My heart's beating like a trip hammer. And I'm about to vomit. A sedan appeared over the lip of the small rise. *Holy shit! How in hell did a Kickapoo County Sheriff's sedan get through that locked gate? And why? No way it's just one guy.*

The car's engine shut off. The driver's door slowly opened. A deputy holding a shotgun stepped out. No one appeared from the passenger's side.

What in hell is Purdy Kendricks doing here? Pete ignored the blood-soaked dishtowel and eased back down the trail. "Purdy Kendricks is standing in front of the house. He's alone."

Laura shook her head in disbelief. *This is getting stranger and stranger.*

The two watched as Purdy walked around the house, shotgun at the ready.

EIGHTY-EIGHT

Present Day

PURDY KENDRICKS

I left the ranch headquarters buildings and slowly followed the
fresh tire tracks winding across the arid pastures. The only other
human living structure on the ranch was the house where Oto and
Raquel had lived, raised their grandson, and were murdered.

My hands were slippery on the steering wheel, and I kept wiping
them, one at a time, on my shirt. It was late summer hot, but that
didn't usually cause the sweat now pouring down my face. My back
stuck to the seat. I was scared as hell. Knowing it was pointless, I kept
checking for cell coverage on my phone.

I had rolled all four windows down at the front gate. My automatic
lay in my lap, and the shotgun, loaded with buckshot, was positioned
next to me, barrel pointing toward the floorboard. The police radio
occasionally crackled with useless static. I turned the volume
completely down.

My sedan dipped into a small draw, and I wondered if I would be
ambushed as I topped the rise. I stopped the car in the swale and
killed the engine. Grabbing the shotgun, I stepped out of the dusty
roadbed and off to one side. I moved around the creosote bushes, bent
in a half-stoop. Reaching the top of the rise, I lay down and peered
toward the Rio Grande. No one.

I backed below line of sight and skittered down the gravel to the
sedan at the bottom of the draw. Topping the rise, I let the car crawl
forward toward the Vasquez house. Twenty yards to the west sat

Otabiano's pickup. Covered in dust, it didn't appear to have moved in a very long time. Twenty-five or so yards further right sat a beat-up Ford pickup I had never seen before. Someone had run it as deep into the salt cedar and catclaw as it would go.

*Well, well, well. Looks like I've stumbled on Pete Vasquez, or Laura, or both of them.*It made no sense. And then it sort of did. Who would think to look for them here?

I holstered my automatic and gripped the shotgun. I didn't think he would kill me, but I wasn't betting my life on it. Given Pete's precarious situation, there was no reason to take a chance.

I walked to a corner of the Vasquez's house. An electric pump hummed as it splashed well water into the cistern. After the bodies of Oto and Raquel had been taken to the medical examiner in San Antonio, we had scoured the house for clues and secured the place as best we could. Now, the old house's sash weight windows were open. Nothing stirred inside, but I ducked as I passed the north and east side windows. The valve on a large propane tank was in the "on" position. The window facing the Rio Grande was near the old stove. A quick peek through its screen revealed the remnants of a meal, dirty dishes, and emptied cans of Dinty Moore stew.

Funny how the mind works. I was scared shitless but thought, *Dinty Moore. That's a shitty brand of stew.* Another quick peek inside revealed a large pot sitting on one of the stove's front burners. I couldn't tell what was in it but felt the stove's radiating heat. *Someone had just turned the stove off moments before.*

Rags covered in dirt lay under Raquel's clothesline. I bent down. *Still damp and warm to the touch. What are these for?* Otabiano's truck was locked. I stepped away from it and back to the front door. Screen closed. Wood door wide open.

"Anyone here?" Nothing. I moved inside and let my eyes adjust to the gloom. I had been inside the old couple's house many times. Living room and kitchen, a bedroom, a bathroom, and a small storage room. Oto's old upholstered chair sat across from the kitchen table. Memories of the old couples' lives ran through my mind. The upholstery on Oto's chair had discoloration on the side of the left armrest. I ran a finger over the smear. Brownish red and still damp. Someone was hurt.

A couple of small bags lay next to the couples' double bed. Dirty clothes were draped on an armless wooden chair. Sheets lay crumpled at the foot of the bed. I glanced under the bed. Dust and lint moved slightly with the draft of my breathing. A large hypodermic syringe for vaccinating and treating cattle lay cradled in a dishtowel on Raquel's tiny nightstand,

I found nothing of interest in the storage room. I backed into the main room. Moving dirty dishes to one side, I placed the shotgun on the kitchen table and opened the refrigerator. Bottled water. Fresh fruit. And a small brown bottle. Veterinarian grade tetracycline, almost empty. God almighty. I shuddered as I imagined the excruciating pain of the syringe's large needle plunging into a human. I closed the refrigerator and turned toward the door.

Pete Vasquez stood there, one hand holding a bloody cloth to his left side, the other hand pointing a revolver at me.

"Purdy, I don't want to shoot you, but I will. And at this distance, I can't miss."

EIGHTY-NINE

Present Day

PURDY KENDRICKS

I had heard victims of armed robberies testify in court in Houston several times. They all said something like, "The barrel of the defendant's gun looked like a cannon." I had wondered how someone fixated on the mouth of a cannon could somehow also be able to identify the suspect holding the weapon.

A small bit of my brain said to me, "Aha, Purdy. Now you understand. That revolver's barrel *does* look like a fucking cannon. And you're not having one bit of trouble identifying the person waving it in your face as Pete Vasquez." I instinctively stood very still, not wanting to die.

Pete's face was ashen. He looked more afraid that I was. I had a thousand questions, beginning with what the hell he was doing anywhere near Kickapoo County to begin with. What came out was, "You look like hell, Pete. What happened to you? And where's Laura?"

As if on cue, she appeared behind Pete.

"Hey, Purdy."

Dirty, no makeup. Hair pulled back into a greasy ponytail. She still looked beautiful. Damn her.

"Hey, Laura. How's it going?"

"Fine. You?"

I'm looking at a badly wounded man waving a handgun in my face, and

423

I'm exchanging pleasantries with a woman whose existence has caused me a shitload of grief. This is surreal.

"Just thought I'd drive around the county to see what was going on. You know, see if there was someone stupid enough to come back here to this godforsaken place where they can get boxed in. With Mexico and the Rio Grande on one side and one dirt road out. Another day at the office."

Pete's right hand was tiring, and he couldn't use the left. It was too busy holding an increasingly blood-soaked towel to a wound.

"You're too close to that shotgun, Purdy. Why don't you sit over there"—he motioned to Oto's armchair "and while you're at it, unholster that automatic and set it next to the shotgun." He turned to Laura. "Get those weapons away from him."

She gave him a fuck you look.

"Please."

She rolled her eyes and retrieved the shotgun and automatic, set them on the concrete floor near the door, then walked to the table and pulled out a chair.

"Pete, I'm sitting down, and you'd better too. I need to take a look at that wound of yours."

He snickered. "Hell, you broke the damned thing open. Not sure I want you near me."

"Suit yourself."

I couldn't help noticing that she was wearing one of Oto's old work shirts. She crossed her arms angrily. She wasn't wearing a bra.

"Good to see you two lovebirds. You're the talk of the town. Come to think of it, you're on every cop's mind between here and Corpus Christi. I never would have guessed you'd come here." I paused. "Why *are* you here, Pete?"

He appeared not to hear me as he shifted hands to keep pressure on the wound.

Laura piped up. "He got shot. Through the side. When they killed the DEA agent. Didn't hit his guts, though. He called me to come get him. I'm not sure I would have if I had known he'd be this much trouble."

Pete looked up, his eyes appearing glassy.

Fever?

"Shut up, Laura. You came and got me 'cause you wanted to."

She started a retort, and then stopped. Something unsaid passed between them.

There would be time to figure out what was going on later. Right now, Pete needed a doctor. Remembering Israel's and the *sicario's* warning about the DEA, I had no idea how I was going get him there. I also didn't know whether there were any charges pending against Laura. I guess I would figure it out as I went. Regardless, the give and take began to wear on me.

"I'll tell you this. My wife just killed a man who was trying to kidnap her and our son. My family's in danger because of you two."

Laura looked genuinely shocked. Pete's expression was harder to cipher.

"The *Zetas* sent two men to grab them, thinking I knew where you were. I didn't. One thing's for sure, I would have traded both of you if necessary to keep Betty and Forrest safe." I was thankful I had never been put to that choice. The depraved barbarity of the cartels wasn't something I would wish on anyone, anywhere.

"Is Betty okay?" Laura asked.

I started to explain what had happened when Pete interrupted.

"I need another shot of antibiotic. I'm burning up, Laura."

She looked at me, almost pleadingly. Remembering the tetracycline, I nodded. She went into the bedroom and retrieved the syringe. She opened the refrigerator, took the medicine, and grabbed a washcloth.

"Here, Pete. Bite on this."

Laura plunged the needle into the bottle and extracted what was left of the liquid.

Intrigued by what I was seeing, I made no move to take the revolver Pete was holding.

"Stand up and drop your britches, Pete, and lean over the table. This is going to hurt like the devil."

He glanced at me, then set the gun on the table. Using his right hand, he unbuckled his pants and pulled them down around his knees. Then he stuffed the rag in his mouth, leaned over and mumbled something to her.

Laura took a deep breath, then jabbed the thick sharpened shaft into Pete's buttock. His face turned purple and eyes rolled back into his head. Quickly pushing the syringe plunger, Laura stepped back.

"He's going to pass out. Please catch him, Purdy."

Pete's head lolled as he slumped. I caught him before he hit the floor. Laura ripped the rag out of his mouth. Mucus flowed down his face.

I reached under his arms and began pulling him toward the bed. The two of us were able to roll Pete onto the bed and prop pillows behind his back. I was worried he would aspirate if he vomited.

Shadows of late afternoon added to the gloom in the house. Laura flopped into Oto's chair. I sat across from her. For several moments we said nothing. It was late, my family needed me, and no one knew where I was.

"Now what?"

I looked up. "Laura, I haven't a clue. I'm still baffled why you brought Pete here. He needs a doctor. There's no more antibiotic, and that wound doesn't look good."

She nodded.

I knew the DEA, or at least Eddleman, wanted Pete dead, perhaps as much as the *Zetas*. I would have to protect him, somehow. Right now, all I wanted to do was leave and with both of them.

Laura read my mind. "I guess you can hold a gun on us and force us into the car with you." Looking at the floor, she appeared defeated.

I stood and walked outside. I had decided to do just that, once Pete woke. I looked north. In the distance, two rooster tails of dust showed someone had entered the ranch and was heading our way.

I ran to the county sedan and reached in the glove box for a set of binoculars. Praying the vehicles meant law enforcement, I focused the glasses. My stomach churned as the sun glinted off the windows of two black SUVs

We weren't going anywhere.

NINETY

Jake Nichols And Johnny Reagan

PRESENT DAY–AFTER PURDY LEAVES

At first concerned, Jake was relieved by Purdy's second call, dismissing earlier worries about the possibility of being followed. Two hours later, Jake finished logging the call times and turned the dispatcher duties over to Fred Clary, working the night shift.

The last call from Purdy, not completed because of the poor cell coverage, gnawed on Jake a bit. But limited radio and cell coverage was a reality of life in the large and sparsely populated county. He asked Fred to keep trying to contact Purdy by radio and cell phone, and to let him know if he was successful in making contact. Normally, Jake would have hung around for a while, but the last few days had left him dog-assed tired.

Clary settled in, opened an old-fashioned lunchbox, complete with a thermos of coffee, and spread paper towels on the dispatcher's desk. It wouldn't do to get pieces of his wife's freshly fried chicken, or chocolate cake crumbs, anywhere on the work area. Fred knew it was Jake Nichols's home away from home.

Dispatching for Kickapoo County's Sheriff's Office, the Department of Public Safety's highway patrol, and the Santa Rosa Fire Department/EMS at night was usually pretty slow. After a good meal, Fred looked forward to finishing a Louis L'Amour western he had started a few days ago, and getting in some reasonably long catnaps.

At 5:30, the phone rang.

"Fred, it's me, Jake. You heard from Deputy Kendricks yet?"

"Not a word, Jake. You want me to try him on the radio?"

"Yes, please."

Fred keyed the mic and requested a response. Nothing.

Five minutes later, the Sheriff called the dispatcher.

"Fred, heard you asking for Deputy Kendricks to check in. Anything?"

Burping the air out of the rubber container of his longed-for chocolate cake, Fred said, "No, sir." There was noise in the background, and Clary wondered where the Sheriff was calling from.

"Who's looking for him?"

"Jake just told me to keep trying to reach him is all. Anything I can do?"

TJ Johnson rang off without responding. Now vaguely worried, he called his chief deputy.

"Deputy Reagan, the night dispatcher is trying to locate Purdy Kendricks. What's going on?"

In his mind, Reagan could see TJ Johnson hiking up his khaki britches, trying to look aware of what was going on in his department. He smiled ruefully. TJ's concern about the welfare of a deputy whose family had just gone through hell was unusual. But then, a tight re-election race might have the Sheriff worried about his public image. TJ rarely monitored radio traffic. No doubt some potential voter with a police scanner must have asked him about it.

"I'm not aware of anything that's going on, Sheriff." *I wonder where that windbag is tonight.*

Reagan's question was answered quickly.

"I gotta give a talk at the 4H-FFA fundraiser tonight. I don't think there's much to worry about, but can you check on it with Jake, and maybe with Kendricks's wife? 'Course, don't scare her or nothing. She's been through a lot."

Reagan stared at his own meal getting cold, agreed to do so, and hung up. He covered his plate and put it in the refrigerator.

"What's that all about?" his wife asked.

"Our gutless son-of-a-bitch sheriff is too busy kissing ass for votes to make sure one of his deputies is okay, is what it's about." He grabbed his hat and pistol belt and left the house.

Reagan called the Sheriff's Office and instructed Fred Clary not to send any more transmissions regarding Purdy Kendricks. *Last thing anyone needs right now is the whole county wondering what's going on when we don't even know.* He punched in Jake Nichols's cell number once inside his car.

"You want to tell me what's going on?"

Jake responded, "He went east toward the county line, thought he was being followed. Pulled over a couple miles west of the county line at the entrance of the county road to make sure he wasn't, then gave me the all clear. Later he tried radioing me, but I lost his signal."

Reagan pictured the broken country. "Let me guess. No cell coverage out there, and you never got a phone call?"

"That's right, Deputy. I didn't."

"What was Kendricks doing? Did he get a call somewhere?"

Jake explained that was unlikely.

"We must have talked for a couple of hours. He didn't get any calls. I don't remember him checking his cell phone for messages while we were talking. He just said he needed to get out of the office and clear his mind." Jake paused and opined, "Which makes sense, given what's happened and all."

Reagan dialed Purdy's cell phone. It went to message. Dreading what was coming next, Reagan called Betty Kendricks.

"I'm looking for your husband. I was wondering if he's staying with you all at Paula's house, and if he's made it there for supper."

Instantly, Betty's voice filled with dread.

"Purdy's not here. He left for the office, and I haven't heard from him. What's going on?"

Reagan kept his voice soft and calm.

"Nothing is going on. I'm just trying to get ahold of him on a case. He's out patrolling, and I thought I'd catch him before he gets too settled in with you and Forrest. Just ask him to give me a shout when he comes in, okay?"

Reagan's bullshit sounded weak to him. He didn't doubt Betty had already gone into panic mode. Nonetheless, he had confirmed that Purdy wasn't in Santa Rosa. He began making phone calls.

. . .

Reagan drove by the Mesa Travel Court on the way to the office. Obvious government-issued sedans and SUVs showed Eddleman and a couple of his agents were still in town. He beat on Eddleman's door. After several seconds, the motel curtains moved. Eddleman unchained the door.

"What's going on, Deputy?"

He stepped to one side and motioned Reagan into the room. Relocking the door, Eddleman set his automatic on the TV stand.

"Like a scotch?" He pointed toward a bottle of Dewar's and an open ice bucket.

Shaking his head, Reagan responded, "We need your help. Deputy Kendricks hasn't checked in."

Eddleman asked, "Where was he last seen?"

"East end of the county. He was patrolling. Noticed some SUVs behind him. Purdy told the dispatcher it was a false alarm. Gave the all clear. Later, tried radioing dispatch, but it was breaking up. Hasn't been heard from in over two hours."

"So, what are we—" Eddleman gestured toward the other rooms occupied by DEA agents "supposed to do?" He rattled the ice in a water glass and splashed in some scotch.

Reagan thought about it.

"I'm not sure if there's a damned thing wrong. However, we owe it to Kendricks to make sure. My sheriff left this to me. He's out campaigning." This brought a snicker. "I'm gathering up as many folks in law enforcement as I can to go look for Kendricks."

Eddleman said, "I'm not sure what we can do, but we'll help." He didn't sound very enthusiastic.

In no mood to put up with the DEA agents' near-sneer, Reagan barked, "Or, you can sit on your worthless ass in a cheap hotel room drinking a shitty brand of scotch." He turned to leave.

"Whoa. Whoa. I apologize. You tell us what you want." Eddleman pulled on a shirt as he realized he had pushed the lawman too far. Eddleman agreed to add his three agents to the search.

Reagan's phone calls produced results. Clete Morales drove up to the sheriff's office in civilian clothes. It was his day off, and he was driving his 4x4 pickup. Ignatius Gonsalvez had just come off shift work with the Border Patrol and was still in uniform. Johnny Bonavita walked into the Sheriff's Office.

Jake Nichols reappeared and pulled up a chair next to Clary.

Reagan asked, "What are you doing here, Jake? You just got off shift."

Jake didn't answer, and Reagan shook his head. Turning to the others, he suggested they start at the east boundary of Kickapoo County and work west toward Santa Rosa.

"We really don't know where to look, and there are plenty of turn-offs toward ranches."

Jake cleared his throat, but was ignored, as everyone discussed the best way to search a huge expanse of territory. Finally, he raised his hand. Reagan couldn't ignore him anymore.

"What, Jake? You got something to say, say it!"

Not sure his hunch was correct, Jake made a suggestion.

"The county road Purdy was stopped at when he called me is the road that heads down toward the Griffin place. It might be a good place to start."

Eddleman gave him a quizzical look but said nothing.

Reagan asked, "What makes you think so?"

Jake didn't know, and with no more than a wild hunch, he couldn't defend his suggestion other than to say, "Well, the ranch is near the end of that county road. Maybe Purdy was just going back for old time's sake?"

All agreed that Jake's suggestion made about much sense as anything.

Reagan nodded. "We'll meet at the US 90 intersection with that county road. I'll start at the county road and work south toward the Griffin place. I'll decide where everyone else goes once we gather up."

Jake's cell phone vibrated in his breast pocket as he stepped into the restroom. *Eddleman. Dammit.*

Jake turned on the ventilator fan to cover the conversation.

"What?"

Eddleman asked, "What do you know that you're not telling us, Jake?"

Regretting that he had voiced an opinion earlier, Jake responded,

"Mr. Eddleman, I don't know anything more than what I'm telling you." He flushed the toilet.

Eddleman said, "You and I have an agreement, Mr. Nichols. You said you'd keep me in the loop, and I haven't heard anything in a while."

Angered, Jake worked to keep his voice from carrying outside the restroom.

"I'm not hiding anything, Mr. Eddleman. Excuse the hell out of me for suggesting something."

"Do you know where Pete Vasquez is?"

Jack didn't, but as he thought on it, he wondered whether Pete Vasquez had for some reason decided to come to Kickapoo County—if Pete was at the Griffin ranch.

———

NINETY-ONE

Present Day

PURDY KENDRICKS

"Get Pete up!"

"How am I supposed to do that? He's passed out."

Exasperated, I shoved Laura toward the small bedroom. "Grab his legs and swing him off the bed."

She looked out the north facing window.

"I'm guessing what you're seeing isn't the cavalry."

I ignored her attempt at humor and got down on my knees, then had her pull Pete into a position where I could carry him on my back. Pete was pure dead weight, so I held both of his hands at chest level after crossing his arms.

"Grab all the firearms. We've got to get out of this house, and now!"

I shuffled under the unconscious man's weight and pushed open the screen door, heading toward the path in the catclaw and salt cedar. Laura grabbed some sort of satchel that she dragged behind her. From its weight, I presume she had loaded up my automatic, shotgun, and the revolver Pete had been holding on me.

She asked, "Why can't we stay in the house. It's got four walls, for God's sake. Maybe we could hold them off."

I didn't have the patience or the breath to answer. The further we were able to get into the thick, unforgiving brush and reeds near the Rio Grande, the better the chance that we wouldn't be found—at least for a while. Totally winded from fear and Pete's weight, I stopped half-way to the opening where Otabiano had kept his small boat. Laura started to say something, and I curtly whispered, "Shut up!"

The two SUVs I had spotted had pulled up next to the house. They both carried bicycles on rear mounts. Not that I needed any confirmation, but I realized that the two black SUVs I had seen earlier on U.S. 90 had been following me. Their occupants had figured out where I had gone and put two and two together.

I heard several vehicle doors slam shut. Whoever occupied the SUVs apparently wasn't worried about making noise. Voices drifted into the brush and reeds. Although the words were unintelligible, they sounded Spanish.

Nodding at Laura, I staggered further upstream past Otabiano's boat. Several hundred yards of tall reeds reached down to the riverbank. On the upside of the trail, catclaw and salt cedar abounded. The slight trail petered out less than 50 yards further.

There were three choices, and none were good. The first was plunging into an evil concoction of thorns and brambles. We wouldn't get far and couldn't do it quietly. The second option was to try to get as far as possible into the sweltering mass of river reeds. Doable, but the reeds were notorious for housing dens of black-tipped rattlers. The third choice was to plunge into the Rio Grande and hope to hide under the overhanging brush all along the banks. To do that guaranteed Pete's death from shock, infection, or drowning.

Automatic rifles opened up in the distance, punctuated by laughter. I could hear glass shattering. The *sicarios* were enjoying themselves as they tore apart the Vasquez's house, which had stood unharmed for decades. I glanced at Laura. Her face slick with sweat, she nodded at me, as if to say, "You were right about the house."

Pete groaned slightly and tried to pull his hands out of my grasp. This wasn't the time for introspection. I planted my feet and pushed into the reeds. The dense foliage almost bounced me backward. Laura pushed against me and Pete. I wriggled in. Her breathing was ragged in what could only be sheer terror.

She whispered, "Further! Further! We're only in a couple of feet!"

I let go of Pete, and his body slid away from my back. The back of my shirt was soaked, and I knew it wasn't just from my sweat. The reeds kept Pete from going totally prone. I turned and grabbed him under the armpits and pushed backwards. Sporadic gunfire erupted, and it seemed to come from somewhere on the trail we had just left.

It didn't matter whether the *sicarios* had seen us or not. The trail was the only obvious way for someone to go in hopes of putting distance between them and the Vasquez house. Movement in any other direction would have been in the open.

The three of us were enveloped in darkness, dust, and overwhelming heat. I couldn't see where we were going, but we couldn't have been more than 10 yards from the riverbank. It might as well have been 10 miles. Gunfire began again. A part of my brain noticed that there were at least two calibers of firearms. They were mostly automatic rifles, but occasionally, some of the *Zetas* discharged handguns.

Stupid shits. Makes no sense to waste pistol ammunition trying to penetrate this heavy stuff. I snorted. *Funny what the mind thinks of. As if I need to go tell those bastards this.*

The rest of my brain was in survival mode. Despite the cane's near impenetrability, fear gave me a new reserve of strength. Pete's groans were barely audible, and Laura shoved at him as I pulled furiously, using my butt to open a small path in the growth. Another yard. Then another. The cane was still as thick, but the contour changed, and I suddenly fell backward as the sandy bank dipped toward the water's unseen edge. Laura tripped over Pete's body and fell on top of him. She rose quickly, and I could feel her edge around his body. Then, she was up against me, and we both grabbed Pete and pulled him into the relative cover of the riverbank.

Laura and I panted with fear and exertion. I felt in the darkness for Pete's face, detecting the slight warmth of his shallow breathing. Before I could adjust my body, several automatic weapons opened up. Despite the muffling of the huge number of reeds, the noise was almost deafening. The *sicarios* were within yards of us. Thwack! Thwack! Thwack! The cane made tearing sounds, as bullets passed through or were deflected by their leafy growth.

I reached in the dark and pushed Laura's head down. Pete made a small grunting noise, and I felt for his face, and then clamped a hand over his mouth, hoping not to smother him.

"Oye, pinche putos! Sabemos 'stan escondidos el la caña. Tenemos tus armas. Si no te salgas, vamos a matarte."

Our weapons? I reached for the satchel that Laura had been carrying. There was nothing in her hands.

She whispered, "Sorry. I dropped it."

Fuck that. If we do come out of the cane, you'll kill us.

Several voices filtered in. The *sicarios* began arguing over who was going into the dense growth. No one volunteered.

Whoever was the boss yelled, *"Buscanlos! Mete adentro y buscan esos jotos!"*

Whoever he was ordering to track us refused to enter the cane. Small wonder. Although the sun had fled west toward the low hills, the heat inside the canes' cocoon had not dissipated.

The chatter began again. Apparently, no one had agreed to plunge into the uncertainly of the cane's darkness. The *sicarios* tried another tack.

The leader shouted in Spanish, "We know Pedro Vasquez is with you. He is all we want. Send him out. We will let anyone with him alone."

As he talked, someone with a machete began whacking at the cane.

More steps thudded on the sandy pathway. The machete wielder suddenly let out a scream, *"Cascabel!"*

He had discovered a rattler. I prayed the snake would bite hell out of the bastard.

"Te mataré!"

The machete clanged a distance away and what sounded like a pistol opened up. The snake's threatening rattle stopped. The man began to curse. He hadn't thrown the machete far, because seconds later he began hacking and screaming at the offending reptile.

"Dejelo, puto! Es bien muerto!"

Dead or not, the machete wielder kept chopping and cursing. The other *sicarios* laughed at the machete wielder and called him a sissy.

The schoolyard-like banter was surreal. I kept my hand over Pete's mouth, making sure I didn't block his airway. The heat of his breath exhaling through his nostrils showed he was still alive. Laura leaned up against me. Her body shook with silent sobs of fear.

A metallic sound grabbed me with renewed terror. Someone said, *"gasolina,"* and there were small splashes of liquid against the cane nearest the trail. Then there was a loud *whoof.* The cane began to crackle as flames crept up it. The smell of smoke wafted over us.

I pulled Pete's body further down the embankment. I noticed my pants were soaked with urine. I had pissed my pants. I had no memory of the sphincter letting go. Too miserable and afraid to be embarrassed, a fleeting thought almost made me laugh. Maybe that part of my body won't get charred.

We were to be burned or smoked out. And not a soul knew where we were.

NINETY-TWO

Reagan, Eddleman, And Others

PRESENT DAY

The seven-vehicle convoy consisted of three DEA vehicles, Bonavita's Sheriff's Office cruiser, Ignatius Gonsalvez's Border Patrol car, Clete Morales's 4x4 pickup truck, and was led by Chief Deputy Reagan. It pulled off the U.S. 90 and stopped.

Several truckers hit their air brakes when they came upon the unusual number of law enforcement vehicles. Some who traveled this border highway routinely weren't surprised by the number. It was the different types of vehicles that puzzled them. CB radios had not picked up any notices of unusual criminal activity or raids on illegals crossing.

Even if curious, no motorist was about to pull over and ask what was going on. The area's proximity to Mexico ensured that, with daylight fading, those familiar with the border and in their right minds wouldn't stop anywhere but well-lit gas stations or restaurants.

Reagan discussed a plan for searching a large and sparsely settled portion of Kickapoo County.

"The question I have is whether we all head south toward the Griffin place, based on Jake's hunch. Jake may think he knows everything," he was interrupted by polite laughter, "but we've got a lot of area to cover, and it's a ways down there. If we guess wrong, we've wasted our time."

Ignacius Gonsalvez spoke up, "There's no way we can cover much before dark, anyway." He motioned toward his Border Patrol cruiser.

"Every rancher on the south side of U.S. 90 has given me keys to their pasture gates, and there are plenty of them. It would take forever to cover even five percent of them if we worked all night. I suggest we head down toward old man Griffin's place and look around. We can always split off if no one is there."

Several grunts of assent helped make the decision easier for Reagan. With the cooling temperatures, perhaps atmospheric conditions would make a radio call possible.

"Fred, you read me?"

"You're ten-one."

That's not Fred, and I've forgotten the damned ten codes.

"Jake, that you? What the hell's ten-one?"

Jake's garbled response confirmed what the ten-one code meant. "Shit."

Reagan checked his cell phone and punched the Sheriff's Office number. It rang through.

"Jake what are you doing there? You're not getting paid for helping Fred out, goddamnit."

Reagan realized he could lose his cell connection while chewing out a dispatcher, so quickly relayed to Jake the group's plan.

"Get ahold of Ranger Selman and let him know what's going on."

Jake asked, "What am I supposed to tell him to do?"

Reagan wasn't sure.

"Tell him we'd appreciate it if he would head this way. I'm putting Bonavita here at the county road entrance. If we haven't come out, he can tell him where we went. If we get down to the Griffin place, we'll lose you. But we can at least reach Bonavita by radio, and he can pass along what we find or where we are."

"That'll work."

"It shouldn't take more than a couple of hours to check that place and get back to U.S. 90."

"What about TJ?"

Reagan almost said, "fuck him," decided against it, and assured Jake that TJ Johnson had other things on his mind that needed tending to.

Jake rang off, thought for a few minutes, and punched in the Sheriff's cell phone number.

"This is TJ. What's up?"

"It's Jake. Half your department and several other folks are in the far east end of the county going to scout out the Griffin place, looking for Purdy Kendricks. I thought you ought to know." Actually, just two Sheriff's Office personnel were looking, but Jake couldn't help trying to goad a reaction from TJ.

"Shit." There was a pause. "Two hundred and fifty." TJ turned his attention to the phone call. "Sorry, bidding on a belt buckle some FFAer made. Three twenty-five!" Again, TJ addressed Jake. "Now, what were you saying?"

You douchebag. Jake sighed and started over.

"Congratulations. Our illustrious sheriff, TJ Johnson, just bought hisself a dandy belt buckle and helped the kids in the process." The auctioneer's announcement over the PA system was as clear as TJ's voice.

There was laughter as the auctioneer poked fun at Clarence Livermore. "Clarence, looks like ol' TJ outbid you. I know you're hoping you'll outpoint him in a couple of weeks."

It sounded to Jake as if TJ had dropped the phone in his breast pocket. Jake was about to hang up when TJ came back on.

"I'll settle up here and see if I can meet up with those folks. Just let me know if they hit U.S. 90 coming back before I get there, so I can turn around and get back to my public."

Nodding at the phone, Jake disconnected and turned to Fred.

"Did I ever tell you that our sheriff is a sorry piece of shit?"

R eagan looked at the group of lawmen.
"Let's go."

Leaving Bonavita and his marked cruiser at the entrance to U.S. 90, the six remaining vehicles drove south. Reagan noticed the multiple tracks in the rutted sandy surface but gave it little thought. There were few roads worthy of the name in Kickapoo County. The surface traveled on was a thin lifeline to several large ranches whose sections butted up against the Rio Grande.

The Griffin Ranch gate stood open. Reagan stopped, walked to the chain and lock hanging from the gate's metal tubing.

"Lock's been cut. Someone's here."

Several trunks opened, as shotguns and high-powered rifles were moved to the passenger areas.

Eddleman walked up to the gate.

"What's going on in there?"

"Hell if I know." Reagan paused and yelled at the others in the convoy. "Y'all come here."

Taking a small dead piece of creosote bush, Reagan began drawing his recollection of the Griffin Ranch structures and layout.

"We'll check the headquarters first. We've all been there, when that Shivelli character's body was found. If we're clear there, we'll head down toward the Vasquez house on the river."

Before driving onto the property, Reagan and several others walked the ranch road surface for 100 yards.

"I count at least four vehicles," Gonsalves said. "Two have wider tires. Bigger vehicles than the other two. One set of tracks looks like worn-out tires and a shimmy." He pointed to a slight wiggle in the sand.

They returned to the rest of the men and relayed the information. Still too light for headlights, a slight haze was beginning to fill the low spaces in the hills hidden from the sun. Reagan led the vehicles to the old ranch headquarters. A single vehicle's tire tracks had pulled up to the ranch house back door. Then the vehicle had backed out and gone toward the Rio Grande.

"Nothing here!"

"Nothing here!"

In less than five minutes, the men confirmed there was no one in the house and out-buildings.

Again, the men huddled up. Reagan looked around.

"Anyone have any clear ideas of terrain features as we come up to the old couple's house?"

Clete Morales spoke up.

"I remember there's a good-sized dip about a quarter mile or less from Mr. and Mrs. Vasquez's home. I walked all over the place the day we found their bodies. It's sort of a dry wash, but not very deep."

Reagan nodded, recalling the feature.

"We stop this side of the draw. Walk down into it and up to the other side and take a peek before we move to the house. Just to be sure someone's not waiting on us."

A mile from the Rio Grande, the men smelled smoke. Moments later, they spotted grey and black clouds billowing up near the Rio Grande. Eddleman turned to a DEA agent.

"Someone's burning cane. Too much smoke for the small house Reagan's talking about."

The Border Patrol cruiser's take-down light flashed on and off, and Reagan waved the vehicles to a stop.

"What's up?" Reagan stepped out of his vehicle as Ignatius Gonsalvez walked up.

"Are any of you making radio contact with Bonavita? He's not answering my calls."

Reagan responded, "I had contact with him at the ranch gate." He yelled at the others, "Someone see if you can raise Bonavita on SO's frequency!"

Eddleman walked back to his sedan, then came back.

"I reached him. Told him what's going on. Just hope this doesn't go all over Kickapoo County. The Patels may get excited about the possibility of charging us another day's rental."

Uh-oh, thought Reagan. *This prick just cracked a joke—I think. What does this mean? The end of the world?*

T he cane's flames leapt 30 feet in the air. The heat reached over 400 yards to the faces of the men, as they crept down into the draw and then up to its lip facing the Vasquez house.

Clete Morales muttered, "Jeez, anything in that cane isn't going to live very long." As if to accentuate his observation, the wind shifted, and the intense heat struck them like a fist.

Reagan and Eddleman used binoculars to scope out the area.

"You've got what looks to be Purdy's cruiser by the house." Reagan continued, "Oto's truck is still where it was when he died. There's a ratty looking Ford truck driven up into some catclaw and huisache." He tapped Eddleman's arm and pointed. "More importantly, there are two new-looking black SUVs over there. Bicycles or no bicycles, those have to be cartel. Unless they're yours, which I doubt." He pointed left of the Vasquez house.

Eddleman grunted, "We can't afford vehicles like that."

Bonavita muttered, "Oh, shit and double shit. This isn't good."

No one argued with him.

Reagan turned to Eddleman. "On foot, or driving in?"

"On foot will take too long. In vehicles, we're defenseless if they open up on us as we drive up."

"Gee, thanks."

Eddleman let out a small laugh.

"Course, we could let them burn whoever's in the bushes and just clean up the mess and whoever comes out."

Reagan couldn't tell if Eddleman was serious or not.

"I'll drive my truck. Clete, how do you feel about using your truck, as well?"

"Aw shit, man! I'm still paying on it. My luck, someone will shoot it up and insurance won't cover it."

Reagan shot back, "DEA will pay for any damage, right Eddleman?" Not expecting an answer, he continued, "Everyone else, follow the two trucks but be ready to bail out if we take shots. When we hit the house, un-ass your vehicles pronto. I don't see anything moving in the Vasquez place, but you never know. We'll use its walls for cover once its cleared and see what's going on in that river growth. Load up as much ammunition as you can. Let's go."

Reagan drove to the top of the draw and instinctively crouched as low as possible behind the steering wheel. Behind his truck at a distance of 10 yards Clete Morales followed in his 4x4. Border Patrol Agent Gonsalves's marked cruiser was third. Eddleman's men crept behind in their vehicles.

As soon as all six vehicles cleared the draw, gunfire erupted upwind from the raging fire. They had been discovered. Reagan floored the accelerator. Behind him, the five other vehicles began to spread out, reaching for the cover of the rock structure of the Vasquez house.

Bullets punctured Reagan's hood and right quarter panel. Steam poured from the radiator as he killed the engine and dived for cover on the driver's side.

Automatic fire now erupted from two different directions. Reagan crouched as bullets impacted the truck bed. *Where are those shots coming from?*

Holy fuck!

"Get down! Get down! They've got automatic weapons!"

The huge fire that stretched upriver cracked and popped. Automatic weapons chattered, and men yelled. Reagan wasn't sure he had been heard. Looking around, he saw his men crouched on two sides of the Vasquez house. Everyone was keeping their heads down.

Good. At least no one has been shot.

"Ummmphhhhh!" Clete crumpled over. He was grabbed by two DEA agents and pulled around the side of the Vasquez house away from the expanse of cane upriver.

A fast tattoo of bullets beat on the chief deputy's truck. Window glass shattered.

Eddleman yelled, "Reagan, get the hell away from that thing and get your ass over here."

Reagan, now on his belly beside the truck's rear tire, turned and nodded. He rose and started toward the cover of the house. He felt a fist punch him in his chest, and it slammed him to the ground. Reagan wondered who had punched him, and things went black.

———

NINETY-THREE

Present Day

PURDY KENDRICKS IN THE CANE BRAKE

nstinctively, I tried to push down toward the river. The crackling of the fire grew louder. The water was down there somewhere. Pulling at cane stalks didn't work. My hands felt shredded, and we hadn't moved an inch. At least with the noise of the fire, I could try to talk to Laura in something close to a normal voice. Besides, the cartel members were whooping and hollering now. They seemed to be having a grand time. No doubt they soon expected to see us running out of the cane trying to escape the heat, or see us on fire. Either way, we would be a source of entertainment before they killed us.

"You have to help me, Laura. We've got to get down to the river, or we'll die." I felt for her. I found her lap and laid Pete's head in it. "Keep him quiet. I'll see what I can do."

Pushing forward on my knees, I angrily shoved the dense growth to each side. Three inches, then six. Then a foot. Then two. Finally, three, then four. Then my left hand felt wetness. All I had to do was push through the cane growing in the river to reach a water level that might protect us from the fire's heat. Making a final push, I reached what felt like two feet of stagnant water. I turned back to reach the others and realized the back of my shirt was dry and singed. I quickly ripped it off, dunked it in the river, and put it back on. The coolness eased the burning on my skin.

Occasionally, bullets ripped through the cane. There was no way to tell how close they came. The roar of the fire concealed lesser noises.

Laura began coughing. The smoke was sifting downward toward us. I took a deep breath, so I would have the strength to push up the bank toward the other two. The heat seared my lungs.

"C'mon, Laura. Stick out your hand. I'll pull you!"

Pushing toward her, I met an arm swinging toward me, trying to reach toward the sound of my voice in the dark and heat. I began pulling Laura until she jerked away.

"We're leaving Pete! We can't do that!"

I wasn't so sure about that, but she wasn't going anywhere, unless I assured her I would take him with us.

"Come this way and low crawl down into the water. Get yourself soaking wet and just keep your nose above the water. Hurry up!"

She responded desperately, pushing past me. I reached up for Pete, not knowing if he was dead or alive. The blood that coated his side and back was almost dry to the touch. I reached for his belt buckle to pull him and burned my hand from its heat.

"Owwww!" I yelped. How could Pete be alive with fire this close to him?

Backing down the bank and pulling Pete's limp body, I began to black out. I fell sideways, then sat up, coughing from the smoke. The flames from the fire were no longer out of sight. They were plainly visible, licking up the long cane stalks. Laura reached for me and began to tug. With another burst of energy, I moved Pete's body several feet. His head bounced on the ground once, and I thought I heard a moan. Laura, soaking wet, grabbed one of his arms. Together we settled into the dirty life-saving water of the Rio Grande.

"Keep his head above water. I can't hold him up" Laura whispered desperately.

I took Pete's upper torso from her, and squatting in the mud, rested his head in my lap until the fire came too close. "We've got to move. Either the fire will burn us, or it'll burn itself out. If that happens, we'll be visible to everyone."

Laura began to sob. "I'm sorry. I'm sorry. I'm so sorry."

Pushing Pete out into deeper water, I wasn't in the mood for her remorse. "For what? Jacking around with this loser? What?"

"No," she said. "We shouldn't have come back here. It's just that... Well, Pete promised me..."

Mexican gunmen are trying to burn us to death and I'm listening to this horseshit?

As I tried to keep Pete's body under water so he wouldn't suffer burns, I asked, "He promised you what?"

Rounds zipped into the bushes, inches from my head.

"Goddamnit! Now, they've got men on the fucking gravel bar in the middle of the river."

Whatever Laura was going to tell me would have to wait.

NINETY-FOUR

TJ Johnson, Abner Selman, And Lowell Johnson, Jr

PRESENT TIME

Lowell Johnson, Jr., knew the *Kickapoo County Register* for what it was—a local newspaper with a tiny circulation, eking out an existence with ad sales that barely covered printing costs. Fortunately, Lowell had ranching income, so he had never counted on the *Register* making money. He just loved the news business and fervently believed that a free press spelled the difference between an open society and oppressive government.

Lowell rarely attended church, describing himself to anyone who would listen as a "deist." His strident beliefs occasionally got his publication in hot water with the powers that be in Kickapoo County, as he wasn't afraid to call a spade a spade. Or, more likely according to one of his critics, he usually dubbed a spade "a fucking shovel."

The pages of the *Register* occasionally thundered about ineptness in county or town government, or exposed some petty theft by a PTA treasurer or county employee. The horrific Vasquez deaths sold newspapers, but there had been no tying up of loose ends.

Then DEA agents floated into town. Ranger Selman became a semi-permanent fixture. Rumors of cartels warring over control of Nuevo Laredo's plaza, and vague talk percolated of connections to Venustiano Huerta's assassination 40 or so miles inside Mexico. However, as he complained to Doc Smithers, making sense of it all "was like trying to nail Jell-O to a wall."

Then, Purdy's wife and kid were almost snatched by thugs who had to be connected to some Mexican cartel, and Purdy had promised him an interview. The attempted kidnapping would be a great human-interest story. Lowell Johnson also had a hunch that it could be the missing thread that would help stitch together the fabric of the last months' events.

Putting the pieces together whetted his appetite for investigative journalism. He was impatient and felt time was getting away from him. After two phone calls to Kendricks that went to voicemail and four Balvenie single malts over ice, Lowell decided he would try to track Purdy down and extract some kind of promise to talk on the record.

Lowell Johnson locked the door of the *Register's* office, climbed into his pickup, and drove to the Kickapoo County Sheriff's Office. Popping two Altoids, he walked in the front door.

"Hello, Jake. Hello, Fred. What's going on in the world of law enforcement tonight?"

Breathe mint or no, Jake knew Lowell's late afternoon drinking habits and could tell he had had a few.

"Nothing much, Mr. Johnson. Just about to go home."

"I'm looking for Purdy, and he won't answer my phone calls. You seen him lately?"

"No, sir." Jake's face flushed. Fred turned his chair, pretending to fill in call logs.

"Uh huh." Johnson looked around suspiciously. "Well, tell him I'm not going to quit trying to get a story, okay?"

Relieved the conversation didn't seem to be going any further, Jake said, "Sure, Mr. Johnson. I think he'll be in tomorrow, if he and Betty and Forrest haven't gone to San Antonio or somewhere for awhile."

"That's bullshit, Jake. They're staying with Paula until their house gets cleaned up. Forrest is horsing around with his cousins in Paula's back yard as we speak."

Disgustedly, Lowell Johnson turned toward the front door to leave. Outside, Ranger Abner Selman was getting out of his state vehicle.

Lowell stepped back, grinning, "Gee, boys, I smell a story. Ranger's here after hours. Is he *just* passing through? Wonder if he needs a motel room, like those DEA agents."

Abner Selman spotted Lowell as he walked in. Seemingly unruffled, he shook hands.

"How's the newspaper business, sir?" He motioned to Jake. "Got a minute, Jake? Just passing through and need to drop a report on your sheriff's desk."

Jake stood up and started for the hallway. Selman followed him into an empty office.

Lowell Johnson turned to the night dispatcher and asked, "Did you see anything in the Ranger's hand, like a report or anything?"

Flummoxed, Fred shrugged his shoulders and picked up his Louis L'Amour novel. A truck door slammed. Sheriff TJ Johnson pushed through the double glass doors, clutching his FFA/4H belt buckle.

"What the hell are you doing in my office, Lowell-no-relation-to-me-thank-you-Jesus Johnson?"

The newspaper editor laughed, "This is getting curiouser and curiouser."

Hearing the conversation, Ranger Selman and Jake stepped into the hallway. TJ appeared surprised to see Selman, but he managed to reach out and shake the Ranger's extended hand.

"Good to see you."

For a moment, there was a pause.

Lowell cackled, "Folks, I've walked in on some kind of police business. Mind if I hang around?"

Selman chose not to say anything. *Let's see the Sheriff handle this one.*

TJ turned to Lowell and said, "I'm going patrolling. You want to go with me?"

Selman's eyes widened in disbelief. TJ's quest for votes was going too far.

"Sheriff-not-related-to-me-praise-be-to-Allah Johnson, since when have you ever patrolled? And after hours at that?"

TJ couldn't resist, "Well, as you know, I'm always concerned for my men. Deputy Kendricks is out of radio and cell phone range, and we were going to check on him. I'm about to rendezvous with others in my department, just to make sure everything's okay."

Selman shook his head. *This dumb shit is an elected sheriff. Unbelievable. But he did pronounce rendezvous correctly, which surprises me.*

TJ turned to Jake and asked, "Where are my men now, Jake?"

"Deputy Bonavita is parked at the county road in the east end that heads down toward the Griffin place. The rest of *your* men drove that road to see if Purdy got stuck or something."

"Why is he there and not with them?"

"No reception, Sheriff. As I'm sure you know, it's bad out that way. They left him so your Chief Deputy could radio, and Bonavita can use his cell phone to let us know if they found anything, and to report when they're coming back this way."

Feeling good after outbidding Clarence Livermore in front of a lot of voters, TJ wanted to extend his winning streak.

"Come on, Lowell. Let's go see what's going on down toward the Griffin place."

Selman shook his head, saying, "I'll follow you out there, Sheriff."

TJ adjusted his hat and headed toward the door.

"We'll just drive that way and meet everyone on their way back. Give me a good excuse to get out and get some fresh air." He checked his cell phone and repeated a number to Jake and Fred. "Is this still Bonavita's cell number?"

"Yessir," replied Jake.

"I'll try to get ahold of him on the way. C'mon, Lowell."

S heriff TJ Johnson took the lead, with Lowell Johnson in the passenger seat. It didn't take long for the sheriff to begin pumping the news editor about his chances of getting re-elected.

Not interested in making him angry, Lowell was cautious in responding.

"TJ, it depends on the Hispanics. If you can get them out to vote, you got a good chance of getting re-elected."

He didn't add that few of the Hispanics gave a rat's ass about either candidate, and were unlikely to make it to the polls.

Ranger Abner Selman called the Sheriff's Office on his cell phone.

"Jake, what's really going on?"

"Ranger, nothing more than what you've already been told. But there are three DEA agents, plus Eddleman, who are helping Reagan. We haven't heard anything from Bonavita." There was a pause. "Just a second. Looks like Johnny is calling in on the other line."

Rather than punching the hold button, he laid the receiver on the dispatcher's desk and answered the other call.

"What? What? Holy shit. Hold on."

Jake picked up the receiver.

"Bonavita just got a radio call from the Griffin place. Shots fired. Shots fired. They've been ambushed!"

"Have him call me, right now!" Selman flashed his headlights, and the two vehicles pulled to the side of U.S. 90. Putting on his flashers, Selman hurried to the Sheriff's pickup truck.

"Bonavita should be calling me right now. Hold a sec."

As if on cue, Selman's cell phone rang. He put it on the speaker and said, "Talk to me, Johnny!"

"Ranger, I just got a radio call from the DEA fella, Eddleman. He said there's a big fire on the river, and they were going to investigate. Then a couple of minutes later, he called back. Said they were taking fire. They had been ambushed." Bonavita's voice broke. "I don't want to sit at this goddamned intersection. I need to get down there and help them!"

Sheriff TJ Johnson looked totally confused. He started to say something, but Selman interrupted him.

"Stay where you are, Deputy. We're about ten minutes out. If anyone goes there, we all go together."

Silence.

"Goddamnit, Bonavita! You hear me! No one is going anywhere until we get there!"

Bonavita's anguish was palpable.

"Yes sir."

Selman rang off and punched in a speed dial number. In seconds, he was talking to the Texas Ranger headquarters in Austin, Texas.

"Get us helicopters, get us backup, get us whatever you can, and fast."

Selman pulled up his phone's GPS app and messaged its map coordinates. Assured of a response, he rang off and turned to TJ.

"Let's go."

Lowell Johnson sat in the passenger seat of TJ's truck, quietly listening. *Holy Mother of God, I'm in over my head.* He turned to TJ.

"You want me to step out when we get to Bonavita?"

TJ was too distracted to answer. The Ranger's vehicle pulled around his truck and with lights flashing, headed east on U.S. 90.

Ten minutes later, the Ranger and Sheriff linked up with Bonavita. It was dawning on TJ that the situation was totally outside his control.

"Deputy, have you heard anything more?"

Bonavita shook his head.

"Let's go, please! We gotta help those folks!"

Selman drove past Bonavita and yelled, "Follow me."

He was 100 yards south before Bonavita could react. The three vehicles sped toward the Griffin property.

NINETY-FIVE

Present Day

PURDY KENDRICKS

Two *sicarios* stood on a small gravel bar in the middle of the Rio Grande. Both were equipped with automatic rifles and were firing into the cane at the water's edge on the United States side. Although less than 50 yards away, they hadn't spotted us—yet.

They continued to shoot, and I wondered when a bullet would hit one of us. Our clothing was soaking wet from wading and swimming the short distance from the Griffin property. Somehow in the craziness I still had time to inwardly laugh at the division between the United States and Mexico represented by the stagnant, muddy water of the Rio Bravo.

I pulled Laura back toward the bank while holding Pete's head above water. In the increasing gloom, a part of me was fascinated by the occasional tracer rounds arcing into the cane on the American side. Both *sicarios* seemed to be keeping their shots low to avoid hitting their compadres. Occasionally, a round zinged off the water and bounced toward the high bank, evoking screaming and cursing. I prayed for errant rounds to kill the bastards near us.

Suddenly, the shouting stopped. Or rather, after a brief pause, it became re-directed. A new flurry of gunshots, but not directed at the water's edge. Over the fire's roar, I heard one of the *sicarios* yell, *"Vienen los pinche gringos. Vengan por aquí. Vamos a matar todos esos culeros!"*

The men on the gravel bar swam back to the American side, then cursed as they were pulled up the steep muddy embankment of the cut bank near Oto's boat. *What the hell was going on?*

"Laura, someone has showed up. Probably someone trying to find me. Whoever it is, this is our chance to get the hell out of here without being burned alive."

She looked at me dully, as if she had already given up.

"Dammit woman! Did you hear me?" With my spare hand I grabbed her shoulder and shook it violently. "We've got to move and now!"

Laura's eyes refocused.

"Where are we supposed to go?"

The gravel bar was 50 yards. A small channel of the river divided the bar from the Mexican side, then there was a gentle slope into brush.

"We go there. It'll be the last place they'll look for us." I shoved through the remaining cane and swam into the muddy current. "Follow me, but check behind us as I go."

I touched bottom 20 yards from shore. The late summer drought kept the current manageable, and within a minute or so I found a footing in the gravel. I turned and began to pull Pete under his armpits. Laura instinctively grabbed his feet. Between the two of us, we dragged him over the gravel and into the shallow water near the Mexican side. Once out of the water, Pete's inert body didn't cooperate with my attempts to pull him up onto the sand shore and into the mesquite.

"Goddamnit! Come on!" Nothing.

"Is he dead?"

Laura slapped Pete's face. A low groan confirmed he was still alive.

"Use some of that anger to help get him up and into the bushes, Laura."

Within 30 seconds, the two of us collapsed over Pete's body, gasping for air.

On the American side, all hell was breaking loose.

. . .

The fire in the cane didn't stay there. A shift in the wind bowed the flames northward, and the blaze jumped the path dividing it from the catclaw, salt cedar, and other foliage slightly further from the Rio Grande. The two *sicarios* scrambled up the muddy clay on the riverbank near Oto's boat mooring and joined three others. The five *sicarios* stood there, looking baffled. They were now prevented from following the trail back toward the Vasquez house.

The sudden flurry of yells indicated the need for the group to head downriver toward the opening near the Vasquez house. The alarm didn't entice any of them to attempt to run the hellish gauntlet they had helped create.

As the gunfire increased, the yells turned to screams. More weapons were needed against someone—I couldn't tell whom, but assumed it was law enforcement.

Four of the five *sicarios* slid cursing down the embankment, trying to keep AK-47s, pistols, and ammunition dry as they plunged into the water. The fifth stood on the shore, pleading with the others.

"No puedo nadar. No me dejes aquí!"

The four in the water ignored him. Their lives were forfeit if they failed to do what they were commanded to do. The abandoned *sicario's* inability to swim wasn't their problem. If he was still there when it was all over with, a cartel *jefe* would probably put a bullet through his brain.

I pushed Laura prone behind some river foliage. Pete remained inert. Slight movement confirmed he was still breathing. Between the raging fire and the gun battle, the four *sicarios* in the river paid no attention to us. Their objective seemed to be avoiding burning to death and joining their *compadres*. I prayed that it would stay that way.

Three of them were indistinguishable. The fourth had a heavily scarred face. His eye on the damaged side seemed to be sightless. The group struggled to reach the gravel bar near the Mexican side.

Yells confirmed my suspicions about the one with the damaged face. He had trouble keeping his head above water. Halfway across the 50 yards or so to the gravel bar, he disappeared. The others screamed that *"el tuerto,"* meaning one-eyed man, was drowning. They reached into the water, frantically searching for him. After several moments, they were successful in grabbing hold of the one-eyed man's hair.

The three dragged him onto the gravel and rolled him onto his side. *Tuerto, as I mentally dubbed him,* began vomiting river water. The rest seemed completely out of breath.

Looking back at their abandoned *compadre* on the American side, one yelled in Spanish, "You won't be left with a set of balls unless you do what you're told. Figure out a way to help us!"

The response was immediate. The man near the mooring grabbed his crotch with one hand and pointed to it with the other. The message was clear. *You can suck my dick.* He put his weapon to his shoulder. I thought he was going to shoot at the four. So did they. With a quick release of the safety, one took three shots in the stranded man's direction. With another scream of expletives, he disappeared from view.

Tuerto continued to vomit. Seeing he wasn't going to be of use, the other three turned their backs to us and plunged into the water again, wading as far as they could before swimming toward the cut bank on the American side.

"Shit," I muttered under my breath.

Laura asked me with her eyes why the whispered curse word. I pointed at the *sicario* lying in the gravel.

I whispered, "We need to get out of here. If he sees us, we're dead." I wondered what was happening outside of eyesight. Slowly, *Tuerto* rolled over onto his back. How long would it be before he was in shape to tempt fate again by following the others downriver?

The three who had abandoned *Tuerto* were now trying desperately to grab handfuls of shrubbery and vines on the steep bank just below the Vasquez house. The cut bank side created swifter current there. They gave up, floating downriver another 100 yards, and then scrambled into the brush and disappeared.

I turned my attention back to the gravel bar. *Tuerto* raised himself onto hands and knees. Spittle drained from his mouth. His head turned toward our hiding place. His good eye stared directly at me. I decided I had to do something.

I jumped up from the brush and ran into the water, making desperately for the sand bar 20 yards away. Five yards, 10 ... for what seemed like minutes. He stared at my desperate, splashing approach. Then *Tuerto* reached for his pistol belt, seemingly forgetting that the others had tried to keep the weapons dry by carrying them over their heads. As they had dragged him ashore, the others had set his weapons on the slight rise of the gravel bar. The *sicario's* automatic rifle and pistol were a few yards from him.

Everything played out in slow motion. My advance through the water seemed endless. *Will I get to the gravel bar before he grabs a weapon and kills me?* The *sicario's* good eye seemed as large as a saucer. He pulled his head away from my look and turned toward the weapons, slowly reaching for the rifle.

It looks like an AK47. C'mon! C'mon!

The water's drag lessened. I made it to the bar. The *sicario's* back was to me, as he bent to pick up the AK47. Bellowing with fear and desperation, I slammed into him, driving the one-eyed man into the water of the river's main channel. The assault rifle clattered on the wet gravel. A part of my mind saw vividly that the *sicario* was wearing a cream colored guayabera. *Awfully nice shirt to be wearing in the river*, I thought.

I wanted to loop my arm around his neck and drown him quickly. At the last second, his body turned, and we hit the water side by side. I started swinging my fists and made contact with his face several times. The *sicario* pushed me away and got to his feet in two feet of water. His one good eye told the story. One of us was going to die in the murky water of the Rio Grande.

Laura was screaming now. I know I heard her. The sound seemed so incredibly unimportant. I drove my shoulder into *Tuerto's* chest. We fell again. This time, I wrapped my right arm around his neck and shoved his head under water with my body and left hand. Both his hands grabbed for my right arm. The *sicario's* head thrashed back and forth. I grabbed a fistful of *Tuerto's* hair to ensure his head would stay down. Suddenly, my arm around his throat slipped upward. Instantly, he bit into the flesh of my forearm. The pain was excruciating.

I heard myself screaming, "Die, you bastard! Die, you bastard!"

Releasing his hair, I drove a fist into his left ear and temporal lobe. Upper and lower teeth seemed to meet. *God! He's taking a huge piece of meat out of me!* I didn't dare let go of the embrace, but my vision tunneled with the pain. I smashed a palm against his left temple again and again.

Suddenly, *Tuerto's* body went still. Holding his hair with my left hand, I pulled my right arm away from his mouth. The *sicario's* body was totally slack. I pushed it into the current. For a moment, his inert body bobbed gently. Then the slow-moving current began to carry it downriver.

Blood streamed down my right arm from the bite wound. He had chewed away a huge chunk of flesh. Trying to ignore the pain, I retrieved the holstered handgun and the AK-47.

I yelled at Laura. "Stay here!"

"Don't you dare leave me!"

"You'll be okay." I wasn't sure about that. I started to explain why I was leaving. Laura's countenance told me it didn't matter. She was beyond reasoning.

I had to assume that whoever was firing from the Vasquez house were rescuers. The three *sicarios* had floated past the Vasquez house and crawled up behind it. The *sicarios* who had climbed the riverbank could kill everyone, taking cover there before they were even aware they had been encircled. I put the AK's strap over my shoulder, stuffed his automatic in my belt, and waded into the water.

NINETY-SIX

Eddleman, Reagan, And The Others

PRESENT DAY

R eagan came to as Eddleman dragged him away from the truck. "Am I dead?" His chest hurt like hell. "Am I dying?" He wasn't making much sense.

"No, you dumb bastard. You caught a round in the chest."

Reagan was puzzled. Body armor wouldn't stop an assault rifle's bullet. As his head began to clear, he scratched at his shirt.

"Quit worrying. If it had been an AK, you'd be dead. Someone must have shot at you with a pistol. If you survive this clusterfuck we're in, you'll feel like hell tomorrow."

Reagan rolled on his side and looked around. The sinking sun left deeper, defined shadows with its departure, making it harder to see. Someone seemed to be trying to stitch holes through the Vasquez house.

"How's Clete?" Reagan had to yell over the gunfire.

"Alive, but not good." Eddleman leaned around the edge of the house, put his DEA tactical carbine to his shoulder, and squirted five quick rounds in the direction of the enemy gunfire. Eddleman then squatted beside Reagan.

"We got two SUVs full of *sicarios* in the bushes near that fire."

Head nearly completely clear now, Reagan remembered rounds coming at them from another direction.

"What happened to the other shooter?"

"Apparently, whoever opened up on us as we drove in, is back with his asshole buddies." He stopped. "We're pinned down here."

Reagan sat up, careful to keep the structure between him and the flying bullets.

"Where is everyone?"

In response, from the other side of the house, a shotgun coughed out buckshot.

"One of ours, I hope?"

Eddleman nodded and pulled the trigger on the tactical carbine.

"We're okay as long as we keep the house between us and them. But they're not showing any sign of giving up. They want us all dead. When it gets dark, it's going to get dicey."

As if to confirm the thought, bullets spanged into the masonry near the northwest corner of the house, sending rock slivers among the men huddled there.

"Is anyone coming to help?"

Eddleman nodded at Reagan again, then winced as rounds shattered the remaining window glass on Reagan's truck.

"They've riddled every tire they can hit. Not that we can drive through this mess anyway. And yes, we contacted Bonavita. Hopefully, he got the word to Santa Rosa."

Reagan stood at a crouch.

"Show me where they are."

Eddleman pointed out the general direction of the gunfire.

"Of course, we've shot hell out of their SUVs. Unless they wade the river, they're not going anywhere, either."

The cane fire still burned, but was running out of fuel. Eddies of smoke aggravated the increasing gloom.

Suddenly, a high-pitched scream broke over the cacophony.

"What the hell is that? A woman?" Reagan peeked around the side of the house.

Engulfed in flames, a blackened human broke from the path, spinning and swinging his arms trying to beat out the fire.

"Christ. Is that Purdy? He's on fire!" The high-pitched agony continued. Automatic weapons opened up from the *sicarios'* position. Dust flew from the burning man as they hit their mark. He dropped to his knees. Looking toward the embattled Americans, he slowly fell forward onto his face.

Shaken, Eddleman muttered, "Sweet Jesus. I don't know. Too burned to tell."

The smell of burning flesh saturated the men at the Vasquez house. Reagan gagged. A DEA agent began to cry.

NINETY-SEVEN

Present Day

PURDY KENDRICKS

T*uerto's* bite had done serious damage to my right forearm. Hoping to keep it dry, I balanced the AK47 with its two jungle-clipped magazines on the top of my head. There was little grip left in my right hand, but enough to keep the weapon positioned. Heavy stamped metal cut into my scalp and hurt like hell. My left arm pulled through the water, aiming toward the take-out point of the three *sicarios*. I swept against the bluff below the Vasquez house and prayed I wouldn't be met by gunfire if I was able to crawl out of the river.

Kicking away from the riverbank, I turned my body upriver and used my left arm to steer. Soon, my feet started dragging in the shallowing river's dirt and rocks. I twisted back, facing downriver and saw why the *sicarios* had chosen this spot. The clay of the cut bank bluff had dipped down here to a small embankment. At some time in the past, a rise in the Rio Grande had flattened and drowned a swath of about 20 yards of foliage. Areas of broken dead reeds and branches showed where the *sicarios* struggled up and away from the river.

With my undamaged hand, I grabbed the assault rifle's gun sling, pulling it over my head. The staccato beat of different caliber weapons above me punctured the dusk. An occasional bark signaled at least one person was using a shotgun. I didn't see anyone waiting to kill me, so I pushed into the mass of dead foliage. It was impossible to get through it quietly. The cracking and snapping of dried brush and cane sounded deafening. *How in hell can those bastards not hear me smashing through this stuff?* I stopped for a few seconds and looked around for some cover once I had achieved clearer ground. Then I thought how stupid I was. Stuck in over two feet of a tangled mass of dead growth, I was a sitting duck.

Purdy, just get your ass moving! Which I did.

Crouching, I ran toward a small thatch of river grass and threw myself behind it, then rolled to my side and pulled the AK free. I felt for the automatic I had shoved in a side pocket. It was gone. But where? I glanced back toward the riverbank. The dead *sicario's* 9 mm lay in the mud, its nickel plating barely visible. It had fallen out of my pocket. *Oh shit.* No way was I going back into the clearing.

I pushed the AK's magazine tab, releasing the magazines from the receiver group. Each looked and felt fully loaded with 30 rounds. I reinserted the magazines and checked to ensure the safety wasn't on. So far, so good, but now what? Cane and salt cedar hadn't taken over this area. Less cover but easier going.

Where in hell were the three *sicarios*? Rolling onto my back, I looked up. A crescent moon with its companion Venus was peeking into the gloom of the early evening. Despite the heat, I began to shiver. It wasn't the soaked clothes. It was the realization that suddenly I had become very good at taking men's lives.

I was almost thankful when my introspection was interrupted. This wasn't the time for a burst of troubling self-awareness. The banshee-like keening of agony assaulted my ears. A burst of gunfire stopped the horrific scream.

What or who was that? I prayed it wasn't someone I knew.

The gunfire stopped for a few seconds. Then an explosion of automatic gunfire erupted from the direction of the burning cane and heavy foliage upriver. Several rounds zipped past, confirming the shooting was directed toward the Vasquez house. One last glance, then I was up on my feet and duck walked toward a thicket of small oaks and mesquite higher up the embankment. Lying prone, the structure was outlined dimly by the burning cane and occasionally lit up by muzzle flashes. If I was this close, the three *sicarios* were closer. But where?

One announced himself quickly, as what sounded like an AK47 let loose 20 or 30 yards to my right-front. The flashes lit up a *sicario's* face. Several yelps of surprise came from the direction of the

Vasquez house. The sharp bark of a 9 mm pistol showed someone returned fire—hardly effective in the gloom and at a distance of 40 yards.

Where were the other two? I expected to feel bullets pound into my back at any second. I crawled on my knees toward the one *sicario* I had spotted. At five yards, I thumbed the selector switch to full-automatic. Shooting semi-automatic in the gloom made no sense. I stood and pulled the trigger, sweeping right to left. My AK's rounds ripped into the man, flinging him backwards into the brush. I had to make sure the *sicario* was dead, so I ran toward the sound and nearly tripped over his body.

Frantically, I crouched and ran my hands over the prone figure, as my eyes adjusted to the shadows. I needn't have worried. He had been hit in the torso several times. His AK47 was configured like the one I had. I released the magazines. Under the *sicario's* body was a 9 mm automatic. My pants belt became a makeshift gun belt. As the extra ammunition was stuffed into one of my back pockets, gunfire ripped into the trunk of the oak tree a foot to my left. Someone at the Vasquez house was shooting at me.

I dived next to the dead man, using his body as a shield. *Just my luck to get shot by my own people.* I almost shouted out, forgetting there were two more *sicarios* somewhere nearby. Fighting to keep my breathing under control, I smelled burning flesh and wondered if the odor was connected to the screams of agony.

A *whoosh* of sound and light swept the area, as the truck nearest to the Vasquez house exploded. Bullets had found its gas tank. Three figures darted away from the inferno and into the shadow at the northeast corner of the house. The truck fire had stolen the concealment of the dusk. One man peeked out, trying to see through the flames and was met by several bursts of gunfire. He pulled back just in time. Rounds gouged the masonry where his head had been seconds before. The rest flew into the oaks and mesquite where I lay.

The truck fire lit up the dark-skinned faces of the other two *sicarios*, as they ran toward the crouching figures and began firing long bursts from automatic weapons. Were there more than three defenders at the Vasquez house? I didn't detect any return fire. Either the three had been hit by the sudden gunfire to their rear, or they had been lucky and dived to the ground. They weren't going to stay lucky for long.

Within seconds, the *sicarios* were going to be on them at point-blank range.

Pushing the release lever, I flipped the magazines and re-loaded, then grabbed the charging handle and rocked it forward to seat a round in the chamber. *Where had I learned this?* Seemingly forgotten skills from police tactical training brought back muscle memory I had no idea existed.

Running toward the two *sicarios*, I began firing on them, hoping to at least keep them away from the three men I had seen in the shadows. One *sicario* fell face down, his weapon flying away from his body. The other stopped and turned. As he turned, he let loose a stream of gunfire. Before the arc of bullets reached me, I plowed into him. The *sicario* let out a curse as he scrambled to his feet.

I jammed the AK47 barrel into the *sicario's* chest and pulled the trigger. The repeated impact of the bullets slammed his body back-wards and onto the ground. For a moment, I stood panting. Then bullets began to zip by.

Shit. I had to do something.

"Hey, it's me, Purdy. Stop shooting at me. I'm coming in."

NINETY-EIGHT

Ranger Abner Selman

PRESENT DAY

T he Ranger's inner voice told him that he was leading three other people into a shit storm—that the best course of action was to hold back and wait for enforcements, air support, anything, before driving headlong into a gun battle against a well-armed cartel group. His emotions overrode good sense, and the undercarriage of the sedan took a beating as it bounced and fishtailed down the gravel road toward the Mexican border.

Selman slowed at the cattle guard into the Griffin ranch, then pulled over to let the sheriff's pickup and Bonavita's sedan drive inside the property.

"Tell me again, Deputy, where did everyone say they were?"

Bonavita slammed his car door.

"Down at Otabiano's old house by the river."

TJ started to suggest something. Selman cut him off.

"We're going to help whoever is down there. We're going in fast."

Remembering the small arroyo Reagan, Eddleman, and the others had probably negotiated, Selman came to a decision.

"When we get near that arroyo, we stop and figure out what's going on." He paused, as TJ handed Lowell Johnson a Kevlar vest. "Before we go further, we see who's where."

TJ pulled a scoped 30-30 Marlin carbine off the rifle rack in his truck, levered a round into the chamber while checking the side ejection port, then half-cocked the hammer onto the weapon's safety.

"All I got for you, Lowell, is this saddle gun. Sorry, but I hope you make good use of what you got. Six shots. I don't have any more ammunition. You can't shoot worth a shit, anyway."

Lowell Johnson set the rifle muzzle down on the floorboard. His hands trembled as he tried to zip up the body armor.

"Hey, I hear my Mama calling. Mind if I take a raincheck on this extravaganza?"

"Lowell, the only thing you hear is the scotch bottle calling."

TJ's starched shirt showed sweat rings under the armpits and made a lie of his outward calmness.

"TJ, I don't remember you breaking a sweat at honest labor since you worked at the service station that summer. Even then, you hardly hit a lick. Where did all that sweat pouring out of your body come from?" Lowell Johnson's voice didn't cooperate with him, his fears turned it into almost a squeak. "Don't tell me, Mister High Sheriff, you're scared of some little ole cartel members?"

Bonavita snorted his disapproval of the banter, as he helped Lowell with the vest, then ran back to his vehicle, while the two Johnsons traded insults.

Abner Selman got back into his sedan. *I'm scared shitless, too. There is no telling what we're getting ourselves into, but I'm not going to join in those two idiots' pissing contest.*

"Let's go, boys! Mount up!"

Past the old Griffin headquarters buildings, Selman waved the group to another stop. Killing their engines, the four heard the *pock pock pock* of gunfire. The darkness accumulating in the lower reaches of hills and arroyos contrasted with the flickering light of the distant fires of Reagan's truck and the cane on the riverbank.

"Kill your headlights. Don't turn on any sirens or overheads. We go in slow and walk down into the arroyo and then up to its ledge."

Selman drove slowly, spying Deputy Bonavita's sedan crowding TJ's truck. *Damn, that boy's gonna get himself shot if he doesn't calm down.* They pulled their vehicles off into low scrub. Selman motioned the other three.

"We move quickly and get out of sight as fast as possible. Any questions?"

TJ pawed at his M-16 and asked, "Why don't we wait for some air cover or something?"

"No time, Sheriff, unless you want to explain to the voters why you sat a few hundred yards away while good men were killed because you were waiting for 'air cover.'"

He wasn't sure, but it looked like TJ may have pissed his pants.

Lowell Johnson snickered.

The four slid down into the arroyo and crouched as they came up the rise. Exchanges of gunfire illuminated the locations of the two forces.

Bonavita pointed toward the pickup, which was engulfed in flame next to the Vasquez house.

"Hey, Sheriff, isn't that Chief Deputy Reagan's vehicle? Jesus Christ, it's lit the place up like a Catholic Church. And he just bought it!"

In fact, the line of law enforcement vehicles that had followed Reagan's charge onto the property reminded the Ranger of combat photos shown on the news during Desert Storm.

Selman grunted, "Looks like the convoy got strafed or something." All the tires were flattened with multiple bullet holes in the metal bodies, and shattered window glass.

Lowell Johnson chimed in, "Looks like our guys aren't the only ones who won't drive out of here."

Otabiano Vasquez's pickup and two black Cadillac SUVs were riddled with bullet holes. An older model Ford truck was parked nose-in to the heavy foliage. Three bullet holes starred its rear window. Its tailgate hung at a 45-degree angle, where a shotgun round had blasted the hinge loose.

The *sicarios* had moved slightly away from the flames and into the cover of small rock outcroppings near the SUVs. One let loose with an AK47. A piece of fascia wood disintegrated on the Vasquez house.

TJ finally spoke up, "What are those bastards trying to do—take Oto's old house down piece by piece? They act like they got all the ammo in the world."

Lowell Johnson stood and pointed toward a blackened object halfway between the two warring groups.

"What is that? A body?"

"Hard to say. It's black and it's smoldering."

Selman got a whiff of burnt flesh. He had no doubt he was looking at a human.

Lowell peered closely and said, "Sure as hell is a body. Christ almighty!"

"Get down!" Selman pulled the newspaperman to the ground.

Several tracer rounds lazily arced toward the arroyo. Dirt and rocks dappled them from bullets striking just in front of where the group lay huddled. Two rounds ricocheted over their heads, announcing their passage with loud *zips*. They had been spotted.

TJ rolled partly down the small incline.

"Mother of our Lord Jesus Christ," he moaned, "I ain't never been shot at before."

Abner ignored TJ's whining and hissed, "Get up here and shoot something." No response. He moved to TJ and grabbed him by the back of the shirt. "We need firepower. Get your fat ass up here."

Selman had always treated him with deference. The Ranger's anger and demeaning comments stunned TJ.

"OK. OK. Let go of me!" He scrambled clumsily up the sand and rocks.

The three lawmen spread out, ignoring Lowell Johnson. Selman quickly decided what they had to do.

"Our people are getting shot up badly. We're going to do what we can to take the pressure off them. I want everyone to aim toward those rocks and bushes behind the black SUVs and let 'er rip."

Bonavita didn't need to be told twice. With a whoop, he opened up with an M-16, and in less than 10 seconds, burned through the ammunition in the first magazine.

Selman spotted the location of one *sicario* and coolly sent round after round toward his target. The shooter disappeared. Selman couldn't tell whether he had scored a hit or not.

TJ closed his eyes and repeatedly pulled the trigger, generally in the right direction. Lowell Johnson couldn't see a target through the 30-30's scope. He set the Marlin in the dirt, rose to his knees and began moving his smart phone from one area to another, alternating between short videos and still photos as quickly as he could. Danger be damned, he had *one hell of a story.*

NINETY-NINE

Present Day

PURDY KENDRICKS

I didn't wait for a response. I ran toward the three men I had seen in the shadows, continuing to scream my name. When I reached the east wall of the house, they jumped and grabbed my injured arm, ignoring my scream of pain.

"Purdy, is it really you?" Ignatius Gonsalvez pounded me on the back.

"We thought you were dead! Where have you been?"

Chief Deputy Reagan actually seemed happy to see me—hard to believe under the circumstances.

I bent over trying to catch my breath. Eddleman was the third man. Three agencies, so far, trying to pull my bacon out of the fire.

"Sorry. Sorry." It was all I could think to say. "Who else is here?"

Someone pulled one of the AK47s off my shoulder.

Reagan was more interested in pumping me for information than giving me an answer.

"What just happened?"

"You had three drift down the river and come up behind your location. They were fixing to kill all of you."

Gonsalvez asked, "Did you get all three of them? Holy shit, Purdy. Thanks."

"Thanks for what? I got everyone in this situation."

Eddleman wasn't interested in salving my conscience and said, "Well, yeah, pretty much, Deputy. Tell us what you've got."

Between intermittent exchanges of gunfire, I gave him the short version.

"Where are Vasquez and the woman now?"

"Hiding in the bushes across the river. Pete's hurt bad. I don't know if he'll make it. You may get your wish, Eddleman."

Almost as soon as the words left my mouth, I wondered if I had disclosed too much to Pete's nemesis.

Someone on the south side of the house yelled, "We've got movement!"

More gunfire. Someone else yelped, then cursed, "Motherfucker! Motherfucker! I'm hit!"

Eddleman suddenly turned loose of me, saying, "One of my men."

He ducked under the bedroom window and began low-crawling toward the sound of the wounded man. Reagan crouched at the south east corner of the building to give Eddleman cover.

I started that way, and Ignatius grabbed me. He said, "We need you on this end. We're outgunned by these bastards. There's not much cover anywhere. They've shot the house to pieces. Can't figure out why they haven't rushed us. Maybe they were waiting for the three to take us from behind."

"Who else is here?"

"Clete's here but hurt. Eddleman's three guys."

"Hurt how?"

"Round hit him in the leg."

Sorry. Sorry. Sorry. "How bad is Clete?"

Before he could answer, a hail of bullets smacked into the wounded house. Then what sounded like three more weapons began firing. These shots were coming from another direction.

Sweet Jesus don't tell me they've got reinforcements.

I edged toward the corner by Oto's bedroom, avoiding its windows. Rounds had gone all the way through the house and shattered the glass.

Again, a flurry of automatic gunfire—the distinctively higher pitch of the 5.56 mm rounds of an M-16. Ignatius and I looked at each other. He appeared as puzzled as I felt.

"Those are new sounds." I took a glance, trying to see past the blazing truck and into the gloom. Another burst of M-16 gunfire. The weapons' suppressors didn't do much to hide the shooters' locations. I couldn't be sure, but it looked like they were on the lip of the small arroyo the ranch road traversed to reach where we were.

The exchange between us and the *sicarios* lulled momentarily. They were as surprised as we were.

Eddleman shouted out, "Were those M-16s?"

There were several acknowledgments. Reagan was the first to figure it out.

"Whoever that is isn't shooting at us! The cavalry's here, boys."

Eddleman's three DEA agents yelled almost simultaneously, "The fuckers are heading toward the river! Shoot the bastards!"

One agent had a shotgun, and I guess it was loaded with double-ought buckshot or slugs. Its heavy cough soon blended with automatic rounds from his partners. Ducking under the bedroom window, Ignatius Gonsalvez and I moved toward the south side of the house.

"Where are they?"

Human forms flitted in front of the burning cane as the *sicarios* made for Mexico and safety. One, near the deep drop to the river's edge, suddenly flung his arms in the air and screamed. Someone's bullet had caught him in the back. I couldn't tell how many others were fleeing toward the river.

I didn't share my rescuers' relief. I turned to Reagan and said, "We've got to go after those bastards. If they find Vasquez and Laura, they'll kill them."

"Purdy, we're not crossing into Mexico. Haven't you had enough of this?"

There was a cessation of gunfire and screams. My ears rang furiously. I wondered if any of us would suffer permanent hearing loss.

Someone from the arroyo began to yell, "There are four of us here."

Vehicle engines started up, and less than a minute later, Selman, Bonavita, Lowell Johnson, and the Sheriff cautiously pulled up to what was left of the Vasquez house.

Bonavita began to whoop, but was shushed by Eddleman, who said, "They may still be out there, and it's getting too dark now to find them."

I grabbed Abner. "I left two people in the bushes across the Rio Grande. One was almost dead. We can't wait to see if they're still alive."

Abner looked undecided, then said, "We'll start an international incident if we cross into Mexico."

I lost it. "Goddammit! I got them away from the cartel, and I'm not leaving them to be killed."

I was tackled before I got five yards. I put my hands down to catch my fall, and my right arm buckled under me from the pain of the bite wound.

In the distance the high-pitched whine of a turbine and the slap of rotor blades signaled the approach of a helicopter. Suddenly, I was blinded, as we were bathed in 18,000 lumens of its spotlight.

"Let me the hell up, goddammit!"

"Shut up, Purdy."

Bonavita grabbed my AK47 and called someone, yelling, "Get this weapon away from him." He locked my right arm behind my back. "I'm sorry, but you gotta calm down."

"Let me up, goddamnit!"

Grudgingly, I felt a new respect for the young officer's assertiveness. No response. Just the whine of the chopper's turbine and the rotors' *whop whop whop,* as it began tracking back and forth, its pilot on the lookout for a landing zone, and *sicarios* wanting to knock it out of the sky.

"At least let me see what's going on." My anger and desperation were compounded by embarrassment at being so easily handled.

Bonavita eased his grip, and I rolled to one side, but he still wasn't taking any chances and remained sitting on me.

The adrenalin in my system dropped, and for a moment closing my eyes and sleeping seemed inviting. Relieved by my change of focus, the deputy turned his attention toward what appeared to be our deliverance.

The helicopter pilot made a tactical ground touch, barely changing rotor speed. Two men pushed off the skids with automatic weapons at the ready. Another person climbed out with a medic's kit bag. Someone, I couldn't tell who, ran up and motioned the three toward the Vasquez house.

"Your arm looks 'bout half chewed off, Purdy. That's a nasty wound. Please, let's get you patched up. We got a medic here for you."

"Forget me. They say Clete Morales is hurt bad."

Someone, it sounded like Ignacius Gonsalvez, added, "And one of the DEA guys is saying he's hurt, too."

I put my head on the ground and turned away. I didn't want to look at Bonavita or anyone else. *This is a nightmare.*

Immediately, the helicopter spun away from the river and began to lift. The rotor pitch change shook me out of the self-pity. I saw a monkey-strapped gunner on the right side with a set of night vision goggles shoved up on his forehead. They were of no use as long as the spotlight overwhelmed its sensors. By the time the chopper passed over the arroyo transecting the road to the house, it had gained enough altitude and swung back toward the Rio Grande. Almost immediately, the brilliance of the spotlight beam flashed by, as it searched back and forth. Then it hovered over the river.

Suddenly, someone yelled, "Oh, no!"

"Goddamnit! What's going on?" Lying on the ground under Bonavita, I had lost sight of the helicopter.

"Oh, Jesus, I don't know, Purdy."

Bonavita released the arm-lock, and I craned to see what was happening. The helicopter spotlight was describing the craft's seesawing, as its bright whiteness stitched an increasingly random pattern.

A spark, then another twinkle on the bird's tail boom.

"Christ, they're trying to take out the tail rotor."

In fact, the chopper was already mortally wounded. The pilot tried desperately to set the bird down in a controlled crash on the American side. The craft started rotating around the axis of its rotor blades. Yawing violently, it made for the clearing where it had just left the three men. The pilot appeared to dump the collective, the lever that controlled pitch, kill the engine, and auto-rotate the main rotor blades. Too many things to do quickly, and too low. It pancaked onto the surface, and a dark dust cloud enveloped the grounded craft. For a moment, I thought the pilot had pulled it off. Then, the right skid collapsed, and the wounded bird tilted. Its rotors struck the ground and broke off. Instinctively, everyone ducked as the lethal blades scissored through the air. The artificial daylight of the spotlight blinked out.

A collective gasp, but the chopper's body seemed to remain intact.

Not waiting to see if the helicopter's two occupants were alive, I rolled and slugged Bonavita's jaw hard, then sprang up and kicked him in the crotch. He doubled over, allowing me to yank his slung M-16 and flee into the darkness. I had to get to Laura and Pete.

It was a short run to the Rio Grande from the Vasquez house. Not a good location, since I would have to move back upriver to where I had left the two, seemingly an endless time before. There was no way to chance it on the American side. One side of the border or the other, odds were, someone would try to kill me.

As I stumbled back through the dead brush near the river, I paused, surprised that I had not been followed, A staccato burst of gunfire confirmed the lawmen had more immediate concerns. I guessed that whoever had exited the chopper had linked up and were trying to clear out the remaining Mexicans. The earlier hope that all the *sicarios* were gone had just been disproved by the savvy attack on the helicopter.

How many are left? Where are they? I had no way of knowing.

I swung the M-16 over my shoulder, waded into the murky waters, and swam for Mexico. Pushed downriver slightly by the slow moving water, I waded ashore wondering how to get upstream without meeting up with fleeing *sicarios* or rounds fired from the American side.

The fury of the gun battle and the noise of the helicopter still rang in my ears. Dense brush, mostly mesquite, catclaw, and creosote, blanketed much of the river's inside bend. The trick was getting across the thorn-covered expanse to where the two were hidden—if they weren't already dead. With no searchlight or night vision goggles, the chances of succeeding suddenly seemed very, very remote.

I stopped and sat down, the latest surge of adrenalin wearing off quickly. A cooling breeze came with the darkness, seeming to accentuate the river's murmurs and burbles. For a moment, I wanted to pretend the tranquil setting held no evil, but I knew better. Exhaustion settled like a heavy blanket, and it seemed almost impossible to move. The pain in my arm and my doubts roared back. Who the hell did I think I was? Some kind of one-man wrecking crew? I shook my head. Maybe the physical effort would make the doubts go away. I had made my choice, and now I would live or die with it.

Hardly a hint of twilight remained in the late summer sky. I took 10 steps and stopped. The gunfire suddenly quieted. Moving any distance in the dark, I had welcomed the noise of the gun battle. In the renewed silence, rodents scurrying in the brush became killers awaiting my next move. Small trees were crouching *sicarios*, knives ready to cut my throat. It took an eternity before I got 100 yards, and I had yet to spot the sandbar next to where Laura and Pete lay hidden.

The Mexican side was in total darkness. Suddenly, a muzzle flashed again from the American side. The rounds zipped across the river. The shooter must have had a night vision scope, or thermal optics, or both.

Seconds later, a heavier chorus of a larger-caliber automatic weapon sprayed toward the Americans. The AK47 gunfire was directly to my front, some 50 yards away. At least the *sicarios* were again occupied elsewhere.

Then it hit me. "You stupid bastard, Purdy! Do you think a night vision scope is going to differentiate between the bad guys and the good guys?"

If a goggle wearer spotted me, he would see a human form carrying a long gun, moving slowly upriver. There was no way I was safe from either group.

If trained in the right direction, either would allow their user to spot Laura and Pete. Remembering Eddleman's hatred for Pete, this knowledge wasn't any comfort. Someone with night vision or thermal sensing ability and a few well-placed rounds toward the darkness of the Mexican brush could end both of their lives, and in this confusion, no one would be the wiser.

I crouched down on my knees and began to dry heave. Nothing came up, thank God. Tears streamed from my eyes, and snot ran from my nose. I became totally frozen with fear. Suddenly, a voice, Abner's, echoed over the river noise. "Purdy, if you can hear me, we need to know where you are. We don't want to accidentally shoot you. You need to let us know where you are."

No shit. And how am I going to do that without getting my ass shot off by sicarios?

Several rounds ripped in the direction of Abner's voice, which sounded upriver from me. I tried to create an image in the darkness. No luck, but just then a small breeze stirred embers from the dying cane fire, about 75 yards from where Abner seemed to be. Now, I knew where I was. Laura and Pete, if they hadn't moved, were about

50 yards the other side of the Mexican shooters returning fire to my front.

There was a pause, then, "Stay where you are now. Let us take care of things."

Tempting, but no.

The Ranger seemed to know I hadn't come this far to quit. Another booming request.

"Purdy, if you can, stand and, knowing that cow college you attended, show us its symbol with *both* hands outstretched."

Oh, sweet Jesus. I set the M-16 in the dirt, quietly stood, and took a deep breath. Hopefully, even if the *sicarios* understood English, they wouldn't figure out what Abner meant. Raising both arms, I made fists with thumbs extended in Texas A&M's "gig 'em" signs and moved my arms up and down. Could a night vision scope spot something that nuanced?

I crouched, and seconds passed.

"Thank you."

They had identified me. Giddy with the small victory, almost involuntarily one hand shot up, and someone got a quick glimpse of a single-digit salute. *Texas A&M a cow college? Selman, you sorry SOB.*

Now what? Why in hell hadn't the shooters on the Mexican side just booked it toward their country's interior. It made no sense that they would continue the fight, especially now that they were outnumbered. Unless the *sicarios* had been given no choice but to capture Pete Vasquez or bring proof of his death. That hadn't happened…yet.

It seemed unlikely that there were any remaining *sicarios* on the American side. When the helicopter came into sight, I recalled they had bolted for the river and the relative safety of Mexico. Now, the two sides were in a standoff across the thin ribbon of the Rio Grande, too dark and dangerous for the Americans to cross.

"We have other resources enroute. Please stay where you are."

However, "enroute" could mean an hour, or six. With the sunrise, Pete and Laura would be easily visible.

A twig snapping, or a rock dislodging, would ensure my death. It was a certainty. Ahead, there was a tall outcropping—probably where at least some of the *sicarios* could have taken cover. Otherwise, shooters on the American side could have killed them by now. Exactly where in the denseness of the jagged rocks were they?

Nervously, my left thumb constantly confirmed that the safety selector on the M-16 was in the off position. Ten yards and then a slight clearing, and I paused. Where was the moon to aid the stars' light wash of the area?

One, two, three? How many are there?

I lay down and tried to control my breathing. Each time I exhaled, it sounded like a gale. Then, a murmur of voices. The flare of a match. Two cigarettes lit off the match. A brief glimpse of faces and weapons, weapon butts on the ground. The Mexicans knew they couldn't be seen from across the river.

But I can see you bastards, and when I pull the trigger....

Partially hidden from the *sicarios'* view, I chanced a wave with one arm, fist and thumb in the familiar position. *Whoever's over there, please see this. And please don't shoot my ass.*

Prone, I pointed the muzzle toward the two shapes. It was too dark to use the sights. I squeezed the M-16's trigger. Almost instantly, four rounds were gone. Shit, I forgot to check if the weapon had a selector switch and expected to squeeze off one round at a time. The thought process and reaction seemed simultaneous. I tapped the trigger. Two. Another tap. Three. Slight movement. Another tap. Two. No movement. Another two.

Jumping up, I reached the outcropping and fired toward the ground. I began kicking in the dark, then let out a curse as a boot smacked into the wood stock of an AK47. Crouching, I felt for the other weapon and instead touched a human form. No movement, and the other AK47 lay next to the body. I picked up that weapon and started firing where the bodies were. In the dark, there was no way I could allow either to live.

Winded and faint, I paused. Someone on the American side opened up on the outcropping.

"Stop! It's Purdy!"

The firing ceased. Two down. Were there others? Again, I dropped and felt the bodies. My hands came away bloody. I took the dead men's weapons and threw them out of reach, just to be certain. I reached into a pocket and found the matches. It took four tries but finally the shaky swipe on the box striker worked. One *sicario's* face was gone. The other appeared unhurt, until the flickering light showed a massive pool of blood growing under his torso.

I shook the light out and listened. Off to my left, someone was pushing furiously through heavy brush.

Daring to expose myself to the American side, I yelled, "I'm coming out of the outcropping to your front. Don't shoot."

Still unsure of exactly where Laura and Pete were, I didn't disclose where I was heading.

"There are two dead ones here. One, maybe more, sounded like they were running away."

Abner again, "They see you through the scope. Stay low. Someone's coming to help."

About damned time.

There were several splashes, as men jumped in the river. Eddleman's threats rang in my head. I needed to be the first to the two hiding somewhere on the Mexican side of the river.

Moving upriver I began to whisper loudly, "Laura. Where are you?" No response.

Again, "Laura, where are you?"

I was at the sand bar next to where they had hidden. No response.

Suddenly, a touch on my shoulder. I swung around, gasping with fear.

"Don't shoot, Purdy. It's me, Laura."

Instinctively, I reached for her and pulled her to me, whispering, "I could have killed you. Where did you come from?" Their old hiding spot wouldn't have concealed them from the goggles.

"Up there." I sensed her arm point into Mexico. A small outcropping dimly contrasted against the night sky. "We lay behind some rocks. Someone's been in the brush looking for us. We had to move."

Her voice was barely a hoarse whisper. Totally spent, she clutched at me, trying to keep from falling head-first toward the river.

Through dumb luck or instinct, Laura had found the strength and saved the two of them from the *sicarios*, and, possibly, Eddleman.

"Yeah, the *sicarios* almost got everyone. But I think we're okay now."

I continued to hold her, whispering in her ear, "How did you move Pete? Is he...?"

She shook her head. "He's still with us, barely. I thought you were coming from upriver. I heard at least two or three come across from that direction" —I felt her arm point toward the burned cane— "just before you yelled."

Four Americans splashed out of the river. One donned night goggles and led the other three toward us. Bonavita was one of them. I started to say something.

"Forget it, Purdy. We've got to get everyone back across to the old U.S. of A."

A medic bag was produced, and a penlight flashed on the fevered face of Pete Vasquez.

"He's not stable, but we can't do anything here. Let's go."

There were sounds of an oar stroking and a boat moving in water. Someone was bringing Otabiano Vasquez's old boat.

Moments later, Abner appeared, stroking upriver against the current. Bonavita ran out, grabbed the gunwale, and pulled the boat onto the sandbar. The medic and I grabbed Pete and dragged him toward the river. We sat Laura in the stern seat, then lifted Pete in. With no room to lay him down, Pete, muttering incoherently, was propped between Bonavita and me. One of the others pushed us off and relieved the Ranger of the oar.

The crack of a single rifle shot echoed across the water, and I felt Pete grunt heavily.

Instinctively ducking, I whispered, "Where did that come from?"

Bonavita answered, "Sounded like it came from the American side, in the brush I think, but I can't be too sure."

"Where did the round go?" Selman shifted on the metal seat, as he peered into the darkness.

One of the goggled men muttered, "Don't know, but we need to get back to Texas ASAP."

In less than a minute, the boat scraped against the bank near its old mooring pipe. We were back on friendlier ground.

No lights were used. Now two men had goggles on and began scanning the Mexican side, as several hands reached to pull Pete Vasquez up the steep embankment.

One man removed his goggles, went into a prone position, and peered through his rifle's heat sensing scope.

"I'll cover. Everyone else, out, now!"

Someone produced a stretcher. We lifted Pete onto it and hurried through the blackness of burned out cane.

We set the stretcher down in the relative safety of the Vasquez house. By penlight, the medic began to work on Pete.

"What the hell?" He held up a gloved hand, glistening with fresh blood. He looked around, puzzled, and pointed to red soaking Pete's shirt. "This guy has taken a round through the chest."

Laura pushed forward. "He only had a wound below his ribcage that was getting infected." She started to cry as she voiced the obvious. "This just happened!"

Quickly, the medic ripped at the buttons and pulled open Pete's shirt. Blood flowed from an ugly wound. The medic then flashed his light in Pete Vasquez's eyes. No reaction.

The last shot had holed Pete Vasquez in the chest, but it looked like an exit wound, not an entrance wound. Before the medic could do anything, Pete shuddered, gasped for breath, and was gone.

ONE HUNDRED

Eddleman

PRESENT DAY

E ddleman moved closer to Kendricks. If Kendricks was about to run, he wanted to find out where Vasquez and the woman were hiding.

Several gasps shifted his attention. Eddleman stood transfixed by the impending crash of the wounded helicopter. He hit the ground as he screamed, "Everyone! Get down!"

Discordant sounds and dust enveloped the Texas Department of Public Safety helicopter, and the main rotor blades broke off. Already prone, Eddleman Instinctively buried his head as a *whew, whew, whew, whew* signaled a main rotor blade scything over the Vasquez house.

On impact, the turbine's whine abruptly stopped, and the dust and debris seemed suspended in the air for an interminable time. Then, yells and screams of the onlookers washed over him, and Eddleman raced toward the crash. The unconscious pilot hung partly out of the sprung left-side door of the cockpit. Ignacius Gonsalvez and a DEA agent carefully unhooked and lowered him to the ground. Others lifted the pilot up and over to the Vasquez house. Eddleman moved under the tail boom and climbed up onto the left side skid. The door gunner struggled to unhook himself from the monkey harness.

"Here, let me help you."

Eddleman reached behind the man, searching for a D ring. The man grunted in pain and vomited. Eddleman grabbed the gunner's night vision goggles and tossed them to the ground, then removed the injured man's helmet. Aviation fuel spilled onto the ground, and Eddleman wondered if he could get away before something sparked a fire.

Two men shouted, "Here! Hand him down to us. You need to get away from this thing before it catches fire."

The voice sounded familiar. Eddleman found the snap link, and the gunner came loose from his tether. As he lowered the injured man, Eddleman was able to discern the two men assisting. Sheriff TJ Johnson and the local newspaper editor.

What in hell is a reporter doing in this mess? Where did he come from?

Eddleman looked inside the helicopter as the sheriff and editor struggled to guide the gunner toward safety. Suddenly alone, he felt around and touched an automatic rifle with an oddly large attachment.

Heat sensor scope. He loosened two Velcro straps and jumped from the skid with the weapon. Turning in the direction of people yelling, he spotted the young deputy, Bonavita, clutching his crotch in pain. He then caught sight of Purdy Kendricks before he disappeared behind the Vasquez structure.

Someone yelled, "He's heading back to the river!"

A brief exchange of gunfire, and no one seemed to pay Eddleman any mind. Guessing that Laura and Pete were upriver from the point where Kendricks appeared to be heading, Eddleman quickly moved toward the dying embers of the cane fire. The smell of burnt vegetation enveloped him as he weaved through what had been a dense stand of river cane.

Eddleman reached Otabiano's upturned aluminum boat and stopped. He took a prone position in some unburned Bermuda grass, slowed his breathing, and peered through the night vision scope, slowly scanning the Mexican side. Vasquez and the woman were there somewhere, but where? No human forms appeared, but heavy brush and rock outcroppings could shield body heat.

Suddenly, movement to his right. Something large was moving near a gravel bar. Eddleman watched, and the white image became a man, holding something in his hands. Was this Purdy? It seemed unlikely that the deputy sheriff had made it that quickly upriver. The man scrambled up the riverbank, paused and faded from detection, as he moved up and out of the Rio Grande's cut.

Sicario, Eddleman thought. *Stealing away. I'd love to kill him, but I've got other things to deal with.*

Selman's voice boomed, and Eddleman jumped at the intrusion on the silence. The Ranger began yelling across the river. Eddleman moved the scope downriver, and it barely picked up the whiteness of a figure whose heat was partially blocked by vegetation. Shots erupted, their muzzle flashes momentarily overloading the scope's optics.

Where were Vasquez and the woman? Suddenly, fast automatic bursts, then a voice signaled the deputy's location. A large collection of boulders shielded Kendricks from the scope's sensors.

More shots, then Kendricks screamed toward the American side. Eddleman felt, before he heard, men moving his way on the pathway.

Time to move. He stood and moved further upstream and away from the burned area. Hunkering down behind some gravel and brush, Eddleman re-trained the rifle and scope toward the voice on the Mexican side.

C'mon, Kendricks. Show me where Vasquez is.

Metallic sounds signaled the old boat being let down into the river, as the scope confirmed several men wading into the Rio Grande. Kendricks—it had to be him—appeared. The deputy stopped, his movements signaling confusion. Voices too low to be heard over the river's susurration, and suddenly, a smaller image appeared.

Laura Griffin Saenz. It had to be. Where was Vasquez?

More figures appeared.

Damn it! Too late!

Two men appeared to drag another toward the river. The injured man had to be Pete Vasquez. And, unfortunately, he didn't appear to be dead.

Eddleman thumbed off the weapon's safety switch, hoping to get a shot. No chance, as it became unclear of anyone's identity other than the woman. Partially blocked by other bodies, Eddleman watched as Pete Vasquez—his inert form was now obvious—was positioned in the small craft's center, sandwiched between two men. Eddleman lay quietly. There seemed to be nothing he could do but quietly make his way back to the Vasquez house. Maybe there would be another chance.

Men pushed the boat into the river, and a man used an oar to push against its current as he aimed the boat toward its original put-in point. Eddleman watched as the boat's bow pointed to him. He now had an unobstructed view of the slumped man being supported by the two men. Eddleman centered the crosshairs on the slumped man's back and squeezed the trigger.

Startled voices mixed with the stroking of a paddle and the slosh of the small boat's efforts against the current. Moments later, everyone was back on the American side of the Rio Grande. Eddleman crouched lower. The figure of a man with night vision goggles seemed to peer in all directions, searching for the location of the gunshot.

Vasquez's body was lifted onto a litter of some sort and carried away from Eddleman toward the old couple's house. The remaining man rose and walked back through the stench of the burned-out cane.

Eddleman threw the scoped automatic into the Rio Grande, pulled his automatic, and quietly walked back toward the Vasquez house. Guessing that he was near the *sicarios'* vehicles, he stepped off the trail and into the ash. He skirted the shot-up SUVs and the downed helicopter and moved toward the house and the sound of a woman crying.

Eddleman glanced around. Seeing no one, he began to smile.

ONE HUNDRED ONE

Three Months Later

PURDY KENDRICKS

"Time for school, young man!"

Forrest groaned and pretended to fall back asleep, pulling the covers over his head. Reaching under the blanket, I found a foot and began tickling.

"Don't, Daddy! Don't! I don't want to go to go to school today!" His attempt at being angry dissolved into waves of giggles.

"Okay, but if you stay home, Mom's going to have you vacuum all the rooms in our new house, and then finish unpacking all your toys." That got his attention. "Oh, and no video game time, either."

"Oh, Daddy. All right."

I pulled his covers off, and Forrest leapt into my arms, wrapping his arms around my neck. "I sure love you, Daddy. What's for breakfast?"

I stroked his head and shrugged away a sudden tear. "Let's go see. But I bet it's going to be waffles today, Sport."

Forrest turned the wrong way in the hallway.

"Your bathroom's the other way."

Within minutes, with hair somewhat brushed, he dug into a waffle, with two strips of bacon on the side.

Attention focused on his food, Forrest missed Betty's look. Unable to be adequately defined, it radiated a mother's fierce love for her son. She glanced at me and nodded as stood at the sink, then turned back and began putting dirty dishes in the dishwasher.

"Hon, you don't have to wash them beforehand. Just rinse them off," I chuckled.

"I'm not at the stage of trusting a dishwasher. It's been so long since I've had one. Houston? Our last apartment there?"

Indeed, it had been awhile.

Forrest finished, slid off his chair, and took his plate to the sink, suddenly energized about school.

"We gotta go, Daddy. Miz Lipscomb is bringing a big lizard to school to show us."

Betty handed him a lunchbox. Going to one knee, she held her arms out for a hug. Forrest wrapped his small hands around her neck.

"Love you, Mommy." Again, our eyes met.

Betty's eyes. So much was spoken through them. And so much hidden. She had killed to protect the two of them. The guilt on my face was evident, but she drove it back inside me with a wink and a smile. A reassurance of forgiveness. But more. Much more. It was a reminder: *We've been to the edge of the abyss. Don't take any of us there again.*

I parked the State car and walked Forrest to his classroom at the Montessori school situated next to an Austin Police Department sub-station. Though early winter, the Central Texas air was still warm, and it was nice to drive something with an air conditioning system that worked.

"When am I gonna get to go to a regular school, Daddy?"

It was a good question. A public elementary school was within walking distance from our new home.

Too soon, son. Too soon. There are monsters out in the world. One step at a time. Your mom and I aren't ready to take any chances just yet.

"Forrest, this is a special place for smart young fellas like you. Don't you like it here?"

The only response was a quick wave goodbye as he bolted for the classroom. Ms. Lipscomb indeed had some kind of creature in a cage. I would hear all about it that night.

Twenty-five minutes later I pulled into the basement parking garage of a non-descript office building owned by the State of Texas. Security on entry and a swipe card for the elevator, then another security station with my ID checked on the first floor. Finally, a quick ascent to the 7th floor.

"Good morning, Commander." The woman at the foyer's desk was old enough to be my mother—or perhaps her younger sister. Her name plate identified her as Alicia Trejo.

"Miss Trejo, I'm having hell with the title. Can I convince you to just call me Purdy?"

For the umpteenth time, Miss Trejo responded, "I'll try...Commander." She gave me a stern look over her reading glasses that told me I would continue losing this argument with her.

I shook my head and walked down a short hallway to my office. I thought I heard a suppressed chortle.

"Oh," she called after me.

I turned quickly hoping to catch some change in her steely countenance. No luck, dammit.

"Don't forget your talk at the Department of Public Safety Academy. It's at four o'clock. You'll need to leave here no later than three-thirty if you want to get there on time."

"Yes, Miss Trejo." The needling had become a daily game. The widow of a Highway Patrol trooper killed by a drug dealer in the brush country of South Texas, she had been raised in a town almost as small as Santa Rosa. Nevertheless, apparently one of her duties was to remind me of how bad Austin traffic was. As if anyone needed reminding.

My office phone had too many messages on it, and once again, I wondered if there were enough minutes I could cobble together without interruption to get any real work done.

Beep "Hey, Purdy, why the hassle getting through to you? Since when did you get so damned important that you can't take my call. In case you've forgotten me, this is that pissant newspaper owner from Santa Rosa, Texas." I caught myself smiling. "Give me a call, if you can spare the time. Got some news for you."

Beep "Selman. Call me, Purdy."

Beep "Commander, this is Glen Hohmeyer. Don't know if you remember me. I'm a detective in Alamo Heights. Can you give me a call?" He gave his number twice.

Beep, beep, beep. More messages dealing with the makeup of the new task force, training, prying money out of the penurious Texas legislature. I decided to deal with those later. First, I punched in Hohmeyer's cell number.

"Congratulations, sir."

"Thanks, detective. What's up?"

"Commander, I'm calling out of curiosity only. If I overstep my bounds, let me know."

"Okay."

"Ms. Griffin slash Saenz is back in Alamo Heights. Installed new security system at her house. Spent a pretty penny doing it. She's got a new housekeeper. Seems to have put things behind her."

"So, why the phone call?"

"Anything we need to know about here? Any concerns we might need to be aware of?"

I couldn't tell whether Hohmeyer was fishing for information on an errant oh-niner, or just trying to do his job.

"Detective, I'm out of the loop on what's going on in any legal troubles she's got with the government." I paused.

Hohmeyer interjected, "Rumor mill is churning out suppositions. One is that she'll do some serious time. One says nothing's going to happen to her."

"Detective, I'm not blowing smoke when I tell you I don't know. When I find out, I'll pass it along. That's a promise." I chuckled. "Sounds like you folks may find out about it sooner than I do."

Hohmeyer laughed. "Commander, you just may be right. About security? Laura is safer in Alamo Heights than on the Mexican border, but…again, I don't know of anything, but I'd sure as hell tell you if I did."

I buzzed Alicia Trejo. "I'm going to be on a conference call for about ten or fifteen minutes. Will you hold my calls?"

"Yes, sir." The inflection in her voice seemed to say, "I *know* you're bullshitting me, Commander."

My old iPod had disappeared in the Rio Grande. After the move, Betty had rolled her eyes when I came home with an expensive MP3 player with all the bells and whistles, but said nothing. Downloading songs off the internet had kept me up late a few nights. My earlier collection had often been a small point of light. I knew I would need something like it in Austin. Different situations, same pressure. At least the one I had bought had Bluetooth. No more winding and unwinding the iPod's wiring.

I scrolled through until I found Jessica Molaskey's version of *Help*

Me. I closed my eyes. She segued into a bossa nova version of *Chelsea Morning. Oh, wow.*

A polite knock sounded on the door. I pulled out the earbuds.

"Commander, Ranger Selman's on the line again, and he'd sure appreciate it if you'd take his call."

It had been less than two months, but Alicia Trejo was making me feel like I was a delinquent kindergartener.

I checked my cell phone. He had called that number also.

"Thanks." I waited for her to close the door. "Ranger, I apologize. I didn't see the missed calls."

Abner Selman was the closest friend I had had in a long time, but after the Griffin Ranch shootout, I had stepped away from him a bit. I needed time to process a truck full of emotions.

"I hear you're coming over to DPS headquarters to talk to a class." It wasn't a question. "If you can pry yourself out of your ivory tower, I'd like to take you to lunch. Just a few things to go over to wrap up the Kickapoo County investigation."

I almost begged off. "I thought we had finished that. What…?"

Abner cut me off, and something told me whatever he wanted to talk about didn't need to happen over a law enforcement land line.

"Sure, where?"

Fifteen minutes later, I pulled into Tranca's Taco Stand parking lot off Cesar Chavez. He was sitting at a table in the back.

"Not exactly on the way to my class."

He nodded but offered no reason for a lunch in East Austin. Pleasantries came along with soft tacos and sweet teas. The Ranger started edging toward the reason for this out of the way *tete-a-tete.*

"How's the job? You happy?"

Happy? Too early to tell, but I had walked away from a pile of horse shit and came out smelling like a rose.

"Abner, I'm over my head, but enjoying the challenge. I owe you a debt of gratitude I'll never be able to repay."

He took off his Stetson. A few Hispanics glanced at the two Anglos who were obviously cops, then went about their business. East Austin was getting gentrified, and they were getting used to *bolillos* of all stripes dangling their toes in multiculturalism.

"Good. Good. We need to keep it that way."

I couldn't keep the concern off my face. "What are you talking about?"

"Calm down. I just need to confirm some stuff. We're dead men talking. Nothing leaves here."

I had spent days, then weeks, debriefing with the State and Federal investigators. What was going on? I set the half-eaten taco back on the paper plate. My appetite had suddenly disappeared. I let out a long breath.

"Okay. What?"

"Laura."

"Laura, what?"

"You talked with her lately?"

"No." She was the last person I wanted to talk to.

Abner toyed with the Stetson's hat band. "She's been back in Kickapoo County. Twice so far. Both times in a borrowed pickup truck. Seen in Santa Rosa at a hardware store buying a sharpshooter shovel and a wheelbarrow."

What the hell?

"Ole TJ, he's beginning to think he's a hero now. Still upset that Lowell's story is closer to the truth. Still mad about you leaving Kickapoo County. Holding to the line that you were washed up, that he gave you a chance, and now you've up and left and getting most of the good publicity. He's mumbling at the coffee shop about "Purdy's old girlfriend coming into some money." To give him credit, Abner Selman looked more and more uncomfortable.

I had finally disentangled myself from my past. Or, so I hoped. Now it was roaring back into the present. I was still being sucked back into matters I wanted to get as far away from as possible. I was angry, but somehow, not surprised.

"Are you asking me if I know anything about any money?"

He shook his head but didn't mean it.

I paused, anger creeping into my voice. Looking around to see if there was anyone within ear range, I bit off my next words in small, terse bits.

"What the hell, Abner. What are you saying?"

"Purdy, I don't know what I'm saying. That's why we're here, talking man-to-man. Did she ever say anything about coming into some money?"

My mind raced, and I began to think out loud.

"No, but as rattled as she was after Pete's death, it never came up." *At least with me, but I wasn't involved in any interviews or statements, as you well know. Especially given the Feds' intention to throw the book at her for helping Pete.* "I've always assumed she would somehow wander back to Alamo Heights and find someone with deep pockets to marry, if she didn't end up doing time in a Federal prison."

"Well, guess what, amigo?" Abner wasn't given to dramatic effects, but he gave me an eyebrow raise now.

"Okay, I'll bite. What?"

"The Assistant U.S. Attorney in San Antonio is looking at her 'alleged' involvement with one Pete Vasquez, now deceased, mule for the cartel and snitch for the DEA, and seems to have some misgivings about proceeding with a formal charge."

Abner seemed pleased by my surprised reaction.

"Alamo Heights Detective Hohmeyer called me today," I said. "Seemed worried about Laura's security as a resident of his fair city. He told me the rumor mill was working overtime, with some saying she'd get off."

Abner nodded. "It's not every day someone helping a fugitive escape from the clutches of the DEA gets a walk from the Feebies."

As in almost never. "What happened?"

"The AUSA wouldn't expand. Just said, and I quote, 'That woman got herself into a pile of doodoo and came out smelling like a gardenia. Told me to pass that along if I ever saw her again."

"Damn." I couldn't think of anything else to say.

"Yep, she had a good defense lawyer. Because of Mr. Eddleman's possible involvement in Vasquez's death, I'm not sure she needed one. Eddleman's needing warmer clothes now, isn't he?" He paused, not expecting an answer. "Which doesn't mean she may not dodge her past. If someone gets wind she's got a stash of money, she'll probably get indicted in State court on some charge, or get dead by the cartel. So back to the original point of this conversation."

"Has she bought any cows, heifers, anything to show she's trying to make a go of it as a rancher?" I started to laugh at the absurdity of my suggestion. "Abner, did she ever make you feel comfortable about her and Pete coming back to Kickapoo County, instead of running to

Canada, or Paraguay, or any place but on the God-forsaken border with Mexico?"

We agreed that probably would have been impossible. Still… "Why would she need a shovel? Unless…."

If we had been cartoon characters, our thought clouds would have sprouted bolts of lightning.

"Holy moley. Pete spent some time with his grandparents. How long had he been muling for the cartels?"

"Good question, Purdy. I'm not sure. DEA debriefed him. He was supposed to give up all money he had made in the drug business to the Feds. But a dope dealer's a dope dealer. Pete had cut a rather good deal for himself, but maybe figured he could do a little better—as long as he didn't get killed. Of course, that didn't work out like he planned." He cracked a small smile. "I'm betting our boy Pete decided not to come entirely clean with the DEA boys." He shook his head. "Hiding money where his grandparents lived. Wouldn't that be something. If so, Eddleman is shitting a brick. If he was around, I'd love to see his reaction. Not that I'm going to look up that so and so."

Perhaps we had put a finger on what Laura was up to. Where to go with it?

"So, Ranger, what are you and I supposed to do with this new-found theory of ours? You want me to call and ask her? 'Hey, Laura. You looking for proceeds from drug sales on your ranch? Surely you won't mind telling me.'"

Abner took a pull of tea, then stretched his legs.

"Purdy, I don't know. If you have any pull with Lowell Johnson, you might want to somehow get him to have a little 'talk' with TJ. The Kickapoo County Sheriff seems to remember his behavior at the Griffin Ranch as above reproach. It wasn't. You don't need rumors following you up from the border."

He was right about Lowell Johnson. He would help get TJ reelected, but he had something on the sheriff. It was worth making a call.

"I can call the newspaper man," I said. "But that's only half of what you're asking, isn't it?"

Abner grabbed the check and stood up.

"Purdy, I believe that you don't know. I truly do. And I know you want as far away from Santa Rosa and Kickapoo County as you can get, at least for awhile." He dropped tip money on the table, and we walked to the cash register.

I put on sunglasses as we walked into the bright sunlight toward my car.

"Purdy, I don't know if you can do it, but I think you still care for that woman."

I shook my head.

"Maybe. Maybe not. But you've got a deep sense of decency and goodness. If you can figure a way, convince Laura Griffin to stay as far away from the border as possible. Eventually, someone's gonna come after her, if what we are thinking is correct."

Sweet Mother of God.

Lowell Johnson

R ecently re-elected Sheriff TJ Johnson wasn't right about many things, but Lowell Johnson had to acknowledge the overweight windbag was right about the *Kickapoo County Register* owner's love for scotch. Single-malt scotch. Balvenie, preferably aged in a rum keg. Lowell propped his boots on his cluttered desk and tilted another splash into a crystal lowball glass.

The fat SOB didn't need to be bothering Purdy Kendricks. Santa Rosa's rumor mill would do just fine without the Sheriff's input. Purdy Kendricks's phone call didn't surprise Lowell in the least. TJ Johnson had a short memory. Lowell called and reminded the Sheriff that between his weak bladder and weaker mind, TJ's ability to look good in a pissing contest with Purdy bordered on slim and none.

He rang off, savoring his final comment to TJ, "I still have pictures of your pants soaked in urine. I've still got videos of you cowering in that arroyo. I'm not going to use them—ever—unless you mess up. And jacking with Purdy Kendricks is messing up."

TJ had sputtered a response, but Lowell disconnected without responding. At least for awhile, Purdy didn't need to look over his shoulder because of TJ Johnson's shenanigans.

He cackled as he took another sip, rolling the amber liquid around with his tongue.

"Ah, the wait was worth it."

A "Closed" sign hung on the front door of the *Register's* office. He had just put the paper's weekly edition to bed and wasn't interested in having someone dropping in and partaking with him.

"This stuff's too good, and damned near nobody in Santa Rosa would know what they're drinking, anyway."

His cell phone chirped—a 212 area code. New York City. Lowell was never averse to publicity, but the last months had been tiring.

Almost not believing he was saying it, Lowell muttered, "Damn. Another publisher I'll bet. Or maybe CBS, or NBC, or ABC. They'll leave a message. I'm taking a break."

He shook his head and lifted his boots off the table. Standing up, Lowell stretched and set his drink down, carefully. It was probably time to head home, but he would take time to re-read—for the umpteenth time—the two letters that had come by Fed Ex in the last week, addressed to "Mr. Lowell Johnson, Jr., Esquire." *Esquire?* He hadn't seen that appended to a name since reading one of the books in the Horatio Hornblower series by C.S. Forester.

The letterheads were inked on expensive bond paper. Although the wording was different in the two, the tenor of the letters was the same. Someone had nominated him and the *Kickapoo County Register* for investigative journalism awards. He had Googled the organizations, and sure enough, they were legitimate. Maybe the James Foley Medill Medal for Courage in Journalism and the Worth Bingham Prize for Investigative Journalism didn't have the cachet of a Pulitzer, but they were the real McCoy. And both prizes even had money awards—just like the Pulitzer.

A tentative couple of knuckle taps hit the front door glass. Lowell was deep into the scotch-enhanced glow of pride and accomplishment and didn't intend to respond to the interruption, but saw it was Johnny Bonavita.

Oh, hell, he thought. I can't ignore the boy. He flipped open the deadbolt.

"Hey, Deputy. What brings you here?"

Bonavita looked down at his feet.

"Mind if I come in, Mr. Johnson?"

"Sure, c'mon in." He thought about it, and then gestured toward the Balvenie on the table. "I'm drinking a scotch. Would you like one?"

"Oh, no, sir. I don't drink."

Relieved, Lowell got a bit more expansive.

"Sit. Sit. What's on your mind?"

Bonavita removed his felt hat and carefully set it on a filing cabinet. As if trying to gather his thoughts, he took time to look around.

"Wow, these frames you got make the *Register* look good, Mr. Johnson."

The front pages of several special editions of the *Kickapoo County Register*, with bold type face, looked down from two walls.

Lowell grinned. "I guess they do."

Bonavita pointed at one. KILLINGS RAISE QUESTIONS ABOUT DEA INTEGRITY. He grinned.

"That got everyone's attention, didn't it?" Not waiting for an answer, he continued. "I've told you this before, sir, but I'll say it again. I think you nailed the story."

Lowell Johnson sensed the deputy was fishing—again.

"No, I'm not going to tell you anything more about Mr. Eddleman, DEA, late of Laredo, Texas. And, no, dammit, I'm not going to tell you all my sources. You probably can figure out most of them. You're getting as snoopy as your illustrious boss."

Bonavita broke into laughter.

"Aw, heck. You and I both know you made TJ Johnson look a lot better than he deserved. That rascal was so scared that he pissed his pants. If the Ranger hadn't darned near beat the hell out of him, he would still be huddled in that arroyo. Probably peeking out occasionally going, 'Can I come out now?'"

Hardly the first time the two had shared that story, but it still was worth a good laugh. After a pause, Bonavita reached inside his shirt pocket and handed the editor a folded letter.

"Read it."

Lowell opened it, grinned, stood, and stuck out his hand. "Congratulations. I'm enormously proud for you."

Bonavita took Lowell's hand.

"Your reporting had a lot to do with it. You made me look pretty good."

"You did it on your own, amigo. And the Ranger had something to do with it, too. So did Purdy Kendricks. But you earned the right to get a shot at it." He glanced at the letter again. "So, you report to the DPS Academy next month? Have you told your boss?"

Bonavita nodded. "I was appropriately respectful, and I told him I owed it all to his leadership." He picked up his hat, moving toward the door. "I just wanted to share the good news with you. I know Austin called you as a reference, and not just as someone writing a story."

Lowell grasped the deputy's shoulder.

"It was an honor. You'll make a fine trooper. I just hope you get assigned here when you graduate."

The two walked into late afternoon coolness.

"I'm not so sure I want that—at least not for awhile. I'd like to make Ranger one day, and there are some ladders I've got to climb to get there. Of course, first, I've got to get through the Academy." He opened his car door. "Besides, after what Purdy Kendricks went through, I think taking a breather from this place might be a good idea."

He turned the ignition switch and watched the editor wave and walk into the office. The "Closed" sign wobbled as the door was locked.

Lowell reunited with his scotch and glanced at another front page of the *Register*. AUTOPSY SHOWS SHOT THROUGH THE CHEST. WHO KILLED PETE VASQUEZ? Lowell Johnson had a very good idea, and he hadn't been bashful about suggesting strongly who had done it.

More to calm his nerves that night, he had stayed out of the medic's way at Otabiano's house, as Clete Morales's leg wound was treated. He had walked toward the dying embers of the burned cane and witnessed Pete Vasquez being carried toward his grandparents' house. Soon, a figure moved around the shot-up SUVs. Afraid it was a *sicario*, Lowell had frozen, praying he wouldn't be seen. In the glow of Johnny Reagan's burning truck, the figure materialized into Eddleman.

Three Months Later

Hohmeyer and the Ranger—from the two of them, I was getting a strong feeling that Laura Griffin Saenz, suspected of abetting Pete Vasquez's escape, had found a treasure trove on her ranch. There was no other reasonable explanation for the sudden financial liquidity and renewed Alamo Heights lifestyle.

What was I supposed to do about it? A borrowed pickup truck, a new housekeeper. It added up. Pete had stashed money on his girlfriend's ranch. Just how much—I didn't know. I didn't much care. But the *sicarios* had come after Pete *and* Laura. The cartel had some idea she was involved—so did the Feds. In this day and age, no one got away with throwing around huge sums of cash. It would get reported to banking authorities, if nothing else.

Abner seemed to be telling me that the Feds had moved on to other targets. Laura was an old topic. With Pete Vasquez dead and Eddleman disgraced, getting involved again would be like playing with Br'er Fox's tar baby. No one in law enforcement wanted to touch it.

So, what to do? I worried about it all afternoon. I thought I had deleted Laura's cell number from my list of contacts. I hadn't, but then, there was probably some subconscious, emotional reason why I hadn't. It was probably not all that subconscious, if I wanted to be honest.

This call wasn't going to be the smartest thing I had done. With a new position in another law enforcement agency, calling the woman who had abetted Pete's escape wouldn't be a career-builder if found out. But at lunch, Abner hadn't discussed his suspicions to me as idle chatter. He didn't work that way. The Ranger knew I would reach out to Laura—that I would do the right thing.

I punched in her number on my cell.

"Purdy?"

Who else would have this number?

"Yes."

A pause.

"How are you doing, Laura?"

"Fine."

I wasn't getting anywhere at this rate.

"I heard the good news today."

"Yeah. I had a good lawyer, I guess."

Maybe she did, but unless the lawyer was so full of shit that she had taken all the credit, Laura had to know she had skated for reasons that had to do nothing with her own innocence or behavior.

"I'm glad for you. I truly am. You've been through a lot."

"I'm relieved, and I'm glad it's over with. My lawyer explained that I had been pretty lucky. I'm glad to be back in my home." Her sigh was audible. "I'm just trying to get back to my life."

I paused. "That's why I'm calling, Laura."

Another pause. I went on.

"I want you to listen to me. Just this once. Please."

She started to laugh.

"Don't tell me you've divorced your wife, Purdy."

Jesus.

"Knock it off, Laura."

She cleared her throat.

"I apologize. That was catty. I just didn't expect to ever hear from you again. What would Betty do if she knew you were calling me?"

Good question. I doubted I would tell her. There was a limit to her understanding of my complicated feelings for an old girlfriend.

"You've been seen in Santa Rosa."

"So what?" Anger seemed just below the surface of her response.

"Like I said. Just listen. I'm not interested in getting into an argument with you, but you need to hear this. You've been back to the ranch. Not once, but twice."

She started to interrupt. I cut her off.

"Don't ask how I know. I just know. It wasn't just Pete Vasquez the bad guys were after. They weren't interested in sparing your life. It's by the grace of God you didn't get your throat slit."

"Blah. Blah. Blah. I know all that."

I was trying to save someone who didn't seem to think she needed saving. I looked around, hoping my raised voice wasn't attracting attention.

"Goddammit. If you go near the border, you could get killed. Don't you get it? Otabiano's house is forty yards from Mexico! There's no one to protect you. You'd be dead for weeks before someone snapped to it."

Silence.

"Another thing, Laura."

I could hear her breathing into the phone.

"What?"

"I know why you went down there. Both times."

She feigned surprise.

"I just wanted to put the place in order a bit."

"Bullshit. You don't give a damn about the ranch. Haven't in years." I wondered how she would respond to what I was going to say next. "Pete stashed money on the place while his grandparents were alive." I paused—nothing. "And he told you where at least some of it is."

Again, nothing said denying it.

"You've gotten access to some money, Laura. I suspect quite a bit. It hasn't gone unnoticed."

Finally, she replied, surprising me. No argument. No lashing out. Just this, "Pete Vasquez put me through hell. I have no doubt that he had a guilty conscience. I'll be careful. Now leave me alone."

She disconnected.

ONE HUNDRED FOUR

Eddleman

E ddleman looked out the window of the small DEA office in
Bismarck, North Dakota.

"Six inches of snow in fucking November." He turned and kicked
at an armless chair next to a government surplus desk. His cell
buzzed. His attorney. "What?"

"Charming."

"Sorry." He wasn't, but it didn't behoove him to piss off an ally.
"What's up?"

"The Assistant U.S. Attorney in San Antonio isn't filing charges on
Laura Griffin Saenz."

Eddleman didn't muster up the effort for additional outrage.

"Huh. She helps a dirty drug smuggling SOB avoid getting
arrested after he causes the death of a damned good agent, and she's
not facing any charges? What the hell?"

The lawyer had heard all this before.

"Are you where we can talk?"

Eddleman looked around. The file clerk and secretary had both
gone to lunch.

"I'm alone."

"You're probably lucky. Your DEA Internal Affairs folks had feces
thrown in their faces. Normally, any 'unusual' incidences are, shall we
say, dealt with quietly, if at all."

The lawyer represented plenty of cops and public officials. He knew Eddleman was aware of this, but wanted his client to understand he hadn't the inclination to waste time holding hands while Eddleman vented.

"No one is saying you killed Pete Vasquez." He was, but wasn't going to just say it. "But the guy had a through-and-through bullet wound from a shot probably fired from the U.S. side, consistent with a smaller bore than an AK47. And there's the supposed eyewitness...."

Left unsaid were Lowell Johnson's deposition, and the *Kickapoo County Register's* repeated suggestions that Eddleman had done just that.

"You mentioned a thumb drive. We both know if you had divulged that, there would have been a much, much closer look into how Vasquez got that second wound. You don't *know* what anything on its file really meant."

Eddleman interrupted. "Yeah, but...."

"No, dammit. You aren't listening. I repeat—you don't *know* what was on that thumb drive, which never existed. *Are we clear?*"

Eddleman got the message. He had never seen a thumb drive possessed by Pete Vasquez.

"Nothing more is going to happen. It's over. Let it go. Lay low. Ride this out. You've got some good years left. Like most of this stuff, it'll blow over. DEA takes care of its own. You know that. A transfer out of North Dakota will happen. Just not for a year or two." The lawyer paused, as if awaiting a response. When Eddleman didn't reply, he continued, "You're a good agent, Eddleman." He tried to sound like he meant it.

"Send me your bill. Thanks." Eddleman tried to sound like *he* meant it.

Neither was buying the other's expressed sentiments.

"Don't worry. I will."

As he disconnected, Eddleman heard the two office personnel chatting, as they returned from lunch.

Eddleman looked out over the bleak landscape. *I'm supposed to interdict drugs coming in to the U.S. through fucking Manitoba? And Saskatchewan? Christ.*

Yeah, the thumb drive does exist. And Pete Vasquez stashed millions of dollars on Laura Griffin Saenz's property. He had taken care of the turncoat, once and for all. Now he was in a crappy office freezing his ass off. There was a lot of unclaimed dope money on that ranch—money that no one ever talked about—money that would sure help with his retirement.

Eddleman would have to think about whether he wanted to "let it go."

ONE HUNDRED FIVE

Laura Griffin Saenz

L aura curled up on the leather love seat with a glass of wine. Purdy Kendricks' phone call had unsettled her.

"You need to stay away from the border," he had said. "Get rid of that damned ranch. If you go anywhere near the border; you could get killed."

South Texas winters weren't usually miserable, but Thursday night a front had blown in, bringing drizzle and a handy excuse to fire up the gas logs in the fireplace. Laura settled back, idly wondering whether she should head to the health club and get in an hour or two of exercise. Taking another sip of a better than decent Argentina Malbec, she decided to take a breather from her self-imposed "time to get back in shape" regimen.

Maybe Purdy was right. Lately, for sure, but Pete Vasquez hadn't been a total asshole. When all hell hit the fan as the helicopter came roaring in, he had roused himself enough to profess his love for her, saying he appreciated all she had done for him. He had mumbled something about a thumb drive the narcs had taken from him. Then whispered that he was fairly sure he still could remember where most of the money was hidden. Then he had drifted back toward uncon-sciousness.

Laura almost felt bad about slapping Pete—hard.

"Wake up," she hissed in the darkness. "You promised."

He had opened his eyes and named two locations, "where we made love."

Ugh. She remembered some places they had sneaked off to. After a day of frantic searching, she had been lucky and found enough cash to get by comfortably for awhile.

And the Feds don't know about it. Nobody knows about it.

Felicitas Gomez came down the stairs, interrupting Laura's reverie

"Ms. Saenz, I've cleaned the upstairs. Is there anything else I can do before I go home?"

Shaking her head, Laura said, "No, except maybe bring me the last of that wine." She gestured toward the bar.

The rather stout middle-aged woman adjusted her work smock and checked the labels to confirm which one was the open red, then brought the bottle to the love seat.

"You want me to pour?"

"No, Phyllis." Laura preferred the anglicized version. It was easier to pronounce. "Thank you very much for bringing it over. Please. Go home to your family."

The woman picked up her coat and purse and walked toward the front door.

Laura stood.

"Phyllis, wait a sec, will you?" She approached and gave the woman a hug. "I appreciate you taking this job. It was such a shock losing Adela."

Laura didn't explain how Adela had been brutalized by a drug gang near where Phyllis was standing now. Some things were better left unsaid.

"You've done a great job. This place has never looked better."

Uncomfortable in her employer's grasp, Felicitas Gomez shrugged free, embarrassed by the display of affection.

"Thank you, Missus Saenz."

Laura stepped back.

"I apologize. It's just that..." She could feel the tears welling up. *Oh boy, here I go again. I've got to stop this.* Quickly brushing away the moisture, Laura held up a hand.

"Wait, please."

She handed the woman an envelope.

"This is for your family as a Christmas gift. I know you have kids and grandkids, and this will help make your holiday season a little brighter."

Phyllis seemed reluctant to take the proffered gift.

"Missus Saenz, really."

"No, I want you to have this. It's my way of saying thank you. Now go on, and I'll see you on Monday."

Reluctantly, Phyllis Gomez stuffed the envelope in a coat pocket, popped open an umbrella, and walked to her car.

"God, I'm so lucky to get some good help around here." Laura closed and locked the front door. It had been hell replacing Adela. The woman quit after being scared half to death by the Mexican thugs. Even a new security system and assurances that nothing like that would happen again hadn't convinced Adela to come back to Laura's house in Alamo Heights.

"Too many bad things and memories, *señora*," she said.

Refilling her glass, Laura caught herself mimicking the woman. "'Too many bad things and memories.' Well, hell, honey, I've had a few bad memories in the last few months myself." She barked a laugh and looked around. "But I'm still here, and life is good again."

It was getting dark, Laura was feeling the wine, and she had no place to go but to bed. Idly, she wandered through the house. *I love this place. Thank God, or Pete Vasquez*—she giggled—*I've got the way to keep it now.*

Felicitas "Phyllis" Gomez, whose name was really Gabriella Saldaña, and who wasn't a mother or a grandmother, drove out of Alamo Heights onto Broadway. Pulling into a parking slot at a convenience store and gas station, she opened the envelope and pulled out its contents. Thirty-seven 100-dollar bills. *Hijole!* She punched a pre-set phone number.

"*Si?*"

"I left the woman's house, and I'm going home for the weekend."

"Did you find anything?" It was a male voice, but she had no idea who it was. Better that way.

"No." *Fuck those* pendejos. *I'm doing their dirty work, and they aren't paying me shit. This cash is mine.* "I told you, that *gabacha* hasn't showed me any cash money except for the weekly pay. She's not taking out for taxes, like I told you, but nothing else, okay? She drinks her *pinche* wine, goes shopping, and lies around her *pinche* house. *Que mas?* Eh?"

The man disconnected without comment. *Fuck him. And whoever thought of Felicitas for a name? Or Phyllis? What names are those?* Gabriella Saldaña drove to her small apartment in South San Antonio, thankful to be away from the *gabachos* in Alamo Heights.

S lightly hung over, Laura got out of bed and into shorts and crocs, drank a latte, and headed for the Saturday garage sales.

God, it is fun having money again.

Finding nothing of interest to buy, she headed to Central Market on Broadway with a shopping list. It was close to lunch, and the deli would have something she would enjoy. She might meet a foodie or two, and possibly, an interesting man, although it was probably a little too soon for that.

She missed her Mercedes, but the impound fees were huge, and there was too much blood on the seats.

That old drunk had actually done what we paid him to do. I hope he enjoyed driving it. The Mercedes probably stank of the old man's booze, as well.

She pulled into the parking lot, locked the spiffy Miata that she had convinced the salesman to let her test drive for a couple of days, and went in.

Fifteen minutes later, a black SUV with heavily tinted windows pulled next to the small convertible. The SUV's driver raised an eyebrow to the two men in the middle seat, as if to ask if they had parked next to the right vehicle.

One of the men, a white dress shirt covering most of his tattoos, answered.

"*Eso es el auto que la gabacha esta manejando.*"

The driver thought so and grunted. The SUV was new and still had dealer tags. It even smelled new. The men watched couples with small children loading groceries into similar vehicles, comfortable that their SUV fit in well in the tony upscale market parking lot.

They would wait for the woman to come out.

ONE HUNDRED SIX

One Month Later

PURDY KENDRICKS

I got the call the day it happened. A Saturday. Which was also the day after I had phoned Laura, warning her to stay away from the border, and especially Kickapoo County. Trying to assure her that Alamo Heights was safer than anywhere next to the Rio Grande and Mexico.

Detective Hohmeyer of the Alamo Heights PD, perhaps knowing it would be better if word of the event didn't come from a San Antonio television reporter, called my cell. I stopped the evening's steak marinade, wiped my hands on a dish towel, and answered.

"Commander Kendricks. I've got some news for you."

The timbre of his voice made it clear something bad had happened. The only person he and I shared in common was Laura Griffin Saenz.

"Laura?"

Betty turned off the kitchen sink tap and stood quietly, looking at me.

He took a sharp breath, as if he wanted to get out the whole story in a hurry.

"Yes. She's dead. I'm sorry."

"How?"

"It'll be all over the news. In fact, CNN and Fox have already picked it up."

"What, dammit!" How? Where?"

"She was grabbed in a supermarket parking lot just outside Alamo Heights. The Central Market on Broadway. Three thugs in a black SUV."

He described how Laura, with two grocery bags, had walked to a small Miata. Two men jumped from the SUV and grabbed her. Groceries went everywhere. Several shoppers witnessed the snatch. One even got the dealer's tag information. Nine-one-one calls brought several agencies to the scene. The SUV headed north on Broadway, blew through a red light, and hopped on Loop 410, heading west.

"We don't know where they were heading, but our guess is that the quick police response surprised them. Probably into a neighborhood south of downtown where they would have had another vehicle stashed." He paused. "Or maybe not."

I took a deep breath and motioned to Betty. She walked over, and I slid my arm around her.

"Detective, I'm putting you on the speaker. My wife's right here. She can hear this too."

"Uh. Okay."

"Go ahead."

Hohmeyer described the SUV being spotted as it turned south on U.S. 281, a route with several exits past the downtown area.

"The vehicle hit 100 miles an hour. SAPD had a chopper up, and there were several agency vehicles in hot, and I mean hot pursuit. Shots were fired."

A mirror in the hallway off the kitchen captured Betty and me embracing. We looked like survivors supporting each other after a disaster. Our eyes made contact in the mirror. The image was appropriate.

"Everyone guessed that the abducted woman was in that SUV, so when its occupants started spraying the freeway with bullets, they backed off. In the meantime, Bexar County S.O. got involved. The plan was to block freeway exits. The SUV passed downtown and somehow managed to keep from flipping when it entered IH 37."

IH 37 was the direct route to the border city of Laredo.

"The driver tried to cut off the freeway. He made it onto the exit ramp and access road. There were two civilian cars at the stop sign at the top of the overpass. The SUV couldn't get around them. The SUV's driver rammed the back of one of the stopped cars, trying to shove it out of the way. Pushed it into the intersection, and another car t-boned the SUV. By that time, police units had time to catch up. Three suspects jumped from the vehicle and opened up with automatic weapons. All three were shot dead. It didn't take long."

"What about Laura? What happened?"

"She was in the SUV. No law enforcement rounds were even aimed at the vehicle. She had been duct taped, hands and legs. She was on the floor behind the second seat."

"And?"

"One of the suspects probably figured they weren't going to get out of it alive and decided neither was she. Put one round into the back of her head."

Betty gasped. Hohmeyer heard.

"Sorry, Miz Kendricks. If it's any consolation, she died instantly."

I thanked the detective and disconnected.

I wanted to feel something. I was troubled that I didn't and told Betty so.

"You will, Purdy. You will. There's too much history there not to."

We moved into the living room. The sounds of Forrest and a new friend we had invited for a sleep-over came from his bedroom where they were watching *Coco*.

"I love you, Purdy Kendricks, and I'm here to support you when you need me." She pulled me closer. "I'm sorry, Purdy. I just don't know what else to say."

Stroking her hair, I said, "Neither do I."

The suspects were identified as gangbangers associated with the *Zetas*. Obviously, they had been sent to grab Laura and deliver her elsewhere. The small consolation of her death was that it had been swift. Had the gangbangers succeeded in the kidnapping, I doubted that she would have been spared rape and torture.

Betty and I attended Laura's funeral. The local Methodist church was packed. Her murder sent Alamo Heights, collectively, into a tailspin. Sure, everyone *knew* the cartels had plenty of family members living in the San Antonio area. However, they were living there because San Antonio was safe from the daily violence in Mexico. And yes, there were plenty of gangs in Bexar County, but they *knew* not to let their disputes slosh into the better neighborhoods.

Even though Laura's home had been invaded before, she hadn't been there—only the help, which was different.

Only it wasn't.

ONE HUNDRED SEVEN

Present Day

PURDY KENDRICKS

I t was three weeks after Laura's funeral. New responsibilities and a busy family life hadn't given me much time to process her death. I felt I was at least partially responsible, but I couldn't wrap my mind around exactly how.

Alicia Trejo buzzed into my office.

"Commander, there's a gentleman on the line, calling from San Antonio. He says he's a lawyer, and he has something personal to discuss with you."

There was no way I was taking a cold call from someone I didn't know. Ms. Trejo was one step ahead.

"I've got his number and said I would pass it on."

Relieved but curious, I thanked her.

"Commander?"

"Yes?"

"I checked the name he gave. I checked the phone number. It goes to a legitimate law firm in San Antonio. Their website says the firm deals in, I quote, 'trusts, estates, and probate.'"

I laughed. "Thanks, Ms. Trejo. At least it's not someone in criminal defense work."

There was a break in my schedule late in the afternoon. I punched in the law firm's number on my cell and asked for the caller, a Mr. Charles Githens. The receptionist took my name and put me on hold.

Within seconds, Charles Githens came on the line. Once assured of my identity, he got to the point.

"Laura Griffin came to our office two months ago. We give free consultations, and I thought she wanted us to draft a will for her. Nothing unusual there." He paused. "She handed me two sheets of notebook paper. She had handwritten an entire last will and testament. Perfectly legal and binding if admitted to probate under Texas law, I might add. She asked me to safeguard her will. Said she would get back with us to execute one we had prepared, with all the bells and whistles, one with witnesses and a notary. Paid me my retainer."

What did this have to do with me?

Mr. Githens sensed my restlessness.

"I'm getting to the point, sir. Just hold your thoughts for bit." He continued. "She cancelled a couple of appointments to execute the new will. Then we got a certified letter from her, a week before her untimely death. It contained another handwritten instruction she entitled, *Codicil to My Last Will and Testament.* The only thing in the codicil, which, too, is valid, was an instruction naming me as the executor of her estate. It seems that she thought a lot of you, Mr. Kendricks. She made a specific bequest to you of certain ranch property in Kickapoo County, Texas."

Holy shit.

Flabbergasted, I blurted out, "I don't want the damned place, Mr. Githens."

He laughed and continued, "Her cover letter to the codicil indicated she knew you'd say that. That's why she wanted me to be her executor. She also paid quite a handsome retainer for me to represent her estate in the event of her death. She was quite a character, Mr. Kendricks. She wrote, and I quote, 'If I die, tell Purdy Kendricks that I have no living relatives that I'd let touch the place. That it's mine to bestow, and I want the son of a bitch to have it.'"

A part from visits to Mama or to Paula and her family, I had no intention of going near Santa Rosa and Kickapoo County ever again.

I had come close to ruining my marriage in Kickapoo County. I almost lost my wife and son to killers there.

With the murders of Otabiano and Raquel Vasquez, and its use in drug cartel warfare across the Rio Grande, the ranch was a symbol of a lost love and betrayed innocence. As a young man, I had loved the Griffin place fiercely. My feelings were substantially more complicated now. Kickapoo County, where I'm from and much of what I am, had become one of the many centers of the border crossfire.

I was about to become the owner of 16,000 God-forsaken acres abutting the tiny ribbon of the Rio Grande's dirty water. It divided two countries but offered no protection to the citizens of either.

It was a puzzlement why Laura wrote her will the way she did. Was it a practical joke? A way to get back at me? Or did she sense there would be a reckoning that would take her life? Perhaps, in the end, Laura Griffin simply tried to make things right.

The End

The End

About the Author

This is the first novel by Todd Blomerth. His second novel, Dalton's Run, was published Summer 2021. He is a retired state district judge and former prosecutor and criminal defense attorney. His previous non-fiction book, <u>They Gave Their All</u>, tells the stories of the Caldwell County, Texas men and woman who died in the service of their country in World War II. He and his wife Patti live in Lockhart, Texas.

The author welcomes comments or suggestions about Border Crossfire. He may be contacted at: **blomertht@gmail.com**

Made in the USA
Monee, IL
17 September 2023